Table of Contents

<u>**Index**</u>

Introduction. As far as you can, do not let your life be controlled by others.
First part. Identify what we already have
    1. What is the brain?
        The brain: a complete DIY warehouse
        How the brain works: the movie projector
        Do you have to use one hundred percent of the brain?
        We wear the tools of happiness as standard
    2. What basic tools do we need to know well?
        Two very mysterious and not at all esoteric instruments
        A work board: short-term memory
        The closet to store memories: long-term memory
        An angular periscope: attention
        A microwave for our goals: concentration
        Aladdin's Magic Carpet: Imagination
        The rechargeable battery pack: the motivation
    3. How to use our tools accurately
        What we continuously transmit to exchange information
        What we think. The manual calculator with several rolls of paper: the reason
        What we feel. A few sirens and light signals: the emotions
        Are you rational or emotional?
        Are you reactive or proactive?
Second part. What we can do with these tools to create happiness to our measure
    4. Set effective goals
        useful happiness
        Taking care of the body to achieve mental goals: food, exercise and rest
    5. Communicate without distortion
        Understanding what is not said: nonverbal communication
        Listen to understand, speak to be understood: verbal communication
        How we usually make mistakes in our communication styles
        How to ensure that we do not end up talking about what we did not plan
        three response styles
    6. Learn from mistakes
        Keys to make mistakes with less frequency and intensity
        the smart mistake
    7. Keys to not make life bitter

Exercise patience, which is the mother of science
Learn to surround yourself with positive people and circumstances
Decorate life to our liking: creativity and art
Laughing even at our shadow: the sense of humor
8. Make the decision to be happy
Define the goal: what?
Generate alternatives: how?
Anticipate the consequences in the short, medium and long term
Choose the most convenient option
Evaluate, confirm or correct where deemed necessary
Third part. What we can do to avoid some psychological upsets
9. Correct some erroneous learning or that no longer serve us
We are not like that"; we have memorized it
The art of implanting and eliminating behaviors from our repertoire
10. Dodging 21st century pandemics
So that the kilos that we accumulate remain in the warehouse that corresponds to them: the supermarket
So that anxiety does not leave us breathless
To walk to the edge of the precipice of depression without being pushed into the abyss
So that our defenses are not engulfed by the all-devouring stress
Fourth part
11. Life as a personal and non-transferable experience
12. Take the bull by the horns: responsibility
Let's talk a little about irresponsibility
Kindness or well-intentioned irresponsibility?
Let's learn to apologize elegantly and effectively
The good vibes that responsibility provides
Epilogue. Say goodbye with our best smile. living is worth it
Bibliography
inserts
Credits

Index

Front page
Introduction. As far as you can, do not let your life be controlled by others.

First part. Identify what we already have
    1. What is the brain?
        The brain: a complete DIY warehouse
        How the brain works: the movie projector
        Do you have to use one hundred percent of the brain?
        We wear the tools of happiness as standard
    2. What basic tools do we need to know well?
        Two very mysterious and not at all esoteric instruments
        A work board: short-term memory
        The closet to store memories: long-term memory
        An angular periscope: attention
        A microwave for our goals: concentration
        Aladdin's Magic Carpet: Imagination
        The rechargeable battery pack: the motivation
    3. How to use our tools accurately
        What we continuously transmit to exchange information
        What we think. The manual calculator with several rolls of paper: the reason
        What we feel. A few sirens and light signals: the emotions
        Are you rational or emotional?
        Are you reactive or proactive?

Second part. What we can do with these tools to create happiness to our measure
    4. Set effective goals
        useful happiness
        Taking care of the body to achieve mental goals: food, exercise and rest
    5. Communicate without distortion
        Understanding what is not said: nonverbal communication
        Listen to understand, speak to be understood: verbal communication
        How we usually make mistakes in our communication styles
        How to ensure that we do not end up talking about what we did not plan

three response styles
6. Learn from mistakes
    Keys to make mistakes with less frequency and intensity
    the smart mistake
7. Keys to not make life bitter
    Exercise patience, which is the mother of science
    Learn to surround yourself with positive people and circumstances
    Decorate life to our liking: creativity and art
    Laughing even at our shadow: the sense of humor
8. Make the decision to be happy
    Define the goal: what?
    Generate alternatives: how?
    Anticipate the consequences in the short, medium and long term
    Choose the most convenient option
    Evaluate, confirm or correct where deemed necessary

Third part. What we can do to avoid some psychological upsets
    9. Correct some erroneous learning or that no longer serve us
        We are not like that"; we have memorized it
        The art of implanting and eliminating behaviors from our repertoire
    10. Dodging 21st century pandemics
        So that the kilos that we accumulate remain in the warehouse that corresponds to
        them: the supermarket
        So that anxiety does not leave us breathless
        To walk to the edge of the precipice of depression without being pushed into the
        abyss
        So that our defenses are not engulfed by the all-devouring stress

Fourth part
    11. Life as a personal and non-transferable experience
    12. Take the bull by the horns: responsibility
        Let's talk a little about irresponsibility
        Kindness or well-intentioned irresponsibility?
        Let's learn to apologize elegantly and effectively
        The good vibes that responsibility provides

Epilogue. Say goodbye with our best smile. living is worth it
Bibliography
inserts
Credits

As far as you can, do not let your life be controlled by others.

Of all the advances that we are witnessing thanks to science, without a doubt the most relevant to our lives is the profound knowledge that has been achieved about the functioning of our brain. It has ceased to be an impregnable mystery to become a fascinating toolbox within our reach that has the most advanced technology. We know what they are, what they are for and, without a doubt, we are already in a position to learn how to use these tools in an absolutely practical way in our day to day life.

In fact, we already know so much about it that we could be tempted to skip the previous step of the correct use of the most basic mechanisms, without mastery of which we will not be able to master the higher levels of its use, which we are so called the attention: knowing how to remain calm in difficult situations, strengthening the will and motivation until we achieve the goals we have set for ourselves, or knowing how to transmit complex messages in a masterfully simple and effective way.

Many times we can have the feeling that "what happens to us" is out of our hands: there are people who believe that their thoughts are swarming through the air and, suddenly, like a virus, they catch them; others think that emotions are like indomitable beings that have their own life inside their body; In general, we believe that "we are" in a certain way because of some genes when, mainly, "we have learned to be" the person we have in front of the mirror, and that we have chiseled through conscious and unconscious habits.

In the courses I teach on emotional intelligence, I often use a lot of similes so that complex concepts about the brain are easy to understand and, finally, we can "wear them", that is, we have an image that makes us quickly and easily remember an idea without having to go look in our library "where I read that about how to manage emotions."

We are living in a privileged moment in history in which we have the opportunity, if we want, to design a life according to our way of thinking, feeling and acting. We have created social models where there is room for a great variability of ways of understanding life. We have all grown up in environments with which we could feel identified, or with which we preferred not to have much reference when we reached adulthood. But changing what we have learned, the style of understanding or approaching reality, the habits acquired or knowing how to project ourselves towards a personal future is sometimes not as easy as we imagined, mainly because we may not know how and what we have to be able to do it with some degree of success. We can wait for lucky breaks or fortunate circumstances to occur,

Actually, the most intelligent attitude is to be willing to be learning all your life and, in addition, to enjoy it.

For this reason, what I want to propose to you throughout this book is an approach that is as practical as possible to all those mental operations that we do on a daily basis and of which we hardly know very well how they occur. We have to stop looking at the brain as if it were something alien to our nature, or as if it were that tremendously complicated "thing" that we will never fully understand. I would like us to open together that little treasure chest that, moreover, is yours. No one else's. But above all with a very clear objective, which is that, once we know what we have and how to work with it, we can each design the person we want to be, with the life we decide to live. Quite a challenge, right?

What we are going to see throughout these pages has to do with the emotional intelligence courses that I have taught for years throughout the entire Spanish geography. Your doubts, your questions, or what you understand more clearly is what will finally be reflected in all these lines. The experience of many people will now also serve as an experience for many more, since we are going to share it in the simplest way possible despite having a background in many areas of knowledge of the psychological discipline.

We will then begin at the beginning, that is, to understand the basis on which all the behaviors that we carry out throughout the day, throughout our lives, are based: what is the brain? We are not going to complicate ourselves with too many technicalities that are sometimes incomprehensible and that are not strictly necessary either, but the main objective is going to be to have a general idea of the nature of this prodigious little machine, and to clearly understand the distinction between what the brain is and what it is. what the mind is, because although they are intimately related they are not exactly the same. Once we have these clear concepts, and before getting down to work, we will go through all those tools that do not stop working inside us, to fully understand how they work. The similes with small instruments of daily use that we use for operations of all kinds are perfectly applicable to brain and mental mechanisms, especially if they allow us, with a single image, to get an idea of how we can work with them. Who has not played as a child with those sand boards that, once the drawing was done, tilted and erased everything we had scribbled? And who today does not have rechargeable batteries that allow us not to be disconnected at the most inopportune moment? We have cabinets to store what we are going to need later, sirens and lights that warn us with different intensities depending on what is happening around us, periscopes to identify what is far away and microscopes to analyze with millimeter detail where a conflict may be generating. We have somewhat rudimentary but very useful instruments, such as manual calculators, and also quantum technology, with automatic pilot included, which before we can realize what is happening has already been in charge of creating and resolving situations of great elegance. some complexity; we carry simultaneous translation and consecutive translation machines, and even some somewhat fantastic surprises: magic carpets that allow us to move at will through the past, present and future, or transport us to our worlds of dreams and illusions. like manual calculators, and also with quantum technology, with automatic pilot included, which before we can realize what is happening has already been in charge of making and resolving situations of a certain complexity with great elegance; we carry simultaneous translation and consecutive translation machines, and even some somewhat fantastic surprises: magic carpets that allow us to move at will through the past, present and future, or transport us to our worlds of dreams and illusions. like manual calculators, and also with quantum technology, with automatic pilot included, which before we can realize what is happening has already been in charge of making and resolving situations of a certain complexity with great elegance; we carry simultaneous translation and consecutive translation machines, and even some somewhat fantastic surprises: magic carpets that allow us to move at will through the past, present and future, or transport us to our worlds of dreams and illusions.

Each of these instruments has its own characteristics, and in order for them to fulfill their functions perfectly, we will analyze them one by one, so that we can understand, when transferring them to our daily lives, how they are operating and, most importantly, important, if we agree and we like them. If this is not the case, we will be able to have a clearer idea of what it is that can be readjusted and in what way. Working with our brain can sometimes give us the impression of working with several people at the same time, although in reality what is happening is that it works on two levels: the conscious and the unconscious. Neither of the two is better than the other and both need each other to optimally carry out our vital projects. There are some things that the unconscious does, like very basic life functions, They hardly need our intervention. Messages and experiences are also recorded in the unconscious that normally allow us to function normally, but other times they produce a series of short circuits that it is essential to identify in order to repair them before they cause major damage. The conscious has a main characteristic, and that is that it is very slow compared to the unconscious, but the great advantage is that it allows us to pull the reins that are directing us towards the objective to which we want to channel all that current of life in which we get involved. Most of the instruments that we have move between both levels with absolute naturalness, and we will see what advantages and disadvantages this happens in this way. You are already seeing that for the brain there are no absolutes. Things are not black or white, good or bad, but will depend on the contexts in which they are applied and the consequences that must be faced after having made a series of decisions. The brain likes to flow, and to flow we must learn to relativize, clearly identify what context we find ourselves in and determine to what extent the situation depends on us, and what part is where our intervention has no place and the smartest thing is let go of reins

Once we are more or less clear about what all this intervention equipment that we have incorporated consists of, we will be in a position to start messing with it. Knowing what we have and how it works does not automatically mean that everything we do is right. Then we have to practice, make mistakes, correct and grow; in a word, to become the great master goldsmiths of our lives; or in the champions of the Champions, whichever you like more. And we will do it in the way that pleases our mind: positively and forward.

To approach this phase, which in the book corresponds to the second part, we must begin to incorporate more complex operations: communicate well, know how to set goals and meet them, learn to make decisions and, a very important one that, in addition to burning calories, is an instant relaxer: laugh, develop a sense of humor and stop living life as if it were a drama, except when it is. And even in extremely difficult circumstances, we will always have one more resource: resilience, a special ability that consists almost literally of grabbing at straws, but blessed nail if it is the one that propels us to continue living fully.

I would also like to clarify that we are going to be very realistic. Not everything in life is paths of roses; sometimes we are wrong, and other times life surprises us and not precisely to give us joy. We cannot always go with a smile in the face of tragedy or laughing at what is not funny at all. Happiness is not a state of frivolity in which everything slips away from us, or in which we have deactivated the minimum survival mechanisms. Sometimes we will have to get angry to mark the limits of who is jumping them; or we will feel sadness for the loss of something or someone significant to us. Happiness will be the result of feeling effective in managing who we are and the goals we are achieving. And for that many times we will have to activate some of the most uncomfortable instruments that we carry,

Therefore, another basic concept on which we are going to base our vital learning is that happiness and easy are not synonymous. Would Rafa Nadal be just as happy if to reach number one and stay there all he had to do was smile and think he was the best? I suspect not. The states of happiness that he experiences are the consequence of many moments of concentration, perseverance, frustration, injuries and mistakes. Let's learn then from the great champions.

That is why it seemed important to me to address a third part in the book, which focuses on how to avoid certain pathologies that are a direct consequence of the lifestyle in which we find ourselves immersed. In addition to being clear about what we have to do with ourselves, we live within certain cultures that drag us along without realizing it like a subtle tide, sometimes to good port, and sometimes adrift. The great pandemics of the 21st century are obesity, depression, anxiety and stress. Most of them, except in the cases that we will indicate when we talk about them more specifically, are avoidable or manageable when we see that they make an appearance in our lives. It is about those delicate moments in which, far from letting ourselves go, we have to take the reins more firmly and manage to get out without the crossing taking us too far from the objectives we have set for ourselves. We can intervene when we are already immersed in them and come out gracefully and successfully, but we can also practice a little preventive psychology that will undoubtedly allow us to mitigate, or even avoid, the effects of going through the most difficult situations in our lives.

There is nothing more worthwhile than learning what our brain is and how it is used correctly so that the journey of our life is finally at the height of our projects, hopes and dreams.

Surely we are becoming more and more clear about one of the main objectives of this book's itinerary, which is none other than to feel like highly qualified experts for whom, from now on, the most difficult challenges will undoubtedly mean a source of inspiration, growth and, of course, enjoyment.

And how to finish this journey? Without a doubt, having understood that happiness is not a path of roses, but it is our path after all, tailored to our needs, with our people and with our tastes. One day we will leave and say goodbye to each other. And when that moment comes —which I hope will catch us with our boots on—, we will be able to look back with the feeling that we did well, the best we knew how and that we were always willing not to leave even a corner of ourselves without travel. For that, we decided one day to stop allowing others to tell us where to go; we took everything we already had inside us and dedicated ourselves to what really is —and I hope I have been able to convey it in these first few lines— our only obligation: to live and be happy, in the sense of being able to create a life that is as close as possible to our deepest nature, and to all the baggage with which it has individually equipped us. And no one can do that for us.

As a note, before starting our journey, just remember that what we will have left at the end of this adventure will be the quality of the relationships that we have been able to create.

There is nothing that gives us greater satisfaction than knowing that we know, and that we are capable of designing a life created by and for us. Or that we can at least manage successfully through all the paths that it presents to us. And from that path, the most important thing that will remain for us will be the quality of the relationships that we have been able to forge with each other.

I am already looking forward to it, and I hope you too, to open the box of our magic wands and staves, which we will learn to understand, control and use to create those states of flow or well-being that only we can design. Go for it.

First part

Identify what we already have

1

What is the brain?

As Mortimer Mishkin (1986) said, mind and behavior are two indissoluble terms. There would be no behavior without a brain; therefore, if we want to know something about behavior, we cannot ignore the study of the functioning of the brain. A writer of the height of Arthur Conan Doyle put it in the mouth of his Sherlock Holmes character: «Watson, I am a brain. The rest of my person is a mere appendage.[1]We live, science tells us, in our own heads.

Starting from this premise, it is clear that we have no choice but to begin this journey by first describing what our brain basically consists of, the operations it performs and at what levels it moves. This will make it easier for us to understand why it is equipped with the tools that we will find in it, and the best way to use them.

The brain: a complete DIY warehouse

A LABYRINTH OF ELECTRICAL CABLES

To make a simile that is not too complex to understand, let's imagine that the entire neural network in our brain is like a complex labyrinth of electrical cables and plugs that are connecting and disconnecting nonstop. These cables that make up our central nervous system extend from that perfect box of bone called the skull to the spinal cord, from where more cables will in turn come out to the skin —peripheral nervous system—, in order to collect all possible information from the brain. Exterior. In this way, the brain obtains data on what is happening, on the one hand, within the rest of the body and, on the other, from the external context in which it is located at all times.

In a very basic way and for the case at hand, we will simply point out that there are three types of neurons or cables:

- The sensory or afferent, which are responsible for carrying information about what happens outside our body to our central nervous system. With this information, the brain will calculate and plan how to direct the behavior at each specific moment.
- The motor or efferent ones, which, once the information received by the sensory neurons has been processed and a decision has been made, are responsible for sending the orders from the brain to the different tissues of the body so that they carry out a certain behavior.

• The interneurons of the brain and spinal cord, which are responsible for transmitting information between the two previous ones.

As we can see, there is no millimeter left undone with continuous information in all directions.

Just like the cables we have at home, in which the copper or optical fiber goes on the inside, and on the outside they are covered by a layer of rubber or insulating materials, our neurons are perfectly covered by a fatty layer called myelin. that allows, on the one hand, that the electrical impulses that run through them circulate at high speed and, on the other, that no energy is lost. The most important neural networks are protected by the skull, which houses the brain, and the vertebral column, which contains the spinal cord. Both have their protection system in the form of cerebrospinal fluid in which, among others, the meninges are found.

In addition, these cables can be short or long, and they are not continuously connected to each other, as Ramón y Cajal discovered, but rather they do so as needed and with what corresponds at each moment, although the general activity is incessant. Each of them can have, in turn, a series of particular branches that make connections with other neurons.

Another characteristic of these connections is that they are not automatic, that is, not all the plugs fit into the same sockets. When two cables come together, if the key on one does not fit with the lock on the other, there is nothing to do. As you will see, very similar to what we all have at home in our toolbox.

At this point it is important that we know the voltage with which our brain works. We can find four brain rhythms that change in frequency and amplitude, depending on what needs to be done. These rhythms are:

•Beta b rhythm
Frequency: 15-30 Hz (Hertz)
Amplitude: 5-10 mV (microvolts)
It is very fast and is characteristic of wakefulness with moderate activity. It occurs mainly in the frontocentral region. When cognitive efforts are made, its frequency and amplitude increase. Its highest frequencies, between 25 and 30 Hz, are produced associated with the consumption of sleeping pills and anxiety.

•Alpha rhythm to
Frequency: 8-15 Hz (Hertz)
Amplitude: 20-60 mV (microvolts)
It occurs preferably during relaxed wakefulness and with the eyes closed. It is related to relaxation, rest and pleasure. It is blocked with the opening of the eyelids, since the entrance of visual stimuli causes it to disappear. It decreases in tasks that require visual imagination.

•zeta rhythm q
Frequency: 4-8 Hz (Hertz)
Amplitude: 50-100 mV (microvolts)
It is a slower pace, but broader. It is normal in states such as sleep, hypnosis, deep meditation, problem solving, etc. It is related to that kind of creative reverie, and it is the moment in which a large number of ideas and solutions usually appear.

•Delta rhythm δ
Frequency: 0.5-4 Hz (Hertz)
Amplitude: 100-200 mV (microvolts)

It appears in certain stages of sleep and is present in infants during periods of wakefulness. If it appears in adults, it may be indicating a tumor, vascular lesions, etc.

One of the great advantages that we have is that the brain is very well organized, and the different compartments in which its tools are distributed are already determined by the factory. And also, just as it happens when we open one of those more sophisticated toolboxes that are displayed on several shelves, our brain also has three fundamental levels or regions, and each of them represents a stage of its evolution. As we can see, our brain is the consequence of a fine and persevering work of nature.

Each of these parts or shelves are: the brainstem, the limbic system and the cerebral cortex. Let's see in a little more detail what its characteristics are.

The brainstem would represent the most archaic part and, why not, the most effective, since it is the one with the greatest capacity to process the information it receives from the stimuli of the environment. For most of its functions, it can do without, a priori, reason and verbal thought, since it has worked for millions of years without them and the incorporation of these "puppies" sometimes interferes with its almost instantaneous decision-making. Let's see what it is mainly responsible for:

- Functions such as heart rate and breathing are controlled in the brainstem.
- At the back of the brainstem and attached to it is the cerebellum, whose main function is to coordinate muscle movement.
- Within the brainstem, the reticular formation controls arousal and attention.
- At the top of the trunk is the thalamus, which is where sensations are collected in the brain.

The next ledge, which we have called the limbic system, is linked to emotions, impulses, and memory. It has a component that we have surely already heard about frequently in relation to emotions: the amygdala. It is very important not to confuse this tonsil with the "other" tonsil in the throat, from which we normally have surgery when we are children. Both receive this name because they are an almond-shaped nucleus, which is what the Greek word from which it comes means. While the second causes annoying tonsillitis, the first are responsible, among other functions, for responses of aggression and fear. As you will see, no direct or indirect relationship between them.

There is also another very important nucleus in the limbic system, the hypothalamus, which is related to maintenance functions, pleasurable rewards and the endocrine system.

The endocrine system is not just about weight gain or loss, which is perhaps why it is most familiar to us. In fact, it is of vital importance, since it secretes a series of hormones that can modify emotional states, growth and other bodily functions. Nothing in the brain is superfluous or for nothing and, due to the size of certain nuclei, we could almost reflect that nanochips, which are those increasingly tiny and imperceptible human-made microchips, still have a lot to shrink to reach this level of natural technology.

We now come to the third ledge in our toolbox: the cerebral cortex or neocortex. This was the last to appear in the evolutionary process and, therefore, is still the slowest in terms of information processing. It has, however, other advantages, which make it an essential complement for this journey towards the fullness of life that we have proposed.

This shelf has, in turn, four very well differentiated departments, each with a series of very specific functions. Although they maintain their functional independence, they continuously interact with each other to continue exchanging information in all directions. These four departments are what we know as the frontal, parietal, occipital and temporal lobes. Let's see what they are and what we find in each of them (see Figure 1 of the color booklet):

—The frontal lobe, which is located just behind the forehead, is concerned with speech, with muscle movements, and with making plans and judgments, that is, with the control of conscious behavior.

—The parietal lobe, located at the top of the head and towards the back, is concerned with sensory functions. In this lobe there is a kind of map according to the number of sensory endings in each part of our body. The end result is an image of how we really are to our brain, which is not very flattering, so to speak.

Homúnculo de Penfield y Rasmussen.

Let's not be alarmed, because nobody is going to see us like this. It simply represents the amount of space that each member of our body occupies in that lobe, depending on the nerve endings from which it receives information. We can see that the back, thighs, calves or arms, no matter how developed they may be thanks to the gym, will always be far from the size occupied by other crucial organs, such as the tongue, lips or hands.

• The occipital lobe, which is located at the back of the head, is responsible for receiving and processing visual information, with the peculiarity that it does so in the opposite field to that which is perceived.

• The temporal lobe, which is located approximately above the ears, is responsible for receiving and processing all sound information.

It is very important that we bear in mind that our brain does not process absolutely all the information that exists around it, but rather it does so according to what we call "ranges of perception", applicable to all the senses: what we see, what what we hear, what we smell or what we feel. Let us say that each of them has a range of perception beyond whose limits, upper or lower, the information "eludes" him. But there is no need to worry either. Outside these ranges, the data are probably not relevant to our survival, although they may seem fascinating to us.

In addition, we still have to see one more division, depending on the place where each of its hemispheres is located: left or right. Each of them, according to studies by Sally P. Springer and Georg Deutsch, has more specific functions, but they are not exclusive. Thus, although the left hemisphere is mainly responsible for linguistic functions, it needs the right hemisphere to capture the musicality of language or all the non-verbal information (mainly tones) that accompany it. The left hemisphere is also responsible for number processing and calculation, and in this case it needs its partner on the right for spatial control of what is being done, such as knowing what numbers are added to or subtracted from. others. For its part, the right hemisphere is responsible for emotion, of spatial and musical processing, as long as we dedicate ourselves to amateur music or humming at home. If we dedicate ourselves professionally to music, the right hemisphere will need the left to process all the logical signs and interpret the scores on which the music is written.

The frontal lobe is particularly interesting to us, because it is where emotions are processed, among other things. The left side would be responsible mainly for the positive expressions of emotions, and the right, for the negative ones. Therefore, to process them all correctly, both sides of the brain are needed.

In summary, we could say that asymmetry is relative, since all functions require both sides, although one of them may be more functionally important at a given time than the other.

An interesting point about this hemispheric specialization refers to the differences that arise depending on whether you are a man or a woman. The male brain has its areas of specialization more localized, while the female brain has its capabilities distributed more bilaterally, that is, between both hemispheres. In addition, since the language areas are more closely linked to the emotional part, it is not surprising that they use language for almost all kinds of tasks, something that does not occur in the male brain, which has its emotional areas more closely linked to motor regions. , something that translates into not speaking —for what?—, but doing. To explain it in a colloquial way, the female brain "thinks out loud" while the male brain thinks inward, in silence. This characteristic is essential for men and women to understand each other better, as some tend to think that their partners have gone crazy because they are continually changing their minds, when really what they are doing is putting their thoughts in order... but out loud . They also think that her husband could really use talking about her problems and insist that they do it over and over again...until they get a snort in response. You have to let your brain sort things out, otherwise there's literally nothing you can say. One of the disadvantages that the male brain has due to this more specific specialization is that if an injury occurs, its chances of recovery are lower,

The great multiplicity of connections allows all these areas to continuously feed each other, so that they all have relevant information on what each of them is dealing with. In addition, there is a hierarchy regarding the level of specialization so that, as the information is integrated, it can be treated with higher levels of complexity. As a result, it is possible that on occasion we have the feeling of being several people at the same time talking to each other: not to worry.

One of the characteristics of our brain is that it works in parallel, so that for different capacities there are several structures working at the same time, sending their respective messages. But we are still one and the same person.

Let's see how he does it.

When the different areas of the brain receive information from a stimulus, it has a series of features that are "compressed" into nerve impulses, so that they can be quickly transmitted to the corresponding place. To get an idea, for each stimulus we perceive there are thousands of neurons talking to each other so that the information arrives as clearly as possible.

And for the nervous system to translate that signal, it must first identify a series of basic features of each of the stimuli it perceives, and they are the following:

- Modality. Each of our senses (sight, taste, smell, touch, hearing and balance) has a specialized organ working at its service: the set of eyes, mouth, nose, skin and ears. And each one receives the information in different energetic modalities. For example, the information that the eyes translate when they receive it through light does not arrive in the same format as the smells that the nose perceives through particles with chemical components in the air, or sounds through sound waves. . Given the complexity of the different energy vehicles that transport information, there are also submodalities.
- Intensity. Not all stimuli are received with the same force. Depending on this, there will be a greater or lesser number of nerve impulses.
- Duration. The time a stimulus is presented is directly related to intensity. At the same time that the force is detected, some sensors are responsible for determining when a change occurs, that is, when that stimulus has ended or has weakened.
- Ubiquity. We have already seen that our brain has a kind of sensory map that allows it to immediately identify where a specific stimulus has been registered.

A very important point to keep in mind is that we do not see with our eyes or hear with our ears, but with the interpretation that the different brain areas make of the information received from these reception centers. That is, if the communication and "chatter" through the nervous system between the brain and the different parts of the body is interrupted, the experiences that could occur in the latter do not exist for the mind. And we can see this, for example, with people who have lost sensitivity in their legs as a result of an accident. The sensory nerves in the skin are intact, but since communication through the spinal cord to the brain has been interrupted, whatever happens in that part of the body does not exist for the mind.[two]The phenomenon of "phantom limbs" also occurs, which consists precisely in the opposite, in having the impression that they still have them, when they have already disappeared. This is precisely because the neurons in the brain that were in charge of that part of the body connect or become electrically excited for some reason, so that part is "interpreted as if" it were intact.

But let's continue with those interesting debates that take place within our organism between some neurons and others.

In the same neuron, tens of thousands of "conversations" can be taking place at a given moment at the same time, which are carried out, on the one hand, through connections of these branches with each other and, on the other, through the exchange of neurotransmitters that occurs between them. Both the fact that two neurons connect, and the place where that connection occurs, are known as "synapses."

Not all the neurotransmitters that are communicating a certain information fit perfectly with each other. They must be properly complemented or, otherwise, the data will not run in that place. Some even order each other to "shut up" by inhibiting their behavior, and others, on the contrary, "jeer" in an excitatory way so that more connections are produced, resulting in a harmonious order in which, under normal circumstances, They all do their job perfectly.

Now let us reflect for just a few moments: if thousands of dozens of conversations can be taking place at the same time in a single neuron, how many are taking place in our entire central nervous system? Fortunately, our ears aren't set up to hear that level of lively chatter, but we can be sure of one thing: we have direct testimony of how we feel, emotionally and physiologically, and how we act from all the chatter that goes on.

And one more characteristic of the brain that we must not fail to mention: its great plasticity. All these connections are unique and individual, tailored to our learning and our experiences. No two brains are the same, even though their basic structure is the same. We shape them through our thoughts, our feelings, and our behaviors. We can recover and enhance capabilities, and also eliminate bad habits. That our brain has this great plasticity is excellent news, because it means that the result of these brain operations, that is, what we are, is also subject to this great plasticity. A priori we have the ability to become our personal design, when and how we decide, starting without a doubt from where our vital experience originates:

THE BRAIN IN "MODE ON": A CONSTANT FLOW OF PERCEPTION AND EXECUTION

By now there is no doubt in our minds that our brain is always on, never rests, and even when we're asleep, it's still multitasking. By way of vigilance, the ears remain open in case there is a need to react to any special noise; The thermal receptors will quickly indicate when the temperature has dropped and you need to throw the sheet or blanket over you, or when it starts to get too hot and you need to uncover. While the reason rests, the brain is in charge of readjusting all the internal processes, such as replenishing vitamins, taking proteins to the muscles or finishing digestion.

Our brain maintains two parallel lines of work active: on the one hand, there is a continuous flow of data reception and execution of tasks that have to do with everything that happens inside our body and, on the other, the same is done regarding our body in relation to the outside or with the situation in which it finds itself at all times.

Our brain does not rest, but there is no need to be alarmed about it. In reality, our only action in this regard is to adequately provide the moments of rest, food and exercise that you need to function in optimal conditions. The rest, to our comfort, do not need conscious control to perform at their best. Simply with us knowing that we are alive and functioning, the rest goes by itself. Isn't valuing it, caring for it and enjoying it a way of being happy? Well, let's not waste it.

How the brain works: the movie projector

Later I will explain how our brain deals mainly with two types of language: one made up of images, and the other, of words. The first is instantaneous and the second requires a long learning period. Images are a universal language, so it is easy to understand that it is one of those mechanisms that we have built into our brain as standard. Words are a cultural elaboration, although what we carry innately is the ability to create grammatical structures with different hierarchies that allow us to distinguish the subject from the predicate, and the coordinated clauses from the subordinate ones. But we will explain this in more detail in its corresponding section.

Now we are going to focus on that prodigious ability to translate events into instantaneous language. For the entire brain to be in a position to understand what is happening and what it has to do, it is constantly projecting internal and external images that are neither more nor less than the result of what we observe or what we "think" .

THE TV SET IS NOT THE SAME AS THE PROGRAM WE LIKE TO WATCH: THE DIFFERENCE BETWEEN THE BRAIN AND THE MIND

We often use the words brain and mind as if they were synonyms, when in fact they are not, although both are closely related. I want to make this clarification at this point in the book because later we will see that the work we do to achieve our well-being is mainly mental, although it needs to have brain support to achieve it, and hence the importance of its knowledge to achieve it.

Well-being and happiness are two highly subjective concepts that depend on our perception and on what we finally decide to interpret about what is happening. Or better yet, what happens to me, in the sense of self-consciousness, of who I am, and of who I can become.

The simile that is probably best understood to establish this difference between mind and brain is that of the television and the program that we like. On the one hand, we have a device full of chips, cables, light bulbs, a screen, buttons, etc. —I apologize to the television manufacturers, who are probably proving my ignorance about the components of these devices—; and on the other is what we see on the screen of that television. As with the mind and the brain, we refer to them in a language in which the nature of one and the other intermingle. For example, if we say "we are going to watch television", technically it would mean that we are going to watch the television set, when in reality we are referring to the fact that we are going to watch the program that we like, and that it has an image format.

In the same way, we could say that the mind is the result of the operations carried out by our brain, and that we interpret it through the images that are generated in that process.

Actually, the mind is not what, but how we interpret reality, and its language is images. Language that, by the way, you don't have to learn, because we all bring it built-in as standard.

When our neurons talk to each other, the language with which we perceive them is that of images that, fortunately, we all understand in the same way.

A very nice example is the one that illustrates how we perceive what happens outside our body, that is, around us. In reality, the images do not come to us from outside, but the information that reaches our eyes through light impulses and is transported to the occipital lobes, is translated there by our brain in the form of images so that we can understand the world that surrounds us, almost instantaneously —we are always, as researcher Ranulfo Romo of the National Autonomous University of Mexico says, a few milliseconds late—. We all see the same thing because all brains are equipped with the same system for translating reality into images.

We can also produce internal images in the form of ideas, dreams, illusions, fantasies or plans, which are generated in the same place where those that came from the outside were translated: the occipital lobe.

Here it is necessary for me to make a small clarification that I hope you will find fascinating, like so many of the things that we are going to learn about the functioning of our brain.

Just as we see the images produced by the television, we also "see" the images produced by the brain. Actually, both images are "seen" or are the mental result of the operations that have taken place in the occipital lobe.

We have the belief that we see with our eyes, and that "seeing" is an automatic process: open your eyes and that's it. Well, neither one nor the other. Arguably, the retina, which sits at the back of the eyeball, is the only part of the brain that is on the outside of the skull. The eyes are prepared to receive all kinds of information from the outside that reaches us transported through light waves: colors, intensity, etc. The retina, which is a nerve ending, sends this information crosswise —that is, what is seen through the right eye reaches the occipital part of the left hemisphere, and what is seen through the left eye reaches the left hemisphere. occipital part of the right hemisphere. The point where both nerves cross forming the chiasmatic nucleus is where the pineal gland is located.

At this point it seems important to me to clarify why it is relevant to know how images are generated in our brain, because later it will make it much easier for us to work with the information that we receive.
provides to make decisions that have to do with every minute we live.

Now that we know a little better about the highly sophisticated technology with which we solve our day-to-day lives, we are going to continue advancing a little more on how we position ourselves in reality and how we are capable of interpreting it. Remember that we are trying to understand first how we work, and then how to optimize the use of the tools that we wear as standard.

As we briefly pointed out, our body does not perceive absolutely each and every one of the stimuli that are taking place around us, but only those that are relevant to our survival or, what is the same, to allow our lives to prosper effectively. .

We perceive what is outside through the senses, but it is the mind that creates our perceptions and is responsible for transforming meaningless sensations into meaningful experiences. Therefore, perception depends as much on how the organism is equipped through the senses, as on experience and what we have learned.

What we do from the reception of a series of sensations is not to add the parts, but rather we organize them into a total set, and we do it through an individual filter, made up of the genetics, experiences and beliefs of each. From here, our brain is dedicated to making a series of inferences that may be logical.

Although it might seem to us that perception is a passive process in which there is not much to do, in reality it is a highly active process in which, on the one hand, the stimuli we receive from the outside and, on the other, are interacting. the filters modulated through experience and the knowledge we have of their nature, and that will suppose an interpretation of reality and, therefore, a specific behavior. For example, if we hear a dog barking, a priori the stimulus will be the same for all those who are exposed to it. But the reaction to it will depend on the filtering that our brain does next: for some it will mean "danger! You have to distance yourself quickly", while for others it will mean a pleasant approach to where the animal is.

Earlier we also discussed that we would talk more in detail about the nature of the stimuli we receive, and how we are equipped to be able to encode them through the senses. It seems to me a very interesting little stop, because we are barely aware of everything we do, with very sophisticated equipment, which I think deserves, on this path to well-being, a certain degree of attention and care.

Let's see then what are the different types of receptors that we have to transform stimuli into information.

- General sensitivity of the body or somatosensory system. To get an idea of what state the rest of the body is in, our nervous system is equipped with different mechanisms: mechanoreceptors (react to movement), thermoreceptors (to temperature) and nociceptors (react to tissue damage).
- Smell. In the nose there is a series of chemoreceptors, which are proteins located in the membrane of the olfactory neurons. That is, what we are going to "smell" comes to us in the form of chemical components.
- Taste. It is a sense directly related to the nose, so it is not surprising that we also find chemoreceptors for stimuli similar to those that will be perceived by smell. In this case, they are located on the tongue, on the palate and in the upper part of the pharynx.
- Hearing/balance. In the ear, two types of information are collected: one referring to external sounds and another that corresponds to the state of gravity and displacement. In this case, we find ourselves with mechanoreceptors, since the information is going to be collected through cells with hairs (ciliated) that are found in the inner ear, and that move depending on the position of our head. Sound waves vibrate these same structures, and their stimulation is interpreted in the temporal lobe as music, speech, or noise.
- View. To perceive the information that arrives through light waves we have photoreceptor neurons that are found in the retina, and that are of two types: cones —very small, responsible for colors, and located in the center of the retina — and the rods —which perceive light and are located in the peripheral part of the retina: that is why we have to open the pupil a lot in the dark, so that they can capture the little light there is—. As we have already pointed out, the retina is the only projected extension outside the brain.

It has also been commented that the senses do not perceive absolutely everything that is around them, but only what allows certain operating margins.

Thus, we have the absolute thresholds, which are the minimum stimulation necessary to detect a certain stimulus (light, sound, pressure, taste, smell, among others). If we are standing on the top of a mountain, on a completely dark and clear night, we can see with our bodily senses the flame of a candle on another mountain 30 miles away; we can hear the ticking of a clock twenty feet away in a quiet room; we can feel the wing of a bee brushing our cheek and smell a single drop of perfume in a three-bedroom apartment.[3]

To open a small paragraph, I would like to introduce here a debate that is reopened with certain periodicity: is it possible, given the subtlety of perception, its speed and the way it is processed, that subliminal messages are effective? We're probably all familiar with an experiment James Vicary conducted in 1957 that appears to have included images that prompted people to drink soda and eat corn. To check whether such a phenomenon existed or not, the experiment was replicated again, much to Vicary's reluctance, and the results were, to say the least, curious. One of the conclusions reached was that the brain, even when we are not aware of it, does perceive. What could not be verified was that this small stimulus had the intended effects on the behavior of those who perceived it, Well, that's where the filter that each subject has and the interpretation they make of the stimulus come into play. What's more, a well-known American advertising magazine carried out a test with subliminal messages. When the subjects were asked if they were able to say what the message consisted of, almost none of the five hundred participants got the answer right. Perhaps conditioned by knowledge of the famous previous experiment, they simply said that they had had a certain feeling of wanting to drink or eat during the program. But this had more to do with their expectations, since the actual message subliminally presented to them was "Phone now." According to the records of the telephone company, the effects of said message were null.

By the way, after multiple replications of the experiment were made, none had significant results. Vicary had no choice but to admit that he had made up the results. No comments, right?[4]

Let's continue then with those sensory thresholds that our brain perceives. Our perception mechanisms are not rigid, and we see that they also have a variable regarding the way of perceiving that has to do with what have been called differential thresholds. In theory, this is the smallest difference a person can detect between two stimuli 50% of the time. The differential threshold increases with the magnitude of the stimulus. This means, in practice, that if we add one gram to a weight of ten grams, we will be able to appreciate the difference. But if we add a gram to a weight of a kilo, that same amount will go unnoticed. According to Weber's law, who was the one who made the observations in sensory perception, for an average person to perceive the differences between stimuli, two lights must have an intensity that varies by 8%, two objects must have weights that differ by 2%, and two tones must differ in frequency by only 0.3%. I leave this information for those who are more curious about this topic and are encouraged to experiment.

And for perception, our brain still has a very useful mechanism called sensory adaptation, which is that our sensitivity decreases to a stimulus that does not vary. This would explain why in front of a neighbor's construction site, or an adjoining building, noises can be very annoying at first, but after hours or days one ends up getting used to them. We have to pay special attention because this adaptation can also happen to us with our partners or our jobs and, if there are no stimuli that cause surprise, novelty or motivation, we can fall into the same tedious habituation.

Although sensory adaptation reduces our sensitivity, it offers an important benefit: it leaves enough room for attention to focus on changes that signify new information in our environment, without being distracted by constant stimulation. This would make it easier for us to react more quickly if necessary to a sudden change in the environment. Our sensory receptors are attentive to novelty; if they are bored with repetition, they will take care of detecting more interesting things.

What our eyes see is not really the color, but pulses of electromagnetic energy that the brain later translates into the different colors that we know, and only a part of the entire spectrum, because for our survival we do not need to interpret all the electromagnetic waves that they exist in nature. Other living beings need to perceive other ranges of the spectrum, such as bees, which cannot "see" red, but they can see ultraviolet light, which is the part of the spectrum that causes sunburn in humans.

There are two characteristics of light that allow us to perceive it:

- The wavelength. It is the distance between one wave and the next. The highest frequency gives bluish colors; the lowest frequency, reddish colors.
- The intensity. It refers to the amplitude of the wave and determines the luminosity. The larger the amplitude, the more intense colors. When the amplitude is low, the colors are duller.

Light enters the eye through the small opening known as the pupil. When passing through the lens, an accommodation to the curvature of the eye is produced, and the concentrated rays are captured by the retina, at the inner bottom of the eyeball.

A series of receptor cells, called rods and cones, are concentrated in the retina, which, as we have previously mentioned, are the only external part of the brain. The cones allow us to see the color, and the rods, the intensity of the light.

In the dark, the cones are not activated, but we can see thanks to the rods, although we cannot distinguish colors. The cones are located in the central part of the retina and the rods in the peripheral part. This explains why, when there is a lot of light and the intervention of the rods is not necessary, the pupil contracts. That they perceive the cones is enough. Conversely, when light is poor and rod action is crucial, the pupil must dilate so that the poor light reaches the peripheral part of the retina. The light received in them is translated into impulses that the optic nerve will be in charge of transferring to the specialized neurons located in the occipital part of the brain, which are the ones that give it meaning as we understand vision.

Vision also requires a learning process. All the connections in the different occipital areas need to be well understood to create images that allow us to correctly interpret the reality in which we move.

When a light stimulus is presented, the brain starts its activity without the need for the subject to be aware for changes to occur. To study the time it takes for the brain to react once said stimulus is presented, experiments have been carried out from a field of psychology known as psychophysiology. Both eyes are stimulated separately, not at the same time, and a flash of light or a chessboard is normally used, with a frequency of one stimulus every half second. That is, when a flash occurs, there are two flashes per second, and when it comes to the chessboard, the white and black squares alternate. These studies have shown that, from the moment the stimulus is presented until brain activity occurs in the corresponding region —that is, since the nervous system collects the information until it reaches the place where it has to be translated, the time that elapses is one hundred milliseconds. This time can vary by about 4 milliseconds (that is, between 96 and 104 milliseconds). Later we will see its relevance, since not all stimuli are translated with the same speed.

Some more interesting observations on visual perception

Surely the following examples are familiar to us, because in environments such as the Internet there are very interesting videos about how visual perception is not as objective as it might seem, and also uses mechanisms to process information in a way that is more efficient.

What we perceive of objects that are outside our body is:

- Figure and background. Perception is responsible for differentiating what is most relevant, called a figure, from what is not, that is, from its environment or background.

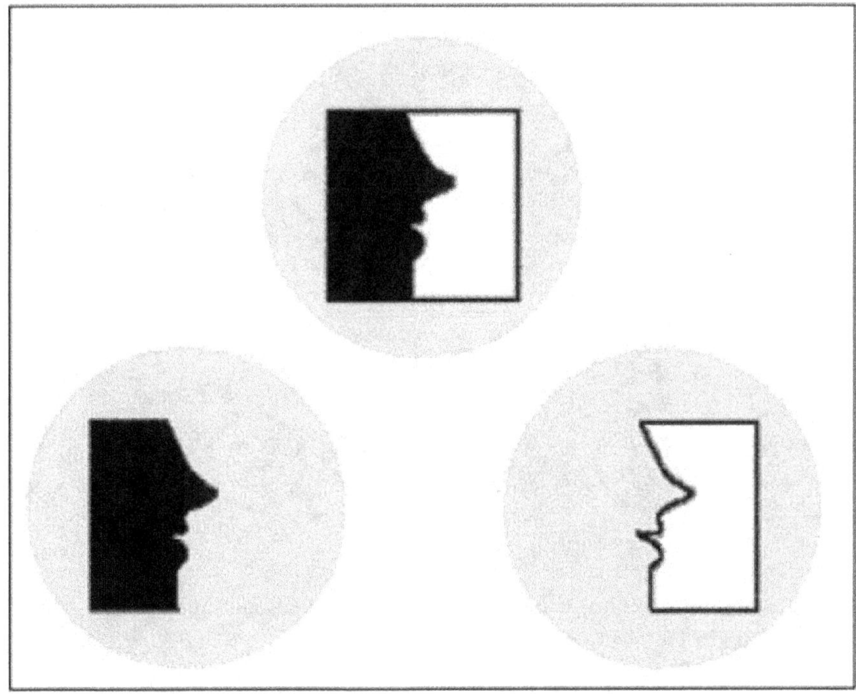

Look at the image. In this case, information about an apparently human face is more significant to us, so we can distinguish it more easily. Actually, what this means is that we give it more informational weight.

- Grouping. The stimuli are grouped in such a way that the information is coherent, so that the perceived whole is not actually the result of the mere sum of its parts.

- Proximity. We group figures that are close to each other.

- Similarity. We group similar figures.

- Continuity. We perceive smooth, continuous patterns more than discontinuous ones. For this reason, although some lines are discontinuous, we perceive them as straight.

- Closing. If a figure has gaps, we fill them in to close a complete and whole object.

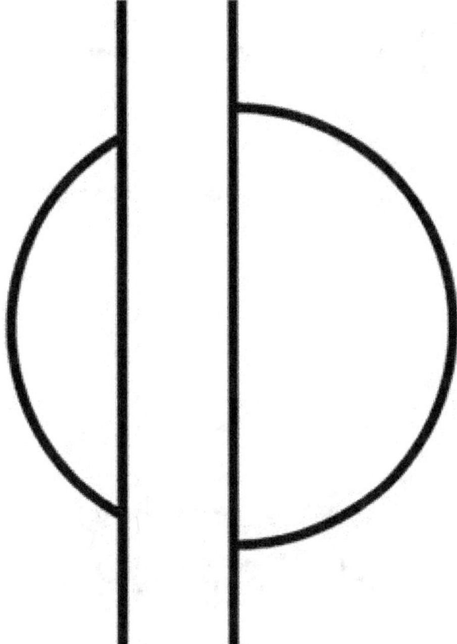

stimulate, there is no circumference, but our brain "closes it" and interprets it as such.
• Connection. We perceive points, lines, or areas as a single unit when they are uniform and linked.

Sometimes the so-called optical illusions occur due to various reasons, such as an overexcitation of the cones or rods. The following experiment is used to see what happens when color vision is "tired" (see Figure 2 in the color booklet).

Other well-known optical illusions have to do with...

-The size. Despite perception, these two lines are the same size.

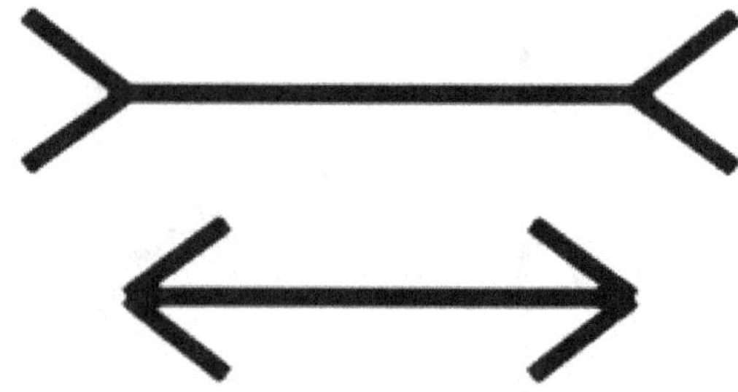

Ilusión de Müller-Lyer.

-Distance. Also these two beams have the same dimensions.

Ilusión de Ponzo.

The lines are straight:

-The movement. Stare at the center point. You will see how the lines move.

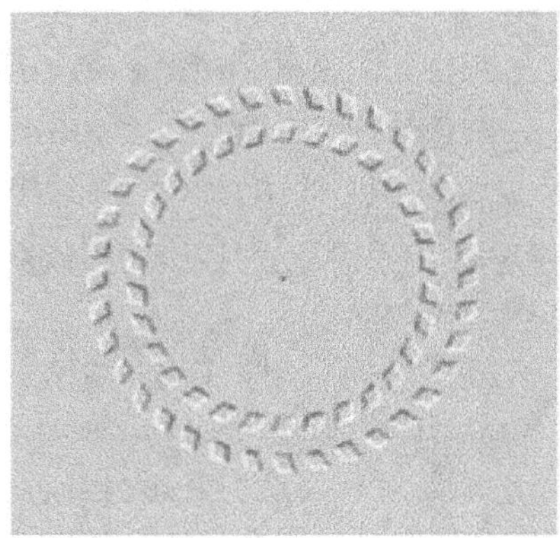

-The perspective. Are we going up or are we going down?

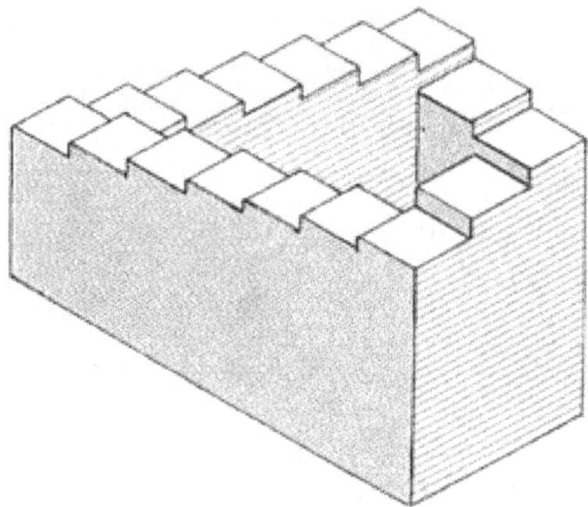

—Colour contrast (see Figure 3 of the color booklet).

Following these characteristics, we are going to see how easy it is to confuse our brain. Let's see in Figure 4 of the color booklet an example of the Stroop effect.

These examples serve to keep in mind that we do not perceive the stimuli of the environment as they are outside of us, but that an interpretation process takes place according to multiple factors that can sometimes lead us to make mistakes.

Optical illusions and misperceptions are normally used by the most famous magicians in the world to make us believe, even though we all know there is a trick, that they have supernatural abilities. Without having to go that far, it is true that sometimes we are convinced that we have seen or heard something that did not really exist, but to the extent that we experience it, it becomes real.

Hearing: how we hear

As with vision, we do not translate all the sounds on the spectrum, but only those that are useful for our survival. Among them, the range of sounds corresponding to the human voice stands out. When the wavelength is short, we hear high-pitched sounds. When it is long, we hear deep ringing sounds. Reduced amplitude gives rise to soft sounds, while higher amplitude gives rise to loud sounds.

To convert sound waves into nerve activity that can be translated by neurons in the brain, the human ear performs a complicated mechanical chain reaction. First, the waves are directed towards the eardrum, which is a tense membrane that vibrates with them. The middle ear transmits vibrations from the eardrum through small bones called the malleus, anvil, and stirrup, and from there they pass to a snail-shaped tube, which makes up the inner ear. In this tube there is, on the one hand, a fluid that reproduces the vibration received and, on the other, a kind of hair or hair cells, which originate impulses in the adjacent nerve fibers, which are the ones that will reach the neurons of the temporal part of the brain.

According to studies carried out by psychophysiology, the time it takes for the brain to receive information from the auditory wave is ten milliseconds. As we see, the brain takes a little less time to translate what we hear than what we see.

Our sense of touch is a mix of at least four different skin sensations: pressure, warmth, cold, and pain. In the skin there are different types of nerve endings specialized in perceiving each of them.

Experiments carried out from psychophysiology indicate that brain activation for touch appears twenty milliseconds after the stimulus is presented.

The sense of taste involves four basic sensations: sweet, sour, salty, and bitter. The remaining tastes are a mixture of those four. Sweet flavors are perceived on the tip of the tongue, and bitter ones on the back. We have already commented that taste is a chemical sense and it is the small activated hairs on each part of the tongue that allow the brain to interpret each nerve impulse.

One characteristic of taste receptors is that they reproduce every week. Hence, when we burn our tongue by drinking something very hot, the injury is not usually long-lasting.

It is important to keep in mind that to determine the taste we also need sensory interaction with smell.

The resulting experiences of smell are far more intimate than one might suppose. It is the sense most linked to our emotions, so we are going to pay attention to it that is surely well deserved.

To smell you have to inhale. The hairs in the nose allow information to be translated by the five million receptor cells found at the top end of each of our nasal cavities. The activity of these cells instantly alerts the brain. Mothers and children, for example, reciprocally distinguish their scent. Surely, many mothers and fathers will identify with the feeling of deep peace that the mere fact of smelling their babies' heads gives them.

The ability to identify odors peaks in early adulthood and declines with advancing age.

It is more difficult for us to describe a smell than a taste or a color. It is possible that, due to the fact that smell is a more primitive element, it is more complex for us to make a verbal description of what activates us, while we can react emotionally in an instant and profound way, whether it is about stimuli that suppose disgust or , therefore, rejection, as if we are faced with something that is deeply pleasurable for us. Smell is also intimately linked to our memories.

If we want to help our state of mind without having to carry out complex self-motivational reasoning, we can surround ourselves with pleasant smells that, on the other hand, improve our attitude and our confidence.

A bit of bad news is that, no matter how much we love a person, if their body odor is unpleasant (it's not that they don't shower, please!), the emotional intimacy necessary to form a couple will be difficult.

Position, movement and balance

In order to determine which movement is the most appropriate at each moment, we must first know what position the body and each of its members are in. For example, to take a simple step it is necessary to receive feedback from about two hundred muscles, to which it is necessary to give very specific instructions.

Human beings are equipped with millions of position and movement sensors. They are distributed over the entire body and supply constant information to the brain. To control position and movement we use balance, whose sensors are found, as we have seen before, in the inner ear, close to fluids and hair endings. We have all experienced what happens to us when we rotate repeatedly: when we stop, the fluid keeps moving. Hence the feeling of continuing to do so, as if our heads were spinning, until everything "falls" back into place.

We have seen that the brain activates more quickly when the stimulus is auditory; then it reacts to tactile stimuli and then to visual ones. This would be indicating to us that for our body the sense of hearing is more relevant than that of sight or touch. One of the reasons that could explain this relevance would be, for example, that from the point of view of survival, it is probably more important for a mother to be able to warn her pup by means of sounds from any distance of imminent danger, so that it can react more quickly.

We can also draw a conclusion for our well-being: setting a place with pleasant musical stimuli can predispose, just at a subconscious level, to be comfortable in a place or not. Paying close attention to the sounds we surround ourselves with, or our own voice, may deserve special attention on our part, since the body is processing them before any other stimulus it sees or feels.

Also, knowing that smells are associated with pleasant moods, we have more tools to feel better in a relatively simple way. When we feel good, we try to prolong the experience as much as possible or repeat it. We have also seen that smells are intimately linked to memories, so we can create, by linking moments to smells, memories that we will be happy to evoke in the future.

However, we must also bear in mind that smells, being linked to the emotional, suppose the most individual and subjective perception, and we can easily make a mistake when trying to provoke a positive emotion through smell, especially if it is in other people. In this case, we will try to ensure that the smells keep a certain concordance with the stimuli that are seen or heard. For example, if we are in a room where wood predominates, we can enhance it with scents related to it (sandalwood or rosewood); or if we have a water point, such as fountains or sounds of the sea, enhance it with fresh or marine scents, etc.

Actually, we work in a fascinating way, continuously, and with great efficiency. So much so that when we realize the prodigy we carry on our shoulders, we feel like exploiting it to the fullest. But is it really necessary? Let's see if it is so or not.

Do you have to use one hundred percent of the brain?

We are now going to address one of those maxims that are part of the repertoire associated with the themes we are working with. Surely, on some occasion, talking to other people about how incredible our brain is, we will have heard that "we are not using it one hundred percent; if we did…!" This reflection usually causes us to remain thoughtful — speechless, most of the time—, and probably with the impression that, if we did so, perhaps we would be people with superpowers capable of extraordinary things. Actually, and I hope we come to that conclusion after reading this book, our brains do extraordinary things pretty much all the time. Another very different thing is that we realize it, we know how to value it and, as we are trying to do in these pages,

This idea of using our brain "to the fullest" comes from those times when there was a significant lack of knowledge about it, while the complexity of all the operations it executes was intuited. Even today, there are still people who continue to think that the brain is "that great unknown", when, in fact, neuroscience has come to unravel in an absolutely fascinating, forceful and extensive way that prodigious network that we all carry on our shoulders. . Yes all.

Now that we have so much information, it may be a good time to ask ourselves the question again: is it really necessary to use all the brain's resources at the same time? Because what would we get out of it? Happiness, wealth, power, love, health...?

Let's start by defining the maxim that governs the functioning of our brains.

minimum energy expenditure for maximum performance.

Although this principle may seem taken from an advanced (or basic) financial management course, in reality our brain has been implementing it for a few million years and, by the way, very effectively.

The incessant activity of our brain needs a good fuel to function smoothly: glucose. With the food that we eat throughout the day, we get the amounts necessary to carry out the daily functions that are required. We are now going to use a simile so that you are the ones who decide what percentage of glucose to take, and if it is really worth it.

Let's imagine that we get home, open the door and turn on the light switch. All rooms have switches, sockets, lamps and light bulbs of different voltages and designs. In principle, we only turn on the light in the entrance and then perhaps the one in the kitchen, if we come hungry, or the one in the living room, if we feel like sitting down to rest for a while. Some of us will have turned off the entrance light and others will almost certainly have left it on. Throughout the day, and as we go from one room to another, we will turn on or off the different switches, depending on the need to have, or not, light in each of those spaces. Sometimes, there will surely be several rooms that are lit, either because there are other members of the family,

If now someone came to tell us: "Hey! Do you know that you can have all the lights in your house on at the same time?", it is evident that, although we do know, we would probably answer: "Of course!, but... for what?". The idea of having all the lights in the house on all the time, far from seeming like a cool idea, probably fills us with astonishment. Just thinking about the amount of the bill that would arrive at the end of the month could even cause some fainting. And, let's remember, just for the light.

Something similar happens to our brain. Its way of functioning tested over millions of years is adjusted so that some parts are working at full capacity (light on) when we are engaged in a specific activity, while the others wait in a kind of waking state, until your work shift arrives. For example, if we are studying, glucose will go to the areas of the brain where it is most needed, such as those related to attention, memory, sight (to read), the motor cortex (to write), etc. If at that moment someone comes to ask us a question and we have to listen to what they say, it will be the parietal area (the one near the ears) that will "turn on" in our brain so that we can attend to what is happening in our context,

In addition, it is very comforting to know that the brain, in addition to the conscious activities in which it is applied for a task, also has a perfectly programmed system to carry out a large number of functions that we do not even have to think about: for example, digesting, beat the heart, regulate body temperature or maintain in good condition the different types of muscles that are distributed throughout our body. Or something even more amazing: a baby growing inside its mother's womb. Can you imagine that we had a system at home that would allow us to save a lot of time, and that would take care of selecting the clothes, putting the washing machine on, drying and ironing them without even having to think about it, and finding them perfectly placed in the cupboards? It would undoubtedly entail an energy expenditure, but in our brain this is calculated to the millimeter, and not one watt more than is strictly necessary will be used. And, definitely, it makes our lives much easier. As it is an ultramodern technology, it is so silent that we do not even notice all the work it is carrying out and, what is more, we have the feeling that absolutely nothing is happening.

Our mistake is "believing" that since we barely perceive what is happening in our brain, it is not doing anything. We are actually running on some really sophisticated and wonderful technology, which requires intelligent maintenance and tuning.

If by using "one hundred percent" of the brain we understand that there are certain types of faculties that perhaps we could have more developed, the answer is clear: without a doubt. But before unnecessarily fantasizing about our super abilities, we must set foot on solid ground and understand that everything that we bring innate and that is capable of being developed to its maximum potential needs good teachers, good practices, regularity and perseverance.

The mental faculties are trained just like the muscles of the body: daily practice, regularity and perseverance.

For example, we may be born with the ability to be good runners, but while, all other things being equal, some dedicate themselves to training daily, eating a diet adjusted to their level of activity and resting so that their body recovers —and probably one day hang the precious gold medal around their neck, or simply enjoy practicing an activity that fills them with satisfaction and happiness, since they have been able to maximize their innate tendencies—others are unable to practice even the slightest physical activity, with the logical atrophy and stagnation in which it ends after years of inactivity. There are also many people who could have been great pianists, but perhaps they were not born into an environment where they had the opportunity to develop this activity. But there is no need to get frustrated: Fortunately, we are gifted to enhance more than one special faculty, and surely, throughout our lives, we feel satisfied with many of the things we have managed to achieve. There are also "plans B", and it is possible that someone who could not be a concert performer has satisfied his innate tendency to become an excellent journalist specializing in this matter.

Something very similar happens with the brain. We are already quite familiar with games for training, to exercise attention, memory, or spatial and verbal reasoning. But the really important thing is that when we know or sense that we have certain capacities for a specific skill, we don't let it accumulate dust in some forgotten corner of our brain mass. With all certainty, it will be an activity that, without necessarily having to become world champions, by the mere fact of practicing, developing and even allowing ourselves some creativity with it, will allow us to enjoy life and, why not, achieve a fairly acceptable degree of happiness.

IS THERE ANY OCCASION IN WHICH WE CAN PUT OUR BRAIN TO ONE HUNDRED PERCENT?

In exceptional situations like the ones we are going to see below, we don't even have to bother to put our brain to one hundred percent, since it puts itself. To understand how our brain works when it decides to turn on all the lights in the house, it is best to illustrate it with an example.

Have you had any experience of an accident or extreme situation in which you were convinced that in the next millisecond the word end would appear in the movie of your life? This is one of the contexts in which it is more clearly perceived what happens when the brain decides that it is in a situation of maximum gravity, and therefore needs the maximum illumination to be fully effective with its objective, which is, let us remember , survival. Now yes, you need all your faculties to be one hundred percent, because you have to quickly analyze the context, understand what is happening, devise a way to get out of it and, finally, act effectively.

If you have had this type of experience, or if you have heard someone recount it, they will tell you that at that moment they see, hear, perceive, feel, smell... everything. It is as if reality suddenly expanded and in a matter of milliseconds the mind opened elastically to collect absolutely all the information that is available and thus be in the best conditions to make a decision favorable to survival. The perception of time and space is altered, because under normal conditions it is neither possible nor necessary for us to think, see and execute with such rapidity.

However, we see that the brain is capable of doing it... and it does. Of course, only when it is absolutely essential. In those moments the energy wear is extraordinary, but the occasion, without a doubt, requires it and in that case not even the slightest resource will be spared. After overcoming this type of situation, the body feels exhausted and needs to recover all the energy invested in order to be able to return to its usual operating levels.

Therefore, the brain does work one hundred percent, and it does it perfectly, when necessary. The rest of the time it is so highly efficient with its consumption and management of energy to allow us to carry out our daily tasks that, without a doubt, it deserves that honors degree that we so often deny it. Our brain works spectacularly, and it is up to us to enjoy such a precise, efficient and extraordinary machine.

The important thing is not to use the whole brain, but to know how to do it well.

Can we now imagine how much glucose we would have to ingest throughout the day if our brains were working at full throttle all the time? Perhaps we would have to be eating without stopping, which would seriously damage the entire digestive system, from the teeth (can we calculate how many times a day we would have to brush them?), to the liver, which, by the way, is another organ that we have to learn to take care with special attention, because it is practically as important as the heart.

Our body is made up of a perfect team that functions with an absolutely prodigious balance, coordination and harmony. And now we are in the task of knowing it, recognizing it and managing it as authentic professionals who enjoy it.

We wear the tools of happiness as standard

We all have a certain idea that we are the owners of our lives. We know that part of the theory well, but when it comes time to put it into practice, good intentions are usually not enough: either we know what we have and how it works, or we will have to let others tell us what to do or why where to go, and many times this does not satisfy us at all, even though we are aware that we have no other choice.

The starting idea is that we are organisms that have to survive in one or several specific contexts: in which we are born, in which we sometimes place ourselves, or in which life has prepared to surprise us.

As Ortega y Gasset rightly pointed out, each of us is "me and my circumstances" and, although his main field of knowledge was philosophy, it is perfectly consistent with what neuroscience tells us today. The rest of the characteristic manifestations of the human being, such as, among others, art and poetry, do nothing more than adorn the only task that interests the brain and in which it has invested all its technology: survival. And no matter how shocking or simplified it may seem to us, it is so.

For this complex task, our particular toolbox is divided into two well-differentiated parts, although they need each other, so that the exchange of information is continuous, reciprocal and occurs at different speeds. For everything to go smoothly, one of these parts processes a huge amount of information so quickly that it is imperceptible to us. We know how it works, but it is difficult to manipulate. It has taken millions of years of trial and error, and has become an almost autonomous and absolutely efficient instrument that handles multiple complex tasks simultaneously without us having any idea of what, why, how or when it is doing it. Can you imagine that we had to control at what rate the heart has to beat at each moment, or what gastric juices must be secreted according to what we eat throughout the day? Fortunately, it is not necessary, because the brain makes sure that everything works with amazing precision. So we have mental resources and more time to do other more interesting activities, or at least they seem so to us, with the youngest part of all that gray matter, which gives us that feeling of "consciousness". Most of what we feel, whether emotions or sensations, are perceived and executed in the most autonomous and "unconscious" part of our body. They can go "automatically", without us having to "think about them", or we also have the opportunity to be able to modulate them with the extraordinary tools that we have been incorporating throughout evolution, and that make up what we have decided to call "reason".

This part of consciousness or reason seems to us to be the great achievement of the human species, but it has a serious drawback: it is still quite slow. It is located in what has been called the neocortex, and has been in the experimental laboratory for a short time. This is quite good for us, because there we can intervene more easily to make the necessary readjustments, as long as we know where we are by turning the screwdriver.

We are going to find things as interesting as working memory, which is what allows us to remember a phone number or make a shopping list, and which is deleted as soon as we have solved the task; attention, which is a periscope or a magnifying glass that sometimes gets foggy, sometimes goes out of focus and perhaps gets stuck on more than one occasion, but which is absolutely necessary for us to use two other wonderful little gadgets: concentration and memory storage long term. And there is still another essential for us to get to where we have marked our travel coordinates: motivation.

Nor do we have to lose sight of the different types of thoughts in the form of verbal language, which are what make up the panel of instructions that our brain executes, and which are usually accompanied by another language instrument that moves quite freely between these two parts of our brain: the imagination.

When we learn to combine all these tools we can do things as extraordinary as setting goals and achieving them; analyze if we are facing a situation correctly; understand the signals that come to us from intuition to modulate them with reason; relate to what —and with whom— surrounds us; laugh and have fun; dance, make music and break sports records; ultimately live.

In the following chapters we are going to approach these instruments, one by one, to learn how to identify and handle them, but above all so that we dare to take our first steps of creativity with our personal work of art: our life.

two

What basic tools do we need to know well?

Our brain also has a series of mechanisms that allow these tools to perform a series of functions, whether we are aware of it or not. We are now going to observe and describe each of them in more detail, so that we understand how they work when they are "in automatic mode", and how we can work with them in a completely voluntary and goal-oriented way.

Two very mysterious and not at all esoteric instruments

A MEGA QUANTUM COMPUTER: INTUITION

We call intuition that "I don't know what, what do I know, what do I know", that makes our stomach shrink, warning us when something doesn't quite convince us, that makes us wince when we think we are being deceived, but we do not have evidence to be able to affirm it, and that makes us relax when we enter a place that gives us "good vibes".

For a long time, "intuition" has been considered the great unknown. The fact that we couldn't explain why we sometimes had a kind of weird feeling about certain people or events gave it an air of mystery. And, certainly, if it was not known what operations our brain was doing when it sent us those messages, the intuition could only be defined as surprising and, in some cases, even "esoteric".

We have already talked about the characteristics, components and compartments of our brain, and we have seen that there is a very archaic part, which has been operating for millions of years and which collects information from the context at a speed that, with the permission of the physicists who dedicated to it, we could call "quantum". I do not want to use this term here in its strictest scientific sense, which refers to the imperceptible how many, but rather in the colloquial sense, which refers to everything infinitesimal that occurs beyond our consciousness and our reasoning, and that encompasses everything that surrounds us, that is, a huge, enormous, enormous amount of data.

For that part of our brain, it is a simple operation that it executes incessantly and humbly: we don't even realize that it is doing it. It deals with both simple issues and managing the most complex information. For example, when we go to a room to listen to a lecture, if the environmental conditions are adequate, we will be able to pay attention without major interruptions to the subject that interests us so much. Specialists in creating suitable environments are great connoisseurs of how our brain works: they know when a light can be annoying if it stays on for a long time, if the sound is at the right tone and volume, if the seats invite you to spend a long time in them, or if the colors and decoration of the environment are appropriate or shocking. Our brain is collecting all this information (and much more) to determine if there is something concrete to do in that context or not. Many of us have experienced on some occasion, suddenly, in the place where we find ourselves, that something changes, we don't know exactly what, but we feel like leaving. There may be some strange noises or silence, the faces of some people may have changed, maybe there is some agitation not too alarming... The brain, which has all its areas in incessant transmission of data to each other, tries to tell us that we are let's march, but he is going to do it in his particular language, which is not precisely verbal: our liver shrinks. in the place where we find ourselves, that something changes, we don't know exactly what, but we feel like leaving. There may be some strange noises or silence, the faces of some people may have changed, maybe there is some agitation not too alarming... The brain, which has all its areas in incessant transmission of data to each other, tries to tell us that we are let's march, but he is going to do it in his particular language, which is not precisely verbal: our liver shrinks. in the place where we find ourselves, that something changes, we don't know exactly what, but we feel like leaving. There may be some strange noises or silence, the faces of some people may have changed, maybe there is some agitation not too alarming... The brain, which has all its areas in incessant transmission of data to each other, tries to tell us that we are let's march, but he is going to do it in his particular language, which is not precisely verbal: our liver shrinks.

What we call intuition is an instant signal from our brain to give us some kind of information, but it does not use reasoning or verbal thought, but rather a sensation sometimes accompanied by emotion. Its language is, so to speak, a kind of very simple binary code: either it shrinks our liver or it makes us relax peacefully.

The truth is that it is an extremely intelligent way of communicating instantly: can you imagine that he had to put us in sentences, with his subjects and predicates, all the information he has collected, what measurements he has made and how he has arrived at the conclusion that "get out of there already"? Too ineffective, no doubt.

There are many people who, precisely because of this non-verbal nature of intuition, have a bad habit of ignoring these signals and, when they want to react rationally to what is expected of them, it is likely that they have already made one or more mistakes. times.

The recommendation that the scholars of this very useful tool give us is that we pay much more attention to what it is trying to tell us; that we trust what our brain is telling us. Its technology is highly refined and extremely precise, except when there is some automated thought, experience or association that distorts the original message it is transmitting to us.

Our intuition is rarely wrong, both in situations in which we can all identify that the answer must be the same, and in decisions that have to do with the particular and individual nature of each person. We will explain this last case better with an example: we arrive at a dinner with some friends and they introduce us to someone who, to our intuition, does not quite convince him, and our liver shrinks. It is very likely that we are not as nice, although we probably keep the minimum forms of education and cordiality, as if our intuition had not set off any alarms or if it had even sent us a signal of relaxation and confidence. We are not in a position to say that this person is not "worthy of mistrust" for everyone. He probably has good friends, work and lead a normal life with other people. But, in this case, our intuition is telling us that "us", with our ideas, experiences, needs, values, etc., "that" specific person is very likely not to feel good at all. And, as we have possibly verified on multiple occasions, intuition does not fail. How many times have we reproached ourselves with a "if I already knew it", or "I should have listened to what I thought"? This is, without a doubt, an important milestone in the process of maturity: we take charge of our lives, of who we are, and of the authorship of our mistakes. If we are going to make mistakes, it is better to do it with our own than with those of others. needs, values, etc., "that" person in particular is very likely to not feel good to us at all. And, as we have possibly verified on multiple occasions, intuition does not fail. How many times have we reproached ourselves with a "if I already knew it", or "I should have listened to what I thought"? This is, without a doubt, an important milestone in the process of maturity: we take charge of our lives, of who we are, and of the authorship of our mistakes. If we are going to make mistakes, it is better to do it with our own than with those of others. needs, values, etc., "that" person in particular is very likely to not feel good to us at all. And, as we have possibly verified on multiple occasions, intuition does not fail. How many times have we reproached ourselves with a "if I already knew it", or "I should have listened to what I thought"? This is, without a doubt, an important milestone in the process of maturity: we take charge of our lives, of who we are, and of the authorship of our mistakes. If we are going to make mistakes, it is better to do it with our own than with those of others. an important milestone in the process of maturity: we take charge of our lives, of who we are, and of the authorship of our mistakes. If we are going to make mistakes, it is better to do it with our own than with those of others. an important milestone in the process of maturity: we take charge of our lives, of who we are, and of the authorship of our mistakes. If we are going to make mistakes, it is better to do it with our own than with those of others.

It is very beneficial to make our intuition a traveling companion to listen to, even if it is in its binary system. It is very comforting to know that we have a very powerful information collection system that is rarely wrong and that it transmits the information to us in such a fast, clear and effective way. Without the set of rules and algorithms by which it operates, we would not be able to cope with the world we are in.

Yes, we carry a quantum megacomputer on our shoulders, which processes a huge amount of information, makes decisions and sends messages. And if all your life you have presumed to have a good intuition, this can undoubtedly mean two things: one, obviously, that your brain works perfectly. !! Congratulations!! And two, that you have learned, fortunately, to decode their messages and, most importantly, to trust them. Keep it up, because that is the correct way to use this not at all esoteric tool, but at least, amazing, wonderful, spectacular, and surprisingly precise, with an almost infinitesimal margin of error.

Let's go for the second of those until now mysterious instruments, but which are no longer so: the unconscious. No, it is not about any person who is close to you, but about a way that the brain has to work so that we can have enough space in the conscious part, which we have already seen is slower and can be misled with some ease. And life should not be thought so much, but experienced more. Or at least that's what our brain teaches us.

The unconscious presides over all the functions of our body, and also the vast majority of behaviors that lead us to meet a series of objectives.

We classify as unconscious all those operations that do not pass through our consciousness, for our reason, that is, those that we are not aware of, but that nevertheless occur. They are like the autopilot of the airplane that, once activated, does not need conscious control by the human and thinking pilot, and is in a position to execute all its functions perfectly. That is why it is so important to know the nature of this instrument well, because sometimes we do things for which we do not have a clear explanation and, nevertheless, if they are happening, it is because they are formulated or enunciated inside our heads. If we do them, it is because, without a doubt, they are. Forgive me for insisting so much on this that seems so obvious, but this redundancy is especially dedicated to all those people who say they don't know why they do what they do. We repeat: because it is stated that way inside your head.

The nature of what we have stored in the unconscious is quite varied: it regulates the most basic functions for our survival, which have to do with all physiological processes, not just the most obvious ones —such as digestion, sleep or blood circulation—but also with body temperature, hormonal regulation, maintenance of tissues and organs, etc. Although health specialists already know a lot about how our brain works in the proper maintenance of all the parts that make up the vehicle it is piloting —that is, our body—, it would be impossible for us to rationally control everything that happens in our body, at that level, every second. So it's great that we don't have to think about how he does it.

We also store experiences and thoughts in the format of our two main communication codes: verbal and image. But it would be tremendously costly on an energetic level to have all these thoughts activated all the time, and they would cause us so much interference that they would only make our simpler daily tasks more difficult. To solve this problem, the brain has a compression process, so that those experiences or thoughts become smaller and smaller for our attention; and more, and more, and a little more. So, when they are the right size, they go into the unconscious format to continue acting from there.

How does the brain compress all this information? In psychology, this process has been called automation, which consists of nothing more or less than the repetition of a behavior so that, by always doing it the same way, the brain no longer has to worry about how to execute it: it It does this automatically, investing tiny amounts of energy in it.

We can learn verbal concepts, but also experiences that, if they are very intense, need few repetitions to pass into the unconscious mode and stay there. And they exert the same type of influence as the rest of the learning that is in that place.

Much of what we do has been automated before we even learn to speak. If, for example, someone asked you what the behavior of walking consists of, what explanation would you give, other than "first one foot forward and then the other"? I am going to make you wait a few more pages to explain to you, consciously, how we do this wonder unconsciously, but learned.

As we have commented in the previous box, we need to be especially careful with what we pass to this format, because once we have made it so small that we can hardly even perceive it, its principles will always be active. It is important that we learn a new skill in the most correct way possible. Sometimes we like to introduce our personal touch, but at the beginning of the learning, when we are automating it, it is not the right time. Let's leave creativity for when we already master the technique.

Let's imagine that we are learning to do a difficult sports movement. Perhaps our coach tells us to put the foot "this way", or the wrists "this way", not on a whim, but because it will be the way to perform the movements correctly without annoying injuries appearing in the future and get the most out of it. benefit of exercise. In the automation process we keep both good and bad habits, and the latter, although they can be changed later, need a slow decompression process (except in traumatic cases), which we usually face with tremendous laziness or reluctance. This is where we clumsily justify ourselves with a "well, that's how I am", when really, and now I hope you understand better how it happens, we have learned to be a certain way: without a doubt,

Three more behaviors that we are very familiar with about how the unconscious works would be, for example, when we are driving and, suddenly, we have reached our destination. "But how did I do it?" If we stop to think, we were so absorbed in other issues that we have not realized the steps we have been taking and, nevertheless, we have done it perfectly. We have not skipped any traffic lights, we have not run over anyone and, on top of that, we have found a place to park. While we were busy with another more interesting or pressing topic, our brain, with its autopilot, has returned us home with millimeter precision. A great resource that has allowed us to address two important issues simultaneously: one consciously and the other unconsciously.

Another example, perhaps not so positive, is that of bad character. There is no bad character gene, but rather we have learned to be that way by intimidating anyone with our insults and getting away with it (this is a great reinforcement to implant a behavior, as we will see in the corresponding chapter). Without a doubt, thanks to its repetition over and over again, we have automated it in our repertoire, so that this habit has become second nature. But we have to be careful: both in private and at work, living with people who have a bad character is quite unbearable and no one has the obligation to put up with them. It is better, perhaps, that we modulate a strong genetically based temperament with learned behavior in a more positive and effective way.

A third example of how our unconscious works would have to do with everything we do that we don't like, and for which we have no explanation, at least consciously and reasoned. Logically, having learned behaviors that are positive for us on a day-to-day basis, far from being a problem, is a real wonder. For example, good eating habits learned in childhood - the appropriate way to relate to food, not eating food with anxiety, not talking about unpleasant or conflictive topics while at the table, eating slowly the right amounts, and everything in its proper measure—will make it easier for us to maintain a correct weight throughout our lives. But, perhaps, at some point of stress, we have taken refuge in pleasant foods, such as sweets or carbohydrates, which are quite pleasant for us. If that stress has lasted a certain duration, it is likely that we have repeated that behavior over and over again... without realizing it. Unfortunately, we will be automating it, as we get the reinforcement of releasing tension and relaxing every time we play it. And its generalized learning can end up leaving us phosphatine facts, since every time we feel angry, frustrated or stressed, we will automatically go to food to solve it. We may not know how we have incorporated this behavior into our repertoire, but if we do it, it is undoubtedly because it is unconsciously stored in our memory store and, without having to spend energy thinking, we execute it. If that stress has lasted a certain duration, it is likely that we have repeated that behavior over and over again... without realizing it. Unfortunately, we will be automating it, as we get the reinforcement of releasing tension and relaxing every time we play it. And its generalized learning can end up leaving us phosphatine facts, since every time we feel angry, frustrated or stressed, we will automatically go to food to solve it. We may not know how we have incorporated this behavior into our repertoire, but if we do it, it is undoubtedly because it is unconsciously stored in our memory store and, without having to spend energy thinking, we execute it. If that stress has lasted a certain duration, it is likely that we have repeated that behavior over and over again... without realizing it. Unfortunately, we will be automating it, as we get the reinforcement of releasing tension and relaxing every time we play it. And its generalized learning can end up leaving us phosphatine facts, since every time we feel angry, frustrated or stressed, we will automatically go to food to solve it. We may not know how we have incorporated this behavior into our repertoire, but if we do it, it is undoubtedly because it is unconsciously stored in our memory store and, without having to spend energy thinking, we execute it. we will be automating it, because we get the reinforcement of releasing tension and relaxing every time we play it. And its generalized learning can end up leaving us phosphatine facts, since every time we feel angry, frustrated or stressed, we will automatically go to food to solve it. We may not know how we have incorporated this behavior into our repertoire, but if we do it, it is undoubtedly because it is unconsciously stored in our memory store and, without having to spend energy thinking, we execute it. we will be automating it, because we get the reinforcement of releasing tension and relaxing every time we play it. And its generalized learning can end up leaving us phosphatine facts, since every time we feel angry, frustrated or stressed, we will automatically go to food to solve it. We may not know how we have incorporated this behavior into our repertoire, but if we do it, it is undoubtedly because it is unconsciously stored in our memory store and, without having to spend energy thinking, we execute it. we will have automated go to food to fix it. We may not know how we have incorporated this behavior into our repertoire, but if we do it, it is undoubtedly because it is unconsciously stored in our memory store and, without having to spend energy thinking, we execute it. we will have automated go to food to fix it. We may not know how we have incorporated this behavior into our repertoire, but if we do it, it is undoubtedly because it is unconsciously stored in our memory store and, without having to spend energy thinking, we execute it.

In other words, everything we do, whether we like it or not, has a conscious or unconscious statement in our brain. If we don't like what we do, we probably won't agree with what we think either. If we are not able to identify what thought is latent, we can describe it with what we do. For example: "Whenever I get stressed, I eat." Well, let's change that thought: "Every time I get stressed, I go for a walk." You have to repeat it, persevere, feel comfortable with it... and automate it (repeat it), replacing the previous one. At first, like all new behaviors that are learned, we can feel a little uncomfortable: "This has nothing to do with me", "I'm not like that", "It's hard for me"... Okay, I'll buy them all! But please, we are going to persevere until the new thinking allows us to carry out behaviors that make us feel proud and comfortable with ourselves. And if possible, that they provide us with the benefits that we long for.

The advantage of applying ourselves well in the learning period, while we are automating a behavior, is that, since there is no loss of time due to injuries, errors or inconveniences, we will be able to develop it more easily to levels of mastery. Surely we will not find a good pianist who plays with the wrists below the level of the keyboard. From there, we can start to introduce our personal touch, our unique stamp and our original contribution. But, for that, it is first necessary to automate all the good habits that have been scientifically proven for thousands of years through the trial and error processes carried out by the human species. Let's not try to skip the steps that facilitate further growth.

A work board: short-term memory

We have many types of memories in our particular toolbox, but we are going to deal especially with short-term and long-term memories, since they are the ones that will allow us to work better with our behaviors.

Short-term memory began to be studied relatively late, and with more intensity starting in the 1960s. In the introduction to this book, we compared it to those little blackboards we used to play with as children that, once the drawing was made, the we moved and it disappeared. They were ephemeral doodles that lasted... almost nothing.

Operationally, it is defined as a store that allows us to retain information for a time, either to work with it or to pass it to the long-term memory store. It is not just an external information receiver, but it is the mechanism that we are continuously working with and filtering information within the system.

It has little capacity and retains information for a short time. It comes into play when, for example, they give us a phone number and we retain it for a few seconds, or when we go shopping and carry the list in our heads... for a short time.

It has an extraordinary importance in cognitive processing, since it works simultaneously with the internal and with the external, that is, with the information that it receives from the outside and with the statements and the rest of the information that it recovers from the interior. Therefore, it participates in all cognitive operations and that is why it is also called working memory. In this blackboard, what is collected through the senses is understood and interpreted.

While working memory is maxed out with all the hustle and bustle of every minute, long-term memory is off, in "power saving" mode. It is the short-term memory that is in charge of activating it when you need it: «Let's see... What was the brand of condensed milk that we bought at home and that we liked so much?», we ask ourselves in the supermarket while we are doing the shopping

SHORT-TERM MEMORY CAPACITY: THE MAGICAL 7 ± 2

It seems that there is a consensus in the scientific community regarding work capacity, which consists of the so-called 7 ± 2. But what does it mean? That 7 refers to units, portions or chunks. Depending on each subject, you can work with 7 + 2, that is, 9 units, portions or chunks; or with 7 – 2, that is, with 5 units, portions or chunks.

Before giving an example that you will understand perfectly, I am going to define some more nuances of these chunks, since they are relevant elements, and then we will return to them.

A chunk, which would be the English equivalent to these portions, is a subjective unit: each individual defines what a chunk is for him.

What is limited is the number of chunks that can fit in short-term memory. The good news is that there is no limit to what can fit inside each chunk: you can put as much information as you want. For anyone it is just as easy or difficult to work with seven books, seven topics, seven sentences or seven whatever.

The limit is in the unit of information, but the information of the unit has no limits.

Now we are going to put a very everyday example: the telephone numbers that we have to remember. Let's take a mobile, which has nine units (7 + 2). Perfect: 713421032 (I hope it's not anyone's...). We can work with it on our board by taking each number individually: 7-1-3-4-2-1-0-3-2. But we can also do it by taking it two at a time: 71-34-21-032 (we have four chunks here, so we could easily work with three or five more units, such as "extension 512", from "7 to 9 " in the morning"). Many people group the numbers in threes: 713-421-032. This way you can even work with two mobile numbers at the same time, and still have room on the board to work with one or three more chunks.

A chunk can also be a complete poem by Neruda, which would allow us to work with seven poems at the same time. Or a completed doctoral thesis. And we would still have six free chunks to continue operating. As we have mentioned, the content of the chunks is subjective and unlimited.

There are certain strategies that help us re-encode information in memory, such as intonation or music. Do you remember the alphabet song? (I had to learn it in English.) Well, that ditty is also a chunk.

So, when you need to work with enormous information in your working memory, you already know: group it by chunks in the way that seems most appropriate to you, but that allows you to have it at hand while you need it, for example, during an exam, the presentation of a job or a trip with many coordinates.

We can imagine the effort that part of our brain makes throughout the day. As it is also responsible for regulating our behavior, what usually happens to us when night falls? Well, we have to let it rest and disconnect it a bit so that it is in optimal conditions the next day. Yes, our prefrontal lobe gets tired too. Have you seen how little children pout and cry when bedtime approaches? Something similar happens to us adults: if we try to talk to our partner or solve problems at certain times of the afternoon or at night... we are not going to do it with the prefrontal lobe in optimal conditions. We're tired, our ability to work with information and solve problems is at a minimum... Can we leave it for coffee the next day or, better yet, for Sunday breakfast? Surely we will work out what is infinitely better, in the right frame of mind and on much better terms. That is what we could truly consider an intelligent and effective use of our short-term memory or multipurpose board.

It is in short-term memory that attention works—and, by the way, it is the only memory that it does. Attention is like a bottleneck, which selects only a part of reality. Afterwards, an encoding process occurs and all the necessary operations are carried out to either discard what is no longer needed, or to make the information be represented or retained in long-term memory.

We are now going towards that other warehouse in which we keep the memories with which we narrate our existence and give meaning to our lives.

The closet to store memories: long-term memory

Long-term memory is the place where we permanently store information, with the advantage that it has unlimited capacity, both in space and time. It supposes, then, storage (unlimited) and retrieval (limited). Both operations can be done consciously and unconsciously. Unconscious processes are much faster and structurally more sophisticated and advanced than those that are under conscious control. In fact, there are encoding and recording channels in the memory system that are independent of consciousness.

With the information that we do not use, recovery force is lost, but not storage. It is like the pot of asparagus that we push to the bottom of the pantry, that we forget is there, but that we can recover the day we need it, when we find it by chance. The advantage of having information in memory is that, even if we are not using it regularly, it can be quickly relearned and recognized whenever it is needed. For example, if we haven't ridden a bike in a long time, but we did when we were little, it will be much easier to catch up on this skill.

We can retrieve information through recognition or memory. This can be serial (in the same order), free (as we want) and with keys or clues. These guide the search processes, but we would need to use our blackboard or short-term memory, since we would have activated our particular magnifying glass or periscope, attention, to search for data in our own store.

In our daily life, memory is usually free with cues ("what did you do with Ana yesterday?"). Yesterday, by the way, was Friday. Do not forget this information for two paragraphs.

"Your face is familiar to me." Why don't we recognize the supermarket cashier we greet every day when we meet her at the movies, dressed differently, with her husband and her children? The recovery of any information will only be possible if during said process the subject has the same keys (context) that were present during the encoding process. We will have to look into her eyes or listen to her voice (cues) from her to be able to match or fit between the person we have seen in the cinema and the one we see in the supermarket.

Let's continue with the example of Ana. When we are asked something and we do not remember it, it is because we do not have at that moment the keys that guide us in the search process. "What did you do with Ana on Monday?" "Me? On Monday...", and nothing is remembered. Information has been crossed. It wasn't Monday when I was with Ana, but Friday. Therefore, I cannot retrieve the information needed by the person who asked me, who — by the way — was very likely to have been clueless as well, and what he wanted to know is what I did on Friday. Alas, these miscommunications! ... Or from memory?

It is then clear to us that when information is encrypted, not only is it stored, but all the keys that surround it. Everything we learn is contextualized. "I am me and my circumstances...", and we are already seeing that the rest too. If it is out of context, it is almost impossible to recover it. If it fails with keys, it is because interference is taking place, since the connection between encryption and recovery is total and absolute.

"If it's a lion, it eats me." Have you tried looking for the jam jar on the fourth shelf when it's on the first? «Yes, but I kept it in the fourth», and in our memory it has been stored in the same place. We direct our attention to where our memory tells us, with its keys and clues. Although it is right under our noses, attention only focuses on specific parts of reality: and memory is telling it to look on the fourth shelf, since it has absolutely no clues to guide it to the first one.

We still have to resolve the issue of whether what we save is rigorously objective, or if we manipulate it in some way to save it. It is like the package of coffee beans that, once ground, we keep in the pantry in a different container.

Memory traces are the result of perceptual analysis. This means that depending on how we perceptually analyze things, so they will be. We can do very superficial analyzes (sensory) and also deeper analyzes (semantic-cognitive, extraction of meanings). The greater the depth of processing, the longer the duration of memory traces. The deeper the analysis, the greater the guarantee that it can be remembered, especially since it has been understood and has involved other brain areas, such as emotion.

Storage is not based solely on repetition. There is a type of maintenance repetition, which is always the same while we use it, and another type of elaboration repetition, which looks for connections and associations with previous knowledge. These contain a great wealth of attributes and, in this case, we can say that they have an absolutely personal touch. The more we elaborate a print, the more distinctive we make it: the fewer features it shares with similar prints, the more distinctive it is. If we have five chicken tupperware in the fridge, one of them can have a special preparation, with curry, fine herbs, nuts and mushrooms; if, in addition, we put a yellow lid instead of blue, like the rest, it will not be lost.

What can we learn from this? That the best memories, the easiest to recover, will be those that we endow with depth, elaboration and distinctiveness. If something is important, we have to make it really special with our personal touch. We remember better what we find congruent.

Long-term memory obviously has to do with learning processes. The great memory researcher, the Estonian-Canadian Endel Tulving, defined memory as the ability of living organisms to acquire, retain and use information or knowledge. This acquisition process is also known as learning.

Some memories have to disappear as learning capacity increases. For example, the primary reflexes, so necessary for the baby, disappear by four months (if not, it would be indicative of brain damage).

As we are seeing, for our survival in optimal conditions we have to take out of the pantry not only cans of supplies, but also a whole arsenal of duly stored memories and learning. Its basic function is going to be to solve problems of the environment in which we find ourselves.

We have good news and bad news. Let's start with the good one: memory, being a recoverable base of knowledge, allows us to modify our behavior at will. Good! That is what this whole book is going to be about.

Now let's go for the bad: human memory is highly fallible. Oh! It seems that all highly evolved processes have a series of restrictions.

We can fail because there was, for example, a miscoding: one of the functions of the brain is to retain traces of all the stimulations it receives, record the intensity and frequency with which they appear, and then give them a meaning. And there are times when each one understands or interprets what he wants.

Another type of error is forgetting, which is neither more nor less than a failure in the information search and recovery processes, not that it has been lost. That is to say, the can of asparagus is in the pantry, it has not disappeared, but we do not know where to look for it and, consequently, we cannot recover it. In reality, forgetting is not a mechanism in itself, but the result or product of the different mechanisms of the memory system.

An advantage of forgetting is that we can consciously activate it at the moment when certain information enters short-term memory and we decide not to activate its repetition. I suggest you read the section on thinking stop, so necessary when disruptive thoughts appear on the short-term memory board, a moment that we have to take advantage of to get rid of them by deactivating them, that is, not allowing them to repeat themselves in an endless loop.

A paradox also occurs in our storage and retrieval system: sometimes we remember what we have not consciously done ("That's right! I took the third left..."), and sometimes we don't remember what we have done. done consciously ("where have I left the keys?").

The advantage is that, after a while, the former is forgotten, and the latter costs us less to learn, which means, as always, a great saving of energy for the brain.

In general, memory, in order to function properly, needs to forget. "Remember your past only to the extent that its memory provides you with well-being," the English writer Jane Austen told us. Therefore, forgetfulness, except in certain cases, is not a memory disease, but a health condition.

We still have to mention a type of maladaptive forgetting, which is going blank before an exam or the presentation of an oral presentation. In reality, it is a task due to the short circuit that produces an excess of stress, or thoughts with a negative statement, for example, about one's own worth. Our memory fails and can leave us in evidence at the most inopportune moments - like saying the name of your ex when you are with another person in an intimate moment. Or is it a failure of attention? That said, in any case, it is a task. By the way, I was thinking about who listens to it..., what about you?

An angular periscope: attention

Attention is the mechanism located in short-term memory or the prefrontal lobe, responsible for collecting and letting —or not— information enter other brain areas, and is at the service of consciousness. It is less efficient than the implicit systems and we have already seen that it operates with very few themes or chunks at a time (remember?).

This high-precision angular periscope called attention is one of the fundamental tools with which we are going to work in practically all the skills that we explain throughout this book. It is interesting to have it at hand and in optimal conditions, because on multiple occasions, if not throughout the day, every day of our lives, we will have to have it.

To understand how attention works, we have to be clear about two concepts that have to do first with our nature and, second, with the context in which we find ourselves. We have already explained before how our brain does not work with all the reality that surrounds it, but only with a part of it, which is the one that encompasses everything that it can perceive through its senses, and these, in turn, fluctuate only in certain ranges of perception that are useful for the survival of the organism. Even operating within those margins, much of that reality is still elusive to you due to the vast amount of information that is available to you and that you have to work with at all times. Without a doubt, it is necessary to choose and select the elements with which you are going to operate.

To get a better idea of how it works, we are going to locate ourselves at a viewpoint, on top of a hill, from where we can contemplate an immense landscape. It is true that we can gloat over the general vision, but if we want to interact with that panorama, we will have to look at something more concrete than what happens in it. To this end, binoculars are installed that allow us to make a more detailed and detailed tour of this immense landscape.

Our attention works in a similar way. We have already seen that there is a part of the brain that collects all the basic and relevant information at an amazing and unconscious speed. At the same time, and in parallel, the conscious part needs "fragments" of that same reality with respect to which it can make decisions about its actions, since it is impossible for it to work with everything at the same time. It is at this point that it could be said that the advantages and disadvantages begin, depending on where our brain is focusing reality at each moment. And, not to vary, to focus on one place or another, you also learn. Let's see what factors influence the degree of sharpness and ability to focus of our particular periscopes.

Faced with the same panorama, individual periscopes stop at a limited part of that reality. That decision will be conditioned by thoughts, moods and learning; but, on the other hand, the chosen part of reality will also condition, in turn, thoughts, moods and behaviors.

The first adjustment coordinates are determined by genes or by inheritance, and here it must be said that some tendencies of our character are encoded in the DNA. Traits such as introversion or extraversion, openness to change, or being more restless or calmer, can condition the part of the landscape in which we decide to stop to, for example, choose the people with whom we prefer to have a good time or go on a trip

The next level of adjustment in focus may be determined by physiological states at a particular time. Thus, the day that our head hurts or we are tired, we probably will not see life in a rosy color and, in the same way, when we find ourselves full of energy and health, we will be in a better position to also see the kindest face of those who visit us. surround, or to interpret certain events in a more resolute and positive way.

The next turn of focus is determined by our emotional states. When we are low in spirits, it is difficult for us to see the bright side of what is happening, while when we are elated by good news, there will literally be some things that slip by or simply do not affect us.

One more spin is determined by the repertoire that makes up our catalog of ideas, thoughts and beliefs. Many of them will have been learned, without a doubt, in the environment of our family or our friends. You can learn to be afraid of other people, animals, diseases... or just the opposite: to relate correctly to each other, not to miss school if you have a headache, or to strengthen the immune system allowing our body to deploy all its resources to environmental stimuli. In the same way, if we prefer to work in silence, we will try to choose an environment made up of people who have a similar concept of work to ours.

Our periscope also focuses or blurs according to our personal needs. The need indicates some lack and, as in nature everything tends to the average to reach a state of balance and well-being, when we perceive that something is missing we will direct our periscope towards the place where we believe that we can supply ourselves with what we need, whether they are caresses , affection, fun, money, understanding, or a very long etcetera to suit the consumer.

All these factors usually act, if we do not intervene in this regard, unconsciously. But we can also do it consciously, for example, when we realize that a certain approach may be causing us unnecessary discomfort.

Let's say that, due to some big disappointment, our mood or physiological state is at a minimum. It is very likely that, in this case, the periscope that we are using from the viewpoint has remained focused, for example, on the dunghill of the city that we have before us. It is evident that this vision does not produce any positive state of mind, although it has its logic and its explanation. At first, the automatic mode directs the attention towards landscapes in accordance with the experiences of that moment, and that, perhaps, even make it get stuck in that part of reality with which it feels identified. We can then intervene consciously by modifying the coordinates in which the blockage has occurred. It is possible that, if the disappointment has been strong, it will be difficult for us to move the objective to another place. In this case, a little oil in the form of positive self-messages seasoned with a dose of perseverance will allow us to contemplate more pleasant places whose observation finally calms our mood and we can manage our structure of thoughts in such a way that we come to glimpse effective solutions to the situations that caused us that unease. The vision of the waves breaking on the shore of the beach is a good tool to put our thoughts in a more pleasant and constructive order. A little oil in the form of positive self-messages seasoned with a dose of perseverance will allow us to contemplate more pleasant places whose observation finally calms our mood and we can manage our structure of thoughts so that we can glimpse effective solutions to the situations that caused us that restlessness. The vision of the waves breaking on the shore of the beach is a good tool to put our thoughts in a more pleasant and constructive order. A little oil in the form of positive self-messages seasoned with a dose of perseverance will allow us to contemplate more pleasant places whose observation finally calms our mood and we can manage our structure of thoughts so that we can glimpse effective solutions to the situations that caused us that restlessness. The vision of the waves breaking on the shore of the beach is a good tool to put our thoughts in a more pleasant and constructive order.

Our periscope will unconsciously focus where experiences, beliefs, needs, or physiological states take it. We can do it, consciously, to where we want our emotions and thoughts to be at each moment.

Now that we know what factors influence the way in which our attention changes coordinates, and how we can also introduce those that seem most appropriate to us, we are going to continue analyzing some more characteristics that will be extremely useful to us.

It is important to keep in mind that, where we put our attention, that is where our brain will go. This always needs a route map and clear coordinates, conscious or unconscious. That is why it is crucial that we learn to correctly state the statements that we put before him, because he is going to fulfill them with millimeter precision.

We will surely remember that, on our first nightly outings with the car, when another vehicle was coming in the opposite direction, the lesson was: "Don't look at the headlights, look straight ahead." Or if we are driving along a tree-lined road, we cannot keep our eyes fixed on the tree that is next to the road, but we must keep our eyes straight ahead. Indeed, wherever we direct our gaze our attention also goes. If we do not want to end up in an accident against the other car or crashing into a pine tree, we must keep our eyes on our objective, on our way, without allowing other elements to make us change our course.

This example will help us to explain why negative statements do not work for us. If I tell you not to think of an ostrich, I don't need to have the ability to read your mind to know that you are thinking precisely what I told you not to do: an ostrich. If what I want is for you to think of an elephant, the statement must be direct and clear: "Imagine an elephant." How does this translate into the small discomforts of our day to day? If, for some reason, the relationship with our mother is not exactly good, and is also emotionally and rationally charged, we may have introduced the following coordinates into our thought structure: "I don't want to look like my mother." Where have we put the focus of our attention? In our mother. Where will our brain go? Towards all those coordinates with which we define our mother. Who will we end up resembling?... Yes, our mother. How is it possible? Well here we have the answer. It is perfectly legal not to want to look like your own mother if you are not comfortable with the idea, but, immediately after identifying the reasons that support the decision, you have to tell your brain who to look like: the mother of my friend whom I have always admired so much? Audrey Hepburn? The teacher who taught me so much during my studies?

We must make it very clear to the brain what is the destination we want to reach, instead of repeatedly repeating where we should not go, because, when we want to realize it, we will be where we did not want. They were the only coordinates available to our attention.

And we still have to solve another uncomfortable situation, which is the one that occurs when our periscope is spinning without focusing on anything in particular, so that we are not able to make any decisions. We feel as if we were going over and over again the ring road that surrounds our city, never getting anywhere and, if the situation continues unnecessarily, even with symptoms of dizziness. It is necessary to make a stop and establish at least a few minimums towards which to start heading. Beach or mountain? Beach. With warm or cool environment? Cool. Well, we already know that, for now, we are going north. Once we are en route and moving towards a goal that is not yet very clear, but at least somewhat more defined, we can decide if we want sand or stones, an urban or wild environment, or crowds or isolation. Surely there is a beach for every taste. Many times, when we find ourselves stuck in a situation, it is better to make small decisions that allow us to get out of that initial quagmire, and then define our objectives with greater precision. It doesn't matter being in Burgos if you suddenly realize that, in reality, where you wanted to go was Almería. Soon you'll be enjoying a nice day at the beach instead of endlessly driving around an already boring beltway that leads nowhere. to then define our objectives with greater precision. It doesn't matter being in Burgos if you suddenly realize that, in reality, where you wanted to go was Almería. Soon you'll be enjoying a nice day at the beach instead of endlessly driving around an already boring beltway that leads nowhere. to then define our objectives with greater precision. It doesn't matter being in Burgos if you suddenly realize that, in reality, where you wanted to go was Almería. Soon you'll be enjoying a nice day at the beach instead of endlessly driving around an already boring beltway that leads nowhere.

Another important characteristic of attention is that it is continually opening and closing or, what is the same, focusing, unfocusing, moving from one side to another according to the stimuli it needs and refocusing. The act of focusing involves an energy expenditure that the brain only does when it considers it strictly necessary. Depending on the degree of focus, you will spend more or less energy and, as we have already mentioned, the mental functions are trained in a similar way to the body muscles and, in the same way, they can cause us the same exhaustion. Have you ever wondered why conversations with certain types of people leave us exhausted? Normally, their themes focus on negative issues, complaints, regrets, etc. Our brain has an innate tendency to pay special attention to negative stimuli, which are the ones it likes to resolve as quickly as possible. When we are with fun, pleasant or pleasant people we go home with a pleasant feeling of well-being and even full of energy. When, on the other hand, we have to pay special attention to negative messages for an entire afternoon, we come back with the feeling that they have sucked us to the core and that we have run out of reserve minimums. In reality, they have not robbed us of energy, but they have forced us to make an overexertion with a continuous maintenance of attention that leaves our brain, literally, exhausted. The learning that this knowledge implies is that, on the one hand, we must apply ourselves not to be burdensome if we want people to feel comfortable when they are with us and, on the other hand, that when we see that someone demands disproportionate attention from us, either we change the subject, or the conversation partner. We don't know what we're going to need our energy for in a while, but it's best to maintain healthy levels. In case you are interested, the person who complained so much, after being with us for a while, will be as good as new. So much attention received is a reinforcement that her brain finds very, very comforting. but it is better to maintain healthy levels. In case you are interested, the person who complained so much, after being with us for a while, she will be as good as new. So much attention received is a reinforcement that her brain finds very, very comforting. but it is better to maintain healthy levels. In case you are interested, the person who complained so much, after being with us for a while, she will be as good as new. So much attention received is a reinforcement that her brain finds very, very comforting.

Another particularity of attention is that we can focus it even more powerfully in extreme situations where we need to be extraordinarily precise. For example, in a top-level competition, or in the execution of a delicate job or situation that practically allows no margin for error, attention can be focused to unsuspected limits, but at a cost: when we are focusing with such precision on one point, the rest of the image is distorted. The brain needs all its resources for an important task and the surrounding stimuli will lose their value. All attention is literally on a single point. We have no more for the rest. But, as we have already seen that prolonged maintenance of attention produces a lot of wear and tear, The capacity that we have just described is extraordinary for exceptional cases, but it is not advisable that it occupy too much time of our lives, because, perhaps, when we open the focus of attention again and look around us, we find that the landscape has changed, and not always to our liking. Some people, neglected, may be gone forever.

Attention is also very important in the processes of storing information in memory. In this case, the simile that we could use is like those machines that have a hook that moves with a lever to catch a stuffed animal or an object. We take a part of reality, and we take it to the memory store. Again, this process can be done consciously or unconsciously, let's not forget that these two mechanisms are continuously active. If we want to retrieve a data package from our store, we will first have to have saved it in it. This, which seems too obvious, is not so in situations, for example, of stress. When we are very stressed, attention is not well focused and, if stress levels rise, we directly leave it out of play: we do not remember where we have put the keys or they have even ended up in the trash "without realizing it", at the same time that we threw away the advertising brochures that we carried in our wallet. How have we been able to do this? Are we going crazy? Or are we suffering from early degenerative processes? Don't worry, it's just that we are not letting our attention direct our actions well or collect the information properly and, not being aware of what we have done with them, there will be nothing to get out of the memory store: zero, in white. Therefore, it is better to regain calm or a rhythm with which we feel dynamic, but not out of focus, and that the periscope opens and closes with its most precise mechanisms, instead of opening and closing the clamp without rhyme or reason. .

In summary, this would be the main decalogue to keep in mind when we are working with our attention:

Decalogue for optimal use of care

1. Attention works in parallel with conscious and unconscious mechanisms.
2. Attention is focused by adjusting according to our genes, our physiological and emotional states, our experiences and beliefs, and also according to our needs.
3. Attention works by selecting "parts of the whole."
4. The activity of attending consists of an incessant focusing, unfocusing, moving in search of stimuli and focusing again.
5. What our attention is focusing on determines our mood, both positive and negative.
6. The brain will direct its action towards the coordinates on which the attention is focused, consciously or unconsciously.
7. The statements addressed to our attention must be formulated in the positive.
8. Attention needs constant and clear focus coordinates.
9. In rare situations, high-precision focusing involves a distorted focus of the environment.
10. Attention is an essential instrument for the correct encoding of information in the memory store.

Closely linked to attention we find in our toolbox another very useful device, which will allow us to achieve more elaborate goals, based on concentrating energy on the constant maintenance of attention: a microwave called concentration.

We have already seen how when we have to carry out complex operations, attention needs to be maintained for a longer time, more focused on just a small part that concerns us, so that the rest of the stimuli do not interfere with what we are doing. In this way, with our entire attention span held at a single point, we "warm up" our subject matter in a way that shortens the time it takes to understand, apprehend, and reach it.

We need concentration to memorize, for example, the large amount of data from a study subject in a relatively short space of time, from an important paper, or from a physical activity that involves many of our muscles with very precise coordination. .

But we can also use concentration to isolate ourselves from surrounding stimuli and be aware only of our state of calm and relaxation.

This is one of the moments when we can imagine all those neurons that we talked about in the first chapter and that are in a constant chatter. When it is necessary to activate this instrument of concentration, some act as support for the others, and silence those whose talk is irrelevant. All energy has to be directed and used in a single task, and the brain understands this. It is also a mechanism that, like most of those we are seeing, needs practice and perseverance so that it becomes easier for us to use it.

We have already commented that stress is one of the great distorters of attention and, therefore, of concentration. This requires a state of stillness that allows the brain to apply itself in the most efficient way possible, so all relaxation techniques will be a good way to enhance this ability. The one that I suggest you mainly has to do with breathing control, performing rhythmic inspirations and expirations that allow you to eliminate contractures of all the body muscles and allow oxygen to circulate unhindered through the bloodstream, nourishing each cell of our body. If when exhaling the air we do it with force, we will feel that a large part of the accumulated tension is disappearing and we are reaching states of deeper stillness. But surely everyone has their own way of relaxing, so we leave it to your choice: some will do it with music, others taking a walk in the mountains or by the sea, or even watching a nice movie. The important thing is that we get our body and brain free of useless tension.

It is true that we can and should also be highly concentrated in very extreme situations, but those who have reached high levels of expertise in a specific skill know that, even in the most difficult moments, a certain degree of relaxation must be maintained so that the mind can focus. and concentrate well on the required operation. It is absolutely ineffective to allow some type of tension, except the positive and necessary one to execute the action, to interfere when we are carrying out a maneuver, physical or mental, of a certain complexity.

Aladdin's Magic Carpet: Imagination

The first faculty of man is the imagination. It is the first language with which he translated and understood his reality and that of what surrounded him.

An imagination adrift or loaded with negative scenes, both from the environment and from itself, or from the future, will undoubtedly shipwreck a precious life project. It doesn't matter if one says he doesn't want something, if he has it encoded in his imagination. When the imagination and the will conflict, the first is always the most powerful and, therefore, the great winner.

In the same way, a correctly educated imagination, which has learned to vary, to move through it like a fish to water, to add or subtract rational analyzes and emotional experiences, allows us to achieve mastery over ourselves, which ultimately is neither more or less than that state of satisfaction that we long for. When the will and the imagination are consistent, the results are not summative, but exponential. The sky, as Dr. Wayne Dyer used to say, is the limit.

TRANSPORTING US TO THE PAST

It is an obvious fact that we cannot change the events of the past. What happened will stay that way forever. At least objectively. As we have already seen when analyzing long-term memory, we keep from reality what we perceive of it through the elaboration that is done in short-term memory. In addition, we usually do a lot of manicures and pedicures for each situation, the consequence of which —as we have seen— is oblivion: if it was a wonderful experience, surely we will keep what we liked the most and, from repeating so much only the good, in the end the we do even better. This also happens with bad experiences: many people tend to forget the bad and keep the good, so they repeat the same mistakes, with the same people or with people of the same type. Or, on the contrary, Faced with those same bad experiences, we can stay over and over again with only the terribleness of the situation, which is why we will probably make it even worse... in our present. If someone has suffered from post-traumatic stress, they probably understand what we are talking about. The past is present again and again, as if it were the first day. Images and emotions return as if they were being experienced at this very moment.

Our imagination then allows us to fly into the past and bring all those experiences, wonderful or not, to the present. Something that has been found is that the more positive the memories, the stronger the self-esteem and life experience of the person. Whether they are true or not.

It is important that we use our imagination when we want to change, not just what happened, but the experience of what happened.

That is why this transport to the past with our imagination is so important, especially in traumatic cases, so that we can unblock situations that emotionally, by remaining in the same painful way as when they occurred, impede the growth and healthy development of the person. in the present and in the future.

How to «fly» to that period of our life? My suggestion is to do it consciously, so that we can control how far we stay from the situation, when and how long we have to make approach maneuvers to analyze something in more detail. If someone is now experiencing scenes of abuse of any kind in their childhood, or accidents in the past, or bad relationships that had negative consequences, we are going to get on the magic carpet without delay and do a flight of inspection.

Imagine that we return to that moment, accompanied by someone who advises us or loves us well, with whom we feel safe. Let's not forget that we are accessing that memory with our imagination. Once we are flying over this place, explain to your companion what is happening (it can be a real or fictional person, or someone you would like to have as a reference, whom you choose). Describe specifically what you are experiencing. It is possible that certain emotions begin to stir within you as a result of evoking that memory. If you feel bad, take flight and look for a few moments at the sky or at some pleasant landscape..., but do not remain unnecessarily in that scene. Now try to fly over it and analyze it from another angle. What would someone who saw it from this other point of view be thinking? Repeat the operation always changing the perspective from which you can observe what happened. There will probably be some that you prefer not to delve into. Take flight immediately and head elsewhere. At some point you will find the weak point of the situation, a place where no one can bother you and where to lay your magic carpet. Then invite who you were at that time... to come up with you. Tell him that you come from his future to take care of the situation. Generate an atmosphere of trust and create a climate of understanding and affection towards yourselves. Tell him that you are going to take a little flight and invite him to visit his current situation. It is important that you understand and help each other: you, to get out of the past; to them (or them) to be able to change your memory and, as a consequence, your present. Go back to the scene from the past and fly over it from all the angles that you have analyzed previously, and explain to it all the things that you have already realized: why it happened, what you could have done, why you could not have done anything else, and what More importantly, what are you going to do from now on? Perhaps it means you have to remove certain people from your life: say goodbye to them or simply leave; In your imagination, you can tell the person who is hurting you in the past that they are not going to be able to do it in the present, because you are taking care of the situation and yourself. That he was unsuccessful in what he did, and that you have made the decision to take care of everything that affects you. Embrace deeply the person you were, create a space just for the two of you; feel how she is comforted in your arms, how you transmit the confidence and serenity that, from now on, everything will be fine; that this experience has made you learn very important things, among others, to love each other; that you will never abandon her and that she can always count on you. Keep hugging each other until you manage to feel that there is peace and serenity in both of you. Stay as long as it takes. When you have achieved it, you can say goodbye to that person, and nobody is going to hurt him. In that same scene he is safe, because you are. Repeat this exercise as many times as you consider necessary until you feel that you no longer have to fly over that scenario again, because everything is in order there and it no longer affects your present. create a space just for the two of you; feel how she is comforted in your arms, how you transmit the confidence and serenity that, from now on, everything will be fine; that this experience has made you learn very important things, among others, to love each other; that you will never abandon her and that she can always count on you. Keep hugging each other until you manage to feel that there is peace and serenity in both of you. Stay as long as it takes. When you have achieved it, you can say goodbye to that person, and nobody is going to hurt him. In that same scene he is safe, because you are. Repeat this exercise as many times as you consider necessary until you feel that you no longer have to fly over that scenario again, because everything is in order there and it no longer affects your present. create a space just for the two of you; feel how she is comforted in your arms, how you transmit the confidence and serenity that, from now on, everything will be fine; that this experience has made you learn very important things, among others, to love each other; that you will never abandon her and that she can always count on you. Keep hugging each other until you manage to feel that there is peace and serenity in both of you. Stay as long as it takes. When you have achieved it, you can say goodbye to that person, and nobody is going to hurt him. In that same scene he is safe, because you are. Repeat this exercise as many times as you consider necessary until you feel that you no longer have to fly over that scenario again, because everything is in order there and it no longer affects your present. feel how she is comforted in your arms, how you transmit confidence and serenity that, from now on, everything will be fine; that this experience has made you learn very important things, among others, to love each other; that you will never abandon her and that she can always count on you. Keep hugging each other until you manage to feel that there is peace and serenity in both of you. Stay as long as it takes. When you have achieved it, you can say goodbye to that person, and nobody is going to hurt him. In that same scene he is safe, because you are. Repeat this exercise as many times as you consider necessary until you feel that you no longer have to fly over that scenario again, because everything is in order there and it no longer affects your present. feel how she is comforted in your arms, how you transmit confidence and serenity that, from now on, everything will be fine; that this experience has made you learn very important things, among others, to love each other; that you will never abandon her and that she can always count on you. Keep hugging each other until you manage to feel that there is peace and serenity in both of you. Stay as long as it takes. When you have achieved it, you can say goodbye to that person, and nobody is going to hurt him. In that same scene he is safe, because you are. Repeat this exercise as many times as you consider necessary until you feel that you no longer have to fly over that scenario again, because everything is in order there and it no longer affects your present. how do you transmit the confidence and serenity that, from now on, everything will be fine; that this experience has made you learn very important things, among others, to love each other; that you will never abandon her and that she can always count on you. Keep hugging each other until you manage to feel that there is peace and serenity in both of you. Stay as long as it takes. When you have achieved it, you can say goodbye to that person, and nobody is going to hurt him. In that same scene he is safe, because you are. Repeat this exercise as many times as you consider necessary until you feel that you no longer have to fly over that scenario again, because everything is in order there and it no longer affects your present. how do you transmit the confidence and serenity that, from now on, everything will be fine; that this experience has made you learn very important things, among others, to love each other; that you will never abandon her and that she can always count on you. Keep hugging each other until you manage to feel that there is peace and serenity in both of you. Stay as long as it takes. When you have achieved it, you can say goodbye to that person, and nobody is going to hurt him. In that same scene he is safe, because you are. Repeat this exercise as many times as you consider necessary until you feel that you no longer have to fly over that scenario again, because everything is in order there and it no longer affects your present. that you will never abandon her and that she can always count on you. Keep hugging each other until you manage to feel that there is peace and serenity in both of you. Stay as long as it takes. When you have achieved it, you can say goodbye to that person, and nobody is going to hurt him. In that same scene he is safe, because you are. Repeat this exercise as many times as you consider necessary until you feel that you no longer have to fly over that scenario again, because everything is in order there and it no longer affects your present. that you will never abandon her and that she can always count on you. Keep hugging each other until you manage to feel that there is peace and serenity in both of you. Stay as long as it takes. When you have achieved it, you can say goodbye to that person, and nobody is going to hurt him. In that same scene he is safe, because you are. Repeat this exercise as many times as you consider necessary until you feel that you no longer have to fly over that scenario again, because everything is in order there and it no longer affects your present.

because you are Repeat this exercise as many times as you consider necessary until you feel that you no longer have to fly over that scenario again, because everything is in order there and it no longer affects your present. because you are Repeat this exercise as many times as you consider necessary until you feel that you no longer have to fly over that scenario again, because everything is in order there and it no longer affects your present.

We will have managed to change not only what happened, but the experience and the memory of what happened. Take advantage of the occasion and this prodigious instrument so that, now that you can, your boy or girl feels as you always wanted: happy.

Overcoming the trauma depends on this trip to the past, on its reinterpretation; In many cases, in addition, the support of the environment is crucial, but not essential.

And, of course, we can use our carpet to the past to remember all the wonderful moments we have lived, as many times as we want, however we want. Invite all your other "I's" to fly with you, to enjoy... and if in the past you had nothing to visit, it is time to start projecting a wonderful future together. Without a doubt, you deserve it.

We changed the flight coordinates...

There is only one way to create reality: by imagining it. Everything that exists was first thought. Everything we do has been designed, consciously or unconsciously, thanks to that trip to the future with our imagination.

We have already talked about the importance of having our mind focused on a goal... which is undoubtedly in the future, even if it is five minutes from now.

I really like using this tool with the participants in my courses, because many of them, despite understanding the difficulties they have at present, do not seem willing to make changes in their lives. That way, if they don't project where they want to be in a while, the repertoire of behaviors they have today will lead them to more of the same than there is now.

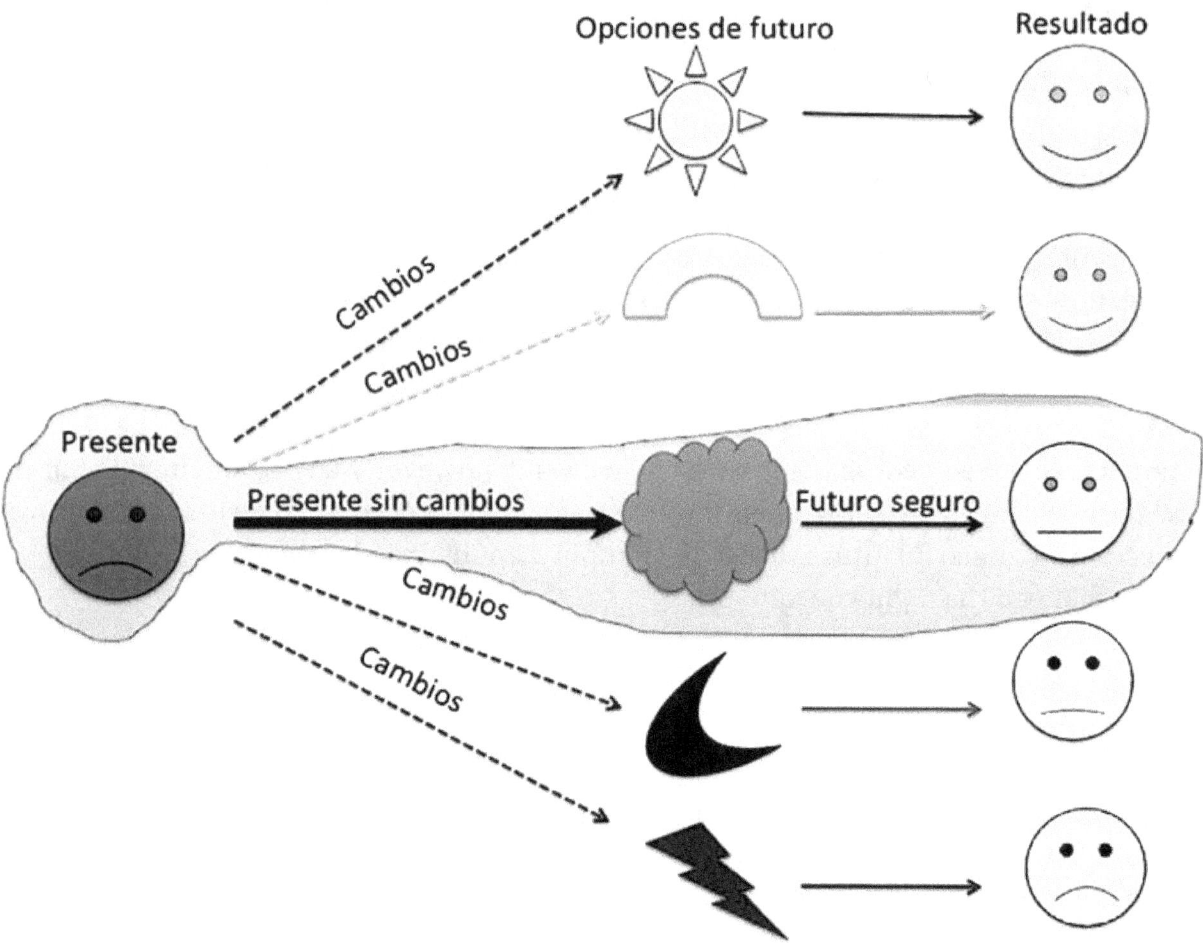

Again, the future is not written. Before us there is always a range of possibilities that our imagination, that "projection", allows us to explore from different angles to finally decide what goal we want to reach. Once the new coordinates are defined, we must check how far we are from them at present, identify what we need to reach our new destination, and set course towards it. Thus, every time we find it difficult to acquire a new habit or learning, the clear and enriched image of where we want to go must be powerful enough (that is, emotionally and rationally charged) to maintain motivation optimally.

When we do this analysis with the people who come for consultation, there are many people who do not want to hear what the reality that awaits them in the future is and that, if no changes are introduced, it is the most probable —and, by the way, we break with the myth that people go to a psychologist to hear what they want to hear. Still, he prefers not to intervene and blocks his ability to understand, emotionally, where he is leading his life. As our intervention capacity is limited, we wait for patients to decide to take charge of what happens to them.

However, the fun part of this job is getting on that magic carpet together and flying over all the options that it is possible to reach, always in the context marked by the person who makes the consultation, not by the therapist. Some alternatives will be more accessible than others, others will have to be discarded and, finally, we will always have a plan A, B, C and even D that takes us as close as possible to where we want to be. From there, we analyze exactly what the current context is, the resources available and a travel plan is designed towards a more satisfying life. It is important to take the time necessary to make a detailed and parsimonious analysis, because, once we start it, the brain will strictly comply with its new travel coordinates,

The design of our well-being well deserves that we dedicate the necessary time to it, so that our energy is, finally, correctly channeled.

Are we so excited that we can hardly wait to get going? One moment, please. In some cases, the path will be uphill or it will not seem as easy as we thought when we started it. But since we carry everything that is essential in our toolbox, we are now going to understand the management and optimization of another tool that we have to learn to use so that, when energy is low, we know how to plug into it and recover energy levels. enthusiasm we need to walk our path...

The rechargeable battery pack: the motivation

As motivation per se does not exist, but rather it is a way of describing the behaviors we carry out through which we achieve goals and carry out a series of actions, we are going to first present you with a set of theories or psychological perspectives that explain how or why we motivate ourselves, to finally explain the practical application that we usually give to this wonderful battery box that, when charged and well focused, allows us to achieve our goals and dreams. Frankly, it is very difficult to explain happiness and well-being without the intervention of this ability that allows us to feel so satisfied with ourselves, with what we have achieved and, why not, with life.

Surely you have heard of a psychologist named Abraham Maslow, whose theories have been widely used in advertising media and business courses. Maslow proposed the existence of a hierarchy of needs, so that as we satisfy the lower level needs, we are motivated to do the same with the higher level needs.

That hierarchy, from the lowest level to the highest, would be organized as follows:

- Physiological needs. Need to satisfy, among others, hunger and thirst.
- Security needs. Need to feel that the world is organized and predictable; need to experience security, tranquility and stability.
- Needs of belonging and love. Need to love and be loved, to belong, to be accepted; need to avoid loneliness and isolation.
- Esteem needs. Need for self-esteem, individual training, competence and independence; Need for recognition and respect from others.
- Self-actualization needs. Need to fully live our individual potential.

Although Maslow's theory is very interesting, the approach that we are taking in this book has more to do with how the brain works and how to use what happens in it when we want to be the ones who direct our behavior, instead of drifting away from automatic operations.

Within psychology, we have a behavioral tradition, for which motivation is an impulse, whose function is to energize or activate and guide behavior towards the desired object. Starting the motivation would help us to recover the balance before the psychological manifestation of need. And among these needs, could be found, for example, those of Maslow.

We also have a cognitive perspective, which tells us that in order to motivate ourselves properly, two circumstances must occur:

- That we interpret what each situation in which the action is going to take place is asking of us, and what the result of that task is going to be.
- That we have a system of beliefs that will determine the value of certain actions and goals.

It could be said that motivation, far from originating at the beginning of a behavior, begins precisely at the end of the process, that is, with the anticipation of the result of what we are going to do.

What really motivates us is the causal explanation that we give to an action, or to put it in a few words: why are we going to do it.

Because we already know that, if it's for nothing, or we don't see or understand why, we don't even bother to mobilize towards that goal.

Another psychologist named Bernard Weiner (1972) went a step further and grouped the explanations we give ourselves when we have to do something into three dimensions:

- Internal-external. We calibrate whether the result depends on what one does (internal) or on the circumstances (external).
- Stable-unstable. We measure whether the action can be changed (unstable) or remains the same (stable).
- Controllable-uncontrollable. We assess whether influence can be exerted (controllable) or not (uncontrollable).

We are usually better motivated to make an effort when circumstances have an internal-unstable-controllable pattern. In other words, it depends on ourselves and that we have a certain level of manipulation, in the good sense of the word, that allows us to adapt the actions to the objectives that we want.

In any case, human behavior is much better explained if we take into account that we all have a set of beliefs that we have patiently internalized throughout our socialization. That is, whether we do something depends not only on the stimulus, but also on what we believe about it.

We are going to go a little further in this framework that explains the way in which we motivate ourselves, because in each of its phases short circuits can occur that prevent us from reaching the goals we have set for ourselves:

- First, we interpret the situation (real or imagined). That is, we have to understand and explain what is happening. In order to do so, we take internal and external elements:
  - The external is not so much what is recognized, but what is built.
  - The internal has more to do with what one feels than with what one knows.
- Second, we feel emotionally in one way or another depending on what we have to do. The goal, which is not the reason (why), but the objective (what), has to be interpreted as effective, has to be liked and has to have some influence on something (for what). For example: «I want a promotion (what), because I have prepared myself and, furthermore, I have been in the company for fifteen years (why); and thus I will be able to have access to another economic, labor and social status (what for)».
  The guidelines for action need to be emotionally charged in order for us to literally move towards the goal we have set for ourselves.
- Third, we think, plan and decide our action. The cognitive or rational part is responsible for planning behavior to achieve what is desired. But there are also times when we decide not to want something, not so much because we don't want it or find it unattractive, but because we don't know how to get it.

Other experiences such as discomfort or pain fulfill the function of helping us define goals and desires. We do not always act to avoid pain. There are situations that put us to the test and overcoming them helps us to better adapt to different circumstances, but as long as the pain has been understood and managed in such a way that the necessary variables have been introduced so that its presence is a transitory experience and, finally, of growth.

Sometimes, for a positive change to occur, a painful experience is necessary that indicates that a necessary modification towards more appropriate behaviors must be made.

For example, when they put an appliance on our teeth so that they are in their place, the pain will indicate the change from an incorrect position to a correct one, and it will soon cease, with beneficial consequences for the organism. We could say that it is a «constructive» pain. But when pain leads to illness or wear and tear, we would be facing a "destructive" pain to which a correction factor must be introduced immediately. If, for example, lettuce, a harmless food, causes us great gastric pain, it is because our body does not feel good, and the smartest thing is to replace it with another type of vegetable. If we persist in its consumption in these conditions, we will only harm our health and our state of mind.

Pain is simply a signal that warns us that we have to make changes to whatever we are doing, that "not like this." If we persist in maintaining behaviors that cause us pain, then suffering and, finally, pathology will arise.

I believe that unnecessary pain is one of the most unintelligent behaviors in any behavioral repertoire.

Other important sources of motivation are curiosity, variety or the desire to cause an impact on the environment, since it assumes that we have some control over what happens.

From here derives the taste for influencing others or the motivation for power. And do you know where it all begins? Well, approximately when we have about eight months of life. If we have had the opportunity to see a baby of that age, for example sitting in his high chair with a toy, we will observe several very interesting behaviors. Until recently, her interaction with the environment was casual: if she hit a toy with her hand, she was not aware that, if she fell, it was due to an action directly related to herself. But our eight-month-old baby is beginning to understand that, if he pulls the toy to the right (and you'll see how he leans hard to the right to see where he's catapulted the stuffed animal), it has to do with his hand. Then mom or dad come and give it back. Immediately, she throws it to the other side. This is great! She looks at him again intensely... And there is dad or mom again to give it back to her once more. He's having a good time, right? Well, best of all, there is a point where he realizes that he is not only able to control where he throws the stuffed animal... but also mom and dad! In addition to being a moment of unconscious joy, it is the beginning of learning about relationships with the significant people in your life. And each one will do it according to the interactions that begin to be created between them. It has to do with your hand. Then mom or dad come and give it back. Immediately, she throws it to the other side. This is great! She looks at him again intensely... And there it is again dad or mom to give it back to her once again. He's having a good time, right? Well, best of all, there is a point where he realizes that he is not only able to control where he throws the stuffed animal... but also mom and dad! In addition to assuming a moment of unconscious joy, he supposes the beginning of learning relationships with the significant people in his life. And each one will do it according to the interactions that begin to be created between them. It has to do with your hand. Then mom or dad come and give it back. Immediately, she throws it to the other side. This is great! She looks at him again intensely... And there it is again dad or mom to give it back to her once again. He's having a good time, right? Well, best of all, there is a point where he realizes that he is not only able to control where he throws the stuffed animal... but also mom and dad! In addition to assuming a moment of unconscious joy, he supposes the beginning of learning relationships with the significant people in his life. And each one will do it according to the interactions that begin to be created between them. And there they are again dad or mom to give it back once again. He's having a good time, right? Well, best of all, there is a point where he realizes that he is not only able to control where he throws the stuffed animal... but also mom and dad! In addition to being a moment of unconscious joy, it is the beginning of learning about relationships with the significant people in your life. And each one will do it according to the interactions that begin to be created between them. And there they are again dad or mom to give it back once again. He's having a good time, right? Well, best of all, there is a point where he realizes that he is not only able to control where he throws the stuffed animal... but also mom and dad! In addition to being a moment of unconscious joy, it is the beginning of learning about relationships with the significant people in your life. And each one will do it according to the interactions that begin to be created between them. It is the beginning of learning about relationships with the significant people in your life. And each one will do it according to the interactions that begin to be created between them. It is the beginning of learning about relationships with the significant people in your life. And each one will do it according to the interactions that begin to be created between them.

Being in contact is another source of motivation, since contact supposes, in the first moment of life, an activation pattern that provides the well-being generated by the physical protection of others. In addition, a well-known hormone is released, oxytocin, which is what facilitates the bond between people, since it produces a pleasant sensation of pleasure. Of the good, we always want more.

We are going to see, finally, two ways to motivate ourselves, depending on the control we have of what may happen around us. According to this, the motivation can be:

– Intrinsic (when we are the cause of what happens). This motivation means:
  • Self-determination: the action is originated and controlled by us.
  • Competence: we have, or believe we have, sufficient skills to carry out the action.
  • Satisfaction: we have achieved our goal.
– Extrinsic (when we let ourselves be carried away by events). How many times do we do something simply because there is a reward? I'm sure many. But for it to take effect, it must have the following characteristics:
  • It is preferable that it be of a social nature (recognition, affection...) than material. We like others to value our merits.
  • It is more effective if we do not expect it.

The goals that we set for ourselves have a subjective component, since we value them not so much based on whether they are good, but mainly on the extent to which they seem so to each of us.

LEARN TO MOTIVATE OURSELVES

Learning to motivate ourselves is probably one of the most useful strategies and it is worth applying ourselves to it with special interest. Normally, we associate motivation with playing sports or passing exams. But motivation comes to mean moving in one direction, and it is directly related to the use we make of another of the brain mechanisms that we have already seen: attention. Let's see how.

When motivation works "on automatic," we find it relatively easy to move toward rewarding goals. We have no problem going to the movies if some friends we like call us, or doing some extra work if we get an economic incentive at the end of the month, or professional recognition. Note that the key is in what we get when we perform an action. If the goal we want to achieve is positive, the brain will be delighted with the idea of going there, and it will take time to get going. But if it's negative or blurry, it will stop dead or spin around avoiding the situation.

There are no lazy people, but incorrectly motivated.

Many students abandon their studies because they do not understand very well why they are studying certain subjects. Although I personally enjoyed mathematics a lot thanks to a wonderful teacher I had throughout high school, it wasn't that many years ago that I understood why it is important in our daily lives. I don't remember that anyone had explained to us, before starting with derivatives, integrals or simply fractions, that mathematics is an instrument created by human beings to measure, describe and even predict what happens in nature. With mathematics we can explain and predict most of the things that surround us at every moment: from the growth of plants to the time the sun will rise the next day.

And what about motivation for dieters! If they do not clearly see themselves at the right weight and in their new lifestyle, they will not give up certain foods with which, at least in the short term, they derive more satisfaction than with a fuzzy future or for which they do not feel trained enough.

Motivating ourselves with activities that we like is very easy. But we don't have to wait for something to simply please us. If, for example, by doing an activity that we don't like we are going to obtain very advantageous benefits, then we will have to learn to like it. You don't stop being who you are by changing or readjusting certain nuances of your personality, but rather, on the contrary, it strengthens it.

An example that I usually use for us to learn to motivate ourselves has to do with an activity that I personally practice regularly, but that is applicable to any other that concerns you directly. Does anyone swim or have to go to the pool due to therapeutic recommendation? I started swimming very early; I like it and enjoy it, but that doesn't mean I can ignore some of its obvious drawbacks which, if allowed to grow large in my brain, would probably dissuade me from playing the sport. For starters, there has to be a swimming pool, not a wading pool or a spa; you have to look for schedules in which no more than three people per street accumulate; you have to cross your fingers not to run into cold water because the acclimatization system has broken down, or that we do not freeze if a door or window has been left open. When we have finished swimming... the hair! We do not get rid of the dryer or the drying time; an hour of chlorine leaves our skin "weird", and if we add the brand of swimming goggles, it's better that we don't meet anyone for a long time; you have to carry shampoos, creams, brushes, towels, flip-flops... in your backpack and return with everything soaked. When the brain sees this panorama, it begins to look for arguments not to go and, if we let it, it will surely find them. That is why it is so important, once we have set ourselves a goal and we have planned it well, not to think. These thoughts are useless, or rather yes: to boycott an action that was probably going to bring us something very positive. When we have finished swimming... the hair! We do not get rid of the dryer or the drying time; an hour of chlorine leaves our skin "weird", and if we add the brand of swimming goggles, it's better that we don't meet anyone for a long time; you have to carry shampoos, creams, brushes, towels, flip-flops... in your backpack and return with everything soaked. When the brain sees this panorama, it begins to look for arguments not to go and, if we let it, it will surely find them. That is why it is so important, once we have set ourselves a goal and we have planned it well, not to think. These thoughts are useless, or rather yes: to boycott an action that was probably going to bring us something very positive. When we have finished swimming... the hair! We do not get rid of the dryer or the drying time; an hour of chlorine leaves our skin "weird", and if we add the brand of swimming goggles, it's better that we don't meet anyone for a long time; you have to carry shampoos, creams, brushes, towels, flip-flops... in your backpack and return with everything soaked. When the brain sees this panorama, it begins to look for arguments not to go and, if we let it, it will surely find them. That is why it is so important, once we have set ourselves a goal and we have planned it well, not to think. These thoughts are useless, or rather yes: to boycott an action that was probably going to bring us something very positive. an hour of chlorine leaves our skin "weird", and if we add the brand of swimming goggles, it's better that we don't meet anyone for a long time; you have to carry shampoos, creams, brushes, towels, flip-flops... in your backpack and return with everything soaked. When the brain sees this panorama, it begins to look for arguments not to go and, if we let it, it will surely find them. That is why it is so important, once we have set ourselves a goal and we have planned it well, not to think. These thoughts are useless, or rather yes: to boycott an action that was probably going to bring us something very positive. an hour of chlorine leaves our skin "weird", and if we add the brand of swimming goggles, it's better that we don't meet anyone for a long time; you have to carry shampoos, creams, brushes, towels, flip-flops... in your backpack and return with everything soaked. When the brain sees this panorama, it begins to look for arguments not to go and, if we let it, it will surely find them. That is why it is so important, once we have set ourselves a goal and we have planned it well, not to think. These thoughts are useless, or rather yes: to boycott an action that was probably going to bring us something very positive. and return with everything soaked. When the brain sees this panorama, it begins to look for arguments not to go and, if we let it, it will surely find them. That is why it is so important, once we have set ourselves a goal and we have planned it well, not to think. These thoughts are useless, or rather yes: to boycott an action that was probably going to bring us something very positive. and return with everything soaked. When the brain sees this panorama, it begins to look for arguments not to go and, if we let it, it will surely find them. That is why it is so important, once we have set ourselves a goal and we have planned it well, not to think. These thoughts are useless, or rather yes: to boycott an action that was probably going to bring us something very positive.

But back to the pool. How to motivate ourselves, then, to go swimming? It is evident that the arguments given by our brain are irrefutable: these disadvantages exist, they are real, and it depends on us what weight or size we are going to give them. It is also just as true and real that when we go swimming, the health benefits are evident: calories are burned, the body is muscled, exercise is exercised without damaging the joints, it helps eliminate fat and other toxins from the body, it is magnificent for the back and the bones in general, needless to say for pregnant women, for the elderly... and in the prime of youth, swimming has the advantage that it leaves you with a "body ten". These advantages are really attractive in every way. Surely if we are now seeing this panorama, our brain will be jumping, wanting to grab the bag and head for the pool. What has happened then?

The reality remains the same: we're going to get our hair wet the same way, we're going to have the same brand of goggles and chlorine, and jumping into the water can be just as cool. Everything depends on where we direct the focus of our attention: if we do it towards the disadvantages, they will be perfectly legible by our brain, while the advantages are blurred or minimized, which will probably disappear from the general image that we are creating in our lives. work board or screen. The important thing is that the same thing happens in the other direction: if we move our periscope towards the positive that we are going to obtain and how well we are going to feel in every way after swimming, we will relativize the weight and importance of what we like less.

Since we can direct this periscope consciously, it is extremely important that we learn to orient it properly. For this, it is also essential to order the internal dialogue that occurs when we have to do something, so that we finally focus on what is going to bring us a benefit, not in the short term, but a little later, in what we call the medium and long term.

Do you see yourself capable of applying this same sequence to your studies, your diet, your work or your relationship? Let's try it with a new decalogue:

1. See the target as clearly as possible.
2. Define very specifically the benefits that are going to be achieved, or the harm that is going to be avoided.
3. Identify what it takes to get there.
4. Repeatedly see the objective and its benefits.
5. Check that you have the knowledge or the means to achieve it.
6. Anticipate possible inconveniences and neutralize or minimize them.
7. Repeatedly see the objective and its benefits.
8. Design, if necessary, an alternative course of action that also leads us to the objective.
9. Recharge ourselves with positive thoughts and emotions that get us going, like joy, love, and sometimes even a little positive anger.
10. Repeatedly see the objective and its benefits.

There are no typos in the above text. It is absolutely necessary to maintain an adequate level of motivation that we keep our attention focused correctly on the objective, we feed it with enthusiasm and give it several touches so that we are not distracted by some thought that intends to take it in a direction that does not suit us at all. .

Wanting is not always power, because it is necessary to know: it is necessary to carefully analyze the objective and the situation from which we want to achieve it, and assess whether we know what it takes to do it or if we need to learn something new. So yes, whoever is clear about what they want to achieve, will find and put into practice how.

Once we have defined an objective, analyzed the way to achieve it by generating multiple alternatives and chosen the most appropriate, the key is not to think, but to act according to the plan that you have set for yourself. Once you get it, you already have permission to think if you wanted to do it or not. All in all, it will be done.

3. How to use our tools accurately

THE SIMULTANEOUS TRANSLATOR: LANGUAGE THROUGH IMAGES

More correct than speaking of a language by images would be to define the images as what they really are: a language in itself, in the sense of a system of encoding and transmission of messages and information, which is neither more nor less than the way snapshot that our brain has to immediately translate what happens both outside (in the world) and inside (in our self).

We could say that images are non-verbal forms of thought, and that they are infinitely more powerful than any words. In fact, each of these has an associated image that is the one that, finally, understands the brain. In fact, a word without an associated image is irrelevant to our system: like, say, supercalifragilisticespialidous. Remember that images are the result of connections between neurons in our brain.

Reality is not what it is, but how it seems to us and how we translate it. That is to say, what we perceive, interpret and, finally, understand, filtered through an absolutely personal and subjective filter.

All human beings see images in the same way, because the medium that produces them, the brain, is the same for everyone. But not all of us select, perceive and interpret reality in the same way. In fact, two people can perceive the same context in a completely antagonistic way. And that will be the individual reality of each of them.

This concept of the image as a language to interpret reality can be shocking, so we are now going to see specifically how it works.

INTERNAL AND EXTERNAL IMAGES

Internal images are generated directly by our brain and may have to do with an internal state, with our own dreams and illusions, with thoughts or reasoning to solve a problem, etc.

In reality, what we are is the result of a sophisticated combination of images that we have about ourselves. These images begin to form when we are children and have to do directly with the messages we receive from the perception that others have of us. That is why it is essential to avoid messages in childhood such as "you are lazy", "you are ugly", "you are fat", "you are bad", etc., because, coming from their reference adults, these messages are loaded with affectivity and they will be recorded in your unconscious as an absolute truth. In their adult life, it is almost certain that a few visits to their therapist will allow them, without a doubt, to modify them in a way that is more in line with their reality: they are neither lazy, nor ugly, nor fat. They will be as they want to be. Or do we not know people who are not physically graceful, but who know how to get the best out of themselves and are terribly attractive to us? And others who are gorgeous, but go through life like a real ugly duckling? Reality is not objective, but rather consistent with the film that each one has mounted in his head.

Let's see another practical example: if you want to work with the thought that you want to be a thin person, but the image learned and that is recorded in the unconscious is that you are a fat person, it will be much easier for us to work with the change first. of image, until it is possible to visualize it with great detail and it feels true and pleasant, since it is the final order that our brain is going to execute. Once he sees it clearly, it will be much easier to maintain motivation while learning the skills that allow us to achieve the goal.

Thinking about things is not enough to create reality, but it is enough to be clear about what you want to achieve, and what you have to learn and do until what we saw in our mind we also see outside of it.

When we talk about external images, we are not referring so much to the fact that the images are outside of us, but to the translation that our brain makes of reality, which is not precisely how we see it. Objectively, outside of us there are no images, but moving particles of a different nature. We have already seen that our ears, eyes, sense of smell, etc., are perfectly prepared to capture this type of information in its different ranges and formats (light, mechanical, chemical, etc.) that they transfer, by means of electrical impulses through neurons, to the corresponding region of the brain. Once there, we have to carry out a process of understanding what we see to give it meaning.

With the information it receives from the outside, our brain composes a series of images that are a simultaneous translation or an instantaneous language that allows it to understand, give orders and react immediately to its environment.

To put it another way: objective reality is not images, but our brain sees and experiences it in that format, which is, by the way, a true marvel of advanced technology. In fact, working with images is the most powerful training we can do to change or correct the course of our lives and, consequently, to achieve well-being and happiness. We will be able to verify that it is present in each of the operations that we carry out with our brain.

Images help us create reality to the extent that we design our goals and push us to act until we achieve them. All our behaviors have been consciously or unconsciously thought of first, and their original format is always in images. Our projects, trips, companies, friendships, etc., have first been an idea: if we don't like them, the time has come to transform those images to consequently change our reality, which, let us remember, is not so much the objective reality, but rather the perceived and experienced.

Many times we use mental images as a state of escape. We move to "realities" where we feel better than the one we are living in. As long as our attention is focused on that creation, if you like it, it will feel good. At least it will have been possible to alleviate the tension produced by situations that you do not know how to deal with. In this sense, the creation of images is another magnificent tool that allows us to relax, enjoy and create moments of well-being. Now, we cannot replace this "virtual reality" that exists only in the images invented by us, for the objective reality that, certainly, we see in images, but that really exists and of which we are a part. Let us remember that when we do not want to face and solve a situation, it is usually because we feel fear, and fear is telling us that we don't know or don't have the necessary skills to get out of it. We will then have to seek advice, ask, train... and take the bull by the horns. When life puts us in the center of the arena, and sometimes not with one bull, but with two, we cannot act as if we were in the sea swimming with dolphins.

The work with the images of the mind is, in any case, fascinating. When we want to explain processes that happen inside our body, we often have to resort to images: our stomach burns, we are floating on a cloud or we have a lump in our throat. The brain, instead of explaining to us that there are too many gastric juices, that we have a state of pleasant relaxation or that our esophagus has narrowed, uses its peculiar language of images so that we understand it without too many technicalities. Similarly, when we want to feel good, we do not give our brain the order to start secreting dopamine or oxytocin, but we create an image where we are, for example, lying peacefully on the lap of a soft and tame tiger. Whatever needs to be segregated for that image, the brain understands it perfectly without the need to have taken several neuroscience courses. Athletes train by visualizing themselves at maximum performance: when the image is perfectly created, focused and microwaved, the brain prepares all the muscular, hormonal and other operations necessary, so that reality is as close as possible to the image. Try now with whatever has come to your mind that you could work in this way.

We are now going to see the other translator of reality that, again, being worked from the conscious, is much slower than the one used by the unconscious: verbal language or sign languages.

Language is a set of rules according to which speech is produced, and which can in turn generate infinite languages and sentences. First, a symbolic function (image) is produced, which is what children use when they point with their fingers; and then language develops. His learning is fast, but not instant.

We begin by making a first distinction: speech consists only of making noises with the mouth. Each language has its particular noises that are not at all genetic, but are already acquired from the child's babbling stage. In Spanish, we want them to learn how to position their mouths correctly to pronounce the difficult jot, and after "mamá", we diligently train them with the word "ajo". When our baby looks at us attentively and puts his mouth in the same way that he is observing us, he is doing a real exercise to be able to pronounce correctly shortly after the language with which he is going to communicate with his environment.

We make these sounds from pressure changes in the air. It seems to provide survival advantages, as it is perceived more quickly in the brain than visual stimuli. Physical presence is not necessary to send or receive messages.

The organs that intervene in the production of language are the left hemisphere, especially the frontal lobes (remember the blackboard at work?) and temporal (mainly auditory); and the buccal tract, which is different from that of other species, and allows certain sounds (especially certain vowels) to be articulated at a considerable speed. It involves the sensory cortices, to listen, and the motor cortices, to speak.

Any type of language supposes a mental process. The meanings are encoded in sounds, which we then transmit by producing them in a chain (phrases that we say). It is also from chains of sounds (phrases that we hear) that we decode and interpret a specific meaning. Simplifying, this means that we convert images into words, and that we extract images from the words that we hear or read. As we can see, all roads lead to Rome: to the original image or language.

When we speak, adults competent in a language select words at a rate of four terms per second with great precision, with only one error for every thousand words produced, and we have a vocabulary of about fifty thousand words, for which we apply a very efficient search and selection system. Communication needs a shared context between the participants, both in terms of the code (grammar) and the external world (semantics or what it means).

Language assumes the ability of a system to refer to something other than itself (signs). No culture teaches another the capacity for language, since it is something that we carry as standard in our brain. Note that we are making a distinction between the language capacity of the brain, common to all human beings, and the language or chain of sounds ordered in a particular way, typical of each group that shares it.

Oral language is acquired spontaneously, but it imposes a series of limitations on memory and attention. We work with him on the short-term memory board, which we have already mentioned operates with the magical 7 ± 2... chunks. A chunk can be a letter, a word, a poem or a complete story. Oral language allows us to refer to absent realities and will also require an auditory analysis from us.

For its part, written language is not spontaneous. It needs learning, but its great advantage is that it has unlimited storage capacity. It requires a visual analysis.

Both auditory and visual analyses, must produce a symbol or image. That is why it is a consecutive and not a simultaneous language. Furthermore, we can decide on a literal interpretation, or attribute a final meaning. For example, if someone tells us "how good that haircut suits you!", first we visualize ourselves with the haircut, and then decide if it really suits us, or if the ditto is taking us.

Language is organized into two subsystems: the phonological, without meaning, since it is a combination of signs; and the grammatical, with meaning, since words and morphemes are combined.

Also, when we listen to a message, people tend to go beyond the perceived information, adding much more of our own. It allows us, for example, to interpret and predict people's behavior using attribution.

We can distinguish the following levels of complexity according to intentionality:

• Belief: «I believe that...».
• Belief attribution: «I believe that you believe that...».
•*Attribution of beliefs to the beliefs of another: «I think that you think that I think that...».*

In this way, we see that language is not only an instrument for communication, since it acts on people's ideas, beliefs, desires and intentions.

Language is then conceived as a very powerful instrument for the functioning of higher cognitive processes. As children, we use the monologues that we internalize throughout development, to turn them into an inner language and, consequently, into a system of thought.

Talking about me, about me and with me is at the base of consciousness.

A particularly interesting concept of language is that it is not a string of symbols, but hierarchical sequences of syllables. To give you a simile, speaking is like playing with cubes of different sizes that we fit together, although their relevance in the sentence is not the same.

For example, if we say "the glass that is in the kitchen is clean", the first is supposes a subordination (second order or smaller cube) with respect to the second is, which occupies a higher hierarchy. Why? Because the main concept is that "the glass is clean"; while the second phrase, "that is in the kitchen", is subordinate to the first. If we only read phonemes in order, we would not be able to correctly understand what they are telling us. But we have the ability to mentally order, as we do with cubes, which ones are more relevant than others, and we order them using our blackboard. It does not matter if the verb goes at the end of the sentence, as it happens in German or Japanese, or after the subject, as it usually happens in Spanish. In the end,

Among the functions of language, we could highlight the following:

- Expressive.
- Receptive.
- It helps us to represent a different reality from the language itself.
- It is a communication tool.
- It helps us to regulate ourselves. First, the adult regulates the child, and then the child learns to regulate himself through the acquired messages.

Verbal language is so "human" that there are certain institutions created by our species that are only possible through language, such as the commitments made when we marry or sign a contract with a company.

The advantage of structured verbal or symbolic language over image is that it allows us attribution, reflection and awareness.

As we can see, there is nothing redundant in our body. These two types of language complement each other again as the best team in the Champions League. With them we form the basis of our thoughts and, ultimately, of who we are.

What we think. The manual calculator with several rolls of paper: the reason

Learning to think properly is a skill that deserves special attention on our part. Thoughts are like the instruction manual that the brain uses to execute an action; or like the post-it that we stick on a board and that our brain picks up to execute what we have written on it. If we think (verbally or in images) "take the pen", the brain will start giving the orders from the motor cortex for us to do so.

When we are unable to identify what we are thinking, we can observe our behavior. It is the direct consequence of the order that our brain is reading on that mental screen with our thoughts. Or if we don't know why we do something, the answer is clear: because our brain is instructed to do so.

If there is something about our behavior that we do not like, we can intervene in two ways:

- Changing the statement of our thought will change our behavior.
- By changing our behavior (with a new order), we will force our brain to change its thinking and put the latter as the main one.

This is brought about by a very simple principle called cognitive dissonance, which the brain doesn't like in the slightest. He is more comfortable with coherence, that is, what he thinks and what he does must be consistent; when he thinks one thing and does the opposite, a great conflict arises within him that he has to resolve, either justifying the behavior with some strange reasoning, or correcting it to adjust it to what he thinks he should be doing. It is practically impossible for us to think that we are disgusted by fish, and that when they serve it to us in the restaurant we are enjoying it while we eat it. Either we argue that this one is particularly well cooked, or we will immediately return it and order a dish, say, macaroni.

In the introduction to this book, we mentioned that many people have the impression that thoughts are a kind of entity that swarms through the air and that at a certain moment they catch them and enter their heads. To others it seems that yes, that they are in their head, but that they are not controllable. The vast majority think that all our thoughts are true: this is false, we will see why.

In reality, our thoughts are the result of one or multiple neural connections. Those connections can produce verbal or non-verbal thoughts, in the form of images. But they are "our" connections, that is, our thoughts, with our copyright and copyright. When this connection occurs thousands of times, thought becomes automated, so that the neural branches are very close and it is very easy for them to connect, that is, to think in a certain way.

Many of these thoughts are the product of learning and, although they occur in our brains, it is true that we could consider them "borrowed", until we have the ability to analyze them and decide whether to keep them, modify them or simply get rid of them. from them.

The good news is that, as our thoughts are self-produced, if we see that some of them we don't like, or are short-circuiting some aspect of our life, we can, and why not, we should, change them. To do this, we have to start by learning to use one of the main tools, we could almost say that the master key of psychological therapy: the thought stop. Once we learn to stop what causes us some discomfort or does not suit us, we can work until we achieve the type of statement we want for our actions.

Many times, our complaints are in the sense of "I can't stop it", "it doesn't come out" or "that's not possible". Why?

When we stop thinking, we are stopping that neural connection that produces it. Quickly, we will turn our attention to another type of thought, that is, we will consciously provoke another different neuronal connection, which neutralizes the previous one that bothers us so much. Thus, to the extent that we repeatedly unplug those neurons, the connection will weaken, it will not be as intense, nor as powerful, nor will it be as easy for these two branches to find each other. Let's not forget either that we have to work as if we were exercising the biceps: repetition, regularity and perseverance.

As we have already seen, learning to stop thinking is the «ABC» of working with our mind, and it could be considered the «mother technique» of a large part of the therapies that are practiced in a consultation, and that form part of what we know as self-control. It is especially relevant, because there are many times when we cannot let ourselves be carried away by a cascade of erroneous thoughts, which give rise to frustrating actions and consequences. You have to stop it immediately, calm down and reformulate it again.

We are going to see step by step the best way to exercise correctly in this technique. Fortunately, we are not going to use ourselves in strange wonders, nor in bizarre formulas nor in complex explanations. Nature, which is generally very wise, works wonders with the simple and everyday.

- Step number 1. When we are aware that a thought is being "invasive" and "annoying", we must say stop, stop, clap our hands, etc. Even a kick on the ground or, if no one is watching us, say loud enough! No, we are not going crazy, but we are getting our brain out of that kind of hypnotic state in which it gets stuck when a thought is making a short circuit and is not able to separate the two cables that originate it. You have to pull them any way you can to unhook them.
- Step number 2. Precisely, at this moment we do not have to relax, because if the connection has been intense, it is most likely that the two neurons look for each other again, so we immediately have to generate an alternative thought to help our brain for a different image to appear on your mental screen.

Depending on the intensity and duration of the thought, we can find ourselves in different emotional states. Thus, if the degree of anxiety is not very high, we will shift our focus to a positive thought, which we will describe in great detail, even the smallest. The more we involve sensory memories, the more we help our brain to generate a more pleasant image that seems more "real" to it: what colors can we distinguish, if there are special smells (of saltpeter, freshly wet grass, flowers, a beach bar). of beach...), what temperature it is, the sounds that we can perceive in that environment... For example, I am on the beach with a blue bikini, with yellow flowers and white edges. Walk through the sand. The sand is fine, yellow and not very hot. I catch it with my hands and it slips. I feel the tingling in my palm and fingers. The water is blue, I put a foot in it and it feels a bit cold. I see fish swimming. Some are brown, some are orange, some are striped brown and white. As I walk, I see the buildings. Some have green awnings with white stripes. Others are blue with a white trim. Some buildings are white stone, others yellow brick, and others red brick. Further on there is a beach bar with people... (and the detailed description follows). and others of red brick. Further on there is a beach bar with people... (and the detailed description follows). and others of red brick. Further on there is a beach bar with people... (and the detailed description follows).

In this way, we are causing our brain to make a small concentration effort, which will help our attention to focus on this new landscape. Probably, those of you who like the beach, by the mere fact of reading the previous lines, will have already noticed a change in mood. Indeed, you have correctly deduced:

We are also well aware that when one is highly upset by a negative thought, it is very difficult to move on to a positive thought, and it can even be annoying or irritating. In other words, we feel terrible when they tell us that "we have to be more positive". In that case, the most appropriate and effective thing is to make an intermediate stop and previously go through a neutral thought that takes us out of the alteration that the negative thought has produced in us. Later, if it seems appropriate and we feel capable, we will take the leap towards a positive or fun thought, which will make it enormously easier for us to finally feel good. Going faster doesn't mean you get there sooner, and the brain has a very particular notion of time.

The way to move to a neutral thought from a negative thought is to use games that do not involve any emotion, neither positive nor negative, so that we give some respite to the intensity from which we come.

The most common proposals that we usually make are the following. The first, whenever possible, change activities, do something completely different. For example, if we are sitting on the sofa at home in a hypnotic state, clap our hands, say stop and, immediately, without thinking, get up, go to the bathroom to wet our face or go for a walk around the block. The changes of stimuli will help our brain to clear. If instead of this, we take the opportunity to clean the shelves in the room or to place the books, the effect will be greater.

There are also childhood games that are purely mechanical for the brain, but that require a minimum of attention and do not involve joy or sadness. Do you remember these?

- Chained words. Start a word with the last syllable of the previous one, and it is not worth repeating: table, toad, pore, clothes, duck, tomato, cloth...). Stay active for a while in this game. Soon you will notice that the alteration has decreased and that, fortunately, we can think with a little more clarity and accuracy.
- Words backwards. It is a variant of the previous game: chair-llasi, table-same, clothing-stop, painting-drocua...

In addition, we can give ourselves self-instructions, which consists of telling us "step by step" what we are doing. For example, "I reach up, grab the door handle, open the cabinet door, grab a cup and saucer, and put them on the counter." "I open the drawer and take out a spoon. I put it next to the plate. I turn around, grab the water heater, go to the sink, turn on the faucet, and fill up with as much water as I want. I turn off the faucet and plug in the heater. I open the box of tea bags," and so on.

We can do it without uttering a word, but we can also introduce the variant of saying it in a low voice or, if conditions allow it, out loud. In this way, we will involve more areas of the brain in this activity: the motor cortex to articulate the words and the auditory cortex, which will be listening to them. If you want to do it in another language, fabulous. It will be the equivalent of adding a weight of one kilo or two when we are doing biceps. Keep you in this action. After a while, you probably won't even remember what was bothering you so much...

We have more playful proposals to help our brain change the focus of its attention, such as engrossing it in cultural thoughts that are not too complex. We can list, for example, cities in the world that start with B. We can limit it to continents and change the letters. More than one will end up going to the geographical atlas if they get "stuck" with the task, but that will be a great indication that they were able to stop a disruptive thought.

Of course, your creativity is always the best. Some people tell me that they start singing and look at the lyrics of the songs; or that a variant of the chained words has occurred to them: for example, thinking of an actor or actress and identifying which movie we saw him in and who his co-star was, or remembering a movie other than this one; and so on. For example, Richard Gere in Pretty Woman, along with Julia Roberts; Julia Roberts in The Pelican Brief, with Denzel Washington; etc.

We also have purely physiological techniques based on the knowledge we have about what things produce a certain state of relaxation in the brain:

- Abdominal breathing. It consists of bringing the breath to the "stomach" instead of the "chest". In this way we release the diaphragm and allow the lungs to fill with air.
- Insalivation. Reduces anxiety. You are probably familiar with the action of "swallowing" in an event in which we are nervous, or wetting our lips with our tongue... It is an automatic way that the brain has to produce, without us noticing, a drop in anxiety levels. Isn't it magnificent? However, and knowing it, we can help him by drinking water slowly, sipping, or sucking gum, candies, lollipops, etc.

In some cases, the degree of anxiety is too high and simply stopping thinking, breathing or salivating are not enough. If the degree of activation has risen to such an extent that tachycardia begins to occur, sweating of the hands or it becomes difficult for us to breathe, we will have to resort to a first home emergency technique. The explanation for this activation is logical: faced with the intensity of a negative thought, the brain interprets that it has to give an effective response, which implies a physical response, either attack or flight. But you have to do, execute some action. To do this, you will need a muscular response, and therefore the muscles will need to burn a large amount of oxygen. To do this, deep breaths are taken as the heart begins to pump blood rapidly, so that it arrives as quickly as possible and in sufficient quantities. The nervous system is also activated (agitation) in preparation for the muscles to respond as soon as necessary. When we get to this point, stopping thought is somewhat difficult and the most effective thing is to use purely physiological techniques that help the brain to get out of the thought that is causing this alteration.

To do this, we are going to use what we know about the body's thermoregulatory system, since maintaining a constant temperature is essential for survival, and we will force the brain as a priority to use resources in this activity, as follows :

- Wetting the inside of the wrists, through which a large number of nerves pass, with cold water for two minutes. It is the equivalent of a cold shower, with the advantage that it can be done anywhere. But if you are at home and a cold shower seems appropriate, do not stop doing it. In addition, according to studies, it is very good for the skin. And the relaxation is almost instantaneous.
- Producing bipolarity. At the same time that we put our feet in hot water, we will pass cloths with very cold water over our foreheads. The brain cannot afford this difference in temperature at two points in the body, so it will activate all its resources, and more importantly, to rebalance this untimely mishap.

If there is some tachycardia, the most appropriate thing may be to do some exercise, walk in the corridor, go up and down stairs, etc. The idea is to put ourselves at the same level of activation that the organism is experiencing at that moment. Once we "hook" that level, when we stop to rest, the negative thought that was causing the situation will also be reduced. Surely those of you who are reading me and do sports will have experienced how good the mood feels for a while of sweating the shirt well...

Once we have achieved that low activation and that neutral thinking, then we will be in a position to move on to positive thinking. This time we are going to go to the mountain; we find ourselves before an immense green meadow, with the smell of the countryside, in which we can see the colors of multiple flowers: white daisies, red poppies, yellow sunflowers, purple lavender... In the background we can see the top of a mountain, and trees of different sizes and crowns. Greens are not all the same, there are lighter and darker ones. The temperature is cool, but pleasant. The light is from a clear day in which we can see a blue sky, with birds in flight or in the branches whose trills we can perceive. Your outfit... I'll leave it to you to describe it! remember,

EUREKA! NOW I UNDERSTAND! CONSCIOUSNESS

Being aware of something simply means "noticing" what it is, and it helps us to recognize it, retrieve it, correct it, and then work with it.

How to incorporate the habit of awareness into our lives? Normally, we become aware of something when it has not turned out as we would like and the situation forces us, yes or yes, to a more thoughtful, deep and conscious analysis, that is, to identify the implication of the self in what is happening. We can then ask ourselves the following questions:

"Has this happened to me before?"
"Were there any negative consequences then?" Can there be short-term or long-term conflicts with the decision I want to make?
"Is it worth acting this way?"
—Have I been able to generate alternatives that are more beneficial?
—Am I able to communicate it from the tranquility that this analysis gives me?

We are unconscious, and never better said, when we go through life without seeming to be very clear about who we are, or in what context we find ourselves, acting without rhyme or reason and without taking responsibility for our actions or their consequences. Turning this sleeve upside down, we are aware when we go through life knowing who we are, or at least trying, in what context we find ourselves, acting consistently and taking responsibility for our actions and their consequences.

Learning to direct the unconscious consciously will allow us to achieve happiness regardless of the conditions in which we find ourselves.

Conscious control and creativity allow us to use reason and emotion, together with their products, thought and feeling, to achieve mastery over ourselves... If we want to, of course!

WHEN WE THINK BADLY, WE MAKE WRONG

Not everything we think is an unquestionable truth. Our thoughts are not always right nor do they carry hidden messages. Nor, of course, are they the masters of our heads. In this one, we rule.

Surely on many occasions we have made mistakes in the approach of certain thoughts, which, on the one hand, have made us feel very bad about ourselves and, on the other, may have ended up hindering our relationships with others.

We saw earlier in this book that the brain applies the premise of "maximum benefit with minimum effort," and thought is no exception to this rule. It would be a considerable energy expenditure to be consciously reasoning every little thing we do throughout each day and, to make things easier, the brain uses a kind of "cognitive shortcuts" that, in general, tend to work quite effectively, but in Many times they also provoke a chain of behaviors that do us more harm than good.

We are going to first identify those most common shortcuts that the brain usually uses so that, when the occasion requires it and it is opportune, we let it go on its own, but when it is hindering us from the coherent and sensible resolution of some situation, we know how to identify it and change the «automatic mode» by the «manual mode» or conscious reasoning. This is one of the great advantages of having a double piloting control system in our brain.

When shortcuts fail, in psychology they have been given the man of cognitive errors, and the most common are the ones we are going to see next.

The starting point is to assume that it is usual to use these paths and that, in general, we do well with them, but on the occasions in which we detect that, instead of serving to make things easier for us, we are skidding with them, the way The most effective way to recover a more coherent type of thinking is to consider them hypotheses, and not absolute truths. In other words, as soon as we identify them and are aware of their interference, we have to think that it is possible that something we are speculating about is happening, but we must also have the good sense to recognize that we are not at all certain that this is really the case. The next step is to devote our energy to gathering as much information as possible in order to reach more objective conclusions.

Once we are able to handle them as hypotheses, we can begin to practice refuting these kinds of thoughts. Roughly like this: "Okay, this is what it looks like to me. But it doesn't necessarily have to be that way. Maybe it's the opposite of what I'm thinking, or even has nothing to do with it. I'm going to stop thinking about it, at least for now."

Let us now see how many of them are familiar to us. We will put the professional nomenclature first, followed by the colloquial one, so that it is easier to remember them when the time comes.

Arbitrary inference or "making the movie"

Who has not ever edited the film when they were, for example, insecure about the reaction of other people? The brain likes to be in control of the situation and, when it doesn't understand it, if necessary, it makes it up. Michael Gazzaniga explains it beautifully in his book The Social Brain,[5] where he gives an account of the work with the divided brain, in which the left hemisphere tells some fascinating stories that justify an action that the right hemisphere is doing and of which it was not aware. Of course, what he tells has nothing to do with reality. I recommend you read it if you are interested in this topic.

So let's continue with the way the brain has to fabulate. As he understands that he has to be prepared for any eventuality, if he does not have objective data, he pulls the subjective ones, which are usually the most varied, based on previous individual experiences and learning.

Let's analyze a classic of this type of error.

For example: "Juan does not call me."

Interpretation: "I'm sure he really likes me and he doesn't want to talk to me."

How the brain fabricates: «The fact is that he told me that he would still be out of town today. But why did he tell me? I'm sure he already planned not to come, but he didn't dare tell me directly. He could have already warned me, because this sit-in really is a bad move. Who would tell me to count on him, if they had already told me to tie short...».

Actually, there is no evidence to support this conclusion, only the data of the call not received. But we don't know anything else... objectively.

This type of chain of thoughts only promotes one's own discomfort, lack of efficacy, poor problem-solving ability, and poor communication with the other person, if it finally appears. Because in what tone do you think we will answer Juan's next call? It's not that we can't tell him that we felt bad that he didn't show up, but the way we communicate it will be crucial for the future of the relationship. And for that we have to try not to feed irrational thoughts that make us jump in the most inconvenient way.

How to handle this kind of thinking?

The hypothesis that must be handled in these circumstances is to say: «Perhaps Juan had thought not to come, but I don't know for sure. I'm going to wait a little longer, and if not, I'll call. If he finally does not come, I can count on Isabel ».

In this way, we eliminate the tension caused by the sit-in and focus on solving the problem, which usually provides more peace of mind and, in general, better results. And we won't answer Juan with a snort when he calls us. Of course, we will ask him elegantly what happened.

Mind reader or "I know what you're thinking"

We make this mistake when, without having enough objective evidence, we conclude that the other person has a negative thought about us. And besides, we know exactly which one.

For example, we are making a presentation at our company, and we see two colleagues talking to each other.

Interpretation: "They don't like how I'm putting the issue. They are commenting that I have not prepared it well.

How the brain fable: "Yes? Well, let's see if they could have done better. Or maybe they're thinking what a roll I'm letting go. Surely they believe that I am not capable of presenting in an interesting and enjoyable way. The same thing always happens to me. Deep down, I didn't feel like making this presentation at all. I'm still playing even my job ».

It's not hard to get used to how bad we can feel if we get caught up in this chain of thought. In addition, the concept we have of ourselves (self-concept) will be seriously damaged by this interpretation of "reality". If we become convinced that what we are thinking about what our colleagues are thinking in turn is absolutely true, it is likely that our attitude will become more defensive or doubtful, which, without a doubt, will show through in the exposure that we are doing, and not exactly for the better. Without a doubt, we will have conscientiously boycotted our professional session.

And do you want to know what our colleagues were talking about? Simply, where were they going to drink their beers at the end of work hours. Nothing to do with us. What a shame of presentation!

How to handle this kind of thinking?

The hypothesis to handle this case would be: «I am doing my presentation and I see two colleagues talking to each other. Maybe I'm seeming a bit boring to them, but they may also be talking about some other issue that I don't know about. Later I will try to know their opinion, or they will tell me about it. Nor is it important. I am going to focus on the rest of the group and on my work, because it is important that points a, b and c are made very clear».

In this way, we protect our self-esteem and focus on what matters: our execution and what we want to communicate. We cannot know what others are thinking and, in this case, the important thing is to transmit the information in which so much time and effort has been invested. And we're going to do it right. We owe it to ourselves and to the rest of our teammates.

Fortune teller error or "I know what is going to happen"

We make this mistake when we anticipate, without objective evidence, that things are going to go wrong, and we take that prediction of the future as unalterable.

For example, we have an event on Saturday with certain people that we don't get along with.

Interpretation: "I'm sure there's going to be a ruckus. They will jump at the slightest and I do not want to shut up this time ».

How the brain fable: «Let's see how we react if we meet face to face. They don't shut up, and Maria's birthday is not the place to argue. Actually, I'm thinking of calling and giving an excuse not to go. That way I avoid disappointment."

We are so sure that things are going to happen exactly as we think that we even prefer to cancel a date with friends to avoid what we know is going to happen. We will look bad with Maria and we will probably lose the opportunity to spend a very pleasant afternoon with other people.

How to handle this kind of thinking?

The hypothesis that must be handled is this: «It is possible that there is some crossing of unpleasant words. If so, I will tell them that Maria's birthday is not the most appropriate place and that, if they want, we can meet at another time. In any case, if the situation arises, I will tell them that it is not there, and I will focus on talking to other people or somewhere else.

In some way we are accepting that things may not go quite right, that the probability of something happening exists, but we will also be able to generate alternative situations to that only proposal made by our erroneous thinking from the beginning. We will feel that we control our performance, with much more bearable consequences and, finally, it is most likely that, if we go with this attitude, the afternoon will be much better than we expected.

By the way, this ability to generate alternative solutions usually has the pleasant consequence of strengthening our self-esteem in a very healthy, almost stratospheric way.

We make this mistake when we focus on a specific detail, which is usually negative. We take it out of its context and ignore other equally or more relevant features of the situation.

For example, Mr. Rodríguez, a client of Mr. Hernández, meets with the latter to comment on the development of the last event and tells him: «Everything has turned out really well: the speakers did not overdo their speeches, the catering was exquisite, the attendees were treated very kindly and felt very comfortable; perhaps some music was missing between the arrival of the guests and the beginning of the meeting, but the objectives of the act were achieved».

Interpretation: after the meeting, Mr. Hernández comments with his assistant on Mr. Rodríguez's impressions: «I think we have made serious mistakes. The client says that he was not satisfied because there was no music until the beginning of the meeting».

How the brain confabulates: "I don't think it's going to call us back. And the worst thing is that he will not recommend us to his acquaintances either. Word will spread quickly that we are a disaster at organizing events.

Of all the information given by Mr. Rodríguez, who, frankly, seems to have been quite satisfied, Mr. Hernández has only kept the negative part. Objectively, only one of the five assessments deserved a comment on what could have gone better, but it was not even seriously serious for the course of the act. However, the rest is ignored and the entire assessment is focused on a trivial detail. Logically, Mr. Hernández goes to his house upset and sad that night, thinking about whether he should change jobs. And, if he's married and has kids, he's probably affecting his relationship with them as well.

How to handle this kind of thinking?

The hypothesis that must be handled in this case would be: «Well, it seems that Mr. Rodríguez likes music, he has a special sensitivity for the musical environment, so, if he were to count on us again, we would take this detail into account. However – and here we focus on the positive – the speeches were adequate, the food was liked and the general feeling of the attendees was quite good. Moreover, Mr. Rodríguez considers that his objectives were met. I'll give you a courtesy call in a few days."

Far from dedicating ourselves to setting up a new company, in this case we recover all the positive part of the context and even our social skills will allow us to call in a few days to comment on a musical suggestion, or to find out more about Mr. Rodríguez's tastes. This detail will probably please you, we will have resolved the situation effectively, and Mr. Hernández's future definitely presents much more promising prospects.

We make this mistake when we extract a general rule from one or more isolated facts. And we probably translate it to similar situations as well. Does it look familiar to us? Certainly, this shortcut is one of the busiest in our thoughts, individual or social. Let's see how it is formulated.

For example: "This is the second time that my neighbor's son has left the front door open."

Interpretation: «It is that in that family everyone goes to his ball».

How the brain confabulates: «Surely at home they do everything with the same lack of coordination. Anyone counts on them for nothing.

This type of thinking probably makes it difficult for us to relate to our neighbors. We assume that they are all the same, that, moreover, they are in all contexts of their lives, and that it is best not to count on them at all. If it continues like this, it is likely that we will not even say good morning. The truth is that, objectively, we don't know how they are at home, if his parents have already caught his attention or if the kid is going through a time of stress or simply a rowdy adolescence.

How to handle this kind of thinking?

The hypothesis that we must handle in this case would be similar to the following: "My neighbor's son is leaving the front door open. I don't know if he realizes it or if he's nervous. I'll mention it to his mother in case she hasn't noticed".

We do not have to have bad relations with our neighbors, as long as we are able to speak understanding that it may be an exceptional situation, or that even the rest of the family may not be aware of what is happening. What's more, even if there is something we can lend a hand with, our home environment would probably be much more friendly.

Sometimes we make the mistake of not giving importance to something that really has it or, on the contrary, we make a world out of something insignificant. We think that if we "dwarf" an important problem, it no longer exists or is more manageable; or that giving a lot of importance to something that does not have it, we will get attention to be able to solve it.

A classic within minimization usually occurs within the couple environment and, sometimes, when we really want to understand what is happening, it may already be a little late.

With this little note made, let's see an example of minimization: a boyfriend brings a gift to his girlfriend.

Interpretation: "I'm sure he does it to look good. Total, if he doesn't love me anymore... I'm not going to thank him ».

How the brain confabulates: "Now it wants to fix things, but this doesn't work for me. I'm not going back to the same kind of relationship we had before, and if he thinks he's going to win me over with a gift... What do you think, that I suck my thumb?

And now one of magnification. Tonight we have an important dinner. When we are going to finish getting ready, we discover in front of the mirror a tremendous pimple on the nose in full boil.

Interpretation: "I'm going to fail today because of this damn pimple on my nose."

How the brain fabricates: "Everyone is going to laugh at me. Surely they will not stop looking at my nose and the speech I made to fire Manuel, who is retiring, is going to be completely lackluster».

How to handle these kinds of thoughts?

The hypothesis to face the minimization would be something like this: «Well, my boyfriend has brought me a present. I don't know for what purpose. I don't know if he wants to fix things or for me to forget everything. I'll ask him or let him tell me about his expectations of bringing me this detail ».

In this case, before continuing to think about what the boy's intention with his gift may have been, let him speak. Once we know what the target was, that is, once we have enough data to react to the gift, then we can decide: if it's a no-nonsense patch, maybe we can return the gift without too much of a charge. awareness; if it is a way of asking for forgiveness, let's hope that the boy takes care and knows how to say where he did damage and how he is going to repair it; it may even happen that it was a farewell detail and surprised us with such an elegant attitude. It is clear that any previous interpretation on our part would have led us to a resounding error.

The hypothesis in the case of maximization would be this: "Well, I got a pimple at the worst time. And I have to give the little farewell speech to Manuel. Today I wanted to be divine, but if I can be nice and funny, I'm sure I'll have more success.

Personalization or "that was said for me"

This error consists in attributing external phenomena to oneself when there is no basis for that connection. That is, we think that what happens, especially if it is negative, has to do with us, or with something we have done or said.

For example, we walk past a group of guys sitting on a bench, and they burst out laughing.

Interpretation: "I'm sure they're laughing at me. I already knew that these pants did not fit me well.

How the brain confabulates: "Of course, that's enough, what a lack of respect! I die of embarrassment. How am I going to go see this client now if these guys have laughed so much at me?

Surely almost all of us have been through this situation or something similar, especially when we were younger or insecure. If it happens to us later, we may not even notice it or have the ability to react not to think that what they are talking about necessarily has to do with us. And if it were, probably at certain points in life we wouldn't care. But it would make us make a mistake if, as a consequence, this fact caused us to go home to change our clothes before seeing the next client, or if we arrived at the office of this one embarrassed, wishing that the earth swallowed us.

How to handle this kind of thinking?

The hypothesis to handle is: "I have no idea why they are laughing. Maybe they're laughing at me because I've reminded them of someone or they don't like something I'm wearing. Or perhaps it happened by chance that the moment of the joke coincided precisely with the moment in which I was passing by».

Sometimes you have to let the boys laugh. It doesn't matter if it's for us or not. Are we sure how we're doing? Well, the rest doesn't matter. And, by the way, if we asked the doorman of the farm next door, he would tell us that the boys had already been in the bank for a long time, dying of laughter, telling each other anecdotes about the last exams they had had. And the pants also suit us quite well.

Dichotomous absolutist thinking or "things are either black or white"

We make this mistake when we classify experiences into opposite categories: either all white or all black. It usually encompasses statements that include the words always, never, everything, nothing...

For example, a teacher, in class, is not able to get her students to keep quiet.

Interpretation: "I am useless. I can't do anything right."

How the brain confabulates: «Surely they don't understand anything I explain to them and my classes are always boring. That way they will never put interest in the subject that I am teaching them. And they will speak ill of me."

This kind of thinking is absolutely devastating. The students do not understand "nothing", zero; the classes are "always", each and every one of them, boring; «Never», not a single day of her lives, will they be interested... If this teacher decides to leave her profession, she would not surprise us at all.

How to handle this kind of thinking?

The hypothesis that we must handle is: "There are some aspects of matter that are probably a little more arid. It is normal that, when the boys do not understand, they may be a little more distracted. Surely there will be a way to find out what interests them so that we can introduce them to the less easy part.

In this way, we limit the problem to the part where the conflict is taking place: not to all the material, not to all classes, not to all the interest of the children. When we focus on the part that needs to be intervened, which is probably not as dramatic as we had planned, it is easier to face and solve it.

We make this mistake when we reject positive experiences, dismissing them with little weight. It may seem incredible to us, but we do it very often. If we pay a little attention, we will see that practically every day someone, or ourselves, rejects or minimizes a good compliment.

For example – do we remember Mr. Rodríguez? – Mr. Rodríguez congratulates us on the good results of our organization.

Interpretation: «How strange it is that Mr. Rodríguez tells me that he thought our organization was wonderful with all the failures that there were!».

How the brain fable: "Maybe he didn't realize, or maybe he just wants a discount on the next job."

Some of us find it difficult to accept that someone tells us how well we have done a job, how good we look or how smart we are. We will always look for an argument that relativizes the flattery and, finally, ends up disqualifying us.

How to handle this kind of thinking?

The hypothesis that must be handled in this case is: «It is possible that we had errors, but it seems that you have been quite satisfied with the result. He probably knew how to contextualize them, but the fact is that it seemed good to him and he has expressed it to us ».

It is also about respecting the opinions of others: not only when they differ from what we think, but also when something related to us seems frankly good to them, although not so much to us. Let's be fair to ourselves: if we accept negative opinions, let's also accept positive ones. The best way to do this is with a simple "thank you".

"I should..." statements

There is a type of thought that adds tension and discomfort to us, especially when it rigidly states the set of rules that we apply to our obligations or those of others.

For example, a person has a behavior that has harmed us.

Interpretation: "I feel guilty; I should have realized what was happening."

How the brain fabricates: "I shouldn't have been so trusting, even though I noticed something odd about his behavior from the start. I have to be careful with new people I meet."

Generally, thoughts should occur in two situations:

—When we refer to something from the past. We think about what we should have done when we expected to have achieved a goal, but when we analyze the present moment we realize that we are somewhat far from what we had originally set out to do. That is, we were wrong: what are you going to do.

Our mistake: ruminating over what should have been done. It is a waste of time in which we can sometimes remain, uselessly, all our lives.

How do we handle this kind of thinking? The right thing is to analyze where we are now and what was the goal we wanted to achieve. Make a new study of what we need to move, physically or metaphorically, to our goal, or to the closest, and get down to work.

For example, we are on the 13th and we have a project delivery date for the 17th. A couple of days ago they should have given us the photocopies we need. Today they call us and tell us that they have had problems and that they will not be able to deliver them to us as planned. We can paralyze ourselves with a should (or should not) thought, or analyze our needs and see what resources we still have to work out where we can get the photocopies we need. Getting stuck on what we should have done and not what we can do right now can lead to unwanted bias.

—When we refer to something in the future. In this case, the thoughts should refer to what one demands of oneself. It is a very rigid thought, because it does not give an option to an alternative action.

How to handle this kind of thinking? The most effective way to reformulate these types of thoughts is to replace them with the statement I would like. This type of thinking does not produce as much tension in the organism, and it is objectively more true. Between "the act should be perfect" or "I would like the act to be perfect", the emotional charge varies considerably, and our performance will be more effective the less tension and stress its mere approach produces.

In short, the foregoing has to do, above all, with how we interpret situations and, in accordance with that interpretation, we make a series of decisions about our own behavior, and about the way in which we are going to relate to each other at that moment. our environment.

What we decide to interpret at each moment is going to be decisive for our action to culminate in failure or in a really graceful and effective exit.

What we feel. A few sirens and light signals: the emotions

Until relatively recently, the world of emotions was a complex universe with which only poets, religions, therapists and some philosophers dared. Not so long ago, trying to talk about emotions in a scientific context was considered sheer nonsense. Fortunately, today, thanks to eminences in the field of science such as Joseph LeDoux or Antonio Damasio, joy, sadness or anger can be understood and explained in a simple way, stripped of all intellectual flourishes. And, much better still, thanks to this knowledge we can readjust, modulate and apply them in such a way that more and more we feel, finally, like the true pilots of our feelings, instead of having the impression that we are drifting with them. .

Have you ever felt swept away by the tide, being aware of what was happening to you, but not knowing how you could take control of the situation? We are going to see in the following pages what I consider to be a beautiful way to regain a sense of control over who we are, and to understand what our brain is trying to tell us.

To understand what they are and what the function of emotions is, we first have to see ourselves in a concrete context. Every minute of our lives goes exactly like this; As already pointed out in the Introduction, what Ortega said ("I am myself and my circumstances") could be considered a neuroscientific maxim. Therefore, emotions help us to live, to adapt to our environment and to communicate. Not in vain, the first thing that arises in existence is the emotional bond, so we could say that "in the beginning, it was emotion."

The concept of emotion is different from that of affection or affectivity. The emotion arises at a certain moment in response to a specific stimulus and has a physiological character. It occurs in our brain and does not necessarily have a verbal expression. Affect is a judgment or an assessment that has a cognitive character and is expressed semantically.

There is a continuous exchange of information between our brain and the context in which it finds itself, so let's remember that the main objective of the first is survival, whatever the circumstances. To do this, it has all its equipment for receiving data (the senses) and responding to them through adaptive behaviors (thoughts and actions). And so that the rest of the parts of the brain understand what they have to do in that context, there are some nuclei in the inner part that emit certain types of signals, like a traffic light, that will trigger one signal or another depending on what is need at all times.

We could say that the main functions of emotion are the following:

- Emotions are powerful communicative messages, because they are interpreted very quickly, and are understandable or recognizable by almost everyone.
- They are a mechanism to regulate our own behavior and that of others, understanding at all times the states in which we find ourselves, and in which others are.
- Emotions facilitate social interaction. The smile is a universal mechanism to start talking to someone. People with emotional problems have more interaction problems.

But, continuing with the simile of the traffic light, what happens when it is unknown, for example, that the red light indicates that we stop? Obviously, we will not, and this can be more than an unpleasant surprise. What if we stop when we have the green light? What a precious waste of time! We'll also see how thoughts can short-circuit the meaning of those signals. What to do if the light is green and a "do not pass" sign appears below? Or if in red we ran into another sign that indicated "cross"? Obviously, the light and the poster have to be in harmony, because when they don't... we have a problem. Sometimes it can mean "going to a good mechanic" so that the sign can be adjusted to the color of the sign.

Definitely, it is very important to know what each one of those lights or emotions is trying to tell us, so that we act in the most effective way possible and do not have the feeling of going through life in stumbles.

There is a set of emotions that have been called basic or universal, which are the ones that we are going to analyze in this chapter, which it is understood that all mammals in nature carry "by default" in the brain, regardless of age, culture , sex or the century in which one was born. There is another set of emotions called social, which can be determined by the codes of coexistence of a population group, and which will not be the object of study in these pages.

HOW DO EMOTIONS WORK?

Let's continue using the simile of traffic lights in an urban environment. If we were observers, from a helicopter that attends to the circulatory movement we would see how the lights are changing in one place or another and, depending on how they are doing, some cars stop and others start, producing a constant and orderly flow that allows for all citizens to reach their jobs or their homes in an organized and consensual manner.

Different lights do not stay the same color all the time. Traffic lights change their colors and signals, and these changes allow traffic or people who have to cross the streets to do so in a natural and extremely effective way, as long as they are acting in accordance with the corresponding meaning.

All the tones are essential, there are no negatives or positives, and, in addition, they perfectly fulfill the functions for which they were designed. Transferring this concept to the world of emotions, I would like to make a clarification that seems very necessary, given that you have probably heard a lot about "positive" and "negative" emotions.

We will soon see what we mean by this forceful statement. But first, I would like us to fully understand how emotions and sensations flow throughout our day, according to a working scheme similar to the following:
- The brain detects something in the context through the senses.
- The brain sends the corresponding signal (emotion).

- The rational part interprets that emotion in that context.
- The rational part (and often also the unconscious) decide what to do with that signal.
- It acts and resolves.
- The end of that emotion occurs (and we would move on to the next one).

Since the examples always better illustrate the theory, we will put a simple one, to begin with:

- The brain senses that it is two in the afternoon, the usual time to eat.
- The brain lowers the levels of certain components in the blood so that it prepares for the intake of nutrients.
- The brain sends out the hunger signal.
- The rational part understands that it is time to eat.
- The context is analyzed. Let's take two different situations: the first, «can I go to eat?»; and the second, "Is there food?"
- Action is taken as analyzed: one option is «I go home, to the restaurant or take out the Tupperware»; another, "I have to finish a job and then eat." If the latter occurs, there is no need to worry: we will all have experienced that, when we cannot eat or sleep, the brain, which is very efficient, readjusts immediately, and after a while the sensation that we had has passed. If you can't, you can't, and you no longer dwell on something that, at that moment, has no solution. Will eat later.
- Once solved, it goes on to the next contextual situation.

In other words, throughout the day we feel endless sensations that we resolve adequately most of the time. I'm hungry? Like. Am I thirsty? I drink. I'm sleepy? I sleep. Do I get angry because I think I'm going to be a little late? I quicken my step. I feel in love? I have a nice gesture with my partner... Well, surely some of us are reflecting that there are some sensations that are resolved better than others: the basic ones, such as hunger, thirst or sleep, do not present a major problem. The emotional ones seem to be handled clumsily at times... But that can be easily fixed as soon as we get to know them a little better, as we are doing now.

Other fundamental principles that we must take into account regarding the way we respond to those signals that the brain sends us would be the following:

- Each signal has its appropriate response (hunger = eat, etc.).
- Eventually, and only temporarily, we may not respond appropriately (not eating because we have other obligations or because there is no food, or eating something unhealthy). The brain is prepared to adapt and has a "normal margin" to deal with unforeseen events of this nature.
- When the response to a signal is permanently wrong, then the pathology appears, physical or mental.

For example, if we don't drink water every time we are thirsty, or don't eat or sleep when we are hungry or sleepy, and if this happens for a long time or permanently, our physical health will suffer even to the point of death. In the same way, when we do not respond adequately to emotions as adaptive signals, pathologies also appear, in this case of a mental and/or behavioral nature: when we do not respond well to sadness and depression appears; when we do not adequately manage anger and provoke serious aggressive situations; or when unresolved fear paralyzes our lives or causes us to go into phobic loops, leaving us in the lurch.

Emotions can be interpreted (in fact, for some subjects with erroneous learning this interpretation is a source of pathology) and can be managed. As a basic principle, when one feels an emotion, the first thing to ask is what part of oneself is feeling anger (or fear, or sadness...).

When faced with an angry situation, a common response —although the most inappropriate for learning— is usually: "I'm angry (scared, sad...) because you... (whatever)". This interpretation is wrong and will take us far from an effective solution. When I feel, I feel, and we have to leave the other out, at least at first. I feel angry because there is a part of me that feels attacked or upset (you know the saying that it doesn't offend who wants to, but who can). I can rephrase my anger: "I feel upset because I don't like what you are doing (to me)", which does not necessarily imply that the other's behavior is good or bad. But if I am aware of what is causing that emotion, I will be better able to find a solution and resolve the situation in the most effective way for everyone.

SOME TOOLS TO IDENTIFY EMOTIONS, WHAT THEY MEAN AND THE MOST APPROPRIATE RESPONSE

How do emotions manifest in our body?

Although it may seem surprising to us, emotions are also manifested in specific places in our body. As we explain them one by one, we will specify more specifically where our brain sends the warning signals.

To begin with, it is important to be clear that we will feel fear, anger, love, surprise, etc., with some physiological reaction, in the same way that we feel hunger as a kind of hole in the stomach, thirst with dryness. on the tongue and in the mouth, or sleep with heaviness in the eyelids.

It is also necessary to know that emotions work like waves or cycles: they have a signaling time and if the brain detects that it cannot respond to the signal adaptively, it will immediately take the appropriate measures by changing its strategy.

Surely we have experienced on more than one occasion being at the house of some friends chatting and the hands of the clock begin to run without even realizing it. It is possible that, at certain hours, we begin to feel heaviness in the eyelids or that our eyes even go a little white: the brain needs some parts of our body to rest. But, of course, we are at our friends' house and it is not a question of lying on the sofa to take a nap or falling asleep until the next day. So, after several attempts, the brain understands that, for whatever reason, it will not be able to do what it wants at that moment. And then what most of us have probably also experienced happens. Suddenly it's like a click and we lost sleep! We can now continue the lively chat with our friends for a few more hours. The brain, in fact, is doing it to see if we take the car and go home in a state of wakefulness that does not put our physical integrity at risk (we already know how dangerous it is to do so when we are practically head butting). And his ultimate goal will be for us to go to sleep as soon as circumstances allow.

In general, these signals do not come alone, and that is why it is sometimes a little more difficult for us to identify what they are, what they are trying to tell us and, most importantly, why. They usually appear accompanied by a nice escort of automatic reactions that will make us have to stop a little longer if we want to learn to detect emotion in its pure state. But there is no need to worry, because we are going to see how we can do it despite all that deployment of means that our body makes.

What exactly are they telling us?

the different emotions?

Well, the time has come to dissect or put under the lens of our magnifying microscope each of the main or basic and universal emotions, so that we fully understand their nature.

The brain needs us to identify the signal as soon as possible, in order to be able to handle ourselves opportunely in a certain context, resolve the situation and continue on our way.

In order for the brain to be able to react better to a situation, it is important that it is clear about what its objective is and what the destination coordinates are. Life, after all, is an ongoing process in which stops are more apparent than real, and the brain knows perfectly well that, from start to finish, it has to be operational. As in our example of the city, while we sleep, the signals continue to change colors incessantly.

Once we are clear about what they are telling us, we will also see what is the most effective way to manage them. I want to highlight a very important point in this regard: learning to manage emotions does not mean never feeling them again. Quite the contrary, we will perceive and recognize them as many times as necessary in order to carry out the vital project in which we are immersed.

The most effective way to manage emotions is to feel them first. And, secondly, decide the most appropriate type of response for the context in which they have been "triggered".

Feeling an emotion consists of letting it flow through our body, identifying it correctly, so that we are in optimal conditions to be able to give it an adequate outlet. We must not make the mistake of anesthetizing them with alcohol, drugs, food, or fantasized avoidance thoughts. The fact that they are not comfortable does not mean that they are not magnificent, because they are helping us to recognize a situation in order to solve it.

Often, when we are training people to better manage their emotions, they usually tell us about situations similar to this: «The other day Fulanito made a most unpleasant comment to me and it made me feel terrible. I feel bad, because I think that shouldn't bother me or affect me at this point. Do you think he may be right? Wrong: if someone has made a comment with the intention of offending us, the brain will send its anger signal, and that indicates that it is working very correctly. Managing emotions well means that, once we hear the comment and identify what really made us feel bad (anger or anger), we are capable of giving an assertive response, instead of an aggressive one. Something like "sorry, but I don't know what you're trying to tell me exactly...".

One of the tools that we are going to see in each of the sections, and which is very useful for identifying an emotion, is to ask ourselves about how we each interpret a context. What affects us is not "because you..." or "because that...", but "because I..." I perceive and understand it in a certain way. In other words, except for general issues, what happens does not have the same meaning, or the same intensity, for some and for others.

Emotions are signals that are triggered individually. They happen to me. Therefore, the most effective thing is to ask yourself why you are feeling what you are feeling, instead of looking outside of ourselves for explanations (such as blaming) that will not allow us to resolve the situation in the way we want. our brain is requiring it.

So let's see what to do with those waves that run through us from head to toe as events unfold throughout each day.

Sadness

How does it manifest in our body?

What we feel in our body when we are sad is the closest thing to a "slump". This means that it is difficult for us to push forward, that there is no energy and that, probably, we do not feel like doing anything. If it is a "minor sadness", it will simply lower our mood indicator a little, but it will not interfere too much with the activity we were doing. But if it's a "major sadness," we'll probably lie down somewhere and don't even feel like getting up. The sensation in our organism is of absolute loss of energy.

What is it telling us?

Sadness in the brain tells us that there has been a loss. And, for him, it doesn't matter what nature it is, material or immaterial, tangible or intangible, what matters is the magnitude of what has been lost.

This means that we will feel sad, although logically not in the same way, when we lose our wallet, the bus or a loved one. But also when we have the feeling of having lost illusion, time or hope.

Sadness is not at all synonymous with tragedy or crying. The latter are behaviors associated with that emotion, and have a large learning component. There are families that take the blows of life with more integrity than others, in which, in the same circumstances, everything seems to fall apart. But it is about different styles of behavior to face the same situation and the same emotion (sadness) produced by an event.

The levels of sadness will depend on how significant that loss is for each specific individual. Losing a belt may not matter. But if it is the belt that someone very dear to us gave us, and if we add that perhaps that person is no longer with us, then we will feel more despondent.

What the brain is telling us is:

- That there is something or someone who is no longer going to be in our lives.
- That you have to accept that whoever or whatever is not going to come back.
- That it is necessary, as soon as we recover our energy, to set ourselves new goals.

There are sadnesses that are easier to manage than others. For example, if we are crossing the street and see how the bus starts from our stop, we will feel a little despondent (we would rather have arrived on time), but we will immediately make a decision about it: wait for the next one, walk or use another means of transport.

If what we have lost has been the hope of, for example, going out with that person we like so much —a mutual friend called us today to tell us that he has a partner—, it is true that we will feel despondency, but the objective of our brain is that Let's assume that you have to discard the idea of conquering that person, in order to set your goals on someone or something different.

When we lose a loved one, not only have we been left without someone who occupied an important place in our lives, but a large part of us leaves with those we have loved: our time, our illusions, our emotions. Those losses are important, but they are not the end. Our body will need some time to get used to the fact that that person is no longer there: there will no longer be neural connections to identify his voice when he speaks to us; we will not pick up the phone to call and consult a problem; our neurons will miss the smell, the touch of the skin; the booster circuits will claim the presence of someone who made us feel so good. But time heals everything, as long as we provide the right remedies.

How do we usually react?

Sadness is one of those emotions that have been called "negative", but which I prefer to call "uncomfortable" and, of course, "delicate", since they must be treated with some skill so that mismanagement does not cause havoc in our lives. .

Remember that the goal of sadness is to accept the loss. If we don't, we'll probably start to "skid".

As we have already mentioned, there are people who have a good training in accepting unwanted losses, and we will soon stop to see how they do it. But it is usual that, after feeling the loss, we begin to let certain types of thoughts take on an unwanted force. Thoughts that do not allow our brain to find a constructive and recovery path, which is exactly what it needs.

Many people opt, consciously or unconsciously, for an interpretation and a narration of what happened that can lead to even more dismal goals. That is why it is so important that we take the reins of what we think firmly and forcefully as soon as possible. If, for example, in the face of the loss of a loved one, or the impossibility of going out with whom we had already begun to forge certain sentimental illusions, ideas such as "I will not be able to live without that person", "my life will not make sense" begin to be associated , «I will never go out with anyone again», etc., the sign that our brain will be reading will be «there is no way out». And then he will begin to activate all the behaviors in accordance with that indication: don't go out, don't have illusions... don't live. The next stop on our life's journey is likely to be a depression. Those who have experienced it know that it is a cesspool into which it is preferable not to fall. Therefore, we are going to correctly follow the indications that sadness is giving us so that our brain does not go towards a destination that does us such a disservice.

We have previously commented on the importance of not canceling what we feel. And even more important is to constructively integrate it into our lives. When we are sad, it is almost certain that we will not be the best company for our friends and family: we will not feel like telling a joke or humming our favorite song. But we don't have to go through life like lost souls either, and if we are generous and kind people, we will surely avoid making life bitter for those around us.

Although we are low on energy, it is important not to stop doing our daily activities. It is evident that we will not do them with the same state of mind, but it is necessary to continue moving forward with our lives. We will probably have dropped from sixty to sixty kilometers per hour, or even thirty, and that speed is, without a doubt, the most appropriate. When there is little fuel left in the tank, there is no need to step on the accelerator. But we will move forward. And a suggestion: when we are close to a person who is sad, the best thing we can do is not insist that they "change that face." Our role will be to understand her loss, while we will play the primary role of entertaining her, distracting her, bringing that spark of good humor, at the same time that we respect the process of habituation to the new situation that is taking place in those who have lost something or someone important. There is no rush, you just have to accompany. And if we also take some time to listen in that recovery process, much better.

But there are other times when it can happen that we feel sad and we don't really know why.

One of those moments of "unidentified sadness" usually occurs in the transitions from one season to another, especially in spring and autumn. In these months, we are going to go from one extreme temperature to another, and the body has to adjust to the thermal changes that are coming. Maintaining a constant body temperature is one of the activities in which the brain is usually busiest, as it is absolutely essential for survival. But in general we are not aware of the hustle and bustle that occurs inside our organism when one day is hot and another, cold; when we leave the house with our coat and by mid-morning we are in a T-shirt... All this implies an investment of energy that leaves us, in some cases, exhausted. And there are many people who interpret that drop in energy as sadness. Those who identify with this symptomatology can reduce it if they spend more time resting on these dates. And above all, let them know that it is not exactly sadness, but tiredness.

On other occasions, the "unidentified sadness" may not be due to physiological causes, but that does not stop us from being confused by that "loss of energy" that we are feeling, without knowing very well why. At this point, we can ask ourselves a question that allows our brain to identify where a void has occurred and what loss is to be assumed: "What part of me feels that it has lost something?" For example, if a coworker has been transferred to another position in a different plant, in principle we would understand that it is something that does not have to make us sad. But we are sad: have we lost that company for coffee? Is there no one to say good morning to us? Is it not possible to raise our heads and ask a spontaneous question? In these cases, logically, it is not a "serious" loss, but our brain for these issues is relatively simple: it identifies a loss and activates its corresponding emotion. This little point of sadness will help us understand ourselves better and identify what and who are significant in our lives, and in what way and measure. Surely we will soon solve it by staying with that person more... or enjoying the arrival of a new one.

A suggestion to optimally manage our interpretation of what we no longer have the possibility of recovering is to keep its good memory. We are who we are based on our memory, on what we decide to remember when something has already happened, and so that the loss can be constructively integrated into our lives, what is usually more effective is that, every time we evoke it, we do so grateful for having done so. lived and, if possible, with a smile of satisfaction and affection.

Little by little, as new habits are incorporated into our daily lives, and these neural connections weaken over time and are replaced by new ones, our brain will regain the ability to focus on new goals. and thus be able to address them. The thermometer of our state of mind will begin to rise, we will begin to feel that we have more desire to do things and soon we will be ready to step on the accelerator again.

Surprise

How does it manifest in our body?

Surprise makes its appearance in the face of an unexpected stimulus or information. It is about something that was out of all expectations and that goes out of the scripts that we had about a person or a situation.

Faced with surprise and the need to understand what has caused it, we quickly put all our resources at the service of identifying the new context or stimulus, and for this the brain is responsible for expanding its receptors a little more: we open our eyes wide (to see more and better), we open our mouths (in case we need to collect more oxygen), and we also open our nostrils and ears a lot, so that the ears can reorient themselves and capture all kinds of sounds better, and the nose is under optimal conditions to detect any odor that is significant. And so that all these organs focus exactly where they are needed and do not move a millimeter, the brain is still in charge of doing something else: it tenses the neck muscles. All ready to analyze the situation.

When something surprises us, the attention has to be at its best and have a clear focus that allows an optimal collection of information, and thus be able to make a quick decision.

What is it telling us?

When something surprises us, the brain stops paying attention to what we were doing to try to understand what the change consists of and if there is something that needs to be done. Again, the best way is to illustrate it with an example.

Let's imagine that we are concentrating on a job, and suddenly we hear a loud noise. The whole body tenses, the attention is directed towards the source of the noise and we try to obtain as much information as possible about what could have happened. The objective is to make a quick and efficient decision: if it is something specific and of no great importance, we will immediately return to our tasks. In this case, it is surely not surprising that, when we return to what we were doing, we have to make a new effort of attention to return to the task that was occupying us previously. This is so because the emotion of surprise has been in charge of sweeping the entire brain so that there would be no thought that could interfere with the instantaneous identification of what happened.

In the event that the noise was indicating to us that what is happening could endanger our lives, we would probably leave the building or the place where we were at full speed. The brain needs all its resources to find a quick way out.

But there are also "mild surprises", such as when something catches our attention (because it is not usual), for example with a friend. Perhaps this person has said or done something to us that "surprises" us. It is likely that first we stay a little tense (although it is not noticeable outwardly), and that, after the initial surprise, our brain is dedicated to pondering what that news may have meant. Sometimes you will not be able to come up with a concrete answer, although it will probably be something that we will remember in the future when, perhaps, it is necessary to tie up a series of loose ends. Once the precise conjectures have been made and after reaching some conclusion, of whatever kind, we feel at least better prepared to face future events, always to the extent that we have been able to foresee them. But whatever

The brain is not very fond of surprises and what misleads it. He prefers to have everything under control. And, certainly, if they are pleasant, it could be said that he digests them better.

When the surprise, far from being something that harms us, brings us some kind of benefit, such as a nice detail on a special day or a well-deserved reinforcement after a job well done, the brain will allow us to relax and enjoy ourselves.

But when the surprise does not bode well, the response of our brain will be the opposite. You will need to activate and feel prepared for a good defense, attack or flight. Perhaps our friend is lying to us and his tricks can get us into a good mess. In this case, the surprise must help us correctly identify what has changed in the relationship, and thus be able to react appropriately.

How do we usually react?

Surprise is an emotion that is highly automated, and that means that it is very important for the brain and for our survival. For instant decisions, sometimes it is better not to count on the slowness of reason. At that time you can not waste time on trifles.

In general, surprise is usually accompanied by some other emotion, such as fear, in case it is something dangerous. In this case, the responses are usually similar, because in reality what is happening is that, after the surprise, the brain has identified a dangerous situation, activates fear, and then we respond to it. This happens in milliseconds. Among the classic responses we find what in English are called fight or flight, «fight or flight». And we also have a third extraordinary response, which is called "talking to someone." When something surprises us, and we understand that there is no need to fight or flee, the next thing we usually do is start asking each other what has happened, if they know something, what have they seen... In this way, a lot of tension is discharged and we feel accompanied in the event that a decision had to be made, of whatever kind, so that responsibility for a possible error can also be diffused. Human beings are a social species and relationships with other people provide us with multiple benefits. And feeling accompanied in difficult times is one of the most rewarding.

We usually respond well to surprise and, if not, there is probably cognitive interference or a short circuit in the form of I don't know thinking. There are many people who have unconsciously learned or think of themselves that they don't know. As a general maxim, they do not know how to respond, solve, deal with problems... In this case, if in the face of a surprising or unexpected situation, instead of flowing with the appropriate behavior, the thought "I don't know" interferes, the person will be blocked, without knowing what decision to make If the context is not dangerous, by this time you will be safe. But if it is something more serious, that thought will really cloud your ability to make a decision and feel in control of whatever needs to be done at a given time. If we identify with this group of people, It wouldn't hurt to consider a visit to a therapist. He usually has a fix and will allow us to stop going around in circles to learn to press only one pedal at a time: the accelerator or the brake. Our brain does know, and a lot.

We can let ourselves be guided by emotion and its co-driver, reason, as long as we are clear that they form a compact and well-coordinated team.

How to manage it effectively?

As previously mentioned, we usually manage surprises well. We put ourselves in a state of maximum perception and attention, we collect information and act accordingly. Both easy and difficult situations do not present too much complexity: if it is not serious, we relax, we are even happy if it is, for example, an unexpected birthday party. And when it's risky, we run or seek help.

In reality, we experience multiple surprises every day: everything that is not planned generates this emotion in us, although sometimes it can be so slight that we hardly realize that it has been activated, because we also solve it, even without having to think too much . It is one of those emotions that, being practically directed by our most unconscious or intuitive part, helps us to better understand how thoughts, and the way we formulate them, can short-circuit a signal that, originally, is perfect. .

And we can also use this emotion consciously, to get the brain out of the state of hypnosis to which situations of boredom tend to lead. Are we starting to get tired of work or partner? That's because the same thing probably happens every day. It is not necessary to change either one or the other. In most cases, if we have the ability to introduce new elements and be pleasantly surprised, the next phase of the journey is usually quite motivating. And much cheaper.

FEAR

How does it manifest in our body?

One of the most uncomfortable emotions that we can feel, without a doubt, in the list of the main ones is fear. To fear we associate a generalized tremor that prevents us, at first, from acting. If you ever have the quick reflexes to analyze where the first "whiplash" of fear occurs, you would feel it in your legs, although it quickly spreads to other places in your body. Why there? Now you will understand why.

What is it telling us?

Once again, and although it may sound repetitive, let's remember that we are what we are in a given context. When the emotion of fear is activated in one of these contexts, what the brain is trying to tell us is that there is something that it does not know how to face, it does not know what it has to do, it does not have sufficient resources to solve something that it has. before himself. In other words, what this emotion wants to tell us is I don't know. Again, let's use some examples to illustrate this.

Do you remember the first time you sat behind the wheel of the car at the driving school? Or, worse yet, the day the teacher told you "today we're going out on the highway"? I do. I thought it was the last day of my life, and my teacher's too. Although I was in the process of learning, I still did not know enough to face the dangers that awaited us in that jungle of cars and people driving at what seemed to me then a great speed. I have no qualms about admitting that, at that moment, I felt very scared, which I resolved with a nervous laugh and a "you yourself...". Now, with the perspective of a few years, we are able to laugh at that scene and the fact of going out on the highway does not produce any fear, because by now we already know what to do. We even go talking with the co-pilot, with our friends, listening to music or the radio, contemplating the landscape... We are the same person in the same context, but with a slight difference: before we didn't know, and now we do. That's why we used to feel afraid, and now we don't.

Regarding jungle, I usually use another example, perhaps a little more metaphorical, but quite illustrative to facilitate the understanding of what fear means. This time we are going to get a little more adventurous, and we are going to imagine that, on the path of life, we suddenly find ourselves before a jungle with five tigers. Except if we are circus tamers, veterinarians or caretakers of these big cats, the brain has to warn us that it has absolutely no idea what to do in a situation that puts its survival at risk: and, for that, it activates fear . It usually reacts with a level of tremor proportional to the lack of resources we have to deal with the situation, that is, if we have never seen a tiger and we do not like animals, we will tremble a lot so that the stopping maneuver is absolutely effective, and if we are somewhat familiar with them, we will tremble a little less, perhaps with some capacity for movement, if the brain has been able to figure out what it can do. The goal of that tremor is to stop. Have you ever tried to walk while your legs shake like castanets? Try it. It is impossible.

The brain is extremely efficient: it detects a situation in a context that it does not know how to resolve and gives the order to stop by trembling in the most appropriate place: the legs.

For now, he has resolved the most urgent situation, which was not to expose himself to risky and unknown situations. But we still have a lot to do and that, precisely, is where we usually mess up. But this mess is, without a doubt, a consequence of not understanding what our brain is telling us. Let's keep unraveling this little mess.

How do we usually react?

We have already commented previously that two of the traditionally typified responses to fear were flight or fight. Then a third was discovered, which was to talk to someone (if you can, of course).

But we also know that there are people who simply get stuck, who paralyze a part of their life either because they don't know how or because they don't want to face a complex situation. Or it stays in circles, unable to find any solution that allows the brain to move in any direction. However, life goes on and, although it may seem so, no one stays in the same place they were; as time passes, one is left, without a doubt, behind. And that's not a good place to feel happy.

We are also currently facing an extensive literature on how to deal with fear. One of the ones that most surprises us therapists is the one that says something like "when you're afraid, ignore it and move on...". Would it make sense for us to follow the advice of someone who told us to run the red light? Well, it comes to the same thing. If we were walking towards the edge of a cliff, surely the brain would activate the "fear" signal at a certain moment. And if we went ahead, without heeding this signal, as the advice we have mentioned suggests, the consequences of our decision would be absolutely dire, except if we are going to paraglide. Let's take a more everyday example:

In the face of fear, there is no need to stop indefinitely —letting life pass us by—, nor to throw yourself madly into situations that pose an obvious risk. We are now going to see in detail what is the best way to face our fears.

Let us remember once again that the emotion of fear is telling us to stop, in order to analyze the situation and correctly identify what our brain has perceived that it does not know how to do.

The next step will be to get down to work to learn what we need and that will allow us to get out of situations that, until now, were unknown to us. In our examples it would be, on the one hand, getting a driver's license and, in the case of tigers, we would probably start by watching documentaries about their life and customs; then it would not be a bad idea to get in shape in case we have to take a little run; It would also be advisable to visit a zoo so that the experts can help us better understand its nature and, finally, decide what is the best way to cross that precious jungle unscathed.

Once the new skills have been acquired, it is true that facing a difficult situation is not, as we have already mentioned, comfortable at all. But we can survive it, which is what it's all about. The positive part of these learnings is that probably the fifth or tenth time we have to go through the jungle with tigers, we may spend some of our time taking selfies with them. We will already know what we have to do, and even how to get the best performance out of each situation.

Can we then say that fear is a negative emotion? Absolutely. Understanding and managing it effectively allows us to learn skills that we lacked, grow as people and feel truly capable of living our own lives, whatever surprises it may bring. It favors our self-esteem and makes our day to day more interesting, because who said that living was easy? But the most exciting challenges always carry that little bit of discomfort.

Fear is an extraordinary emotion: it tells us where our shortcomings are, it makes us grow as people, and it increases our confidence in ourselves and in our ability to be willing to learn what is needed at all times.

Feeling fear when we have to raise a conflict with our boss, or when the time has come to end a relationship, is normal. We probably never would have done it and sometime it had to be the first. If we prepare well what we want to say, for what, how and when; if we practice it until we feel safe —that is why we have felt fear— and, if we manage to get out of situations that offered little with dignity, surely on the following occasions our fears will be reduced to slight pangs in the stomach, because our brain will have more and more clearer what he has to do and, in addition, well.

The feeling of fear is directly proportional to what we can and know how to do in each circumstance.

HAPPINESS

After an uncomfortable emotion —not a negative one, as we have already seen—, we are now going to tackle another much more pleasant one: joy. This emotion is very pleasant for us, because it gives us a feeling of fullness and calm, while we feel full of energy. If we look closely, it is the opposite of sadness (loss) during which the energy had drained from us and we were barely below the minimum of activation.

The relaxation that joy produces allows the blood to flow throughout our body with hardly any tension or obstacles, which in turn makes it easier for oxygen to perfectly reach all the body's muscles, which is thus ready for us to celebrate our birthday with our loved ones. state of satisfaction, we move or set new goals. Undoubtedly, joy is one of those green lights in our lives that tell us that we can and should move forward with confidence.

What is it telling us?

We usually feel happy when the plans we had turn out exactly as we had planned, when our expectations and reality coincide in a positive way or when we successfully achieve our goals.

Joy is telling us that things have gone well, that what has happened is a sum in our lives or that we have successfully achieved some of the goals we had set for ourselves.

It is about those moments in which we can breathe fully and fill ourselves with satisfaction, because we are facing one of those emotions that fill the reservoir of our illusion and make us feel that our life is going smoothly, or that at least its circumstances have improved significantly. It is, without a doubt, the moment to enjoy every pore of our skin.

How do we usually react?

To be honest, we usually manage this emotion well. We let ourselves be carried away by this powerful vital current, to which it is easy to surrender and surrender. It is extremely rewarding and that is why it is included among the so-called "positive" emotions, but I prefer to describe it, in this case, as extremely comfortable and pleasant.

However, there are cases where joy is not managed properly. For example, when there have been traumatic experiences and learning in which any manifestation of joy was likely to be punished with criticism or a bad face. One grows then thinking that, when the good times arrive, one cannot relax and feel full and satisfied, because it is associated in his head that, shortly, the punishment will appear. "Better not to throw the bells on the fly", and instead of allowing life to run through our body from end to end, tensions are generated that attenuate what should be moments of fullness.

On other occasions, learning associated with an emotion such as joy can lead to adopting certain types of violent attitudes in a euphoric state. In general, this occurs when the emotion feeds on irrational thoughts that overactivate the body, so that all that accumulated energy is channeled, either against other people, or against oneself. It is then when a magnificent emotion like this ceases to be positive, not so much for what it is in itself, but for the consequences of its management. Again, we can clearly see that emotions are neither negative nor positive in themselves, but what we do after feeling them is. And that depends a lot on our learning.

How to manage it effectively?

Since joy means goals achieved or added surprises in our lives, the best thing we can do is fully enjoy the moment, and for this we have to be able to fairly assess what we have achieved. When our favorite team scores the goal that will give them the Champions Cup, we can jump and shout at will, as long as we don't start punching the fans of the opposing team. When we have been able to pass that exam that is so decisive for our professional future, the normal thing is to run to enjoy it with those who love us well and value us, with those who are happy from the heart for our successes. But it would not justify anyone belittling or looking down on those who have not managed to overcome it.

Properly channeling the energy that gives us a powerful emotion such as joy can make us feel doubly satisfied: first, for what has been achieved; secondly, because the intelligent management that we have made of it will prevent the most rewarding moments of our lives from tarnishing.

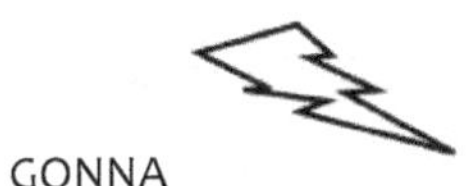

GONNA

How does it manifest in our body?

Let's now examine another of those emotions that I call "uncomfortable," but don't think of as negative at all: anger. We refer to it not so much in terms of anger or aggressiveness, but of the anger that we feel throughout the day at all levels, from the mildest to the most intense.

A first necessary note when talking about anger is the distinction between it and aggressiveness. Anger is an emotion whose meaning we will see below. Aggressiveness is a learned behavior that is often associated with anger, but is not exclusive to it. There are people who are aggressive when they are sad, when they are afraid or when they are happy. And there are also other people who when they get angry are not aggressive at all and know how to express their discomfort without hurting or offending anyone, neither with their words nor with their actions.

How do we feel when we are angry? We are going to remember the last time something bothered us deeply, and then we are going to look inside our body. What was happening? Probably, we feel like a coffee pot with boiling water about to spurt. Internal activation has risen above normal and something needs to be done. But what exactly? If we recognize what that anger is telling us, we will probably solve the situation in which we find ourselves immersed much more effectively than if we let ourselves be carried away by uncontrolled "impulses".

Anger management is one of the most important lessons that we need to incorporate into our lives, because it is so powerful that it often propels us to places where we did not plan to go and that we may not like at all. Fortunately, we are in time to learn to take control of our anger, and make it take us exactly to the point where we have programmed our goal coordinates.

What is it telling us?

There are two main assumptions in which the brain activates this emotion. To understand them well, we will first take into account that our brain is very territorial: «I am me». A priori, he knows perfectly well what corresponds to him and where the limits of his identity are. Later, certain types of learning and experiences can have the consequence that those limits are blurred and one does not know how to mark them properly. For example, children who have suffered abuse of any kind often have problems with these delimitations, since the abuse itself means that the other person has not respected the child's physical and psychological spaces, so that he has no idea when he can say "enough" or simply "no". Actually, instead of learning about who he is, he's learning about who he's not.

Therefore, knowing that our brain has a border to defend in order to guarantee the survival of the entire system it represents, one of the situations that will activate the emotion of anger will be the perception of a physical, psychological or emotional threat. This, which sounds perhaps a little strong, is so subtle that it jumps out at a "you will believe that what you are wearing looks good on you!". Obviously, this is not a constructive criticism, but an ambiguous comment —they do not tell us directly that they do not like what we are wearing, or that it makes us feel very bad—, probably with the intention of offending. Bother us. We do not interpret good intentions and, furthermore, we are not very clear about what they are actually telling us. There is a certain point of manipulation so that we are the ones who give the final interpretation to the message, freeing the person who issued it from guilt: «I never told you that it made you feel bad...». And it will be true. So, does our brain have more than enough reasons to send us a signal that tells us "be careful"? Fortunately, yes, and he usually does it quite diligently. Another thing is that we understand it and that we know how to give an appropriate response to that context. Later we will see in more detail how.

A second situation in which the anger signal is usually activated is when our brain perceives that its expectations and reality do not coincide. The level of anger will be proportional to the distance between what we expected and what has really happened. Surely the following scene, which is familiar to all of us, can help us to better understand its meaning: we go with our euro to the drinks vending machine, because we are quite thirsty. We hope that when we insert the coin through the slot and press the button of the bottle we choose, it will fall and we will be able to satisfy our desire to drink. However, we throw in the euro, we hit the button... and nothing falls. Surprise... and a little anger. The activation that is generated in our body (small dose of anger) is what allows us to hit the button repeatedly... It continues without falling. Now we get a little more angry, basically because we need to do something more forceful and the body needs more activation: we try to shake the machine, so that the bottle falls, that is, so that expectation and reality coincide. The next reaction I'm often offered in courses is "kick the machine." Deep down, it is what we would like to do, but finally our education prevents us from consummating this gesture. However, the brain is still activated at the level of the action it would like to perform and we get much angrier. At that moment we have to use the co-pilot: the reason. Let's see: maybe the machine is broken or the drink has finished. Why not call the concierge (if we are in a local) or the phone number that is on the plaque above the buttons? They are two good options. It is also true that we will most likely turn around and give up the euro for lost. We will soon tolerate the little frustration we just suffered, and we hope that it will pass in a short space of time.

Now let's see this same reaction with something that can happen to us, for example, when the weekend arrives. We have seen that a film that interests us a lot has just been released and we thought it would be a good plan to go see it with our friend Pepe. We have already consulted the schedules, the cinemas and the means of transport. We called Pepe with the idea of going together. But Pepe tells us that he can't — it's the equivalent of when the drink doesn't fall out of the machine. «How not? But what a great movie it is!" We hit the button several times. "Look, I can't go, thank you" —the bottle still doesn't fall—. «But, man, I've already bought the tickets» —little lie to force a guilty conscience in Pepe—. From then on, depending on how assertive Pepe is, he will give in or not to our request to come with us to the movies.

To be honest, generally bad. And "bad" refers to aggressiveness, verbal or physical, indiscriminate, which usually results in normally unnecessary damage and which, moreover, can be perfectly avoided. But let's see why it's so hard for us to control this runaway foal.

We have already seen that the physiological reaction when the brain triggers anger is an activation similar to a boiling coffee pot. Both in the event that the brain perceives that it has to defend itself against aggression, of whatever type and intensity, and when it perceives that it has to match its expectations and reality, the fact is that it has to do something. And for the brain, doing translates into muscular activity. For the muscles to work at maximum performance they need higher doses of oxygen, and for this we will begin to breathe faster, and the heart will be in charge of beating faster to quickly pump the blood that has to transport the oxygen recharges to all that musculature . Depending on the action that the brain perceives that it has to perform, the activation level will be higher or lower. And here we come to the point where we have to learn to release that tension in the best possible way.

As we have also explained previously, for the brain, the perception of "attack" and the "defense" response can correspond both to physical aggression —which we hope will be exceptional—, as well as to verbal or psychological aggression. If we feed these small activations, in turn, with negative, irrational or inappropriate thoughts, the level of activation will increase, so that we will inevitably reach what we call the "point of no return", in which, yes or yes, You have to release all the accumulated tension. And usually we do it against others or against ourselves. Obviously, once the storm is discharged, we will have managed to lower the activation levels, but at the cost of unwanted collateral or direct damage that little by little will leave a deep mark on our lives.

An inappropriate reaction, for example, would be to launch insults with someone who questioned whether the clothes we were wearing fit us well. And, of course, it is absolutely absurd that we get angry with Pepe or, worse still, that we hurl some insult at him, simply because our plans have not gone as expected. Pepe is not responsible and much less guilty of our frustration.

So that the emotion of anger does not make us react like an uncontrolled shotgun firing left and right without any sense, we need reason to become the best co-pilot we could have ever imagined. It depends on it that well-managed anger becomes the propellant that drives us to achieve our goals, instead of the stumbling block that prevents us from achieving them.

How to manage it effectively?

Before we see how to manage anger more effectively in the contexts in which we usually move, it should be noted that, exceptionally, aggressiveness may be the appropriate response in a given context. If, for example, we suffer an attack because someone is trying to steal our wallet in the middle of the street, or in the face of an attempted rape, aggressiveness can be one of the responses that allows us to resolve that unpleasant situation in the most effective way (by pushing or screeching, for example) or at least try. But these contexts are extremely delicate to analyze, and they are not the object of what we need to learn now.

A very effective way to lower the physiological activation that we feel when anger has been activated is to physically put ourselves at the same level of that activation, thus generating alternatives to physical aggressiveness. When we are angry, the best thing we can do is take a long, brisk walk; take the dog out; go do some sport; up and down stairs; cleaning shelves, or any other activity that we know will cause us some physical fatigue. Once we have managed to get rid of the excess energy and recover more or less usual levels, then the time has come to analyze what has really bothered us so much.

Continuing with the questions that allow us to identify the reason for an emotion, in this case we should ask ourselves "what part of me is feeling attacked or attacked?" or "what did I expect to happen and how did it actually happen? Is there anything I can do to match what I want with what I get?" In this way, the issue of clothing, for example, we can manage it in various ways. From the outset, what we are not told clearly we do not have to understand. If someone tells us that if we think that what we are wearing suits us very well, with irony, our response may be a succinct "yes, of course I think so!". We can also reply that "we don't quite understand what exactly you want to tell us." In any case, whether we are doing well or not is something that we must decide,

About Pepe, there is little to say. Pepe is completely out of the speculations that we are doing for the weekend. If he agrees that he can share with us the moments that we propose, magnificent; but if he can't, we'll still love him just the same. And we will try to call, perhaps, Manolo. We still have a pleasant surprise.

LOVE

How does it manifest in our body?

Love produces one of the most pleasant sensations that a human being can experience. When we feel loved and when we love, a wave of order, satisfaction, relaxation and confidence runs through our body. We feel full of life and desire to live, we breathe deeply and our heart beats at full capacity. When we talk about love, we are not only referring to the love of a partner (to learn more about it, I invite you to read my book Good Love, in which I go into much more detail on the entire journey that has taken place since we felt love , until we are able to develop and integrate it as a positive and constructive experience in our lives), but to all those contexts in which we feel loved, for example, by friends, siblings, parents, children, colleagues, teachers, etc.

It is true that when we are in love we feel butterflies in our stomachs, we smile for nothing or we are absorbed and sometimes distant from what is happening around us. Our brain is tremendously active and begins to secrete a large number of substances to spice up the moment, including a good amount of dopamine that makes us want more, much more of the same. So much so that we are unable to see if there is something that does not suit us. At that moment, the lens of our attention is completely distorted and focuses only on what we like so that it continues to provide us with that well-being.

But let's continue with love as an emotion. We feel love for what makes us feel alive and full of hope. Love facilitates approach behavior, because we want to be close to what provides us with so much well-being.

We directly associate this emotion with our most important vital organ: the heart. Is this relationship a myth? Maybe not so much, and we'll see why.

The first and very important point I want to make regarding this emotion is that, in our physiological structure, love is a source of pleasure, not of suffering, this being the consequence of errors in learning or, in the worst case, of any personality disorder.

The brain activates this emotion in any context in which it identifies that the necessary conditions exist to be able to be without there being absolutely no risk to its survival. Quite the contrary, these are environments in which, in addition, the best that we have inside will be enhanced and brought out.

We all want to feel loved, because our main objective is to "live" in the most appropriate context possible: where we are respected and the best of us are enhanced, in a safe environment.

Where there is love there is life. And the organ directly related to it is, without a doubt, the heart.

The signal that turns on in our brain is green, green and, once again, green. If we take into account that the main objective of our brain is survival, it will not be strange for us to understand, then, why it seeks, yearns and wishes to find itself in contexts in which it is assured. If there is a context that means "life", with all its letters, that is without a doubt that of love. And that is why he dedicates himself to experiencing as many times as possible that signal that means "live".

Now we come to a delicate part, in which we must make an important distinction, as we did with the emotion of anger, which we separate from behavior such as aggressiveness. And for this we need to understand that love is not the same as loving.

Love is a feeling. Loving is a behavior.

When they ask me: "Hey, do you think that person loves me?", my answer is the following: "He probably feels that he loves you. No one can affirm that for us and, therefore, we cannot deny it. But another thing is if he knows how to love you or not, because it is something that will depend on what he has learned, what he has practiced and the type of relationship he wants to have with you. This would be a conduct and, therefore, observable, measurable and valuable".

Of all the emotions, the one that presents the most cognitive short circuits for its correct identification is, without a doubt, love. There is so much written about him, from so many fields of knowledge... or from the purest ignorance; so many interpretations have been given to it; is confused with so many other behaviors, such as passion, sex, domination, submission, obsession, self-immolation, convenience, etc., that we have to disperse many mountains of straw to literally keep the most important thing: the grain .

Depending on our learning, our experiences or the vital moment in which we find ourselves, we will react to love in very different ways.

Some of the things we learned during our childhood may no longer serve us well when we are older. There are people who identify that being in a loving environment means that they can display all their bad character and that those who love them have to put up with them like that; or that they have to become submissive people as proof of their deep and true love. For others, the contexts of presumed love cause mistrust and fear, and they will activate defensive behaviors with those who share their intimacy.

We also have a whole repertoire of crazy ideas about love that literally drive our brains crazy: that if love is unconditional, even if they are physically or psychologically abusing you — here the brain is surely sending continuous signals to run away, that, obviously, we ignore—; that if there are half oranges or soulmates, who delimit the experience of a couple to a single person, if you are lucky enough to find it in this life - we are complete people in the process of evolution who can share wonderful experiences with other people who they are like us: getting to know each other and trying to get the best out of themselves—; that if we die of love, that if we are nothing without the other, that we cannot live if we do not have who we want... —in short, a whole range of immaturity, for not accepting that the other does not love us, and for selfishness, because we are capable of putting whoever we say we love in the moral dilemma that our life depends on succumbing to our blackmail—. Clearly none of this has anything to do with love.

However, there are many times when we probably do very well, although we may not know how to explain it. We are going to see what happens when we respond with what our brain needs when it activates this emotion at certain times or with specific people.

Loving well consists of being able to give to whom we love not so much what we believe or want to give, but what the other really needs to develop and get the best of himself.

Many times we think that we love a person very much because we give them what we think is good for them, or what we want to give them. Without a doubt, we are thinking about ourselves, but not about the well-being of those we love, because we are not taking into account their needs, but ours.

Surely we live with the conviction that, as we feel love, only for that reason we already know how to love well, and we want to do it the best we can. However, good intentions are usually not enough if we don't learn how and practice a lot. To practice we do not necessarily need many people, but the most important thing is to have good teachers and, sometimes, one is enough.

Now it has become very fashionable to say "I love you" with some regularity. In principle, there is nothing to object to, except if the words are empty of content. When we are in environments where we feel loved and feel love as the emotion we are describing of trust and safety, the words "I love you" are a nice embellishment to what we already know we have. My suggestion is not to make them a pounding background music if we have no intention of dancing with the one we love.

So how do we know when we're doing it right? In my book Good Love I gave the example of a cactus and a hydrangea that were quite successful because of how well they understood their relationship. In order not to repeat myself, I will give you two examples here that will surely also help us understand if we are acting correctly.

- How do we know if a child is being raised in a loving environment? He probably smiles, plays, is healthy and handsome. And that is a consequence of the care of his guardians, who probably give him mashed food, milk adapted to his stomach, caresses, hygiene, shelter and a lot of security, even if that means that they cannot take a nap at the hours they would lie down a snooze and, of course, not to serve the steak "round and round". One more point related to children, regarding relationships of quantity or quality. Unfortunately, diapers must be changed when appropriate, not when it suits us adults, even if we use luxury wipes and expensive creams. The best in this case is not the most expensive, but the most timely.
- How do we know if a plant is in an environment where it receives love? Without a doubt, because it receives the elements it needs for its correct development: adequate light, water, good fertilizer, regular pruning, insecticides, etc. The result will be a plant that brings out all the flowers that its genetic equipment gives of itself when the

When we are loving well, it is because we are giving the subject/object of our love what they need, also creating the appropriate environment to bring out the best of themselves. If it is a relationship in which we also have to be loved - usually those between people - the correct attention must flow in both directions.

From a certain emotional maturity, the task of getting the best of ourselves, that is, of loving ourselves well, corresponds to us individually. Although if it is in the company of others, the result will be exponential.

HATRED 

How does it manifest in our body?

Hate is another of those emotions that share the podium of what some call negative emotions, and that —as you already know— here we are treating as uncomfortable. And hate is, and a lot. Among other things, because it causes us to be in a state of agitation, of high activation, which we already know means for the brain that it has to do something and, in this case, important. Sometimes we confuse it with rage, but its function is not exactly the same, as we will see below.

What is it telling us?

If we use some classics that are closer to the proposal we are making in this book, such as the philosopher René Descartes, hate is conceived as the awareness that something was wrong, combined with the desire to withdraw from it; for the creator of psychoanalysis, Sigmund Freud, in Instincts and their Vicissitudes (1915), described it as an ego state that wanted to destroy the source of its unhappiness.

Let's see why we have chosen these authors to explain the best way to understand hate in a positive way.

When the emotion of hate is triggered in a context, we are probably faced with something or someone that literally short-circuits our neurons. Whatever causes hatred in our lives is surely telling us that, in its presence, it is difficult to be oneself, or carry out personal projects. This does not mean that we are right or that we are not, but that we perceive it that way. The brain then decides that, whatever it is that is such a detriment to its projects, it has to come out of its environment of influence or its psychological intimacy.

Hatred, like anger, is one of those emotions that we don't manage really well. We confuse it with revenge, with resentment and, once again, with aggressiveness. Again, we have to make it clear that what we feel is not the same as what we do. The latter is determined by the thought or interpretation of the context, and what has been learned about what to do in these situations.

Hate is an emotion. Aggressiveness, resentment or revenge are behaviors that are not always associated with hatred, nor are they synonymous with it.

As we have seen, hate is telling us that it is necessary to vary the distance at which certain elements or people are located in our lives. Nothing more. Where does the problem arise?

In consultation, we usually work with a kind of concentric circle in whose center we place ourselves, leaving the rest of the elements or people in our life around us. Some can get quite close without causing us any discomfort or, on the contrary, we appreciate their presence in our lives. Others, however, as we bring them closer, we understand that there is a point from which their presence is unpleasant or uncomfortable. That is, it "short-circuits" us.

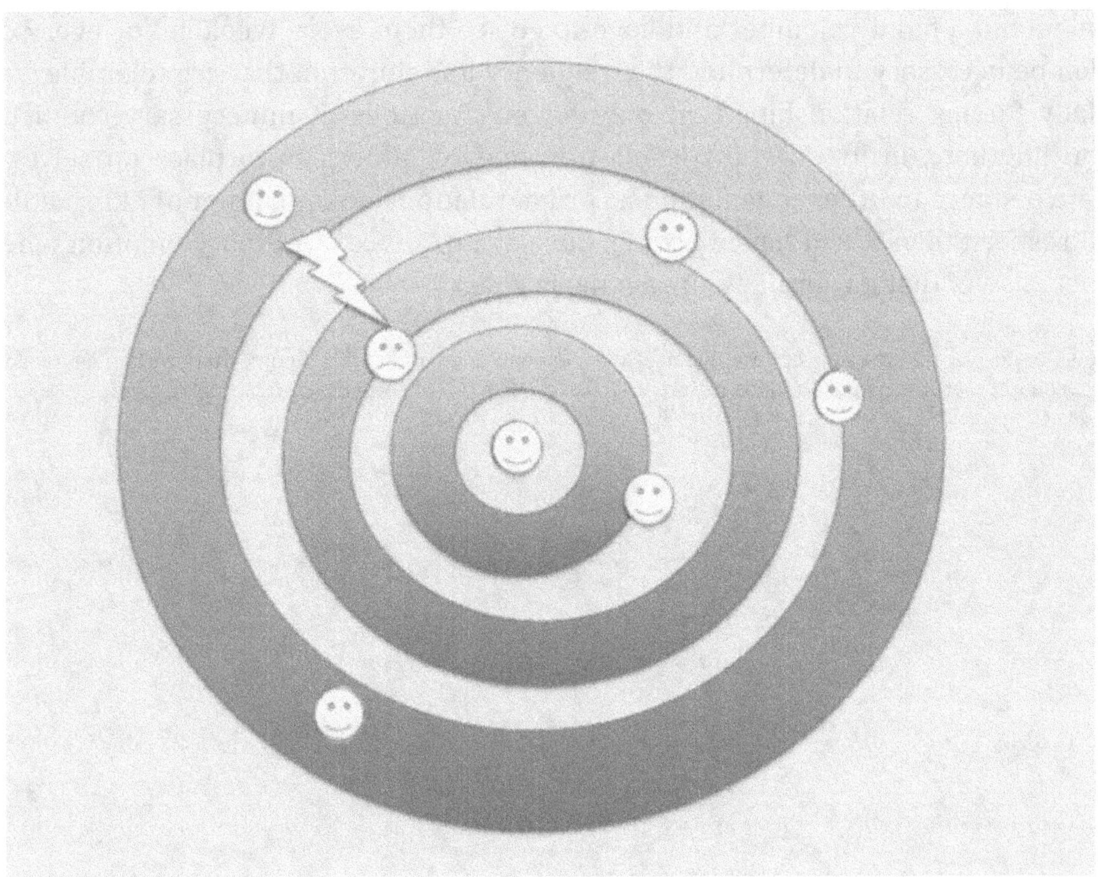

That is precisely the point that we have to learn to detect, simply to understand what is the appropriate distance at which each person in our lives should be, to treat each other with the degree of civility that is presupposed to all of us. But the usual thing is that in the face of inability or ignorance about how to manage this emotion, we fall into aggressive behaviors, such as resentment, revenge and aggressiveness, either verbally —through insults—, or physically. None of them supposes a correct management of an emotion that, in principle, is not inviting us anything more than to put an adequate distance between us and the stimulus that generates so much rejection.

How to manage it effectively?

Neither can everyone like us, nor will we like all the people we meet in life. Frankly, it seems immoral to force someone to like someone who deeply dislikes or who has been the source and cause of deep suffering. We all have the right to decide what we like and want to have around, as well as what we don't want to have present in our lives. What we never recommend or suggest is that, in the face of this emotion, you enter the chain of ineffective behaviors that we mentioned earlier.

Can't stand a family member and have to go see them every weekend or every day? It will then be necessary to determine the frequency and duration that are tolerable, without artificially forcing relationships that only foster situations of unnecessary conflict. If an emotion like hate, in its different levels of intensity, allows us to place ourselves at an adequate distance in order to maintain a cordial relationship and, if not of liking, at least of mutual respect, then it will have become, once again, an extraordinary emotion whenever the exact answer that our brain is suggesting is given.

Hate allows us to place at the appropriate distance the elements or people with whom, after certain limits, sparks fly. Learning to detect that correct point of interaction facilitates a minimum of cordiality and mutual respect.

Cómo gestionar eficazmente nuestras emociones

Emoción	Cómo se manifiesta	Qué está indicando	Gestión ineficaz	Pregunta	Gestión eficaz
Tristeza	Abatimiento	Pérdida	Añadir gran cantidad de pensamientos catastrofistas	¿Qué parte de mí siente que ha perdido algo?	Asumir que lo perdido no volverá y fijarse nuevos objetivos
Sorpresa	Apertura máxima de ojos, boca, nariz y oídos; tensión en el cuello	Algo inesperado, distinto	Bloquearse	¿Qué me resulta inesperado o extraño de esta situación?	Recabar información y decidir si es relevante o si podemos seguir con nuestra actividad
Miedo	Temblor, principalmente en las piernas	No sé; parar	Seguir adelante como si no pasara nada; quedarse parado para siempre; dar vueltas como una peonza	¿Qué parte de mí no sabe gestionar esta situación? ¿Qué parte del contexto es la que no me siento capaz de afrontar?	Aprender lo que requiera la situación, y solucionarla estando mejor preparado
Alegría	Relajación, plenitud	Objetivo cumplido, objetivos que suman en nuestra vida	No creerse merecedor de lo bueno	¿Qué parte de mí siente que sus objetivos han sido alcanzados?	Valorar lo conseguido, tanto si es por méritos propios como si es fruto del azar. Disfrutar de ello

Cómo gestionar eficazmente nuestras emociones (cont.)

Emoción	Cómo se manifiesta	Qué está indicando	Gestión ineficaz	Pregunta	Gestión eficaz
Ira	Activación, el corazón late más deprisa y respiramos más rápido	Se percibe una agresión física, psicológica o emocional; nuestras expectativas no coinciden con la realidad	Agresividad, sumisión	¿Qué parte de mí se siente agredida? ¿Qué es lo que yo esperaba y qué ha ocurrido de otra manera?	Asertividad, resolver sin agredir, pero con firmeza Analizar hasta qué punto puedo hacer que realidad y expectativas coincidan, o se acerquen el máximo posible
Amor	Calma, confianza, seguridad	Aproximación; no hay ningún peligro; podemos desarrollar nuestro potencial	Dañar, descuidar, agredir; llamar amor a muchas conductas que no lo son	¿Siento que este contexto saca lo mejor de mí? ¿Me siento seguro en él?	Proporcionar todo lo necesario, potenciar la vida y la identidad del sujeto/objeto de nuestro amor
Odio	Gran activación	Alejamiento; colocar a la distancia adecuada a los elementos más conflictivos de nuestra intimidad psicológica	Venganza, agresividad, rencor	¿En qué punto creo que puedo colocar a esta persona en mi vida sin sentir que se producen cortocircuitos?	Tantear e identificar cuál es el punto exacto en que debemos dejar las relaciones con cada persona

Hate also becomes extraordinary when it allows us to properly distance ourselves from people whose behaviors have caused profound damage to our lives. Feeling that they are not close enough to pose a continuous threat will allow us to move on and, why not, forget what happened. But our brain will always be alert with this emotion so that, if by any chance, the healthy limits are skipped, we can mark them again as soon as possible. Obviously, it is uncomfortable, but negative?

Let's give our beautiful life project a chance and let's not let anyone ruin it. And let's do it effectively, without falling into irrational behaviors, such as resentment or revenge, which, as we have seen, are not a direct consequence of hatred, but of its incorrect management.

Are you rational or emotional?

It gives us a certain peace of mind as human beings to label everything we find in our path, although we may not like being labeled so much. But, in principle, it seems like a good strategy that helps the brain not to have to pay much attention to someone or something, and to solve it with some speed and even accuracy. For example, when we say of someone that he is "intellectual", a series of characteristics are attributed to him, such as that he spends his days reading, or in libraries, or that he only talks about profound topics. It seems that this makes it easier for us to approach that person, bringing up conversations that we think are of interest to him, or not placing expectations on something that he can do. And surely we have also lived the experience of being surprised the day we saw that same person winning the half marathon in their city, or dancing wildly in the fashionable beach bar. It is not that the other has broken our schemes, but that they have broken ourselves. The label that we have put, obviously, does not fit us and, of course, it has to do with our way of perceiving the world, not with how the other person is in reality. «It is that I believed that...» Well, what each one decides to believe is his responsibility.

This brief introduction will help us to better understand why we need to put labels, and how it especially affects the subject of emotions. It seems to be better seen that men are more "rational" and women more "emotional", although now trends are changing and we find women who like to boast of being "rational", just like many men of being "emotional" .

But what does this actually mean? We «assume» that being more rational implies not flinching when something serious or of a certain importance happens, that one is more reflective or thinks about situations more; we also "assume" that you are more decisive and get to the point without getting lost in unnecessary digressions. About. On the contrary, emotional people are, first, the ones who most easily cry about anything, or simply about everything. They are immediately noticeable when they are sad or angry and, in addition, they tend to give quite a "grime" with their emotional states. When they are happy they are the bell that brings a smile to everyone who crosses their path, and when they get angry they get carried away by the first thing that comes to mind without thinking about its consequences. Also more or less.

If we have reached this page without skipping any of the previous ones, we probably don't have to go too far to have the clarity and conviction that we are all rational and emotional at the same time. And we cannot be otherwise. The difference is not so much the amount of emotion or reason that we put into our behaviors, but the ability we have to properly manage one and the other.

And now we are going to stop to analyze a little more one and the other.

We have detected that, in general, people who poorly manage their emotions, who overflow, who are impulsive, and who do not know how to properly channel what is happening to them, are called "emotional". This, which can happen to anyone at specific times, seems to be the natural state of those we label, or are labeled, in this way. On the other hand, we could say of the so-called "rational" people that they neither feel nor suffer, their face is impassive and they pass everything through the filter of their prefrontal lobe. Except, everything must be said, the day they burst. Because the emotional style of rational people is not that incessant chirimiri of emotional people, but theirs is more about storm, lightning and thunder and, sometimes, with hurricane wind. Of course, after the storm there is always calm, surely accompanied by some collateral damage in the form of puddles. Could we say that it is not a purely emotional reaction in a runaway state? As in the first case, these are inadequately managed emotions in which, of course, there is little reason left in a show of lack of control.

Then...?

We can free ourselves as soon as possible from any type of corseting in the form of a label and to the question about whether we are rational or emotional, our answer may be the following: «It depends». Yes, it depends on what context we find ourselves in and what we consider most relevant in each situation: whether emotion guided by reason; if reason seasoned with some emotion, or if a healthy fifty/fifty balance between the two.

Not all contexts are the same, and moving only by a unique and exclusive way of being is going to provide us with more inconveniences than advantages. This does not mean that we are turncoats or weather vanes, but rather that we have to take advantage of the opportunity to use these two tools well, depending on the situation in which we find ourselves, and feel free to decide if at a specific moment we give more weight to our emotion. than to our reason, or vice versa. And, most importantly, how we do it.

Surely we will understand it better with several examples.

Let's imagine that we have just found out that someone whom we deeply and sincerely appreciated has been deceiving us and, moreover, harming something important to us. At first we will go through a phase of stupefaction, which will be followed by another of pain when we are aware of what has happened, and then an intense feeling of anger and/or sadness will probably come. The level of rage will be proportional to the importance of the betrayal. Obviously, in this case the emotion will be overflowing and all kinds of probably unexecutable thoughts will go through our heads:

- If we are presumably emotional people, we probably enter into a tidal wave of feelings, which can go from deep hatred to forgiveness, trying to justify the other's action, to later cry inconsolably, and then return to feeling disproportionate anger, probably accompanied by questions. and reproaches that, in general, do not lead to anything clarifying or decisive.
- If we are in the group of those who are presumably rational, we will probably react with a deathly silence, and with a muscular contraction similar to a reinforced concrete wall. It's going to hurt us the same as the emotional ones, but we're going to swallow it. We will put our reason to work to try to know how, when, where, in what way, why, what for... the deception occurred.

Actually, we all feel emotions about different events, and we all rationalize in some way what we are feeling. We differ in the way we manage emotion and reason and, within what we call a margin of normality, we will have a wide range of behaviors in which the weight of one or the other will be more evident, but not so much that we put on unnecessary labels.

In any case, it is also important that we do not limit ourselves to being one way in all situations. Probably, some of them will allow us to give more room to emotions than to reason, such as the loss of someone we love, and others in which reason supports the management of emotion, such as the frustration caused by being told in an important test that perhaps we have not done as well as expected. Of course, here, the most appropriate thing will not be to cry in a childish way, but to understand that perhaps our performance was not good enough.

As a conclusion, we will be left with the idea that we live in emotion, that we are continuously responding to signals from our brain and, in that sense, we are all emotional; and that this emotion requires the correct control of reason, which on occasions will have to hit the brakes and, on other routes, will be able to go carefree with the cruise control activated. In any case, let us allow ourselves this interesting journey through all those nuances of our personality.

Are you reactive or proactive?

The correct management of emotion and reason is essential for a personal skill that is related to the way we respond to events that happen to us, so that some people do it by reacting automatically and others by analyzing what the behavior of our most appropriate repertoire at all times.

We are reactive when, faced with something that activates us, we respond to the millisecond, without thinking and, almost always, with the same type of behavior. Of course, what we do is always the fault of others, "who make us jump or act in a certain way." His argument is "I wouldn't have done or said this if you hadn't...". That is, our behavior is directed by the other, not by ourselves. We would like that to exempt us from responsibility in a futile attempt, since we are always responsible for our actions. In many courses that we give in companies we can see that there are people who believe that by being more reactive and quick they are acting in a more efficient way. When we explain to them how easily someone who detects their behavior can manipulate them at will, they are frankly surprised. If someone knows that by pressing button A our answer is inevitably B, when they want to annoy us, it will be as easy as putting their little finger on A in a context in which B will probably leave us phosphatinized. Therefore, and to avoid being so easily manipulated, our goal will be to ensure that even if someone presses the A button, our response can be B, but also C, D or E, as we see fit. In more colloquial language, we will avoid whenever possible to enter the rag and, as a gift, that they put the banderillas on us. our goal will be to ensure that even if someone presses the A button, our response can be B, but also C, D or E, as we see fit. In more colloquial language, we will avoid whenever possible to enter the rag and, as a gift, that they put the banderillas on us. our goal will be to ensure that even if someone presses the A button, our response can be B, but also C, D or E, as we see fit. In more colloquial language, we will avoid whenever possible to enter the rag and, as a gift, that they put the banderillas on us.

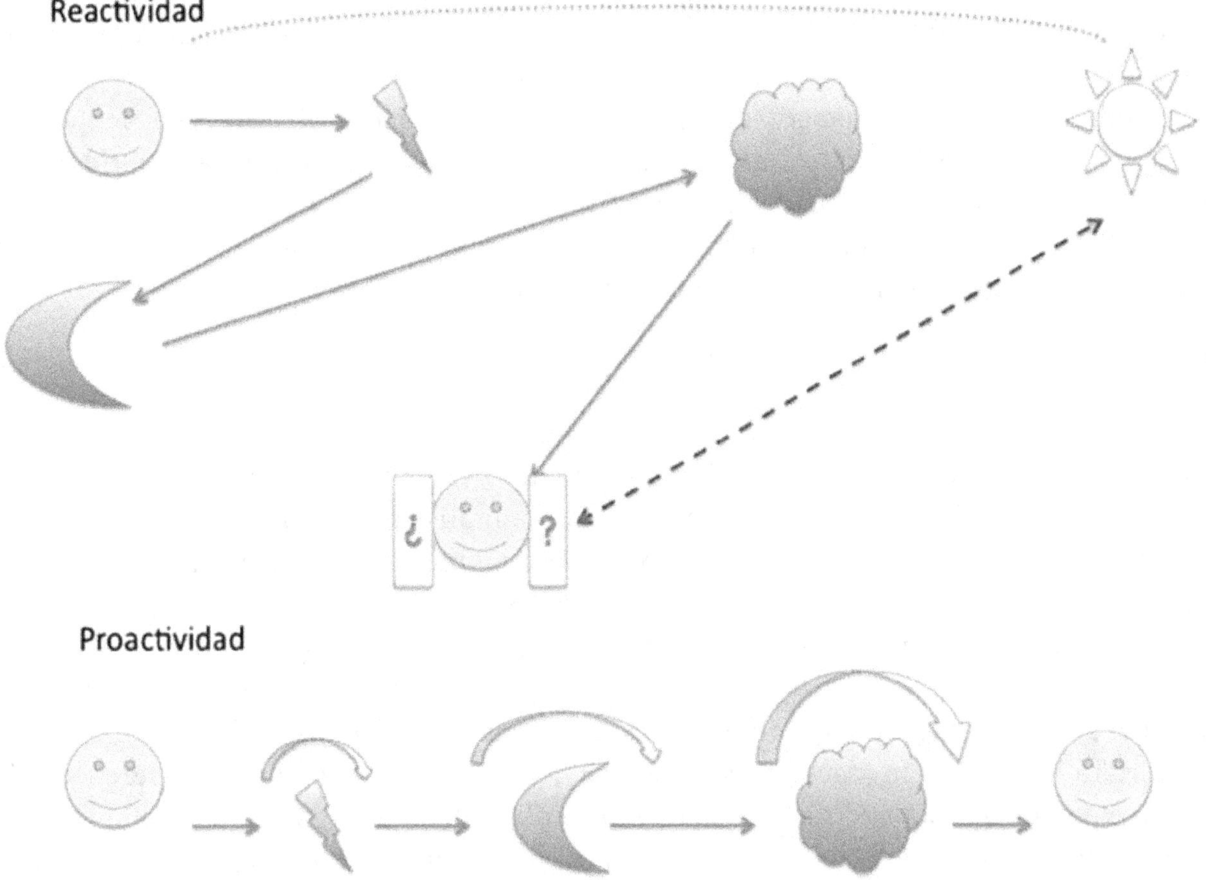

Being reactive also has its drawbacks for our day-to-day lives and, in general, for our lives. When we have goals that we would like to achieve, by acting reactively, any setback can repeatedly divert us from our goal and when we want to realize it, we find ourselves very far from what we intended. On the contrary, the proactive person sets some objectives and, whatever the circumstances that arise, meditates or reasons his action and gives a response that allows him to move in the direction that has been proposed, without being exposed to the different eventualities that may come their way.

The success of the proactive person lies not only in their ability not to react automatically to a doubtful situation, but also in being able to plan and anticipate their behavior in the possible scenarios that may occur in the face of an important event.

Let's take an example once again.

We have an important conversation with our work team. We want them to do a task for which it is essential that they leave other activities and give it absolute priority. The reactive person goes to the meeting thinking only of what he is going to propose and, in any eventuality, he will probably impose her criteria, or have to postpone the meeting because different types of conflicts arise with the employees. The proactive person will be able to prepare in advance not only what he has to propose, but will make a descriptive sweep of all the possible inconveniences that his team may raise. For all of them, he will prepare possible lines of negotiation that will allow the initial objective of the meeting to be achieved.

In addition to the advantages in terms of the effectiveness of proactive people, the emotional exhaustion is minimal and, in most cases, they generate greater confidence in their teams, who feel heard and participate in solving the problems they have to face. together. We can apply it, in the same way, to the context of the couple or other types of relationships in which more than two people are involved.

Reactive people are controlled by circumstances, while proactive people are able to make any circumstance work for their goals.

Being proactive has absolutely nothing to do with being assertive or hyperactive. Quite the contrary, they listen, observe, describe and meditate appropriately on the decisions they have to make, regardless of the circumstances in which they develop. They are able to anticipate events, prepare the most appropriate responses as they unfold, and maintain them without losing sight of where and how they want to achieve a goal.

Reactive people are controlled by their emotions and automatic thoughts, while proactive people identify their emotions, reason about the context and decide on the most appropriate response in each circumstance. The reactive person may perceive the proactive person as cool and rational, and will think of themselves as emotional. In reality, being reactive or proactive has to do with lack of control in the first case, or with control in the second, which is displayed in circumstances that are difficult to pilot.

By the way, the term proactivity was coined by the neurologist and psychiatrist Viktor Frankl in 1946, in his well-known book Man's Search for Meaning.[6]And there is definitely no gene for proactivity or reactivity, that is, we were not born that way and we will stay that way: these are learned behaviors that, like all others, can be corrected, taught and assumed.

And, now, knowing the above, it is up to us to decide how we prefer to be.

Second part

What we can do with those tools

to create a happiness to our measure

4

Set effective goals

useful happiness

Once we know the instruments we have and how to use them, there is no better use for them than to use them to achieve a life in optimal conditions. We all aspire to a happy life, but it is often difficult for us to define how and what steps must be taken to achieve it.

We live in a time of official pursuit of happiness; Multiple study frameworks have been developed from practically all disciplines and, consequently, there has been a healthy debate about the message that we are transmitting about the ability to be happy. If you want to delve deeper into this topic, I recommend you read Smile or Die: The Positive Thinking Trap, by Professor Barbara Ehrenreich.[7]

In his line, the proposal of a useful happiness is very far from that frivolous idea of happiness, in which «nothing has happened here», «everything is fine» or «everyone is good». Being positive is not synonymous with being unconscious or amoral, ignoring —if applicable— behaviors that are unacceptable for the healthy development of the life of any being.

Useful happiness consists of achieving goals as a result of effective behavior, in which the benefits are inversely proportional to unnecessary and useless harm and pain, and independent of external conditions.

Not all situations require interventions consisting of burying their heads in the ground like ostriches or smiles out of context. As we have commented in previous chapters, sometimes the path to happiness needs a positive and well channeled rage that helps us to persevere when the road gets difficult, a sadness that allows us to leave behind what can no longer be in the future or overcoming fears that have forced us to get to know each other better and obtain what we needed to continue on our way.

It is easy to buy the concept of cheap happiness at zero cost, but tremendously useless and empty to avoid all the learning we need to enjoy the path to self-realization. I am absolutely convinced that most of us who are sharing these lines have experienced the storms, hurricane winds and typhoons with which life sometimes surprises us. Was it then time to smile and pretend nothing was wrong? Precisely what professional and personal practice tells us is that in those moments we have to demonstrate the expertise in handling what we are and make external conditions subordinate to internal ones. There is a phrase from Kabbalah that has always fascinated me and that seems to me to be the best way to illustrate this idea: "The wind and the waves always go in favor of those who know how to navigate." A storm is not always a negative event, although it is tremendously uncomfortable. In adverse circumstances, a good captain knows if it is time to keep the rudder steady (stay focused on the objectives) or if, on the contrary, to lift the oars, wait for it to subside, and not exhaust energy against a powerful tide for which our efforts are insignificant; The time will come to row hard when we can glimpse our new position and readjust the destination coordinates. we must raise the oars, wait for it to subside, and not exhaust our energies against a powerful tide for which our efforts are insignificant; The time will come to row hard when we can glimpse our new position and readjust the destination coordinates. we must raise the oars, wait for it to subside, and not exhaust our energies against a powerful tide for which our efforts are insignificant; The time will come to row hard when we can glimpse our new position and readjust the destination coordinates.

A saying from a good friend with a great sense of humor says that after the storm there are always puddles. At first it is possible that yes, but then the calm arrives, the sun... or perhaps another storm. Life sometimes wears a very particular irony. The winds leave the sky clearly clean and clear, the water humidifies the environment and the tornado spins everything that is weak or redundant. Do you remember what your great heroes do in difficult times? Face them, concentrate and, if necessary, enjoy the challenge.

Happiness is made up of placid moments and moments of learning, and its state is one of fluidity and development proportional to that of confidence in one's own ability to get out of each situation what allows us to continue growing.

One of the sine qua non conditions to be happy goes through self-esteem and the level of esteem in which we have ourselves, since it supposes that, no matter what happens, we will trust our abilities so, far from causing us any harm, provide us with the best conditions available at all times.

Since we are going to be our best company from the time we are born until we die, let us dedicate ourselves to correcting and perfecting behaviors, while valuing and protecting what we are in essence.

Learning a healthy self-esteem does not consist in thinking that one is always the best, the most handsome and the most effective. Learning to love and value ourselves has more to do with those moments in which things go the other way than we had thought, or we have exposed ourselves with a ridiculous or ineffective performance and, instead of attacking the central core of our being , we use ourselves to correct what made us err.

Although we have analyzed in the previous chapters what are the instruments to achieve that useful happiness that really enriches our lives, we can briefly review them again:

learn to think
- Thoughts do not occur, they are your own creation, and can be stopped and modified.
- We are as we have learned to be.
- What a person really thinks is observed in what he does, not in what he says.
- Thoughts, verbal or nonverbal, are the statement of each and every one of our behaviors.
- Thoughts are not always true.
- Our brain uses cognitive shortcuts that sometimes lead us to the wrong destination.
    - We experience life through our thoughts.

Learn to manage emotions
- Emotions are signals produced by our own brain.
- They help us to adapt correctly to a given context.
- Emotions are not the same as the behaviors we activate to respond to the context.
    - All emotions are positive if we know how to interpret what they mean and give the appropriate response.

And we are going to take the opportunity to advance some of the strategies for happiness that we will see in chapters after this one.

Learn to respect criticism
- We can't please everyone, it's not good, and it's not real.
- We don't like everyone.
- Criticisms are opinions of others, given from their perspective.
- An opinion is not an imposition or an absolute truth.
- The judgments of others tend to catch us off guard, which is why we tend not to like them, and they tend to have a negative connotation about us.
- It is up to us to agree, or not, with a criticism.

Learn to correctly communicate what one feels or thinks
- Each person has their own perspective of reality, which changes by experience or intention. Therefore, from the only place from which we can speak is from the "me", not from the "you".
- The goal of communication is to find solutions, not blame.
- What we did not like can be described, it is not necessary to accuse.
- We are only entitled to talk about our feelings and our opinions, not those of others, which for us are just hypotheses.
- Before speaking, you have to carefully think about what you want to say, why, when, how and for what. With practice, it takes about a second.
- Insults and yelling, although they have a speech format, are just offenses and aggressions. We can cut communication.

Learn to accept mistakes
- Mistakes are a normal and necessary part of the learning process.
- Mistakes are made and corrected. When you mess up you have to get it out as soon as possible and, if possible, elegantly.
- We must learn to minimize the probability and size of the error.
- You have to set goals and objectives.
- Our body and our life will be directed towards the thoughts with which we have stated our objectives.
- Short-term goals must be accessible, possible and realistic. They help us stay motivated.
- We need to review our results as we move towards our medium and long-term goals. A mistake midway can take us far from our dreams.

Learn to troubleshoot and correct errors
- Define the problem.
- It proposes a wide range of alternatives, starting with the most extreme, which are usually discarded, to continue with the intermediate ones.
- Examine the pros and cons of each alternative.

- When you make a decision, execute it and correct it if necessary.
- Take responsibility for your own life.
- Life is a personal and individual matter. It is never too late to design it at will, to taste and with your own perceptions.
- Irresponsibility consists both in not taking responsibility for what belongs to one, and in taking responsibility for what does not correspond to one.
- Game and trial/error methodologies help discover what a full and satisfying life means to you.
- We are not better people when we prevent another from learning to take charge of their life. Support and responsibility are not the same.

Learn to tolerate frustration
- Frustration tolerance is a nice way that psychologists define patience.
- Things are not usually as they should be, but as they are, whether we like it or not.
- Life is neither fair nor kind. It is how it is. Justice and kindness are provided by us.

learn to love
- I don't know who said it, but let's take good note: it is preferable to be parents of our future than children of our past.
- Power the best you have inside.
- Give yourself experiences of growth and wisdom.
- Be useful to your peers.
- Trust in your ability to be your best caregiver and partner.
- Respect your own freedom and that of others, to the extent that it does not cause any harm.
- Properly manage the circumstances around you.
- "Think of yourself" properly and "experience yourself" with satisfaction.

Happiness, like everything else, is thought, but it is mainly the satisfying experience as a result of what is done in the right way at the right time.

Do we want to learn to be happy? Let's act accordingly.

Tras dos semanas recordamos...		Tipo de involucración
90% de lo que decimos y hacemos	Situación real	ACTIVA
	Simular la situación real	
	Representar la situación real	
70% de lo que decimos	Dar una charla	
	Participar en un debate	
50% de lo que oímos y vemos	Ver los hechos in situ	PASIVA
	Observar una demostración	
	Ver una demostración en un lugar de exhibición	
	Ver una película	
30% de lo que vemos	Ver fotografías	
20% de lo que oímos	Escuchar a alguien	
10% de lo que leemos	Leer	

(Adaptado de Dale, 1969)

Taking care of the body to achieve mental goals: food, exercise and rest

The Irish satirist Jonathan Swift, author of Gulliver's Travels, already said it in the 17th century: the best doctors in the world are the diet doctor, the calm doctor and the joy doctor. Anything to object? For my part, of course not. And any physical and mental health professional will surely not either.

I am not going to dwell much on this point, which is more the domain of medicine, but, without a doubt, there are foods that make us feel better and worse. When we are in a suitable weight we feel more active and full of energy; moderate physical activity allows our body to distribute all kinds of nutrients through the bloodstream to all the cells of the body, and eliminate what is not used or left over. One of the usual recommendations for people suffering from depression is to do some exercise that raises their energy levels.

Taking care of the body does not refer only to the size of the clothes we wear, nor to personal sports brands, but to ensuring that it functions for as long as possible in the optimal conditions that allow us to achieve our goals and dreams. Without him, we won't go anywhere.

The brain is also our body. I would dare to affirm that our body and, therefore, our life, are the result of the thought patterns and habits that make up the mold in which it becomes. Those of you who are interested in this concept can delve into it thanks to the work The molds of the mind, by the professor at the University of La Laguna, Professor Pedro Hernández, Guanir.[8]

Despite the fact that in the culture in which we live immersed it seems that we have forgotten, health is the normal state of the organism, and disease is an anomaly. We have to provide our body with resources for health, not only with remedies for illness, which, on the other hand, most of the time is a consequence of bad habits practiced for many years. Our thoughts and our actions, once again, are more fearsome than many viruses and bacteria.

It is difficult to find happiness when our habits of life and thought go against our very nature.

Good learning from childhood makes adult life much easier. Do you remember when we talked about the automation of behaviors? The child who learns good health habits and maintains them throughout his adult life is more likely to lead a happy life. That is why it is important that we not only love them very much, but also that we become their models of mental, emotional and physical health.

If there are three things that affect our mood almost automatically, those are, without a doubt, a good rest, a good diet and adequate exercise. Not in vain, when we explore the history of the people who come for consultation, one of the keys that we cannot ignore are the habits regarding these three behaviors. If they are the correct ones, many discomforts disappear, returning them to an adequate order and measure.

With both food and exercise, we have to adapt their intake and practice to what is more in line with our tastes and personalities so that, by becoming powerful reinforcement systems, they are integrated naturally and routinely into our lives. "To our liking" does not mean "what we want", but what "keeps us in optimal conditions within a pleasant eating experience".

In turn, sleep and rest play another fundamental role in mental and emotional well-being. Seven to nine hours a night give the brain the time it needs to do all the replenishment work our body needs. In addition, sleep has other important functions that we are going to briefly review so that we can better assess it.

The REM (rapid eye movement) sleep phase has a clear function of memory consolidation. Some theories argue that we dream to forget, to get rid of useless information, or to reprocess useful information. Both approaches agree that REM sleep is an endogenous mechanism for processing surplus material collected during the waking state. On the other hand, the researcher Gary Lynch proposes that during REM sleep the emission of a series of neurotransmitters is triggered that will allow the consolidation of memory traces. A curiosity of REM sleep is that it is a paradoxical phase, because, despite the fact that brain activity is almost waking, it is in this phase when it is more difficult to wake us up.

What we finally find is that there is a principle of coherence between the body and the mind. A poorly treated and poorly cared for body is the biggest obstacle to our mind being able to focus correctly on realistic and satisfying goals. It is completely irrational to think that by unbalancing the entire chemistry of our body with food and toxic substances, we can maintain control of our thoughts and actions. In the same way, a mind shaped by toxic thoughts and emotions will result in a body prepared to go nowhere or to the wrong place.

We are perfectly equipped to successfully take care of our physical and mental health if we learn to listen and correctly interpret the signals from our brain.

When our body is full of life, our mind is full of happiness.

5

Communicate without distortion

I know from clinical practice that one of the lessons that gives our patients the most joy is that of fluid, clear and constructive communication. And, in addition, it is one of those that are assimilated more quickly. At the same time that we say things differently, the diametrically different consequences that occur in the context can be observed and measured. We went from a boxing ring to a boat ride on the Retiro pond in just a snap of the fingers. In psychology we don't call it magic, but assertiveness.

We are permanently communicating, in one way or another, with our environment. Sometimes in a very basic way, with perception and behavior, and sometimes in a much more complex way, through language. What is clear is that the human being cannot not communicate. We do it even when we don't intend it to. All social groups need communication to survive and to exist, since their function is to regulate the interaction between individuals, and make possible the development of agreements between its members.

There is no interaction without communication.

Understanding what is not said: nonverbal communication

A facet that we are passionate about and whose knowledge is usually quite in demand is that of non-verbal communication. We want to control our context and we like to be clear not only what they tell us, but also what they do not tell us.

An important fact that we tend to ignore is that most of what is transmitted during verbal communication is precisely non-verbal. Surely we have experienced at some time that someone is telling us something and, "for some reason", we do not quite believe what we are hearing. That "motive" attends to non-verbal elements of communication, which our unconscious brain, but very quickly, captures at first and twists the gesture a little. We are going to analyze them with one of our instruments, although we already know that it is a bit rudimentary: reason.

Young children, especially those who have not yet extensively developed verbal language, and therefore do not yet distort communication with it, perfectly understand the non-verbal messages of the context. If one day we are not well, they are the first to detect it. They clearly translate our moods through our facial expressions – we have a specialized area of the brain for precisely this – and through our gestures, movements and mouth sounds. What father or mother has not experienced the following situation? We are trying to put our son to sleep, and as we shake him like a mixer while he groans, we say "hey, easy, go to sleep, hey...". While we continue with our compulsive movements, the little one, far from falling asleep, will show more discomfort. Why? Because the real message that we are transmitting to you is not one of calm and tranquility that you need to relax and sleep, but of pure nerve that, on the other hand, upsets you and prevents you from falling asleep. If we really relax ourselves, the children will too. Let's not make the mistake of getting angry with them without first taking a look at what we are doing.

Nonverbal communication uses a wide range of communication channels whose combined use can favor the elaboration of a clear and intelligible message. These channels correspond to the different parts of the body.

Let's see which are the main ones.

THE EYES: EYE CONTACT AND CONTEMPLATION

- In eye contact, both people hold their gaze simultaneously, while in contemplation, only one of them «looks». In turn, the contemplation can be a brief glance or a more prolonged approach.
- Between 30 and 60% of group communication is accompanied by glances that last less than a second each, which is the time with which we do not feel intimidated.
- Dominant people, and also those who occupy a higher status, tend to look more at their interlocutors.
- Looking into the eyes usually generates positive evaluations and, obviously, it is an unequivocal way to increase the degree of intimacy in a relationship.
- On the contrary, the fixed gaze indicates that we are facing hostile or fearful feelings.
- When we look away, we are giving symptoms of shyness, occasional superiority or crestfallen submission. In this case, we have to analyze the rest of the paraverbal elements.

THE FACE: FACIAL EXPRESSION

- The muscles of the face allow us to know the basic emotional states.
- It is so important that in the occipital lobe there are areas dedicated exclusively to the recognition of faces and facial expressions.
- The recognition of emotions immediately is a primary survival strategy, since it does not mean the same to be in front of a hostile person, as in front of a person who shows us sympathy and relaxation. In fact, in a large group of people we will distinguish more quickly those who are angry than those who are happy. "Just in case", the brain likes to always be prepared. A face that expresses anger will modify the behavior of the interlocutor, since he will take precautions against a possible aggression or will try to modify his state of mind. Are you familiar with always wanting to please others? A part of that attitude has to do with avoiding situations in which the other person shows anger or anger. However, this strategy, which in specific situations can come in very handy, in the long term,
- The smile, however, is a reinforcer of the actions of others. When we do something and another person smiles at us in a complacent or approving way, we will undoubtedly repeat that behavior over and over again. For a child, a smile from her parents is the best invitation to continue taking small steps; For those who are in love, a smile from the loved one is a source of satisfaction. You see how simple and how cheap!

– Gestures are the perfect complement to verbal information, and replace or emphasize the message.
– Through gestures, we can distinguish if a person is inhibited (withdrawal movements, stereotyped, unnecessary, gestures with the hair...), depressed (slow, few, hesitant movements...), excited (fast movements , expansive, rhythmic, categorical, emotional...) or anxious (movements of twisting or intertwining hands, opening and closing fists, touching up eyebrows, scratching face, pulling hair, aimless movements...).
– When the person has a higher status, the postures are usually more open and relaxed and, when it is lower, they will be more closed and rigid.
– Changes in posture also give us information about the content of the conversation. When these are large, it is usually indicative that the subject has changed and, when they are small, they are modulations while speaking.
– The subject of bodily contact usually attracts a lot of attention, and, in addition, receives an opposite assessment depending on the sex of the people who are communicating with each other. Women get closer, and people generally get closer to women than to men.
– We have already talked about the sense of territoriality that our brain has ("I am I") and the issue of distances is usually quite clear. As "getting too close" can be offensive to the other person, let's see what are the distances with which we feel most comfortable according to a study by Edward Hall in 1976:

- Intimate distance = 0-45 centimeters.
- Personal distance = 45 centimeters-1.20 meters.
- Social distance = 1.20-3.35 meters.
- Public distance = 3.65 meters, to the limit of what is visible or audible.

Another researcher, Nancy M. Henley, in 1977 was able to verify that people are more likely to touch when...

- Gives information or advice more than when asked.
- Gives one more command than when responding to one.
- Asks for a favor more than when responding to this request.
- Tries to convince someone more than when persuaded.
- The conversation is deep rather than casual.
- You attend social events, such as parties, more than when you are at work.
- You transmit arousal more than when you receive it from another person.
- You receive messages of concern, more than when you send them.

– And we still have to see how we orient our body during a conversation. We will show that we are attentive when we approach the other person or lean forward. When we don't care or don't like what they are telling us, we will back off, or even turn the other way. If we go a little too far in front of our interlocutor, our chest will expand, the trunk will be straight or inclined backwards; the head, erect, and the shoulders, elevated. However, if we feel inferior, our posture will be contracted, with the trunk leaning forward, and the head and chest sunken.

We often think that words are simply relevant to the message we are conveying. However, the meaning of these is the last thing that our brain processes.

By the time we want to know what they are saying to us, we will already have perceived the volume, tone, fluidity and speed with which they have addressed us and, obviously, we will have already become defensive or relaxed, depending on what we are saying. all these elements that accompany the message.

For example, the statement "how well you did!" it will not mean the same depending, not on who, but on how they are telling us.

Let's see what our brain detects before using the simultaneous translator.

In principle, the obvious function of the volume is that the message reaches the person who has to receive it. If it is too low, we will not achieve our goal, so we can either be ignored, or we will cause the irritation of whoever is trying to listen to us. If it is too high, we will undoubtedly be bothering both our interlocutor and those who have nothing to do with our conversation. Changes in volume allow us to emphasize points or make a presentation more enjoyable. Let's remember that the brain gets used to a constant stimulus or, what is the same, "gets bored" and small nuances that call your attention will keep it in an optimal state.

Tone

The tone of our voice has to do with the quality of our vocal cords or with the resonance that occurs in our oral cavity. It is also quite related to our emotional state.

We identify the following shades:

•High-pitched voice: described as complaining, helpless, or childish.
•Flat voice: interpreted as lazy, sick or helpless.
•Hollow voice: with few high frequencies, interpreted as lifeless and empty.
•Robust voice: it makes an impression and is successful, it is common in healthy, confident and extroverted people.

How does it affect us? When our tone of voice is transmitting something that is not in line with what we want others to receive from us, the impression we are making is not exactly what we are looking for. One of the advantages of taking the time to get to know each other well is that we can make great works of art out of our small flaws. We can work with our voice until we achieve a cadence or tonality within our characteristics that, finally, is pleasing to our interlocutors. Just like we do with other facets of our lives, be it clothes, manners or hairstyle. It is very difficult to be with someone whose tone of voice is unpleasant to us.

We can upload an extraordinary physical image with a lousy soundtrack.

Fluency

When the conversation goes smoothly, we are comfortable with our interlocutor. But when periods of unfilled silence begin to occur, for example, the situation can become somewhat embarrassing. People who introduce many filler words that force us to make a special effort of attention to try to follow the thread of what they are trying to tell us also make us a little nervous. Needless to say, we will quickly tire of their conversation. The same will happen with those who constantly repeat themselves, mispronounce or use nonsense words.

Speed

Speaking slowly can sometimes be very pleasant, but if it is made "too" slow, our attention will soon seek out a better entertainment to focus on. If, on the other hand, we find ourselves with someone who speaks too quickly, again it will require an effort of attention that will tire us in a short space of time.

We can talk fast when we are happy as well as when we are sad, but it is extremely ineffective when we are trying to ask for a favor, meet someone or flatter someone. It is possible that he does not even realize what we are telling him and in this case the repetition would not play in our favor.

As with the volume, we can use changes in rhythm to make our speech or talk more interesting, but, again, we have to measure the times and the effect it causes on those who are listening to us very well.

We see, then, that non-verbal communication probably gives us much more information than the words that are being said to us. Through it we can detect the state of mind, the attitude or the relationship that the other person intends to establish with us; we can know when it is our turn to speak and when to listen; It allows us to establish hierarchical structures with a simple glance and, if we do a good body reading, we will be able to modulate our speech so that it is effective with respect to the person with whom we are communicating.

Without a doubt, our great pending subject is to be able to put our feelings, our thoughts into words and learn to listen to the messages of others.

Let's move on, then, to that other part of communication to which we give so much priority: the one we carry out verbally.

Listen to understand, speak to be understood: verbal communication

Talking does not necessarily mean communicating. Sometimes two people are trying to transmit messages to each other that, finally, are incomprehensible or difficult to decipher for various reasons. It is possible that whoever is speaking is not having the ability to make himself understood correctly, or that whoever is listening does not have the resources to understand exactly the content of the words of his interlocutor.

We will be communicating well when the message we want our receiver to understand is clear and understandable, and when we confirm that it has been received without distortion or interference.

We will hardly interact with our environment if we do not make ourselves understood, and if we do not understand what the people in that context need from us.

We can speak impulsively, without any control over our message, or we can think about what we are going to articulate, in the following way - although it may seem a bit exhaustive, it is undoubtedly the most effective way to communicate and, after a period of practice , we will be able to execute it in milliseconds, exactly the same time that we need to communicate inappropriately, but, this time, with better results.

WHAT DO WE WANT TO SAY

Important conversations should not be the result of improvisation or a momentary heat. When they occur in this way, they are usually quite imprecise, very incomplete and, why not admit it, serve little purpose.

It is often difficult for us to identify what exactly we mean. For example, when we live with a person and this person is in charge of making the meals, we are surprised that, time and time again, they make them too salty. If we react impulsively, we may say something like this: "What's the matter, that they had shares in the salt flats at your house?" Is this what we really mean? Certainly not. We have to correctly identify what is happening ("there is too much salt for my taste in the food"), and what we would like ("a little less salt").

Once we have identified what we want to say, we will go to the next step.

HOW WE WANT TO SAY IT

I like to pose the following question: do you think everything can be said? Yes? Nope? Let's think about it a bit.

We have already seen how poor management of anger leads us to inappropriate behavior. In this case, distaste for a food we don't like may make us scream it out; sometimes even offending. Is it really essential?

Let's remember that it is not necessary to be aggressive when something bothers us, so we are going to try to do it in another more appropriate way, following the following guidelines:

- Describe what happens ("I've noticed that your cooking style uses a lot of salt").
- Express what we think or feel ("I find it very unpleasant and I can't eat it").

• Express what we would like ("I would like the meals to contain a little less salt").

Now that we have communicated what we want and we have done it quite decently... are we done? Actually, not yet.

But before continuing, we are going to answer the question that we posed at the beginning: everything can be said, depending on how. Someone can tell us something completely banal and yet cause us deep harm; and we can also be told very serious things about ourselves that, if done with love and respect, we can hardly feel offended and, even in certain circumstances, we will be deeply grateful.

Let's see the next step that is usually as essential or more than the previous ones.

We rarely ask ourselves what the goal of our communication is. Talking for the sake of talking, to let off steam, not to shut up, to stifle... Or better yet: to introduce changes, to reach agreements, so that what bothers you finally stops doing it.

Surely, we do not want to speak to insult, but when we do, we are not communicating any message, but only offending the other person. The best way to manage this discomfort is to go for a walk and review the previous points (what we mean and how to do it).

We probably don't want to hurt the other person either, but if our message comes in the form of screaming and uncontrolled voices, we're definitely doing it, and this really has nothing to do with salt. We can go out for the same walk and do the same review, and we will extend the time that the walk is necessary until we are very clear about the content and form of our message.

The objective is to express what one wants, that the other person understands it, and that between them it is possible to reach agreements that are satisfactory for all. To reach agreements you have to propose alternatives and solutions, and you also have to listen to what the other person proposes.

In the example we used earlier, what we really want is less salty food. For that we can propose adding less salt, or separating the dishes so that each person seasons theirs to their liking.

Once we have more or less clear what, how and why we want to talk, are we ready to do it? Stop! Let's stop for a moment, because there is still an important step that we must not skip.

WHEN ARE WE GOING TO TALK

In general, we tend to think that now is always the best time and, unfortunately, this is not the case. For example, the evening of a weekday is not usually the best time. We are too tired and there is not much time (physiological reasons). The car is also not a good place. Many of the necessary elements for communication are violated: the posture is not one in front of the other, there is no opportunity to look each other in the eye or attend to non-verbal communication that allows understanding the "complete" message of the other person (physical reasons). And if, in addition, you are in a traffic jam, there is little time and some tension (psychological reasons). If we are accompanied, it may not be necessary to make involuntary participants or witnesses to others of problems that do not concern them (psychological reasons).

Saying things at the right time denotes not only intelligence, but also consideration, a good capacity for self-control and adequate time management for each circumstance.

Ideally, agree or find a time when you can be free from interruptions and distractions, and can focus on paying attention to the message and the solutions. They don't have to be four-hour long conversations. Sometimes, with a well used can be more than enough.

The opportune occasion is the one in which we find ourselves with the physical, physiological, psychological and emotional capacity to listen to ourselves.

How we usually make mistakes in our communication styles

We are now going to see a few styles of communication with which we will surely feel identified. This is probably not our usual way of communicating, nor do we feel exactly proud of having acted like this.

COMMUNICATE EXPLOSIVELY

This type of communication seems to be very fashionable lately. Since psychologists have explained how good it is to get emotions out of the inside, it seems that it has been interpreted that there is a green light to do it right and left. I will break a spear in favor of my profession, because we also place special emphasis on the fact that emotions must be managed properly, and must never affect the way in which we wish to communicate them. For this we have coined a term, assertiveness, which we will talk about later, but which consists precisely in expressing what we think and feel without offending or attacking others.

It is true that the lifestyle we lead today does not allow us much time to speak with the calm and pause that we suggest and, in addition, sometimes we keep quiet about what really bothers us over and over again. When, finally, we say it, we usually do it wrong and at the wrong time, and with a good dose of accumulated rage that usually propels our words without stopping through the prefrontal lobe —where reflection and analysis reside—, which would allow us a little more coherence in the message.

The problem with uncontrolled propulsion is that it tends to drag other elements unrelated to the situation behind it, so that when we should be talking about salt, we end up talking about the number of times the other is late for work. And we can finish with a "so far we have come".

Let's take five steps back and remember that effective communication sometimes requires taking a walk or even calling friends who can listen and get our heads together. We need to somehow lower our energy levels, calm our minds, try to be objective and give the problem the relevance it really has. And that depends on us, not on the circumstances.

If possible, our suggestion is not to wait until you have no choice but to do it explosively. When problems are, or seem to us, small, they are better handled. And with the keys that we are seeing to be as descriptive and decisive as possible, we will be able to correct, communicate and negotiate without long periods of time.

Anger is not indicative of a bad relationship with others. They are simply telling us that there is something we do not like or that we would prefer it to be different, and we need to agree with those who are involved in the situation. In general, well-resolved problems result in improved relationships with others, as confidence is gained that, even in difficult situations, far from causing harm or offense, everyone can feel safe.

When we feel that we are about to explode, it is necessary to properly manage and balance emotions and thoughts, lower energy levels, be clear about what we want to say, why, when and how, and reach solutions and agreements that are satisfactory for all. .

And do you know the best thing about doing it right? That what is propelled into the stratosphere are the levels of self-esteem, well, who doesn't feel good about themselves after having passed such a test?

CONTACT US, WHAT FOR?

There are people who are very good at talking, but communicating what they feel, what they want or their most intimate experiences is an exercise of extreme difficulty, which they usually resolve with "there is nothing to talk about" , "it's all right" or "you know what I think". His interlocutors, however, often experience that they are constantly bumping into a reinforced concrete wall. Needless to say, this style makes relationships difficult, whatever their type.

In explosive communication, we practically have to catch the words on the fly to take them to the "management office" of the prefrontal lobe and put them in a little order; in this type of non-existent communication, we have to get feelings out of the deep well in which they are entrenched so that, when passing through that same office, they get a little moldy and we can give them that shine and splendor that they surely have, but that nobody sees . You will have to start little by little, because when you are not used to it, you have to go through the phases of trial, error and correction.

Living from the trenches is typical of someone who experiences life as a war. When you spend too much time in them, perhaps the time has come to consider another way of enjoying life.

COMMUNICATE AMBIGUOUSLY

Sometimes we don't realize it, but when we don't complete our sentences properly, we leave the message to the interpretation of whoever listens to us. This can be done consciously or unconsciously.

When we do it consciously, it is a strategy of throwing a stone and hiding our hand, because if the other interprets our messages and rebukes us ("it's that you told me that..."), we can calmly respond: "No. , I didn't say that...» And, unfortunately, for those who «believed that...» it will be true.

At other times, a kind of parallel communication occurs. Messages occur bidirectionally, but without any coordination. Let's see an example. Ricardo and Antonio have to deliver a job next Monday:

—They have asked us to finish the report on the RexStocks company on Monday.
-Yes it's correct.
'I can bring the car and we'll take it in the middle of the morning.
"I think there's a meeting with the production team.
-In agreement.

Antonio and Ricardo continue chatting about other topics and on Monday Antonio picks Ricardo up from his office to take the report.

—Well, I have a meeting with the production team...
—But what if we had agreed that we would take the report together!
-What do you say? I told you no, that I had a meeting.
"You told me, but you gave me to understand that it did not coincide with the delivery." In fact, I brought the car so we could both go...
"It's impossible for me to go, and I already told you about it."

This type of communication can continue explosively if each one continues to give their arguments in parallel, to become non-existent if they do not speak in the next few days. And the relationship, without a doubt, will be affected: «He goes to his ball», «He does not comply with what he said», «He cheats on me», etc.

The most appropriate thing in the first conversation is that it would not have been settled until both parties confirmed that what each one had understood was coincident. It takes about a second and the benefits are incomparable.

Does it seem familiar to you that when a comment does not sit well with the person it is addressed to, and especially if the latter reproaches it, it seems to many that the best way to come out on top is to blame the misunderstanding on the lack of humor of your interlocutor with an "if it was a joke..."?

If our joke has gone wrong, we have certainly made a mistake. And if it only amuses us, too. To be really funny, you need to be found funny by those who are listening to you. And if we have to admit that we have been wrong, we will probably even win their affection and affection.

We can't expect others to laugh at what they don't like or, worse yet, make them feel guilty about it.

COMMUNICATE IN AN OFFENSIVE WAY: IT TAKES FIVE COMPLAINTS TO REPAIR AN INSULT

Sometimes the way we deliver our messages has more to do with a boxing ring than a nice dance of words. We can be offensive not only by what we say (a hurtful content), but also by using a tone that is too strong or showing the intention to offend. Having a powerful voice does not have to be synonymous with annoyance, and it cannot serve as an excuse. When a loud voice is annoying, you have to analyze why and modulate it according to its characteristics.

We can reply that "I am like this", but the truth is that we have learned to be like that, and it is possible that this learning still needs some more polishing so that it works in our favor, instead of against us. Seen this way, we should be the first interested in getting to communicate in another way.

We use a lot of messages of the type «it is that you...», «because you are...», «because you do or say...», that is, in the second person singular, which the brain receives as an extremely subtle aggressiveness, in the sense of invasion of their personal territory. We will be unable to hear what follows this use of verb tenses without immediately erecting a defensive wall or loading the machine gun with bullets. It is convenient for us to remember, then, what we have already seen in the keys to effective communication: speaking to others from our place, without invading their space, and allowing the other to express themselves without having the feeling that they have to defend themselves. With a "it seems to me that..." or "in my opinion..." we will be saying the same thing, but in a more effective way.

One of my patients understood it perfectly: "I'm talking about myself. Thank you".

The next level in the gradient of offense is when you go directly into the insults. Sometimes we are not able to reflect, before launching them, if what we really want is to harm the other with our words, if we are realizing what we say, and if we are aware of the consequences that it will have once we we've thrown the first left hook. Otherwise, prevention is better than cure, as recoveries are usually slow and expensive.

One of the most followed psychology professors on social media, Richard Wiseman, from the University of Hertfordshire, has developed an interesting line of research in which it has been found that five compliments are needed to make up for an insult. Let's do a little math exercise of what this means, which may help us understand why people can get tired of us, or why, even if they want to excuse us, their brain (we usually say that "our little heart") does not allows us. Imagine a conversation in which we use a disrespectful word and, moreover, with the intention of offending. We have just taken five steps back in the other person's perception of us. In general, we pretend that with a simple "excuse me" the thing is solved, but in reality it is only a small step forward, and the brain, which works like this, still needs four more. Or at least four gestures that balance the offense made. We go for −4. A couple of days later, we let out some more insults. We have to add 5 to the 4 that we had accumulated: that makes a total of −9. If we realize our mistake, we can dedicate a week to being especially kind -by the way, it has to be true, because the brain, with its intuition, usually perceives when it is a simple posture-, and let's say we stay at −2. Oh! Another insult escapes us. Again, we are at −7. We have to add 5 to the 4 that we had accumulated: that makes a total of −9. If we realize our mistake, we can dedicate a week to being especially kind - by the way, it has to be true, because the brain, with its intuition, usually perceives when it is a simple posturing -, and let's say we stay at −2. Oh! Another insult escapes us. Again, we are at −7. We have to add 5 to the 4 that we had accumulated: that makes a total of −9. If we realize our mistake, we can dedicate a week to being especially kind -by the way, it has to be true, because the brain, with its intuition, usually perceives when it is a simple posture-, and let's say we stay at −2. Oh! Another insult escapes us. Again, we are at −7.

It is really exhausting, both for those who have to be making the effort of kindness due to their previous clumsiness, and for those who are waiting for things to balance out, or if what is intended is that the relationship works in numbers with the positive sign. It is more than evident that, in this way, there is no way to get any type of relationship forward.

Frequently, speaking "sincerely" is confused with saying everything that comes to mind, without first stopping to reflect on the harm it causes to others or the consequences of what we say.

It would be desirable that we take into account the following appreciation: the truth, in general, is our truth, not a universal truth. Our interlocutor may consider it true or irrelevant. And that will be the truth of him. If someone brags about "being very sincere" and that means that he can say in the name of that truth that, for example, "you are very ugly", without meaning and without a constructive objective, it is possible that he has gone with the truth. ahead, excellently well accompanied by his own selfishness. He has prioritized the well-being that comes from saying things as he thinks about the unnecessary damage it causes. And, yes, everything can be said, but let's remember: when, how, why and what for. Of course, never to hurt and then stay wider than long.

If telling the truth becomes an act of aggression, that form of sincerity has absolutely no value, nor is it something to be proud of.

How to improve the way we communicate
1. Always speak from the self, in the first person, about our feelings and opinions.
2. Don't yell. Talking loudly is another form of aggression.
3. Do not insult. Offending is not communicating.
4. Reflect and analyze what we want to say.
5. Identify well why we want to say it.
6. Why do we want to say it?
7. Choose appropriately when we are going to say it.
8. And choose the most important thing: how.
9. Be clear about the main ideas that you want to convey.
10. Make sure that we listen and that they listen to us; that we understand and that they understand us.

Jack, horse and king of communication
1. Describe the situation: «When it happens…».
2. Say what we think or feel: «I believe/feel that…».
3. Say what we want: «I would like that…».

Without a doubt, effective and positive communication contributes a lot to our happiness and well-being. We like to be understood, we give others the opportunity, by doing so, to please us and, reciprocally, we will be in a better position to make those around us happy, with the deep satisfaction that this, in turn, produces in us.

We have already seen that messages usually have an objective, even if it is the most banal of distracting each other. However, you will have found that there are people who have the enormous ability to make us say just the opposite of what we really wanted. And after having done it, we feel really bad. This is not the best way to be happy either, but fortunately we have a few ways to better deal with these situations.

The most used techniques to avoid being taken where we do not want are the following.

BROKEN RECORD

This tactic consists of making the subject sound —as its name suggests— similar to a broken record.

The key phrase is "yes, but...". By now, we want to say "I understand what you are saying, but...". It is not at all a matter of nodding or agreeing with what our interlocutor says, but of understanding his position. The subject listens, but does not respond to something outside of what he wants to deal with.

Regarding the but..., it must always sound the same. To do this, this part must be concise, clear and identical.

The effectiveness of this strategy is very high.

Let's look at some examples:

—It's your fault that we're late, as usual.
—Yes, but today I had to do a job that I couldn't leave unfinished.
—But we're always late everywhere and I'm fed up.
"That's true, but in this case I had a job I couldn't leave unfinished."
"You always have some excuse for not being on time.
—You're right and I understand your anger, but in this case it was a job that I couldn't leave unfinished.

ASSERTIVE AGREEMENT

In this case, we recognize that the other person is right, but we do not admit the way of telling us. We agree on the part where it's obvious we've made a mistake.

Look at this example:

—It's your fault that we're late, as usual.
—You're right, today, of course, we were late because of me. But, normally, I tend to be punctual. So, as usual, I think it's over.

ASSERTIVE QUESTION

It consists of "thinking well" of the person who criticizes us. We will ask her to give us more information about her arguments, to be clear about what she means and what she wants us to change.

The key questions are:

"What exactly do you mean?"
"What bothers you about what's happening?"
"What do you suggest to make this stop bothering you?"

Let's look at an example:

"You'll think the act was wonderful."[Objectively, the person is not saying anything and is leaving it to our interpretation.]
"Sorry, but I don't understand you.[This is essential when you ask: not knowing what they are saying to you, even if you understand it perfectly.]
"What exactly do you want to tell me?" Do you have suggestions to make? You seem upset. I can help?

If the criticism is malicious, the person will soon run out of arguments, basically because it will be difficult for him to express in a clear and diaphanous way what he wants us to understand.

It is very important not to interpret the messages of others: what is not said clearly will be treated as an unreceived message. Otherwise, when interpreting something that has not been explicitly stated, we run the risk that the other person will deny it outright. And the serious thing is that, on top of that, he will be right.

This technique breaks the schemes of the interlocutor, because we neither defend ourselves, nor do we respond aggressively nor do we give in, since we are limiting ourselves to asking.

TO IGNORE

With this strategy, the responsibility falls on the other person. It is applicable when we see our interlocutor too angry and his attitude can end in a chain of insults, and we have not yet lost our nerve, or we have not entered into the same dynamic.

Take a look at a conversation like this:

—It's your fault that we're late, as usual. [The statement is issued loudly and with an insulting tone.]
"I think you're too angry, so we better talk about this later."

ASSERTIVE POSTPONEMENT

This response is very useful when you are not quick to react and do not have an answer at hand, or simply in situations where you do not have the ability to respond clearly. Also when, without realizing it, "we enter the rag" and put ourselves at the same level as our interlocutor.

It consists of postponing the response until we feel calmer and able to respond correctly.

Note:

—It's your fault that we're late, as usual.[As in the previous case, it is said loudly and in an insulting tone.]
-Me? And what about you? Are you never late anywhere? [Also loudly and with the same tone, until he realizes the dynamic he has entered.]... If you like, we'll leave it now and talk about it more calmly tomorrow or at another time.

In the two previous cases, it is important to bear in mind that, when one or more people are upset and a dynamic of voices and insults has already entered, it is better to stop, because each word of the other will make the degree of irritation go away. raising. In addition, at this point the main act of the conversation, communicating, will have ceased to occur, giving way to offense and aggressiveness, so it is necessary to stop the situation, because objectively it no longer makes sense, or at least it is not solving effectively.

The golden rule: he who postpones, resumes. In other words, if I ask that you stop talking now, I will take the initiative the moment I perceive that it is possible to speak calmly. It is best not to let too much time pass.

THE INVESTMENT

It consists of simply asking the interlocutor to say «yes» or «no».
Let's look at another example:

—Do you think we meet on Tuesday to see the first data of the event?
—Man, if the computer technician didn't come, it wouldn't be a bad idea... [?]
[At this point, we run the risk of interpreting the message again, but maybe he is trying to tell us no, but it seems that he is telling us yes. To argue later who is right would be a losing battle.]
"So we meet Tuesday?"
—Well, tomorrow the technician calls me and then we'll see...
"So I take that as a yes?"
—No, Thursday suits me better.
[Finally, we got a clear answer before going to his office on Tuesday and having to come back with justified irritation.]

THE REPEAT 1

It is used when the subject thinks that the other person is not listening or understanding. You are asked to repeat what you are saying. As doing it directly could be a bit impolite, we will use questions such as "what do you think of what I am saying?", "do you understand my position?", etc.

For example, we are trying to explain our project to a client, and he does nothing more than list everything he wants, and does not refer at any time to what we are proposing, so that it is difficult to advance in the planning. The best way to approach this situation would be the following:

—Excuse me, perhaps today I have a somewhat dense day and it is very possible that I am not explaining myself clearly. As I have a special interest in this project going really well, I would like to know what you have understood so far of what I have proposed to you, in case it is necessary to point out any details.

Our interlocutor will have no choice but to refer to what we have said, and it will be more difficult for him to get away from our proposal.

THE REPEAT 2

It consists of repeating exactly what the other person has just said. Note:

"You should have called me when Perez told the stewardess to let that guy in."
—You're telling me that I should have called you when Pérez told the stewardess to let that individual in. Is it so?

Using this strategy has a double objective: on the one hand, if what our interlocutor is saying makes no sense, make the mirror effect so that when he hears him he realizes his words; on the other, it allows us to save time and prepare an effective response.

One last note on the above strategies. Although at first its use supposes some tension, especially if one is not used to it, with practice and as one experiences the magnificent results of its use, it can be done with a certain sense of humor. I recommend it to you.

three response styles

The following table presents the types of responses that usually occur most frequently and will allow us to recognize our behavior or that of the person before us.

No asertivo	Asertivo	Agresivo
Demasiado poco, demasiado tarde, nunca.	Lo suficiente de las conductas apropiadas en el momento correcto.	Demasiado, demasiado pronto, demasiado tarde.
Conducta no verbal Ojos que miran hacia abajo, voz baja, vacilaciones, gestos desvalidos, negando la importancia a la situación, postura hundida, puede evitar totalmente la situación, se retuerce las manos, tono vacilante o de queja, risitas «falsas».	*Conducta no verbal* Contacto ocular directo, nivel de voz conversacional, habla fluida, gestos firmes, postura erecta, mensajes en primera persona, honestidad, verbalizaciones positivas, respuestas directas a la situación, manos sueltas.	*Conducta no verbal* Mirada fija, voz alta, habla fluida/rápida, enfrentamiento, gestos de amenaza, postura intimidatoria, falta de honestidad, mensajes impersonales.

No asertivo	Asertivo	Agresivo
Conducta verbal	*Conducta verbal*	*Conducta verbal*
«Quizá», «Supongo», «Me pregunto si podríamos...», «Te importaría mucho...», «Solamente», «No crees que...», «Eh», «Bueno», «Realmente no es importante», «No te molestes».	«Pienso», «Siento», «Quiero», «Hagamos», «¿Cómo podemos resolver esto?», «¿Qué piensas?», «¿Qué te parece?».	«Harías mejor en...», «Haz...», «Ten cuidado», «Debes estar bromeando», «Si no lo haces...», «No sabes», «Deberías», «Mal».
Efectos	*Efectos*	*Efectos*
Conflictos interpersonales. Depresión. Desamparo. Imagen pobre de uno mismo. Se hace daño a sí mismo. Pierde oportunidades. Tensión. Se siente sin control. Soledad. No se gusta ni a sí mismo ni a los demás. Enfado.	Resuelve los problemas. Se siente a gusto con los demás. Se siente satisfecho. Se siente a gusto consigo mismo. Relajado. Se siente con control. Crea y fabrica la mayoría de las oportunidades. Se gusta a sí mismo y a los demás. Es bueno para sí y para los demás.	Conflictos interpersonales. Culpa. Frustración. Imagen pobre de sí mismo. Hace daño a los demás. Pierde oportunidades. Tensión. Se siente sin control. Soledad. No le gustan los demás. Se siente enfadado.

I hope that this brief review has helped us to recover and value the importance of communication in our lives and in our happiness, and so that we take a little more care of our language, what we say, the tone of our voice... At last and in the end, speech is nothing more than a series of sounds with which we can compose the pleasant soundtrack of our lives.

It is preferable to speak little and clearly, than a lot and in a turbulent way. Our brain will thank us.

6

Learn from mistakes

I recently heard a phrase from the writer Albert Espinosa that seemed to me the best to introduce this chapter: "Error is appropriate behavior in the wrong context."

Let's be honest: nobody likes to be wrong. We tend to think that it is a very serious offense and makes us feel guilty. And, we have no choice, let's continue to be a little more honest: the only way to learn is by making mistakes.

We tend to handle making mistakes in a "regular" way, especially if the mistake is evident to other people. It seems that our ego has it a bit wrong and, even when we have no choice but to admit it, we tend to be quite resistant to giving our arm to twist or correct, instead of trying to solve our mistake immediately and, if possible, with the best of our smiles. What a pleasure to be with someone who acts like that, right? Could we be that someone? Surely yes. It does less damage than it seems.

We are going to de-dramatize first what an error consists of. Actually, except on the occasions that we will see later, we cannot know a priori if we are making a mistake. Only when things happen differently from what we had anticipated can we verify that we have made a mistake. Therefore, making a mistake is closely linked to the word after, since it is at that moment that we are able to interpret what happened. It is advisable that, in order not to put our finger on the wound that it produces in our vanity, we do not stir up discomfort with qualifying adjectives such as good or bad, and we change them, considering whether what we did was prudent, effective, convenient, correct, etc.

The attitude that we must adopt from now on in the face of the appearance of future errors is that we will be willing to admit them and, far from entering into subjective and personal considerations (do you remember the «personalization error»?), acquire the commitment to analyze and describe them in detail. as objectively as possible in order to be able to consciously detect where we made a wrong decision, and how we can correct it. Otherwise, we will be forced to make the same mistakes over and over again. And that, in the long run, is tremendously frustrating and boring. Also, do you know what we are automating? Well, neither more nor less than always making the same mistake in the same way. The best we can do is get out of this useless loop and allow our brain to dedicate itself to the task that fascinates it so much:

Errors are an absolutely essential requirement in any learning process, since we will not be able to acquire knowledge or a skill without making mistakes. We are now going to do the exercise of remembering how we learned something that we are deeply proud of today. Surely, we were wrong at the beginning, and also during the learning process. When we reach high levels of mastery, mistakes even give us a certain joy, since they indicate the path to deeper knowledge.

Let's take good note: if we can't stand making mistakes, we will hardly learn anything, we won't be able to feel proud of ourselves and, surprise!, we won't be able to enjoy the happiness that achieving goals means. And that's why you're reading this book, right? Well, now is the ideal time to correct an attitude that blocks the path to that well-being.

We make mistakes for many reasons and it would probably be very useful for us to identify where the origin of each mistake we make is, so that we are able to introduce the appropriate correction factor at that point.

Sometimes we make mistakes because, really, we don't know how we have to act in the situation in which we find ourselves. If we do not have someone to ask, our brain will use the scientific methodology par excellence: trial and error. We will try to put into practice something of the repertoire that we have, to see if it works and, later, as we have already seen, we will check if it has been enough or not. And, it must be said, although we could have asked someone, there are things that we can only learn from our own experience: no matter how much we attend childbirth classes without pain, or read books on education or cooking, or watch animal training documentaries , until we get down to it and, of course, we are wrong, we will not be in a position to learn and apprehend it.

Other errors occur due to the ability of our brain to forget some negative experiences of the past, or simply to turn the page. Memorizing and remembering require effort and energy consumption that sometimes our brain prefers to save for certain things. The advantage is that, if it does not happen again, its memory will not embitter our existence; but if similar conditions occur again... well, we already know the song of tripping again and with the same stone. If it's something that only happens once in a while, we'll definitely get over it. If it starts to be something recurrent, surely the brain will no longer do this exercise of forgetting and will get down to work to try to solve it as soon as possible.

There are mistakes that are directly due to our stubbornness, for refusing to admit the negative consequences of something that happened before. In this case, we find several types of thinking short-circuiting each other: we will deny the mistake because we don't want to or don't know how to face the change it needs. For example, when they ask us to moderate our bad character. "Me? My behavior is perfect. It is you who has a susceptibility problem. Go get it looked at." Without a doubt, a big mistake. And we will also deny it when we are moved by a greater need that will blur the ability to make a more appropriate decision. For example, the woman who returns to her abusive husband because she does not feel capable of facing life alone, or she does not have economic capacity or she is distressed by the loss of socioeconomic status.

The icing is found when we make mistakes because we have learned to make mistakes. How is it possible? There is a type of thoughts or behaviors that inevitably lead us to make mistakes, and they have to do with our inability to analyze the consequences of the decisions we make or, worse yet, to understand that when we are not making our own decisions and we let let others do it, convinced that we have nothing to do with it, we are deciding that it is someone else who is wrong —although, by the way, it will also be our mistake—. If when our travel companion asks us if we have to go to the coast by one motorway or another, and we answer "wherever you want", if he makes a mistake, it will not only be his mistake, but also ours, because in the end and in the end we found ourselves on the wrong road.

If we are going to make mistakes —which, without a doubt, we will—, at least it is because of our own mistakes, not because of those of others.

The good news is that we can handle errors correctly, giving them their fair value and freeing them from their negative connotations to see them in the light that gives them the opportunity to correct and improve. Quite simply, errors are giving us information about what works, what we know or what is appropriate to do, and what is not. We must not associate them with our own worth, or our intelligence or the sense of ridicule. And, objectively, it's just about the steps we have to take when we move towards our goals. I'm sure they're seeming a bit more friendly to us now, I hope.

One of the interpretations that we can make of the error is to consider it as a kind of warning. Some of what we do does not fit the context in which we find ourselves. Let's remember that our brain wants to solve the difficulties as soon as possible, because it doesn't like anything, and the best way to do it is to identify and recognize that warning or error, without allowing any subjective, personal or emotional consideration to interfere in the process of efficient fix. When it is solved, we can already think about how bad it felt when we found out, but, at this point, who cares! No longer exists. How good we feel when we act so diligently!

The error, furthermore, lies at the base of a behavior that we tend to appreciate a lot: spontaneity. This consists not so much in saying things "clearly", but in not being afraid to express our opinions and, if necessary, modify them. When we act spontaneously, we are presenting ourselves honestly: "This is what I know how to do, or this is as far as I can go… and that's fine. I am not ashamed and, if possible, I am willing to learn. In the courses I really like to use the example of spontaneity of a person who won the hearts of almost all of Spain: the singer Rosa, with her beautiful voice and way of singing. I don't know if you will remember that occasion in which she, still competing, in the middle of a song she made a mistake and with an innocent face she put her hand to her head and said: "Oh, I was wrong!" with his endearing Andalusian accent. The teachers told him that he should have continued and that the audience—meaning us—probably either wouldn't have noticed or cared. The reality was the second: that we did not care if Rosa was wrong. She seemed delicious to us even in her mistakes. Logically, she took note of it and those small steps took her to the privileged place where she is today.

I hope that each time we feel a greater tolerance to commit a certain percentage of errors and move away from the idea that they can all be avoided. Of all the behaviors that we have throughout a day and, therefore, of our lives, one to three out of ten decisions will be wrong. And nothing happens. Well, yes, they will make us, if we are emotionally intelligent, so much better than we are now.

Another premise that can put us at peace with the idea of making mistakes is that everyone does it. Let's think of one of our favorite characters: an actor, an athlete, a politician, a doctor, etc. Someone for whom we feel true admiration. Let's do a memory or research exercise, and analyze what mistakes you have made. Let's stop for a moment to make a list, however small, enumerating them. How have they helped him become who he is today? Do we value him for his ability not to make mistakes or to correct when he was wrong? Do we judge ourselves in the same way? Do we allow ourselves that margin of error and growth?

The example in this chapter is going to be ourselves. Let's make a list of what we consider to be the three biggest mistakes we've made in our lives. We have to be able to place ourselves in the way of thinking, acting and feeling that we had at that time, in the circumstances in which we found ourselves. Do we act without thinking or reflexively analyze the consequences that could occur? Could we have generated more alternatives? Could we have prevented or reduced the harm suffered or inflicted? Would we do the same if we found ourselves in the same situation and circumstances?

Sometimes we need to understand each other to forgive each other. We have already suffered the consequences of the error, so there is no need to continue beating ourselves up with messages of a certain harshness towards oneself. If we are aware that the consequences affected another person, the best way we have to ask for forgiveness is to repair the damage caused until there is no trace of what happened. Words are unnecessary.

We were not born knowing, and as long as we continue to learn, we will continue to make mistakes. But even in this one can become a master. Let's see how.

Keys to make mistakes with less frequency and intensity

As when we make mistakes we like to see them little, we are going to learn to do something that we will probably like:

• Minimize the probability of error.
• Minimize the size of the error.

This is already sounding better to us.

Minimizing the probability of error consists of ensuring that the possibility of making a mistake is small. And in this way we will also ensure that the frustration we feel if it were to happen.

Minimizing the size of the error usually pleases our brain quite a bit, since it is not the same to have to tackle a great task that will require a lot of effort and time, and that may take us quite far from the desired goal, than to make a small mistake, which supposes a small readjustment of some aspect, but that neither takes us away from the goal nor does it imply a great loss of energy, enthusiasm and spirit.

We have already commented that the error warns of what does not work or where there is a problem, and the most effective thing is to start solving it as soon as possible. Let's see how (if you experience a situation that you don't know how to resolve, now grab a pen and paper, and manage what is currently worrying you in parallel):

1. Define or describe what concerns you. What is it about? From how many perspectives could you describe it? What do you need to take into account? Who or what is involved in the problem? Answer these questions:

   -What's going on.
   "What is it that bothers me?"
   —What is bothering the others?
   —When does it happen?
   —Why it happens, what happens before it is triggered.
   —How it happens.

   It is important to remember that we are looking for solutions, not blame. We will try to be as objective as possible.
2. Generate alternatives. Open the full range of possibilities that may occur in this situation. We will start by formulating the most extreme ones, as this will help us better define the intermediate ones. We will also include the most elaborate, rare or crazy, because, although it is possible that they end up being discarded along with those that are at the extremes, they can help us generate alternatives that perhaps we would not have thought of a priori. The goal is to find as many possible solutions as possible.
   You have to let your imagination fly and generate what is known as brainstorming. Say everything that comes to mind. There is always time to discard.
3. Study the options in detail: look for the pros and cons of each one. We have to take each alternative one at a time and make two columns for each case: one with the advantages and one with the disadvantages. It is a way of seeing "from outside our head" which option is the one that is going to suit us best.
4. Make decisions. It is necessary to choose the most appropriate solution for the way of being of each one. If you are not sure, go back to step 2, and imagine new possibilities. Examine these points if you are not willing to do anything to solve the problem:
   — Can it be a way to entertain yourself without moving forward?
   — Is there something you don't know how to face and that scares you? (Review again the chapter dedicated to its effective management.)
   — What are the pros and cons of doing nothing? Remember that doing nothing is also an alternative that has its advantages and disadvantages. Write them down.

Even if you have to give up something, try to find a win-win solution for all, giving priority to the perspective that a win-win solution is better than a win-win solution.

Win-win solutions improve relationships and are often more durable and effective.

5. Implement the chosen solution. The time has come to lose your fear and launch into an action. Prepare well each and every one of the steps you must take. With everything you've done, the chances of you making a mistake are small, and if you do, the mistake will probably be quite manageable.

6. Verify. Evaluate the result of what you have done. Now is a good time to confirm if you've made the right decision, or if any timely fixes need to be made.

As we have seen that no one is exempt from errors, minimizing the probability of its occurrence and, when it does happen, its size, will probably make things much easier for us and make us feel much better.

the smart mistake

We still have one more step to go for optimal error handling. So far we have seen how to accept them, assume them, handle them, minimize them and try to make them happen as little as possible.

But, sometimes, far from avoiding them or suffering from them, it can be wonderful for us to be used to managing them, because, surely, they can get us out of some quagmire.

It is possible that some of us have found ourselves in situations that, despite much analysis, we are not able to find, not just a viable way out, but not even a solution without some minimal collateral damage. What's more, sometimes there will be no choice but to cause an error in order to unlock situations that seem immovable.

If there is no other choice, the best way to do it will be to follow the same steps that we have seen in the previous section:

- To analize the situation.
- Generate error alternatives.
- Analyze advantages and disadvantages.
- Anticipate the consequences in the short, medium and long term.
- Decide which error to apply.
- Determine when, once the situation has been unblocked, the correction factor or new analysis can be introduced.
- Put into practice.
- Verify.

Once we have left the impasse in which we found ourselves, it is more comforting to find ourselves in a situation of error that allows us to generate alternative solutions and progress, than in another of «functional death».

Again, we have been able to verify that the brain does not move by parameters of good or bad, positive or negative, but rather efficient or ineffective. Thus, mistakes —that great "bogeyman" that everyone tries to avoid— are, without a doubt, the best allies we have to advance towards the objectives we have set for ourselves, if we know how, if we do it well and if, on top of that, We enjoy overcoming the challenge they pose.

We all seek success, but it only comes when we learn from mistakes.

7

Keys to not make life bitter

Exercise patience, which is the mother of science

One of the reasons why it has seemed appropriate to dedicate a special section to patience is because it seems that we live in a society in which there is a rush for everything: to form relationships, to get rich, to cure an illness, to lose weight. , to learn languages, so that our children learn to shower on their own, to become director of the company where they work, to get divorced and remain friends, etc.

This chapter is, above all, a reflection. From everything I have learned in my life, both personally and professionally, I dare to say that, without a doubt, one of the jewels in the crown is patience. I would define his contribution as a rewarding combination of freedom and strength, which allows you to act when appropriate and not get carried away by apparent short-term failures, or when it is completely inappropriate.

Although it comes from the Latin patire, which means "to suffer", and therefore the patient is "the one who suffers", I would like us to end up giving this word the positive connotation that, in my view, it contains and that, without a doubt, I believe is the key to wisdom. I prefer to associate it with "peace" than with "suffering." Isaac Newton himself attributed to this talent the ability to have provided humanity with his invaluable discoveries.

What in psychology we call "frustration tolerance" is only a part of patience. It is true that it is an attitude that allows us to endure setbacks and difficulties to remain firm in a purpose, but we must recover the function that it has of knowing how to wait placidly, allowing everything to take its course, until our intervention is necessary, or they affect us. positively or negatively their results. The apple that grows on the tree should be picked only when it is nutritious. That we see things clearly does not mean that it is time to intervene in them. That attitude, once again, is neither intelligent nor will it make us happy.

The philosopher Immanuel Kant said that patience is the strength of the weak, and impatience, the weakness of the strong. I rather believe that patience strengthens the weak, and impatience weakens the strong.

From everything we can learn in the pages of this book, I just want to point out that some techniques will probably be easier for you than others, but it depends on your patience that those that need more time to be acquired also have the opportunity to integrate into your lives. , if you work with this highly advantageous capacity.

Patience will free us from being manipulated in a hurry, leading us to make decisions that later on we will not understand how we were able to admit; It will allow us to adequately know and analyze everything that has to grow before our understanding; and it will provide us with the right rhythm to enjoy everything that can be apprehended by our five senses.

The chapters on the proper and effective management of emotions and thoughts, and on decision-making, will be the instruments that will help you the most to perfect this skill that, given its humility and simplicity, we tend to undervalue.

I am going to dedicate only these pages to him. Do you know why? Because they are so important that I want you to tear them out and put them somewhere where you always have them visible.

Nothing that is really worthwhile in this life is achieved without having made patience our great ally.

We have to take a few deep breaths and wait. I assure you that, far from despairing, we will enjoy everything good much more.

Learn to surround yourself with positive people and circumstances

If we have clearly understood that our vital experience is us along with our circumstances, this chapter will not only seem logical to us, but —I hope— also essential, since our context can be the environment in which we find the support, respect and affection that we need. sustain us and enhance our personal project, or it can also be the executioner who aborts it. It will then be up to us to remain in it, modify what is possible or kick off our shoes and seek, find or create new physical and psychological spaces where we can be and grow in the circumstances most appropriate to our nature.

The study of the group is important mainly due to the impact that groups have on our behavior, as well as society. The formation, consolidation and expression of our values, attitudes, thoughts, feelings and behaviors and the patterns of social interaction are largely determined, directly or indirectly, by the influence exerted on us by the groups to which we belong. or with whom we identify.

As humans, we have developed a group structure to survive in adverse conditions, but in group membership we also find the basis for the consistency of our psychological structure. This herd instinct conditions the fact that people are susceptible to influence and, probably, it is found in the biological structure of individuals.

The dichotomy between actions aimed at meeting the group's objectives and those aimed at satisfying personal needs and interests does not appear with the same strength in all situations. We want to be accepted by ourselves, we seek respect, intimacy, identity, authenticity and satisfy other needs of a personal nature.

Depending on our relationship with the group to which we belong, it can be:

- Reference. It is taken as a frame of reference regarding aspirations, values, norms, behaviors, etc., but there is no obligation regarding it.
- Of belonging. It is to which we belong and with which we usually relate.

However, both groups can coincide.

It is also important that we fully understand what functions the groups to which we belong perform, and that we observe how they may be influencing our behavior and the decisions we make. They are the following:

- Normative function. The group proposes or imposes models and rules of action to its members, establishes the principles, rules and forms regarding what must be done or avoided, and also ensures compliance with the established rules, and even sanctions conformity. and deviation from them, thus guiding the social behavior of its members.
- Organizing function of the world. The group offers its members a vision of the world and of themselves, and the frame of reference in which to integrate and organize their perceptions.
- Comparative function. The group provides the criteria against which its members establish comparisons, judge and value different aspects of social reality.
- Socializing function. The group contributes to the generation and development of the social nature of man, through the acquisition and internalization of norms, values and social roles, through the usual interactions that are manifested within the group.

In general, people feel compelled to carry out the decisions we have made as a group. So the group norm influences individual behavior.

Another important aspect that is worth mentioning is that of the roles that we may be playing in the group in which we are immersed. Many times we are not aware of it, and other times we are, but we do not know how to change its nature.

We would define a role as the set of behaviors and functions that are expected of the person who occupies a certain position within the group. The different types of roles can be organized around three criteria, according to a 1948 paper by Kenneth Benne and Paul Sheats:

1. Roles related to the group task:

- Initiator. He is the one who proposes new ideas, has different initiatives to achieve the objectives of the group.
- Requester of information. Find information needed to solve a problem.
- Opinion tracker. Look for the values that underlie the goals of the group.
- Informer. Informs about the topics that the group deals with.
- The one who thinks. He gives his opinion on the different alternatives to solve a problem.
- Developer. Support the group's suggestions.
- Coordinator. Organize the ideas and suggestions, and try to coordinate the group.
- Counselor. Analyze the group discussion and define the group's position with respect to where it is in order to achieve its objectives.
- Critic-evaluator. Assesses the effectiveness of the group in meeting its goals.
- Energizer. Activates the group towards decision making and action.
- Procedures technician. He is in charge of more routine tasks, such as distributing the material, but necessary for the group activity.

2. Roles related to the formation and maintenance of the group:

- Entertainer-inciter. Maintains group solidarity.
- Harmonizer. Reduce the tension in conflicts and try to mediate them.
- Deal maker. Responsible for keeping group commitments.
- Ordinance. Motivates and facilitates participation and communication between the different members of the group.
- Ego-ideal. Uphold group norms.
- Commentary observer. Take note of the various phenomena of the group process.
- Follower. Is carried away by the group accepting the ideas of others.

3. Individual roles (they satisfy particular needs that have nothing to do with the task or with the cohesion of the group):

- Aggressor. He attacks others, disapproves of their opinions and actions, and lowers the status of others.
- Blocker-blocker. He usually disagrees with the group, without giving reasons; it is negative.
- The one who seeks recognition. He draws attention to himself, behaving in an unusual way.
- Self-confessor. Uses the group to express their feelings and beliefs.
- Playboy. Shows lack of involvement with the group and develops behaviors inappropriate to the context.
- Dominator. Try to impose your criteria, manipulator.
- The one who seeks help. Insecure, confused, with little confidence in his abilities.
- Defender of their own interests. Try to cover up their needs or goals as if they were group.

Another classification made by Pichon-Rivière (1975) distinguishes three essential roles that appear in the group dynamics: the spokesperson, the scapegoat (guilty of group failures), and the leader (responsible for the positive and successful aspects of the group). . Moreland and Levine (1989) also introduce the figure of the newcomer.

The differentiation of roles is a very important phenomenon in the life of the group, because it implies a division of labor among its members, which will facilitate the achievement of goals. In addition, the roles help maintain a social order within the group, are part of our own self-concept and give a sense of who we are, which contributes to our own identity.

If we find ourselves in a group in which we feel happy and in which we can express our identity, logically our life will have more chances of success and happiness than if we feel constrained and exposed to non-constructive criticism, explicit prohibitions and rejection. lack of understanding or space to express one's identity.

Although the mistake could be in the group, there is another that we usually make and that I think it is important that we correct as soon as possible. In general, we waste too much time trying to please someone we are never going to like. It is not that the other person is "bad", but - as we saw when we analyzed the emotion of hate - simply that our mental and emotional schemata short-circuit each other and the relationship is not viable, for whatever reason. Our brain has a mechanism for detecting emotions that it considers dangerous and we have a certain ability to quickly detect "who doesn't like us", before "who likes us". In perfectly natural behavior, as we have seen throughout the book, we try to control the environment and we try to influence that person's opinion of us so that, at least, it stops seeming like a threat, however slight or subtle it may be. We would like that whoever had to love us (the family, in general) did it from the heart. However, it is in the close environment that we can find our worst enemies, and severe mood swings occur if the situation is unnecessarily prolonged. It also occurs in groups of friends, reference or at work. and severe mood disturbances occur if the situation is unnecessarily prolonged. It also occurs in groups of friends, reference or at work. and severe mood disturbances occur if the situation is unnecessarily prolonged. It also occurs in groups of friends, reference or at work.

What to do then? We must take care of our mental health, and this also depends on the messages we receive from those who are closest to us. If they are people who express their opinion or negative attitudes towards us, our day to day will be heavy, slow, sad and, sometimes, annoying.

If, on the other hand, we accept the opinion of those who don't like us, we put aside the stubborn idea of wanting to change what they think of us, and dedicate ourselves to the wise task of surrounding ourselves with those who love us, to who we like and who will provide us with a safe space, we will change and, without a doubt, our lives will change.

Surrounding yourself with positive people, or people who have positive effects on our way of being, feeling and living, is a matter of absolute importance and very healthy, since all parties benefit from the relationship. We can quietly forget who does not love us, because, fortunately, in this world there is room for everyone. Our brain needs us to provide it with the right context in which to develop. If you are a rose, do not go to the desert. And if you are a cactus, do not insist on being happy on top of the mountains. If you have no choice, try to create the conditions most similar to what suits you best. And you will always have the option to ignore what I am saying, and live where you please.

That is precisely what we are talking about.

Decorate life to our liking: creativity and art

What is most fascinating about this whole process of happiness is that it involves a component of creativity that we rarely apply to our way of being. Behavior is also an art, as long as we master the basic technique and then develop it with our personal originality.

All the great geniuses of art, even those who showed their talent as children, such as Mozart or Jane Austen, began in the same way: by copying. And if the masters from whom they copied were possessors of the best techniques, genius soon found its way into original expression. There was little to correct and much to enhance. Hence the importance of surrounding ourselves with people from whom we can learn correctly, especially since the most powerful mechanism we have to do so is what is known as "modeling" thanks to some curious neurons that we have in the brain that allow us to copy what we see.

Parents... look at the data! Our children learn from what we do, not what we say. The human being is the best imitator of nature. Some years ago, in the 1930s, Dr. Kellogg and his wife carried out one of those experiments that could only be done at that time: they decided to raise their baby together with a baby chimpanzee. Everything went wonderfully well for the first few months, until they watched in amazement that while the little chimpanzee had already given all he could give, the little human was beginning to imitate the language of his foster partner. The parents immediately stopped the experiment without much further explanation, and left us for posterity the confirmation of the great plasticity and adaptability that humans have thanks to our ability to imitate.

Do you remember the phrase that we already mentioned, "I don't want to look like my mother"? If the model that we put in our mind is our mother, our brain will take good note, consciously or unconsciously copying everything it has to do to comply with the coordinates that we have indicated. It does not matter that we have put it in the negative: he is seeing our mother, and that is where he is going. And we proposed that what we have to do then is to immediately provide the model that we want it to copy, but in a positive way: «My friend's mother, my neighbor, Audrey Hepburn...», in short, to suit the consumer.

When we want to change a behavior and we don't really know how, the best we can do is choose a model and copy, copy, copy until we have the perfect replica. Once we have fully mastered it, the time has come to play and create: with our tastes, with our dreams and with our abilities. Actually, the same tactic is used to learn to draw, to play instruments, to dance...

The creation involves a process of trial and error, sometimes controlled and sometimes risky, from which the genius, the masterpiece or the supine blunder finally emerges. In the latter case, we will review the bug fixes chapter and, if possible, also the humor chapter, and continue with our creative process.

Let's remember the steps:

- Copy.
- Copy.
- Copy.
- Make an exact replica of the model.
- Become an expert.
- Create "to suit the consumer": play and trial/error are the most appropriate techniques. And lose the shame once and for all, of course.

One of the advantages of the creativity process is that we exercise a feeling of freedom that allows us to be in a state of permanent change and transformation. Each person perceives reality in a way to later project with their individual touch what they have interpreted from it. His emotions, his experiences and his thoughts are reflected in that original work that can only exist if the filter exists, that is, the person who created it. That's why it's so important that we don't miss out on being whoever we want to be—or at least trying to be. Don Quixote is the creation of Cervantes. Without him, there would be no hidalgo knight, because no one would have gone through the experiences and interpretations that led Don Miguel to create him as only he could.

Artists are characterized by their own style and we all like to observe each other to see how we are managing to solve this fascinating adventure of survival. We copy each other until we dare to take the leap of creating and expressing our own personality.

We do not have to think that the creativity process is only possible if we are from the field of fine arts or letters. If you consider yourselves to be people of science, you have no excuse to get away from this personal self-exploration: science requires extremely creative people, capable of going beyond the obvious and of proposing hypotheses that allow society to advance. All scientific processes consist of testing a series of original ideas that have to be confirmed or falsified, in infinite trial/error processes. You just have to know how to move between the criteria of truth, goodness and beauty, and lose the fear of experimenting with all our subjective references.

One of the fundamental tools to develop creativity is imagination, as a form of non-verbal thought capable of projecting images in the format we want. As we already discussed, everything that "is" had to be thought of first. In the process of creativity about ourselves, our brain has the ability to combine in infinite ways all the elements that make up its perceptions, emotions and experiences.

The creativity process is also necessary to generate alternatives that allow us to find adequate solutions to our daily problems, and also to surprise those we love with beautiful details, to explain the most complex concepts to our children and to facilitate relaxation in daydreams of escape. .

The qualities that we can specifically work on are:

- Fluency to generate a large number of images, alternatives and relationships of all kinds between them.
- Flexibility to explore everything that can be done with the same element in all the different ways we can think of.
- Originality to get out of the hat all our singular, rare, personal and distinctive ideas. These can be new (they did not exist previously), unpredictable (they do not have a cause-effect relationship), unique and unrepeatable, surprising, etc.
- Sensitivity to perceive and understand the essence and go beyond appearances.
- Tolerance to frustration, since the creative process, being mainly trial and error, implies many possibilities of making mistakes before reaching a success or final result. But you have to learn to move in ambiguity, in the unknown and uncertain, and embrace challenges as pleasurable and stimulating experiences.
- Spontaneity, which is nothing more than the freedom and autonomy necessary to detach oneself from what is supposed to be, to start experimenting with what one wants it to be.

Everyone, absolutely everyone, is creative. The changes that we are able to introduce in our behavioral repertoire —which includes thoughts, feelings and behaviors— must be accompanied by a strong motivation that leads us to the acceptance of who we are, of our destiny and meaning and, finally, of our self-realization .

I can tell you that there are few things that are more moving to me than when new people literally bloom before our eyes, with lives to suit them and full of happiness. I have always considered that it was a privilege and an honor for me to witness first-hand the spectacular works of art that those who lose their fear of facing their ghosts return to us after arduous journeys through deserts of pain and, sometimes, despair . It is not necessary to reach this point to decide to take all the tools that we have proposed in this book and start working on our own personal work of art. At least it will be fun.

> The best way to enhance creativity is to cultivate as much inner joy as possible and give ourselves permission to enjoy life to the fullest.
>
> DR. HAROLD BLOOMFIELD

Laughing even at our shadow: the sense of humor

This section is not going to teach us to develop a sense of humor, but to remind us of its importance for our mental health and our happiness. As Groucho Marx said, "Humor is reason when it goes crazy." Although in the prologue of my previous book, Good Love, María Jesús Álava Reyes had the surprising detail of highlighting a sense of humor among my presumed virtues, frankly I am not very clear how I acquired the ability to laugh at myself and my circumstances, so I will rely on better comedians than me and other wiser or more elegant people to refresh some key concepts about this wonderful ability that, as Democritus pointed out, makes us wise. Laugh at yourself, at your shadow and this way it will never reach you. And have fun with it.

I know that it may be surprising for lovers of Eastern philosophies to learn that there is a Hindu belief that "an hour of laughter produces more beneficial effects than four hours of yoga". One of the best relaxation techniques that exists is a good time of laughter. So many muscles in the body and face are activated that when one stops laughing, the next state is one of pleasant relaxation. And we already know that, to the extent that we learn to reduce our stress levels, we will also be working for our health. You have probably heard that the main reinforcers of our brain are food, sex and exercise. Well, there is one more that makes the brain secrete dopamine with real delight: a good laugh. In fact, the Dalai Lama himself admits that it is his favorite pastime.

The sense of humor, like any other behavior, is learned, practiced and taught, both the bad and the good. The good news is that there is no better antidote to anger than a good laugh. "Man should know that our pleasures, joys, laughter and jokes, as well as our sorrows, pains, afflictions and tears come from the brain." This is a matter of Hippocrates, who knew something about medicine. And Sigmund Freud, who was one of the first to try to explain what was happening in the brain through psychoanalysis, considered humor "the highest manifestation of the individual's adaptive mechanisms." This is another of those traits that all human beings share, because, at least in basics, we can laugh at the same things and we all understand what a laugh means. Definitely, a smile is the best way to establish communication and links, even if you don't speak the same language. It is about those experiences that feel much better in company than alone. And the prognosis for couples who are able to make love with humor is unbeatable. "Laughter is the shortest distance between two people," said the pianist and comedian Victor Borge.

One of our national psychologists who is experts in humor is Eduardo Jáuregui, who on his website, <www.humorpositive.com>, which I recommend you visit, tells us about the many benefits of a sense of humor:

- Reduces stress and allows better coping with problems, failures and even the worst crises.
- Enhances the health and capabilities of the human being.
- Attract and retain the most valuable human resources.
- Strengthens individual and collective motivation.
- Stimulates innovation and decision making.
- Optimize communication.
- Promotes learning.
- Unites human teams.
- Enhances the persuasive impact of any message.
- Strengthens relationships.
- Create a more pleasant and human environment.

If you think that this is the skill that you lack in your repertoire of behaviors, or that you simply want to enhance, you will be in the most appropriate hands.

One of the keys to developing a sense of humor is, without a doubt, the game, the optimal strategy by nature for any type of learning. The game is a test without falling into the drama of error, even if it happens. One of the quickest ways to detect a person's intelligence is their ability to correct their mistakes and often laugh at themselves. According to Nietzsche, "a man's intellectual power is measured by the dose of humor that he is capable of using." The anecdotes of our lives that we most like to evoke and with which we have the best time are those in which a mistake happened.

And what about the role of humor when life is really uphill for us and we feel like we can't take it anymore? There is no better medicine or "shot" that gives us more power than laughter. India's former prime minister, Indira Gandhi, admitted: "If it hadn't been for my sense of humour, I would have committed suicide a long time ago." Probably half humanity, too. Humor allows us to turn the coconuts that are our problems into little gnomes that won't bother us as long as we keep them the right size. If we laugh at them, we will have won the battle. Humor cushions bad drinks, or as Plato said, "it is the rest of serious things." It is a power tool and gives us a different perspective on our own problems.

There is a definition that I particularly like, and it is the one made by one of the great comedic writers on the Spanish scene, Don Miguel Mihura, who has given us such good times: «The only thing that humor aims at is that, for a moment, let us get out of ourselves, tiptoe about twenty meters away and take a walk around us looking at ourselves from one side and the other, behind and in front, as before the three mirrors of a tailor's shop and discover new features and profiles that we didn't know." I can promise that I had not read this quote when we talked at the beginning of this book about our periscope in charge of attention and the flying carpet that allowed us to travel through present, past and future reality, from all possible angles, including the most remote parts. of our whole being.

Be careful, you don't have to go overboard. Trivializing everything can take us to the opposite extreme and make us fall into a state of neglect in which we do not give a damn about everything. And neither so much nor so bald. Humor, like everything else, needs its fair measure and you have to know how to apply it —let's remember Nietzsche— intelligently.

And only someone as elegant as the Uruguayan writer Eduardo Galeano could make such a delicious description of the sense of humor: «Humor has the ability to give you back the certainty that life is worth living. And one is saved, sometimes, by the joke, by the magical sound of laughter, which may not be your laugh; for the hidden ability to tease you, to see you from the outside and laugh at yourself».

And one last fundamental point: do not confuse a sense of humor with ridicule. The latter is poisoned and is usually toxic. And, above all, very crappy. A good laugh is an elixir for those who produce it and for those who enjoy it. Actually, we have not discovered anything new, since Cicero told us that "there are two kinds of jokes: one uncivil, petulant, malevolent, obscene; another, elegant, courteous, witty and jovial».

Well, come on, practice. Did we laugh today for a reason? Have we set out to get a smile out of someone we care about or, perhaps, someone we don't? What happened when we did it?

Be wary of those who never laugh. They are not serious people.

JULIUS CAESAR

8

make the decision to be happy

You have to see how little we like to make decisions and, however, it is something that we cannot escape from and that, in reality, we do every minute of our lives, including not making any.

It is also considered to be making a decision when you do not want to solve a problem or do not acquire the necessary skills to be able to do so.

Do you remember the explanation about how we walk? It is an unconscious but learned process, thanks to which we move towards goals and also jump, dance and run. Decision making is in a certain way the psychological equivalent of the steps we take every day to resolve from insignificant issues to others of greater relevance in our lives. Most of the time we do it unconsciously, with autopilot and, when we consider that a situation needs more reflection, we activate the brainy conscious.

We decide in which cup we are going to have breakfast, if we add one or two spoonfuls of sugar, if we give our partner a kiss or not, if we are going to spend a week without speaking to him..., and so on throughout the day until It's time to decide when we're going to sleep.

From all these small and big decisions our habits end up being formed, which we have already seen are the consequence of the repetition with reinforcement of some type of behavior, and that, unfortunately, we do not always take the time to reflect on whether its consequences are how positive we wish they were. When we get up in the morning and look out the window to see what day it is, seeing the overcast sky we can think that it is a great day or a calamity; when we go to breakfast we can decide to have two churros instead of six; and, at work, we can decide whether to make that call to a potential client or leave it for another day.

One of the difficulties that we frequently detect with some of the people who come to consultation is the blockage when making decisions and the discomfort that it produces, especially when it comes to complex issues and when they involve more people. We don't care too much about making a mistake in the color of the shirt we have chosen, but doing so in a separation process or in a professional career change can mean literally turning our lives around, and we want the changes to always be for the better. or, at least, for the better.

One of the emotions present in these moments prior to making a decision is fear (remember: I don't know what I have to do), which translates into an attitude of insecurity. But we also find a logical desire, supported by a thought that, at times, can become irrational: "I don't want to be wrong." As we have already seen when we deal with the issue of mistakes, indeed, we do not want to make them, but it is in our hands to minimize both the frequency with which we do it, as well as its size. If we start from a good preparation of the decision that we must make, and if, if necessary, it is feasible to correct it, surely our objective will be clearer for our attention, and then fear can be replaced by motivation to get where we have proposed. .

We are now going to suggest a series of steps so that the route is the most appropriate, allows us to gain security and relocate our life in what should be its natural state: moving and advancing.

Define the goal: what?

Let us remember once again that we make things much easier for our mind if we clearly define why it is going to have to deploy a whole series of mechanisms and actions in which it is going to invest a lot of energy and that should not threaten its survival. Therefore, as we advance in the first chapters of this book, we are going to try to make this objective consciously explicit: what is it that we intend to achieve? Where do we want to go?

To answer, we have to fine-tune a lot. Sometimes we think we want something when, in reality, we only want part of it or, perhaps, our desire is not completely well stated.

Let's see what happens when what we want is actually a part of the whole: "I want to lose weight." A priori it is a lawful and apparently correct desire, but losing those extra kilos also implies changing other habits and even a lifestyle. Do we also want to change them? Have we clearly defined and visualized them? Are we clear about what this new way of life is going to consist of? Losing weight can then be an objective, but above all a consequence of the modifications that we have defined and introduced in the whole context, which has to be consistent with the weight we want: exercise, pantry, habits, etc.

This example also helps us to find out if it really is the exact objective that is intended. When someone tells us that they want to lose weight, at least we psychologists must understand why, what the objective is, because sometimes we find ourselves with irrational ideas such as "if I lose weight, I will find a boyfriend (or girlfriend)", "I will find a job" or "I'm going to have more friends". We cannot deny the obvious, which is that if it improves physical appearance, we facilitate certain personal and work interactions, but these do not depend exclusively on one's weight. Therapists cannot feed the expectation that only by losing weight will a series of objectives be achieved. The goal of losing weight must be accompanied by equipping that person with other skills that will be the ones that, ultimately,

Another example that we often use a lot in training courses has to do with the explicit objective of this book: the feeling of happiness, of a full and satisfying life, endowed with meaning. And the truth is that it is really curious. At a certain moment we ask: "What do you really want?", and the answer is: "To be happy". Our faces light up and we all point to each other with a certain glee: «I...», «I...», «Me too...». Cool! The brain jumps for joy: it has heard something that it really likes! Luckily, we have that other part of the brain working in parallel that tells us, "Great idea. Now please tell me how. I have to adjust coordinates so I can give the appropriate specific commands." And then they change faces again. Is it possible that we don't know how to be happy? That we are waiting for someone to give us the recipe?

In this book we are not saying what it takes to be happy, but how each one can achieve it according to the way in which he decides to use all the instruments that "we carry as standard".

Those who have been through a psychologist's consultation will know that we ask many questions, apparently banal at times and very insidious at others. We may seem too gossipy, but what we are trying to do is obtain as much information as possible about how the person functions, what their emotional and thought structure is, and what context they are in and what needs our intervention. We need our patients to come down to earth, to put their feet on the ground and take the bull, their bull, by the horns. This is their life, their responsibility, and they have to carry it out with their own resources. There are people who find it difficult to go into detail, but without this level of specificity we cannot give the brain the right coordinates to make the right decisions to achieve its goals.

Our life is a consecutive process of milliseconds and each of them is relevant.

We already talked in another chapter about the importance of forcing ourselves to carefully break down each of the steps that must be taken, and for this we use as an example the objective of going to the beach to unblock a situation: which one? ?, with what type of sand?, by what highway?, etc.

We have also seen that communication is strongly affected when we are not clear about the message we want to convey, because the messages do not arrive with the appropriate clarity, and finally each one of the people involved in the same action activates their particular route map, in instead of using a common one for all.

As an extra bonus in this first section, we are going to suggest something that is usually very useful: when we want to confirm if someone has correctly understood what we have told them, we will ask them to repeat the information ("well, tell me how you are going to do it" , or "what did you understand from what I said or how did you do it"). Of course, in a good way. If they answer exactly what corresponds to us, then the communication, the personal relationships and the results will be extraordinary.

Generate alternatives: how?

Once we have defined the objective, we have to put on the table all the possible ways we have to achieve it. This phase is absolutely crucial because, yes or yes, we are going to have to go through one of them. The best option will be the one that we have analyzed in detail, foreseeing the advantages and disadvantages and preparing ourselves adequately for each of the possible scenarios, instead of leaving it to chance and solving without any foresight, depending on what is presented to us. More time is wasted, without a doubt, trying to solve it by infused science, than the time we use to prepare ourselves for possible eventualities. It is preferable to invest that time in choosing the most appropriate option, as it is, ultimately, infinitely more comfortable and effective.

Let's return to the example of weight loss. Not all people achieve this goal in the same way and hence the failure of most regimens; In addition, as we have already seen, sometimes the initial error lies in not having correctly defined the exact goal that is intended to be achieved. The issue of being overweight may have a medical or genetic origin, but in a large number of cases it is a matter of relationship and interaction with food and with the act of eating, mediated by the cognitive and emotional filters learned by each person . Therefore, it will be necessary to define if the way to address it is going to be with medical help or support, or if the emphasis should be placed on the psychological aspect. In general, the correct interventions are those that include both specialists, as well as a good physical exercise monitor,

That the diet has worked for our neighbor cannot be the only argument with which we start ours. We have to analyze the pros and cons, if it suits our tastes or if it is necessary to introduce some variable that adjusts to our personality and lifestyle.

Personally, I am more in favor of what we call the "tailor made suit". After all, our body is. Choosing a way of eating is very similar to choosing a partner: each one has to do it according to their own characteristics and what suits them. The ideal relationship occurs when food provides nutrients and pleasure to those who eat it, and the latter, in turn, consciously values and enjoys what he is receiving. After all, eating cannot be torture, but rather a source of satisfaction, because our brain expects it that way. Right on.

Therefore, generating alternatives taking into account all the circumstances involved in the objective we want to achieve will allow us to find the right way to make it a reality.

Anticipate the consequences in the short, medium and long term

This step is really interesting and it is where the success of the decision we make will lie. It is surprising, perhaps, that we do not do something so obvious with the necessary regularity, nor with the interest, nor with the time that we deserve.

Once the previous step of generating all the possible alternatives to reach our objective has been carried out, whether we like it or not, we will dedicate ourselves to analyzing the foreseeable consequences in the short, medium and long term, the most relevant being those that occur in the short and long term. long term, each for different reasons.

Let's take a look at the following box first, and then develop its content:

<table>
<tr><td colspan="4">Consecuencias de una decisión
en cada tramo de su trayecto</td></tr>
<tr><td>Opciones</td><td>Consecuencias a corto plazo</td><td>Consecuencias a largo plazo</td><td>Conclusión</td></tr>
<tr><td>A</td><td>Negativa</td><td>Negativa</td><td>Directamente no se hace</td></tr>
<tr><td>B</td><td>Positiva</td><td>Negativa</td><td>Error asegurado</td></tr>
<tr><td>C</td><td>Negativa</td><td>Positiva</td><td>Hay que sufrir un poco, pero es una buena opción</td></tr>
<tr><td>D</td><td>Positiva</td><td>Positiva</td><td>La ideal, la que a todos nos gustaría</td></tr>
</table>

The consequences of option A do not usually present us with any problem. We don't make a profit at any point along the way, the goal our brain sees isn't attractive at all, so it just doesn't work. It's easy to dismiss this option without much thought. Do you remember the example we gave for the motivation to go swimming in the pool? If we wet our hair, the water is cold, the chlorine affects us, we go with the bag full of creams and dryers, and on top of that we do not improve physically, it is evident that we will stop doing it sooner rather than later.

You have to be a little careful with this forecast, because people who present a depressive style usually see the future in this way: whatever you do, things are going to go wrong. This is what is known as learned helplessness. It goes without saying that a good training with psychological support usually strengthens your mood.

Option D is, without a doubt, the ideal one, the one that we would all like. Sometimes, life pleasantly surprises us by making the path towards our goals well accompanied by positive consequences. If when we go swimming, the water is clean and at an ideal temperature, if it is not necessary to carry the whole arsenal of subsequent equipment, and if our health and our appearance improve, maintaining regularity in the exercise will not only be guaranteed, but also It will provide us with deep pleasure and well-being.

Option C is not ideal, but it is the most advisable when we want to be successful in the decisions we make. In general, why deny it, it is usually the most common. We have to go through somewhat more unpleasant consequences in the short term (efforts, discomfort, etc.), but in the end all this has the reward of achieving what we wanted. Learning new habits, such as eating more slowly, with fewer amounts and different doses of each type of food, will seem like smart actions when we manage to reach the desired weight. And, if we repeat them, we will have easily acquired the habits of a new lifestyle.

Option B —we are not going to deny it either— is usually one of the most common, and also the one that causes us the most frustration, remorse and discomfort, because the results we obtain are not what we wanted.

We often call the temptation to succumb to short-term gains instead of keeping our attention focused on long-term gains a lack of will.

Examples of option B are the chocolate donuts that we eat when we are on a diet, or the weekend with the couple with whom we have already broken up four times, and with whom we know that from Monday there will be more of the same .

Option B not only leaves us with the feeling that we have gone backwards or that we have wasted time and energy, but also produces an effect on our self-esteem that lowers us to the sub-basements for which we will also have to put in place a good rescue team. And practice option C more.

Remember, we are training for our happiness.

Choose the most convenient option

Needless to say, the best options are C and D. B is used for small unimportant whims, and A is automatically discarded, except in cases where it is the only possible way. Life, sometimes, also uses a fine irony. If this were the situation, although logically we do not want the negative consequences in the short or long term, they usually serve to start the journey and analyze without delay the opportunities that allow us to give the necessary turn to our action plan and «redirect» to positive consequences. Once again, it is up to us and our abilities to turn something that initially seems negative into an opportunity that works in our favor.

For example, if we have already made up our minds that we have to go to the pool yes or yes, and we don't like it or get anything positive, it may happen that —maybe we hadn't noticed before—, a couple of blocks further where we usually park when we go swimming there is a fitness center where some classes are taught that could perhaps interest us more, and even help us to achieve our goals. Goodbye at last to the flip flops and here are the sneakers! But if we had not activated plan A, we would not have discovered this new route that is opening up before us.

Evaluate, confirm or correct where deemed necessary

Once each action plan has been started, it is convenient to analyze if everything is going correctly, or if there is any unforeseen event for which we can immediately introduce our correction factor. Let's remember that errors are solved more easily and with less investment of time and energy when they are still small and we can handle them.

What decision do you want to make right now about your own happiness?

"Me? The one to be happy. Because I want. And because I have decided so.» Marching one of positive rage and smiles in bulk to achieve this beautiful dream!

Third part

What we can do to avoid some psychological upsets

9

Correct some erroneous learning or that no longer serve us

At this point in the book you will be familiar with the idea that we are not "like this", but that we have learned to be. Most of what we think makes up our personality is nothing more than a series of behaviors that we have automated based on a lot of practice over the years.

The learning of many of them has begun even before leaving the pacifier and we have developed our thinking in verbal format. That is why, when we reach adulthood, and we try to explain why and how we do certain activities, it becomes difficult for us to explain it.

We will return to an example that we have already discussed: the behavior of walking. I am going to propose the challenge of explaining how we do it. Before reading on, I invite you to stop reading here and try this exercise: how do we walk? What does walking consist of?

Well, I hope you have taken at least a minute of your time, and let's see if your explanation matches the one we are going to see next. The most generalized is usually "putting one foot forward and then the other". And this is where our discourse usually ends. Actually, the act of walking requires precision and even a certain daring. For this reason, the age range in which we usually learn to do it is the ideal one, firstly, because of the reasonable height from which we fall and, secondly, because of the unconsciousness of our actions, which makes us even have a lot of fun learning something so rugged. Actually, the act of walking consists of intentionally causing an imbalance that we correct by throwing one leg forward, we recover balance by stretching the leg and advancing the rear, that we immediately launched to compensate for the new imbalance that we have caused. Observed like this, it is a real wonder that we have automated by repeating it daily: calculating the appropriate degree of incline, the power of our muscles and developing our sense of balance. And we do it so well that, balancing and unbalancing our position, we also learn to dance, jump and run marathons.

Perhaps this example is somewhat neutral, but it will allow us to understand how we also learn and finally automate traits of our character that we think are innate, when in fact they are acquired.

Let us now imagine that in a family of five siblings a sixth arrives, with parents absolutely overwhelmed with the care of all their children. The latter, still with the pacifier, will begin to display various types of tentative behavior to see when his parents are more diligently attending to his needs. He realizes that when he cries, he joins a chorus of different voices in which his doesn't exactly stand out; if he keeps quiet, it is possible that on some occasion they will forget about him; one day, by chance, he discovers that, with a huge smile, his parents think he is an angel and they find it very funny. And every time he laughs he gets exactly the attention he needs, and probably more. Without a doubt, this little boy will learn to be a nice man. But we will not be able to ask him why this is so. I'm sure he doesn't even remember.

Likewise, we learn bad character and other skills for which we may have an innate natural tendency and that the reinforcement of the environment makes it easier for us to develop and enhance, sometimes unlimitedly.

Many of these behaviors can be useful to us during a certain period of our life and, when we reach another, they can be completely inappropriate. However, we are so used to them that we think we cannot change our way of doing things, despite the fact that, as we have already seen, most of what we do is learned. However, there is nothing more ineffective and less intelligent than insisting that, by applying behavior that does not correspond to the context, things turn out the way we want, that is, well. It is not necessary to think that we are useless or that those around us are terrible: let us simply apply ourselves to identifying what is the right thing to do at each moment and, if we do not know, we must be willing to learn it.

Have we mentioned in any of the previous lines the word reinforcement? Here we have another of those terms contributed by psychology to colloquial language that, without a doubt, we use a lot, but in which we may have to delve a little deeper to know exactly what it is and how to use it properly.

What we are going to see next I usually give to my patients "like gold on cloth". It is about understanding how our brain activates two extraordinary mechanisms to implant and eliminate behaviors, applicable both to ourselves and to the people around us and, in this second case, both in their relationship with us and with themselves.

With them we can unlearn bad habits and implant new, healthier ones; we can change learning that we no longer like or that are not worth us and change them for others more adapted to our dreams, illusions and possibilities; In short, we have the ability to become whoever, from the depths of our being, we want to be.

Now yes, with all of us: reinforcement and punishment.

The mechanisms of implanting and eliminating behaviors from our repertoire work in our brain absolutely free of prejudices; therefore, not all the behaviors that we establish are the healthiest, nor all the ones that we eliminate are the worst. Sometimes just the opposite happens, with the uncomfortable consequences of inadequate learning and, above all, the effort that must be made to change them when they already have their entire neural circuit perfectly mapped and are automated in the warehouses of the unconscious.

That is why it is important, when we are facing a new learning of something that interests us, that the first steps are slow but sure and, above all, correct, because once we begin to repeat and reinforce, we will incorporate them into our repertoire. As with other skills, it is preferable to dedicate some time to adequate preparation that allows us not to undo anything we have learned.

Let's go now step by step, with a certain parsimony, to fully understand the concepts with which we want to work. At the end of this explanation, you will find a diagram that I hope will be useful to you and, above all, very practical, and we will also see some examples that illustrate and help us to better integrate what has been explained.

We begin by defining the two basic concepts of these mechanisms:

- Reinforcement is the mechanism that allows us to implement behaviors.
- Punishment is the mechanism that allows us to extinguish or eliminate behaviors.

If what we implant or extinguish is good or bad, it is something that we will decide according to our scale of values and with the consequences that we obtain once we carry them out, but, a priori, the brain is simply in charge of activating one or the other, regardless of its later meaning.

As already mentioned, at this time we cannot speak of good or bad, so when we use the two terms that we are going to see next, it is important that we do not confuse them with these two meanings.

Reinforcement and punishment have two modalities:

- Positive. We repeat, this time it does not mean good. It is used in the sense of "managing" something.
- Negative. It is not synonymous with bad. It is used in the sense of "removing" something.

Let's pause briefly to explain what in neuroscience is known as "reinforcement circuits" of the brain, which are precisely what physiologically support these learning mechanisms.

Nature has found a way that certain activities that are absolutely essential for our survival are so pleasant that, yes or yes, we repeat them and learn them correctly. The most basic: food, exercise and sex. And for this there are some centers in the central nervous system, mainly the ventral tegmental area and its projections towards the nucleus accumbens, which release a neurotransmitter that is surely very familiar to us, dopamine, responsible for the pleasant sensation that will make us repeat a behavior determined. This same circuit, which is so useful for the implementation of new learning, is so powerful that it is also the center where addictions are generated. But we are not going to stop at this last aspect,

This stop was important to explain the following concept that we must be clear about: what is pleasant and unpleasant. Without a doubt, this is a very subjective question, and it does not have to be the same for everyone. Therefore, when we refer to this term, it will always be in relation to what it means "for the subject" who is learning or eliminating a behavior.

So far, we have seen that we have two types of reinforcement to implement behaviors: positive, which will consist of administering something pleasant to the subject; and the negative, which will consist of removing something unpleasant for the subject. Let's see it better with a couple of examples.

Positive reinforcement is easy to understand. If this week I have learned a new recipe to make chicken and, when I serve it at the table, my whole family congratulates me (adds something nice) for how delicious it is, surely next week we will have chicken again. I will definitely repeat the behavior.

We also implant undesirable behaviors with this type of reinforcement. We are in the bakery and, suddenly, a boy tells his mother that he wants a bun and she denies it. The child insists and the mother continues to deny him. Then the crying, the fights and the tantrums begin. The mother continues to resist, but the child drops to the ground and begins to put on the show. The mother, embarrassed, while she tells him off, asks the clerk to serve her bun. She is useless the sermon that she is giving him: a deplorable behavior has achieved something that pleases her. In the future, the same behavior will be applied to obtain what is desired. Unfortunately, what our mothers or fathers put up with us as children is absolutely unbearable for our peers and, if we don't change it, definitely the difficulties that we will have to relate to each other will not facilitate our happiness at all. And, obviously, we were not born that way. We have been taught it and we have learned it at some point in our lives.

We can also use it when we want to change something in ourselves, for which it is very important that we give ourselves positive self-instructions and value each time we carry out the behavior that we want to automate, especially in the first phases in which the effort can play tricks on us. make us throw in the towel. Statements like "come on, I'm doing very well, this is what I like and it makes me happy..." will help us keep our goal well focused (remember?), until we incorporate the new attitudes into our nature .

We also have a second type of reinforcement: the negative. With this one we usually get involved a little more, especially because of the semantic issues that we have already clarified previously. But we will soon see that it is also easy to understand. In this case, we are going to implement a behavior based on removing something "unpleasant" for the subject.

Imagine that we have an obligation to mow the lawn on Sunday mornings. One day we realize that, when we prepare breakfast for the whole family, someone is in charge of carrying out this tedious task, and they do it with more pleasure than us. Without a doubt, we will repeat the behavior of preparing breakfast for everyone as many times as necessary. We just got rid of it!

How do we implant inappropriate behaviors with this type of reinforcement? If we discover that a skillful lie has saved us from a well-deserved reprimand, we will certainly use it as many times as necessary.

Now, this process is not that simple. The reinforcement can sometimes lose value and not produce the effect we expect. Let's see then what is the ideal way to implement behaviors.

What usually happens when a behavior is positively or negatively reinforced each and every time it happens? In this case, a phenomenon known as habituation occurs in the brain, which consists of the brain stopping paying attention to the stimulus in order to use it in things that produce more surprise or novelty. Thus, the reinforcement loses its value and, let us remember, the important thing is that it be significant for the subject. If it ceases to be, it will not matter if you receive it or not. At least for now. This is what usually happens when, after a long time bringing your partner breakfast in bed every day, one day, tired, you stop doing it because you see that the other person does not value it or takes it for granted, without give you a sad thank you or an affectionate kiss. Although your intention is good, the effect is not what you wanted. Y,

What happens if a behavior is never reinforced at all? Let's go back to the case of breakfast. The person has managed to get her partner to stop doing a behavior that perhaps he liked, but by ignoring her and not making any kind gesture (reinforcement for the partner), she stops doing it. All for what? The brain cannot be wasting energy in a useless way and clearly this behavior does not serve, it seems, neither to please the person we love, nor to make them love us more. It is, in short, very ineffective, not even for the relationship to be healthy. I know that many of you are now thinking that when you love someone "you don't expect anything in return." Sure, you don't expect it, but if over time we don't "receive" anything coming our way, the brain gets bored too, and for good reason.

But let's continue with the best way to implement behaviors. We still have a case that is not usually effective. What happens if we reinforce a behavior with a fixed interval? That is, if, for example, we always administer something pleasant "on the third" occasion that it occurs. The brain, which is usually very aware of these things, realizes that the reinforcement "falls" every three times, no matter what you do. Therefore, it will only do the expected behavior on that third occasion. The other two, it will do as it does, but probably not the same as in that third. Or, in any case, we are missing the objective, which is to implant a behavior. Let us remember that reinforcement only serves us so that a behavior is repeated over and over again, so that we automate it and thus remain integrated into our repertoire of habits without us having to think about it. If we know that, no matter what or how we do it, right or wrong, the third time we get something we like, the implantation will be quite weak. And, in addition, the reinforcement, although we like it, loses value, because it is not conditioned by our execution, but by when it happens, and we don't like that so much anymore. Can you imagine that your football team, yes or yes, won the Champions League every six years? They probably wouldn't make an effort at all to play a good game of football, or to put on a good show with the best they know how to do, because they're going to win the cup anyway. Can you imagine that your football team, yes or yes, won the Champions League every six years? They probably wouldn't make an effort at all to play a good game of football, or to put on a good show with the best they know how to do, because they're going to win the cup anyway. Can you imagine that your football team, yes or yes, won the Champions League every six years? They probably wouldn't make an effort at all to play a good game of football, or to put on a good show with the best they know how to do, because they're going to win the cup anyway.

But what happens if we don't know when we're going to get the booster? What if it happens sometimes yes, other times no, we don't know how often, but when we receive it we do it with great pleasure? Definitely, not being certain when we are going to get what we like will make us do it right each and every time: just in case. It is not that the reinforcement was going to fall on us just the day that we do not make an effort in the task and we miss it. In this way, we will do the behavior well repeatedly in the hope that something will happen to us and, when we want to realize it, it will already be part of our second nature. This is called a "variable boost interval." Actually, it's like a game that, by the way, is nature's quintessential learning methodology. Let's recover it with our children instead of giving them sermons that serve little purpose. The results are usually spectacular. So spectacular, it must be said, that they are also at the base of what they have learned, unconsciously, those people who spend hours in front of the slot machine hoping that sometimes five will fall, other zero, other ten, other five hundred, other three, and so on. What behavior have they automated? Take the coin, put it in the slot and hit the lever or button. I leave you the comments for when you close the pages of this book, which focuses precisely on learning to use the instruments and mechanisms we wear to be happy, and also so that we learn to avoid unnecessary slavery. So spectacular, it must be said, that they are also at the base of what they have learned, unconsciously, those people who spend hours in front of the slot machine hoping that sometimes five will fall, other zero, other ten, other five hundred, other three, and so on. What behavior have they automated? Take the coin, put it in the slot and hit the lever or button. I leave you the comments for when you close the pages of this book, which focuses precisely on learning to use the instruments and mechanisms we wear to be happy, and also so that we learn to avoid unnecessary slavery. So spectacular, it must be said, that they are also at the base of what they have learned, unconsciously, those people who spend hours in front of the slot machine hoping that sometimes five will fall, other zero, other ten, other five hundred, other three, and so on. What behavior have they automated? Take the coin, put it in the slot and hit the lever or button. I leave you the comments for when you close the pages of this book, which focuses precisely on learning to use the instruments and mechanisms we wear to be happy, and also so that we learn to avoid unnecessary slavery. another zero, another ten, another five hundred, another three, and so on. What behavior have they automated? Take the coin, put it in the slot and hit the lever or button. I leave you the comments for when you close the pages of this book, which focuses precisely on learning to use the instruments and mechanisms we wear to be happy, and also so that we learn to avoid unnecessary slavery. another zero, another ten, another five hundred, another three, and so on. What behavior have they automated? Take the coin, put it in the slot and hit the lever or button. I leave you the comments for when you close the pages of this book, which focuses precisely on learning to use the instruments and mechanisms we wear to be happy, and also so that we learn to avoid unnecessary slavery.

We are now going to turn to how to extinguish behaviors from our repertoire, or from the repertoire of the people around us. Again, let us remember that these mechanisms can always act on two levels: the conscious and the unconscious, that is, we can be implanting or extinguishing behaviors without realizing it or, better yet, by our own will.

To eliminate behaviors, the mechanism we use is called punishment, which is a word that sounds pretty bad to all of us. I'm sure more than one of you have already cringed when reading it, but I hope we can learn how to use it in the most effective way possible, and with beneficial consequences for the management of our lives.

The punishment is also presented in a positive way, that is, administering something unpleasant for the subject, and negative, which is when we remove something that is pleasant for him. It happens the other way around than with reinforcement.

The example that we are going to see may not be familiar to some people, but I remember when, as teenagers, we had a time to arrive home —something that has practically disappeared now— and if we were late, the one that fell on us was good. What was happening? Our parents wanted to eliminate that behavior. For that, they had two ways of acting, even if they had not studied psychology:

- By means of a positive punishment, that is, administering something unpleasant to us, like a good rant of those that are difficult to forget.
- By means of a negative punishment, which consisted of withdrawing something pleasant from us: «And tomorrow you won't go out with your friends».

Double dose. To make sure we didn't do it again.

But sometimes we also eliminate good behaviors, without being aware of it. For example, it is common for many couples who come to consult to report that the wife was very affectionate at first, and that the husband has long missed those kisses and caresses. During our exploration of the case, we detected that when her wife came home every day, she gave him a kiss. His response used to be a "oh, what a pain you are!" (manage something unpleasant) or, worse yet, ignore it. In this subtle and unconscious way, it is possible to eliminate from the couple's repertoire of behaviors one that, over the years, he misses because he liked it. Is love over? Be careful, sometimes we put it out with jugs of cold water.

The problem with punishment is that, like all double-edged swords, you have to be very skillful in its application. Well used it can be an extraordinary instrument, but badly used its consequences can be disastrous, causing unnecessary and sometimes irreparable damage. I was going to use the simile of the knife, but surely more than one by now will have crossed his mind.

What are those essential characteristics that we must take into account to make masterful use of such a delicate and sharp instrument?

First of all, the punishment has to be immediate. That is, when behavior occurs, punishment follows. The brain needs to make the correct association of what behavior is not to repeat. We are going to continue using the theme of couple relationships, which give us a lot of play. How do we feel when, when arguing about the famous extra salt in the food, we are scolded for that time we were late —by the way, something we have done on more occasions—, and for that comment in front of the mother of our partner? But what does one thing have to do with the other? Of course, we are not going to resolve the issue of salt by talking about other issues that have nothing to do with it. In either case, this "punishment" (something unpleasant is being administered to us) is supposed to resolve four behaviors at once. And that, unfortunately, it is one hundred percent ineffective. Better one by one and, as we have mentioned, immediately. If not, it is better to wait for another more opportune occasion.

The same thing happens with the education of our children. If we are going to take away their cell phone (negative punishment, because we take away something nice), let it be immediately after the behavior we intend to eliminate. If we do it three days later, the effect will be less or null.

A second characteristic of punishment is that it has to be proportionate. The problem is that when a behavior makes us angry (remember the chapter on anger management), depending on the type of thought that we associate, we can considerably vary the importance of what is happening, applying a punishment of the same size as the value that we put on it. we are bestowing, not the one you actually have. Let's go back to the example of the mobile with the child. At one point we are so angry because it has brought us two failures that, instead of applying a punishment for a few days or a week, we let out a bravado with the intention not only of eliminating a behavior, but of annihilating it: «Now you are not going to use mobile throughout the year!». For a whole year? This punishment is unreal, because the one who will not be able to comply with it in the first place will be the one who imposed it and, therefore, it is completely ineffective. It is preferable to apply small touches in which the brain understands exactly what is expected or not of it, than these enormities that sometimes only cause the laughter of those who listen to them. This is as ineffective as spending a fortnight without talking to your partner (withdraw something pleasant) when there is an anger. Or give voices (we manage something unpleasant) for any trifle. We must find another way to resolve disagreements, quickly, before love dies under these slabs of irrationality or mismanagement. than these enormities that sometimes only provoke the laughter of those who listen to them. This is as ineffective as spending a fortnight without talking to your partner (withdraw something pleasant) when there is an anger. Or give voices (we manage something unpleasant) for any trifle. We must find another way to resolve disagreements, quickly, before love dies under these slabs of irrationality or mismanagement. than these enormities that sometimes only provoke the laughter of those who listen to them. This is as ineffective as spending a fortnight without talking to your partner (withdraw something pleasant) when there is an anger. Or give voices (we manage something unpleasant) for any trifle. We must find another way to resolve disagreements, quickly, before love dies under these slabs of irrationality or mismanagement.

The third characteristic for punishment to fulfill its task of eliminating behaviors is that it must be sporadic. Again, when punishment is applied in a continuous, repetitive and sometimes harmful way, far from eliminating a behavior —which sometimes it does not achieve either—, it causes unnecessary resentment in those who are continually exposed to the administration of unpleasant stimuli, or to the withdrawal of pleasant stimuli. Thus, a child who is daily exposed to bad words, bad gestures, insults (administration of something unpleasant) and deprived of affectionate words, understanding and respect (withdrawal of something pleasant), will grow up with a fragile and weakened self-esteem that will not exactly facilitate the healthy path to self-knowledge and development. As with variable interval reinforcement, if we don't know when something we don't like is going to fall on us, or when something we like is going to be removed, just in case, we don't do it. And in this way we eliminate that behavior from our repertoire.

However, we must say that the optimal way to extinguish a behavior is, without a doubt, to ignore it. We have already seen the effect of the husband's indifference to his wife's kiss. And it will have the same effect on the child who, when thrown to the ground, is ignored by his mother and goes on her way. If he were to get aggressive and destroy things, then an immediate, proportionate punishment, at that time, would be most appropriate. When the brain sees that activating a series of resources does not achieve anything, it tries to find other more efficient ones. Perhaps the child will learn to ask for things in a more polite way, and the husband would gain much from just a wink or a complacent smile.

By the way, a suggestion before punishing our children that also contributes to their maturity process is that we explain to them what the punishments and reinforcements will consist of depending on their behavior. In this way, if they know that suspending two means they will not have a mobile phone for a week, they are the ones who decide if they want to have a mobile phone or not. Our desire is not to take it away, quite the contrary. We would be happy if they had it if they were able to organize their time to pass and to enjoy the mobile. If they bring two fails, we will understand that they did not want to have a cell phone that week because, if they had wanted to, they would have made an effort to pass. That is, not having a cell phone for a week, rather than the consequence of a negative punishment (withdrawal of something pleasant) imposed by us, it is from your decision not to have done what was necessary to enjoy it. Then the prayers and supplications are not worth it. They must learn to be responsible for their actions, especially when they already know the consequences. Trust me, you'll save yourself a lot of hassles and unnecessary discussions.

Next, I leave you with a summary that I hope you hang with a good couple of magnets on the fridge, as it helps us to change what we want from our repertoire; to educate our children; to strengthen our affective relationships, whether as a couple or as friends; to modulate behaviors that we dislike from colleagues or other people around us, etc. In short, to mold the person we want to be, along with the people we want to live with, according to our design.

Refuerzo ➜ Implantar conductas

Castigo ➜ Extinguir conductas ➜ { ➜ inmediato / ➜ proporcionado / ➜ esporádico }

(+) Positivo ➜ Administrar algo

(–) Negativo ➜ Retirar algo

R +: Implantar conductas administrando algo agradable para el sujeto

R –: Implantar conductas retirando algo desagradable para el sujeto

C +: Extinguir conductas administrando algo desagradable para el sujeto

C –: Extinguir conductas retirando algo agradable para el sujeto

Forma óptima de extinguir conductas ➜ **IGNORAR**

Forma óptima de implantar conductas ➜ **REFUERZO DE INTERVALO VARIABLE**

Avoiding the pandemics of the 21st century

The habits of each century brought their diseases, turning some of them into authentic epidemics: thus, when there was not enough hygiene, the plague spread; the lack of precautions in sexual relations brought, at one time, syphilis and, at another, AIDS; In the 21st century, the World Health Organization has declared obesity as one of the pandemics on which to intervene, as well as depression, anxiety and stress. All of them closely related to the psychological resources of the people who suffer from them.

As we mentioned when dealing with responsibility, when things go wrong it is more comfortable to blame external causes that prevent us from facing what we could avoid with our own individual resources.

Our health, physical and mental, is our business.

So that the kilos that we accumulate remain in the warehouse that corresponds to them: the supermarket

The subject of body weight is quite delicate and it must be taken into account that research is being carried out from practically all disciplines of science to provide solutions that may be definitive.

We are going to continue with our line of work, which consists of understanding the responses that our brain provides when it is in a given context. In this sense, the accumulation of fat in the body is an extraordinary strategy that has allowed human beings to survive the harshest conditions in their history on the planet. When food has been available, it has been taken directly from nature, but for times of scarcity, what better place to take it than incorporated into the body itself! This is an absolutely prodigious survival strategy.

In this sense, maintaining an adequate weight would depend on our ability to determine what corresponds in each context according to the circumstances: whether to wear the reserves or leave them in the supermarket. Our abilities to focus, analyze, make decisions and tolerate frustration must work properly so that food intake corresponds to the needs of a given moment and fulfills its function of facilitating our survival.

When the body needs to accumulate energy, it does so considering that these are transitory situations, since the foreseen food shortage will cause the deposits to be used in a short space of time. In this way, energy continues to be managed effectively, in a constant and balanced flow between what is required and what is used. We have already seen in the first chapters of this book that energy management is one of the strengths of our brain. And, in fact, when we correctly attend to its signals, it works with amazing perfection. But when we introduce conscious control and the automation of incorrect behaviors enunciated by irrational thoughts, then it is, as usual, when the pathologies begin to appear.

The study of the psychological resources involved in maintaining a correct body weight has been one of the objectives of some of the research that I myself have carried out at the Autonomous University of Madrid, based on the hypothesis that, except in medical cases diagnosed, the cause of the difficulties in maintaining a correct body weight was not found on the plate, nor in the supermarket nor in advertising, but in the content of what we think, what we feel and what, finally, , we decide to do: that is, inside our heads.

With food we have to have a more careful handling, since, as we have already seen, along with physical exercise and sex, they are the most powerful reinforcers for our brain, since they are behaviors that it needs to do, yes or yes. It will always want more, it is prepared to do so without limits... except if our reason gives it a little tug and says «Enough!». As always, in a good tone, because we must treat ourselves with the consideration we deserve.

We know that it is healthy to follow a varied diet, in which we eat vegetables, fruits, proteins, carbohydrates and fiber. What foods? The ones we like the most. Eating must be, above all, pleasure, not torture. There are some that, given their high energy content, we can eat from time to time and in moderate amounts, but we should not give the brain an absolute ban on eating them. Have you experienced what happens when this is done? When we tell the brain "there will be no more of this", the mechanism is triggered "because I have to start up my accumulation resources of that until further notice". If we tell him: "Don't worry, we'll find the right time to eat and enjoy it", he'll calm down quite a bit and wait for us to decide to give ourselves that little treat. But of course it won't trigger a series of extreme survival auto-resources that will push us into mass storage. More than anything, because it is a false alarm, because in reality if we like that food, at some point we will give ourselves the healthy pleasure of eating it. Why not be more consistent then? Are you one of those who likes sweets, but you should take them in moderation? It recovers, for example, one of the healthy customs of years ago, when cakes were bought for dessert for the family meal on Sunday and enjoyed as a family. Why not be more consistent then? Are you one of those who likes sweets, but you should take them in moderation? It recovers, for example, one of the healthy customs of years ago, when cakes were bought for dessert for the family meal on Sunday and enjoyed as a family. Why not be more consistent then? Are you one of those who likes sweets, but you should take them in moderation? It recovers, for example, one of the healthy customs of years ago, when cakes were bought for dessert for the family meal on Sunday and enjoyed as a family.

One of the sayings that it will not be difficult for us to remember about the measure of what to eat, of proven effectiveness in regards to health, is the one that says: "Eat breakfast like a king, eat like a prince and dine like a beggar ». The body needs more energy during the day than at night, but above all it has to be used in tasks that are not, precisely, having to deal with heavy digestions. If we were the managers of a bread factory, we would not put our workers to knead and put bars in the oven at the time they have to be distributing and distributing them.

Another way to reach the right weight is to return to good habits, such as eating calmly. When we sit at the table in a calm state, we are more aware of what we are eating and when our brain indicates that it has had enough. Two of the bad habits that we detect quite frequently are eating in a hurry and generating arguments at the table. Our body is doing something very important and that, in addition, it likes. Why not spend those little moments doing it with the resources we have to enjoy it and do it correctly?

In addition, and this is a personal note, I believe that we must recover the awareness that food is not "things" that we eat, but that absolutely everything that we are going to integrate into our organism has previously had its own life, be it vegetable or animal, and that in some cases it has also needed the work and knowledge of other people to reach us. For some, all this may not mean anything, but if it does, it will surely change the meaning of eating.

Finally, we have to move and put all that energy into circulation. In addition to the well-known benefits of aerobic exercise, you may have heard of "basal metabolism". To explain it in a simple way, it is the amount of energy that the body uses when it is at rest, that is, when we do nothing. And how does our brain use that energy when we do nothing? We are going to see another of those interesting activities that happen in our body and that we probably did not understand very well what it consisted of.

Our body invests all its energy in maintaining the smooth muscles (liver, intestines, kidneys...) and striated muscles (extremities...), which must always be in optimal conditions so that we can move and thus achieve our goals. Do you know how much energy the body spends on stored fat deposits? Zero. The energy goes into the pantry, and only goes there to get it out. Just as we do with what we put in the pantry of our house, we only turn on the light when we go to look for something. The rest of the time it is off. For this reason, many of the people who are morbidly obese or simply overweight have a large volume, but very little muscle, so they need very few calories for maintenance. If they overeat, they will continue to accumulate calories endlessly. Secondly, In these cases, the ability to move and to generate muscle mass decreases, which would force, precisely, to increase energy consumption for its maintenance. For the same reason, people who are pure fiber can eat more, since their body, when at rest, will be using large amounts of energy to maintain all that muscle in optimal conditions, with practically no need to store anything anywhere. Deposit.

From psychological tools, it is very important that we learn to say no and change certain ideas about food. Going to a restaurant or to dinner at a friend's house does not mean "permission granted" to eat without limits or to see ourselves obliged to finish everything they put on us. In that case we are transferring the control of what we are going to eat to the circumstances, or to other people, and that, in the end, especially if the consequences are harmful to us, is very frustrating and considerably separates us from our objectives and, why not to say, of our self-esteem. Not so much because of the accumulated kilos, but because of our inability to treat ourselves properly. We cannot always be satisfying the needs of others without attending to our own. And being overweight is a big enough reason for us to learn to say no. You already know what the "house brand" is: good vibes and giving thanks, if possible. But not.

It's also important to practice one of the tools we saw in previous chapters: the thought stop. When we are trying to modify our weight, the best thing we can do is not to constantly think about food. You don't have to think about her. Spot. Stop thinking and focus on another goal. In this way, if when it comes to the mid-afternoon cookie, we have not thought about it, it will be easier for us to eat only the one that corresponds to us: one. But if we have thought hundreds or thousands of times about the mid-afternoon cookie, when it comes time to take it, the brain will try to ingest something similar to what it has been visualizing (remember how important images are for our brain? And how is he usually coherent in thought and action?). Managing this instrument well is much more effective and cheaper than anything else we ingest. It is true that you have to practice and strengthen the stop of thought and focus, but it is just one more exercise of the table that we probably have to do.

When food is "emotional", we will review the chapter on the effective management of emotions: are we eating due to impulses that do not correspond to hunger? What are we feeling: anger, sadness, fear? In general, food is an instant way for the body to induce a state of relaxation. If we are not able to relax on our own, we gorge ourselves on eating — remember that it is a reinforcing activity for the brain— and the consequence will undoubtedly be a feeling of drowsiness due to the digestion process. One of the causes may be the activation produced by anger, which requires an action that facilitates venting and, if it is also reinforcing, much better. In the short term, the consequences are wonderful, but in the medium and long term they produce deep frustration, regret, self-reproach and low self-esteem that must be prevented from undermining the foundations of our state of mind. Identifying the emotion, managing it and, above all, sticking to the rule of eating calmly will help us doubly: on the one hand, to solve the problem that is really bothering us and, on the other, to properly manage the food we eat.

Health is in food, and so is disease. Once again, the decision and effective management of our kilos are in our minds, not on our plates.

The lifestyle generated by the obligations that we have created for ourselves can lead us to states of extreme concern, sometimes disproportionate to reality, so that we can perceive it as a threat and cause a rather unpleasant emotional state. This disproportion even affects the ability to distinguish what is real in our concern, and where the imagined or fabled begins.

There are other factors that can trigger anxiety, such as high consumption of caffeine, certain medications, drugs or alcohol, or some diseases such as those related to the thyroid gland or respiratory problems. Some are more controllable than others; We will focus mainly on those that have their origin in our way of interpreting reality, so that at least to the extent that it is in our hands, we do not make it easier for anxiety to make an appearance in our lives.

Not all people generate a state of anxiety in the face of worries, since it is a very subjective personal experience, which has to do with negative past experiences, or with learning styles in which the model indicated negative connotations about the past, the present and future. Anxiety appears when, in the face of normal concerns related to important issues, such as work, health, children, etc., what has been learned interferes, generating perceived threats that rarely have anything to do with reality.

It is possible that in some situations in which we feel fear or stress, anxiety responses are triggered, but they are not exactly the same. Anxiety will be directly related to negative, disproportionate or unrealistic thoughts associated with situations in which we do not know what we have to do (fear) or in which we have to attend to multiple responsibilities with a certain degree of difficulty (stress). But not everyone who is in situations of fear or stress has anxiety.

The best way to prevent it is to learn to modify our irrational thoughts, as we explained in the corresponding chapter. States of anxiety, except in the cases we have mentioned above, are the consequence of an interpretation, that is, of specific thoughts, about our past, present and future.

To walk to the edge of the precipice of depression without being pushed into the abyss

I want to clarify from this first line that there are depressions of endogenous origin (from the interior) that are caused by physiological conditions, some even of unknown origin. And I want to take this opportunity to pay my respects to all those patients I have had the privilege of dealing with, with whom I have traveled through these arid landscapes of depression, and who have shown me that this was not the place they wanted to go, not even in the that they wanted to be, but that they had no choice but to endure, against their will. You have all my admiration and affection, and, if you are reading these lines, you will know exactly who you are. We keep fighting together.

However, it has become one of the pandemics of the 21st century, not so much because of irrefutable medical issues, but because of cognitive and emotional styles that, inevitably, lead us to this pathology. Martin Seligman, who provided us with one of the theoretical frameworks for the study and treatment of depression, that of learned helplessness, described the cognitive structure of people who suffer from it as "whatever you do, it's useless; I am unable to control myself, the circumstances and their consequences, positive or negative. Why do anything? Consequently, there is a loss of energy in 97% of the cases studied by him, sleep disorders (in 80%), anxiety (in 90%), appetite disorders, sexual disorders, etc.

When we talk about control, we do so in the positive sense of the word. We have already seen how we like, as children, to be aware of the ability we have to influence the environment, ourselves and others according to our will. It is the opposite of impotence. Like everything, it has a limit beyond which it becomes manipulation and perversity. If you want to delve into these issues, I recommend the book Moral Harassment, by the French psychiatrist Marie-France Hirigoyen, an essential that everyone should read.

We can control:

• Our actions.
• Our way of living.
• Our behavior with others.
• How we make a living.

How we think we can do it can enhance or reduce our ultimate ability to implement it. We generate irrational expectations that, when they are not met, make us angry and sad, but, in addition, we usually lack the necessary calm to restructure those thoughts and give them a format that helps us contemplate alternative solutions and set new goals more in line with the reality. We get into loops of negativity that, far from propelling us into the future, bore our lives into an endless pit.

I can put my hand in the fire without fear of being wrong that more than one of you who are reading these lines will have gone through vital circumstances in which you will have felt that you were walking on the edge of the precipice of depression, to which life seemed to be pushing you due to multiple circumstances. Appropriate habits of thought and behavior have probably enabled you to remain sane on the edge of the abyss.

Do you know what you have to do to climb to the top of the pyramids of Chichen Itza, to climb to the top of a mountain or to cross a suspension bridge? The key is to always look up. If we remember the chapter dedicated to attention, surely it is not necessary for us to repeat here what mechanisms are set in motion in our brain so that, regardless of the circumstances in which we find ourselves, we always have an advantageous way out. And the first is a positive goal to which to direct our action and our movements.

Therefore, I suggest that you put into practice what you have seen in the chapter on managing thoughts, how to stop them, how to focus them, how to maintain motivation and how to create attractive images; the management of emotions, decision making, internal dialogue and the importance of maintaining good physical exercise, sleep and eating habits.

Thus, if the depression pushes, it will not be stronger than you.

So that our defenses are not engulfed by the all-devouring stress

Stress is the result of exposure to various difficult situations that are not easy for us to handle fluently, sometimes due to ignorance and others due to overload.

We want to do everything and, in addition, well. We have to be good professionals, dedicate endless hours to our jobs and earn good salaries; we have to take care of our children's homework (surely I don't have to mention to you, on the one hand, the amount and, on the other, the modern obligation of having to sit down to do it with them), their leisure time (children no longer go out to street to play with their friends and hardly ever with their neighbors), their sports activities and their daily habits (in a short space of time, from when we get home from work until we go to bed, they have to do their homework, take a shower , dinner and, of course, we must read them a story). And the couple's relationship? Languishing in some corner of our affectivity, since we only have a few minutes and little energy left.

There is a stress that is very, very positive. It is the spark that gets us going and lights the fuse so that we do a lot of activities. Pathology always appears when we exceed certain limits or make inappropriate steps. The natural state of the body, in which oxygen and blood flow through every cell in the body to adequately nourish it, is that of relaxation. The stress maintained over hours, months and even years generates blockages and obstacles (such as contractures) that cause wear and tear on the body, which has no choice but to pull everything it can until it settles: psoriasis , hair loss, body hair, irritable bowel, stomach ulcers and endless ailments that could be avoided if we just changed our lifestyle,

We barely give ourselves time to let our minds go blank, as happens when we look at the sea or walk through nature. Go out to your office window and stare at the sky for a few minutes and take a deep breath. Exhale forcefully and unblock your entire body and your thoughts. Stress is a bottleneck that makes us highly manipulable, since we barely have time to reflect and make the right decisions.

stop Take your time. Nothing is that important. You do not deserve any of the diseases that stress will cause you. The goal of your life is health and well-being. Breathe and think if this is what you wanted, and if there is something you can and should do to change it.

Happiness, too, is an experience of delight when we are able to stop time.

Fourth part

No one is going to live your life for you

Life as a personal and non-transferable experience

How good the word life sounds together with experience, personal and non-transferable! Of course, we want everything that living implies to be an experience that resonates throughout our bodies, that fulfills our aspirations and that, in the end, has meaning and has served a purpose. And let it be "ours".

We associate the fact of living our life, and in our own way, with the beautiful idea of freedom and happiness. In fact, we would not understand freedom without the ability to live according to our tastes and aspirations, and be happy. And we would not understand happiness without a good dose of freedom to live it. Three concepts that resonate in harmony, intertwine, feed off each other and form a perfect combination. However, we still lack a basic ingredient for all of them to have a consistent foundation.

We have already talked about the responsibility of assuming the consequences of our actions. And to the extent that we understand the authorship of our thoughts, our emotions, and our attitudes and behaviors, the essence of what our vital experience actually consists of, whether we like it or not, is revealed to us: loneliness. Oh! But are we going to talk about this? », You are probably wondering. I would do it. In fact, it is the concept that must be clear when we try to address all our psychological and mental processes, since they refer only to us, and from there to their relationship with those around us. I understand that being as we are, a fundamentally social species, the term, a priori, is not very attractive to us, although there are exceptions to everything. What produces deep unease to many, seems to others an unattainable reality. They can't wait to be alone and finally be able to do what they think is best. But I would like us to take the opportunity, once again, and as we have already done with other concepts throughout this book, such as emotions or errors, to understand that all those instruments that are usually categorized as "negative" are not so in reality. absolute. Quite the contrary, understanding their nature and managing them properly is the real key for us to live that life to our measure that we so long for. and as we have already done with other concepts throughout this book, such as emotions or errors, understand that all those instruments that are usually categorized as "negative" are not so at all. Quite the contrary, understanding their nature and managing them properly is the real key for us to live that life to our measure that we so long for. and as we have already done with other concepts throughout this book, such as emotions or errors, understand that all those instruments that are usually categorized as "negative" are not so at all. Quite the contrary, understanding their nature and managing them properly is the real key for us to live that life to our measure that we so long for.

Now let's look around us for a moment: all the people around us are living their lives alone, whether they are aware of it or not, just like us. Each one is fighting their own battles, surviving and wanting to discover where the best of themselves and of life is. We are all immersed in our processes of learning, maturation and, finally, fullness and satisfaction.

For those who find it difficult to integrate this concept, the best way to analyze it is to think of extreme situations, such as birth or death. The latter may be happening simultaneously to millions of people, and yet each one will be experiencing theirs in their own way, and in an act of deep intimacy with themselves: what we decide to do at that moment will depend on our internal dialogue and how we have understood our vital experience. And although we have spent our lives allowing others to make decisions on our behalf, no one can pass on to a better life in our place. We do not remember the moment of birth, but, without a doubt, that first cry after cutting the umbilical cord was our first act in solitude. How sad it sounds! TRUE...? Or not?

Loneliness forces us to look at ourselves in the mirror and understand that we have to be the best travel companion for this adventure, from start to finish. It is loneliness that allows us to affirm "my life is mine!", and begin to assume the responsibility of taking care of ourselves, of loving ourselves, of understanding ourselves, of experiencing ourselves and of getting where we want in the way we decide. There is nothing! The other option seems much sadder to me: letting others design our route plan. That said, everyone has the right to be happy in the way they choose: from consciousness or from unconsciousness; from the responsibility or from the apparent comfort of being in tow of whoever pulls us.

The fear of loneliness can lead us to make somewhat unwise decisions, such as pairing up with the first person who walks by —anyone goes— and then expecting them to become who we would like them to be. I suppose that by now you are capable of analyzing the succession of irrationalities that are chained in this behavior that, by the way, has a large number of followers. Loneliness is experienced as an experience of deep restlessness, instead of the tranquility from which we project who we really are outwards.

Once we understand that we are all alone, we are in a position to understand each other better, to respect differences and individual decisions, to accept the states of mind of our interlocutor, and to interact on equal terms.

We could define loneliness as a process:

- Inevitable. Whether we like it or not, loneliness and life are inseparable. By accompanying us throughout the life experience, it is not strange that we have to face her at critical moments, such as illness, bankruptcy or a sentimental breakup. Actually, it's a good place to start putting yourself back together with some foundation.
- Constant. Absolutely each and every one of our thoughts, emotions and behaviors are acts of loneliness, even if we are in the company of other people.

- Necessary. Our solitude is the laboratory where we develop our most intimate desires, our illusions and our projects. It allows us to take control of our lives and decide with whom we want to live it.

The fact that life is a solitary experience does not at all mean that we have to live it alone. Moreover, the human being is a social species, which owes its survival to the work it does in a group, to the support they receive from each other and to the perfect team they form, reciprocally taking care of the different needs. The doctor is as necessary as the plumber, the carpenter or the engineer, the dancer or the comedian. We are all pieces of a perfect gear. The important thing is that we have the ability to decide who we want to be in this complex puzzle, and be able to contribute the best that we have inside.

It is logical that we abhor imposed solitude, but not chosen and sporadic solitude. In fact, learning to experience healthy loneliness allows us to avoid the unpleasant loneliness that comes with a lack of support, friends, or social isolation.

Life is simultaneously an experience of solitude and mutual support, in which we all take care of individual and group needs.

Let's see, then, what are the advantages of assuming our vital experience as a process of healthy solitude that allows us...

- Recognize the authorship of our decisions.
- Correct our mistakes without the need to blame anyone.
- Do not feel guilty for mistakes that do not correspond to us.
- Model our life to our liking.
- Experience our autonomy and freedom.
- Being able to make our life a happy experience.
- Being able to make our best travel companions happy.

When we learn to positively manage loneliness, we are also in better conditions to avoid precisely everything that we dislike so much as...

- Feel isolated. Without a doubt, we will be able to identify more clearly when we need to be with other people and we will have no problem going out to meet them.
- Feeling that we have no friends. Looking for people related to our way of being will be the best of our experiences. At the end of the day, what we will have left in the end will be the quality of relationships that we have been able to build.
- Suffer from superficiality in relationships. Feeling that we can trust is one of the most pleasant sensations we can experience, but it takes a certain degree of depth. Once we know how to identify who suits us and who doesn't, it will be easier to achieve that feeling of fullness and well-being.
- $ $$ Fall into emotional hooks. Our happiness is our own business and we cannot leave it in the hands of other people, nor should we allow someone to make us responsible for what legitimately belongs only to him or her. Suppress dependencies, own and others.
- Suffer unreasonable demands. No more asking for the moon or being asked for it. It is better to walk the path together.

In short, the path to happiness passes inexorably through the understanding of loneliness itself, seasoned with the best company we can provide ourselves.

Solitude is that cozy room from which we design and experience our lives. In reality, our loneliness is us in its purest form.

12.

Taking the bull by the horns: responsibility

On the podium of the aspects that are most difficult for us to manage consciously, in addition to the ability to accept mistakes and make decisions, shares honors with the ability to take responsibility for our thoughts, our feelings, our actions and, ultimately, our life.

We live in the dichotomy of leaving it in the hands of other people, while pretending to be happy with what others decide for us. And this, to be honest, I find very, very difficult. I think that, although some people don't like the word responsibility too much, it makes the path to self-realization and happiness much easier. At least, to that of conscious happiness.

If you are reading these lines and you consider yourself responsible people, you may like this brief review that we are going to do to the concept of responsibility, because sometimes, with good intentions, we can be doing other things.

Once again, let us remember that we are not born being responsible or irresponsible, nor is it something that "happens", or that is acquired over the years. Responsibility is a behavior that is learned and that is indicative of our degree of maturity, which, by the way, does not depend on age.

Furthermore, responsibility is by no means synonymous with seriousness, boredom, or seriousness. The sense of humor that the irresponsible person has to resort to so that his environment swallows the little pills of his immaturity has nothing to do with it and is much more tiresome than that used by the person who knows how to make others pass pleasant moments and light of unnecessary loads.

We have already mentioned just a few lines ago the first step to becoming responsible people: understanding that what we think, feel and do is one hundred percent homegrown. And when we detect what is not, have the ability to replace it with what seems most convenient and appropriate for our personal project.

The second and logical step is to accept the consequences of what we do, whether we like it or not. If they occur after careful decision-making, we will undoubtedly be in optimal conditions to assume what happens. One of the characteristics that describe responsible people is that they accept their mistakes and take care of what is necessary so that they do not happen again.

Let's talk a little about irresponsibility

An important point about irresponsibility is that we tend to associate it with those who do not do what they should do and, finally, force other people to deal with it. A classic would be the colleague who leaves certain tasks assigned to him unfinished, and has to be continually replaced by the rest of the team. Coexistence, both professional and personal, with these people usually ends up boring, exhausting, and generating conflicts and distance, especially if they tend to blame others, or if they use blackmail in the name of love or friendship to take care of others of what they should do.

There are other reasons for shirking responsibilities: finding yourself in a particularly difficult situation or lacking—or believing so—sufficient skills to deal with it. On some occasions, it will not be particularly serious and it will not be difficult for us to find, for example, someone to sew the buttons on our shirt. But in significant situations, such as when we have children or we are going to take the step of getting married, it is better to fully understand the implications of the steps we are going to take and, ultimately, the responsibilities that they will entail. If we are not ready for it, or it is not the right time, the most responsible action is not to commit if it is not yet appropriate.

We can also help in cases where it is possible to address the situation, creating spaces in which the other person feels safe and can develop skills for personal growth. Suppose, for example, that one of our subordinates at work is not doing a task that he has been asked to solve. There is the possibility that he does not know how and that is why he is giving the long walk that is irritating us so much. In this case, far from reproaching uselessly, we can sit down and talk with that person, create a climate of trust in which what is being detected is described and in which they can express in which points they recognize that they do not have the skills to solve what is being detected. has asked you, and thus create the best conditions to indicate the resources you need, allowing you to take care of it at all times,

As we have already mentioned before, there are people for whom the term responsibility is a bit jarring, as they associate it with loss of freedom or not doing what they most want at all times. In fact, in this book we are advocating that each one do what satisfies him the most, provided that he has made a detailed analysis of what is required for it and the consequences that it will have. If everything is correct, then go ahead! Stopping what we don't like (let's remember negative reinforcement) is very pleasant, but it is even more so if its consequences, especially in the long term, are positive. But this is not what usually happens in the case of irresponsibility. Now let's return to the decision-making process: it is usual to opt for plan B, in which short-term positive consequences and long-term negative ones prevail. If, for example, we have agreed with our partner that on Wednesdays and Fridays we take care of the food and, when those days come, we don't do it, and we look for a sweet way for our partner to take care of it, short term we will feel very good: we have gotten away with it. But the day our partner—tired, bored, and disappointed—tells us (in the long run): "Look, there you are," we probably won't like the consequences so much. in the short term we will feel very good: we have gotten away with it. But the day our partner—tired, bored, and disappointed—tells us (in the long run): "Look, there you are," we probably won't like the consequences so much. in the short term we will feel very good: we have gotten away with it. But the day our partner—tired, bored, and disappointed—tells us (in the long run): "Look, there you are," we probably won't like the consequences so much.

This same example serves to illustrate one more form of irresponsibility, which consists in not accepting one's own mistakes, surely because it is painful and humiliating, and, instead of feeling what corresponds to that moment, we anesthetize it by pointing an accusing finger towards other side. How? The day our partner tells us that he is leaving, instead of understanding that he had already told us about it on multiple occasions, then he had gotten angry, later he had reproached us and, finally, he has thrown in the towel with all reason, we jump indignantly saying: "You don't love me anymore... You have looked for another person". I mean, it's your fault. Without a doubt, a nice icing on a lackluster cake.

The modalities used by irresponsible people to transfer their responsibilities to others can range from despotic imposition, such as "you do it because I tell you to, period", to a very subtle form that probably will be very familiar to more than one of us: the consented futility. Yes, consented by the other person. Let's continue with the example of the Wednesday and Friday meals, still in the phase in which the couple was still together. "Oh, today it burned me." "I went over salt." "I forgot to defrost it." "I fried it in a pot instead of a frying pan." "I didn't know that cannelloni stick in boiling water." And a long etcetera, until our partner tells us: "Come on, I'll do it." Mission accomplished... For now. We have already seen one of the possible endings of this story—"I am leaving"—,

- "Don't worry, honey, you'll see how one of these days you'll end up doing it like a great professional. Don't worry about me, in the meantime I can eat the twelve macaroni that are stuck together with a knife and fork. The sauce, by the way, turned out delicious." That is, encourage the other to try until it works out and learns, as we have all done.
- «It has occurred to me that, since cooking is not my thing, and I don't see signs that I will ever make something really edible, what do you think if I take care of taking out the garbage every day [or hanging the washing machine or taking the dog for a run in the morning]?» If cooking is really not your thing, why not suggest to your partner a change for another activity that she is assuming and that you would willingly do?

And we are still going to raise one more situation, which has to do with the management of emotions and communication. Let's continue with our example of task sharing. We have already seen that there is one of the members who has every reason to feel annoyed or even quite angry, and one day he raises his voice and even insults his partner. Although the justification will be given by what the other person is not doing and it should have been, in this case it is important that we assume that each one is responsible for the tone of voice they decide to use, the words they use, and the moment and the manner in which it is said, regardless of the circumstances in which the conflict is taking place. We are not screaming «because you...», we are doing it «because I can't take it anymore...», «because I'm fed up...», «because I don't know how to say it anymore...».

Kindness or well-intentioned irresponsibility?

We are seeing a form of irresponsibility that consists in not doing what corresponds to each one, and there is still a second one that consists in taking care of what does not correspond to one.

This way of acting can be understood in two ways:

- As an unacceptable invasion. Imagine that we are carrying out our work assignment and we have a colleague who is always in charge of doing our thing. His motives may be that he wants to make merits, that it serves as an excuse not to do something that he likes less or that he considers us to be truly inept. Whatever the case, it is inadmissible behavior that we must eradicate as soon as possible. This example is also applicable to cases in which someone forces you to take care of your money (quite common in a couple), or other matters that, if they have any legal implication, we must take up with full responsibility, whether the other person likes it or not. No.
- As an exercise in well-intentioned kindness. Sometimes it seems to us a "gesture of love" that someone takes care of what is not theirs. Responsibility supposes autonomy in all senses, physically and psychologically speaking.

A large part of the goal of educating our children is for them to be able to become autonomous adults: to earn their money, to form their own family, to make their own decisions and, logically, to live their lives to the fullest and with satisfaction. If we don't do it this way, we will be generating insecure adults, frustrated and with a load of anger (not aggressiveness, mind you!), towards us perfectly justified: «Why didn't you let me do it? Why didn't you teach me how to do it if you already knew? Why have you forced me to depend on you?». It is not pleasant to feel useless when life brings us its difficulties. However, when someone accompanies us in our learning and teaches us to be autonomous and responsible, we feel deeply grateful,

When we care for our elderly in their old age, we try to ensure that they maintain their degree of autonomy in each of their capacities as long as possible. They want to feel useful and capable, and that feeling brings them great well-being. Their mood plummets when we begin, with all our good intentions, to take care of everything that they are still in a position to do perfectly, or to the extent of their abilities.

One of the disadvantages of someone assuming responsibilities that do not correspond to them is that, sooner or later, they usually present some kind of bill: either in the form of emotional blackmail ("with what I have done for you"), or in form of psychological abuse ("I gave it to you and now I demand that you return it to me"). As we can see, we are already far away from what at first seemed like acts of kindness.

In any case, it is important to understand that we are not really doing anyone a favor, nor are we better people, when we take on the responsibilities that correspond to others who are in perfect conditions to assume them for themselves. Quite the contrary, we are standing in the way of your path to happiness. True kindness is support, not substitution.

Finally, a special warning, especially for all those people who are strong, decisive, generous and autonomous, as they tend to have a certain tendency to carry their own and others' on their backs. Everything has a limit that we must not exceed.

Let's learn to apologize elegantly and effectively

The topic of forgiveness is usually quite tricky and we will find multiple theories about it.

It seems appropriate to point out at this time that in nature the phenomenon of regression to the mean usually occurs, that is, a return to balance, which is where the sensation of well-being is produced. Imbalances, thanks to which we advance, are a stimulating challenge, but fullness comes to us with balance.

Once we have eliminated from our repertoire the prejudice by which admitting a mistake is inadmissible or humiliating, knowing how to ask for forgiveness can make us grow exponentially before those to whom we have unconsciously caused harm or harm. If we do it correctly, what will be perceived of us is that we are taking into account the feelings of others, that we are willing to introduce the appropriate changes and that there is the will to maintain a relationship, of whatever type, on the best terms.

To ask for forgiveness, we must assume responsibility for anything that has happened as a result of our conduct, accepting reality, whether we like it or not.

The best way to ask for forgiveness is to repair the damage we caused and leave it, if possible, in better condition than when we found it.

There are people who solve it in an extraordinary way and they usually do it in the following way:

- First, they describe the scenario in which they believe or know for certain that the offense, harm or harm has occurred ("Look, yesterday when I insulted you that way at the meeting…").
- Second, they understand why, how, when and where they have hurt ("I guess you felt really bad because my anger had nothing to do with you directly, although I took advantage of your mistake to unload the bad mood I had…") .
- Third, they present what we call a heartfelt and sincere proposal to amend ("I'm going to try to make sure it doesn't happen again, but if you see that I don't notice, I'd like you to let me know. However, at the next meeting I'll ask you to apologies in front of everyone who was present at the previous one").

This sequence is very far from the typical ones that we already know and that we like so little of "but if it was a joke, how do you get on!"; «Yes, yes, will you forgive me?»; or "I don't have to ask for forgiveness", so proven ineffective. And its consequences are infinitely better.

I would just like to make one final reflection: before demanding that the damaged person forgive the person who attacked them, let us have the courage to ask the person who caused the damage to correct it. It is fairer and, without a doubt, much more balanced. And the brain understands it much better.

The good vibes that responsibility provides

Somewhere we already commented on the perfect compatibility between responsibility and sense of humor. When one is responsible for his actions, one can laugh, calmly, even at his shadow. Total, it is his, so he will decide the best way to manage it.

When we are surrounded by responsible people and we are also responsible, life becomes a much easier, pleasant, bearable and fun experience. Even if it is only for the fact of removing the psychological burdens that guilt, unnecessary overloads or unpaid bills entail, it is worth the effort to take our life where it has to be done: because of the resources that, fortunately, we carry in our brain. A place very close to the horns, yes, but not exactly the same.

Life becomes an absolutely pleasant journey when, at the same time, we assume our responsibilities, we allow each one of us to manage their own and, finally, we share them in an exercise of balance that is beneficial for all.

Epilogue

Say goodbye with our best smile. living is worth it

Cycles of life and death occur in all living beings, on all biological scales. Our body is made up of small cells and other elementary particles that have a complete biological cycle, with their date of birth and probable death. Each one of them has to take care of their own life and this depends on the instructions that are marked genetically, and also by our habits. Our brain is the little god of all those little living beings on whose management their survival depends. And we are not an exception. But we are not even aware that this is going on all the time inside us.

Farewells should always be short. What we have done is done, and the end will only seem happy to us if we give authentic meaning to all our actions, if we feel that we never betrayed ourselves, even if we could be wrong, and if we knew how to surround ourselves with people who really loved us, whose well-being we contribute, thereby making ourselves happy.

I think this is the moment in the book in which I can recognize —but, please, let it stay between us—, so that everything does not sound like pastelón and absurd happiness, that a few years ago I visualized that moment of farewell with a wide smile , yes, but it was because it was accompanied by a good sleeve cutting at the last minute. So I shared it with my good friend Lord Kermitt, who didn't exactly have more constructive ideas than mine. And we laughed a lot, for a long time. Life was hard and potatoes had to be peeled. One was alive because he was not dead.

What I want to say, in the end, is that we have not only the permission, but the obligation to get angry, to laugh, to cry, to despair and to get up again. Without all these emotions in their proper dose and management, there is no possible path to happiness.

I must not go back on what was promised. Farewells should be short. Just to tell you that it has been a real pleasure for me to share these pages of experience and, to the extent that they are useful to some of you, I will take a portion of my heart full of satisfaction and gratitude.

And, please, once again, do not deprive yourself —or us— of the opportunity to enjoy yourself as you are.

Don't take life too seriously; you will never get out of it alive.

ELBERT HUBBARD

Bibliography

Álava Reyes, MJ, The futility of suffering, Madrid, The Sphere of Books, 2010.

—, The psychology that helps us live, Madrid, La Esfera de los Libros, 2011.

—, Recover the illusion, Madrid, La Esfera de los Libros, 2013.

Bachevalier, J., and Mishkin, M., "Visual recognition impairment follows ventromedial but not dorsolateral prefrontal lesions in monkeys," in Behavioral brain research 20(3), 1986, pp. 249-261.

Baddeley, AD, Human Memory: Theory and Practice, Madrid, McGraw-Hill, 1999.

Baron, R., Psychology, Mexico, Prentice-Hall Hispanoamericana, 1996.

Benne, Kenneth D.; and Sheats, P., "Functional roles of group members," in Journal of Social Issues, Vol. 4(2), 1948, pp. 41-49.

Branden, N., The psychology of self-esteem, Barcelona, Paidós, 2012.

Cahue, M., Good Love, Madrid, JdeJ Editores and Communication Attitude, 2014.

Cahue, M.; and others, Tales to eat without stories, Madrid, La Esfera de los Libros, 2007.

Cart, L.; and Iglesias, J., Psychophysiology: methodological foundations, Madrid, Pirámide, 2000.

Correas, G., The company and its protocol, Oviedo, Protocol, 2004.

Coast, P.; and McCrae, R., "Influence of extraversion and neuroticism on subjective well-being: happy and unhappy people," in Journal Of Personality and Social Psychology, vol. 38, no. 4, 1990, pp. 668-678.

Coué, E., La Méthode Coué, Paris, Nouvelles Editions Marabout, 2009.

Dale, E., Audiovisual methods in teaching, third edition, New York: The Dryden Press, Holt, Rinehart and Winston, 1969.

Damasio, A., In search of Spinoza, Barcelona, Crítica, 2007.

Diener, E., International College Alumni Survey, Urbana Champaign, University of Illinois, 2001.

Diener, E.; and Diener, M., "Cross-cultural correlates of life satisfaction and self-steem," in Journal of Personality and Social Psychology, vol. 68, 1995, pp. 653-663.

Diener, E.; Suh, E.; Lucas, R.; and Smith, H., "Subjective well-being: three decades of progress," in Psychological Bulletin, vol. 125, no. 2, 1999, pp. 276-302.

Diges, M., The false memories, Barcelona, Paidós, 1997.

Domjan, M.D., Bases of learning and conditioning, Jaén, Del Lunar, 1998.

Freud, S., Instincts and their Vicissitudes, Standard Edition, Vol. 14, London: Hogarth Press and the Institute of Psychoanalysis, 1915.

Fuente, C., Techniques for organizing events, Oviedo, Protocol, 2004.

Sources, N.; and Rojas, M., "Economic theory and subjective well-being Mexico," in Social Indicators Research, no. 53, March 3, 2001, pp. 289-314.

Hewstone, M.; and others,Introduction to social psychology: a European perspective, Barcelona, Ariel, 1993.

Hewstone, M.; Stroebe, W.; Codol, J.; and Stephenson, GM, Introduction to social psychology: a European perspective, Barcelona, Ariel, 1993.

Huertas, JA, Motivation, Buenos Aires, Aique, 2000.

Hirigoyen, M. F, Moral harassment, Barcelona, Paidós, 2013.

Jáuregui, E., The sense of humor, Barcelona, RBA, 2007.

Kandel, ER; Schwartz, JH; and Jesell, TM, Neuroscience and behavior, Madrid, Prentice Hall, 1997.

Loftus, E.; and Ketcham, K., The Myth of Repressed Memory, New York: St. Martin's Press, 1994.

Seligman, M., Learn optimism, Barcelona, Debolsillo, 2004.

McKay, M.; and Fanning, P., Self-esteem: evaluation and improvement, Madrid, Martínez Roca, 1991.

Montorio, I.; and Izal, M., Psychological intervention in old age, Madrid, Síntesis, 2000.

Morales, JF; and others, Social Psychology, Madrid, McGraw-Hill, 1997.

Moreland, R.L.; and Levine, JM Newcomers and oldtimers in small groups, 1989.

Pichon-Rivière, E., The group process. From psychoanalysis to social psychology, Buenos Aires, Ed. New Vision, 1975.

Pinker, S., The language instinct, Madrid, Alianza, 1995.

Reeve, J., Motivation and emotion, Madrid, McGrawHill, 1994.

Ruiz-Vargas, JM, Human memory: function and structure, Madrid, Alianza, 1994.

—, Keys to memory, Madrid, Trotta, 1997.

Sacks, O.The man who mistook his wife for a hat, Barcelona, Muchnik, 1987.

Sachter, D.L.; and Tulving, E., Memory Systems, Cambridge, MA, The MIT Press, 1994.

Tanori, B.Psychometric properties of an instrument to measure subjective well-being in the Sonoran population: an ethnopsychological approach, unpublished thesis, Universidad de Sonora, 2000.

Tarpy, RM, Basic principles of learning, Barcelona, Debate, 1993.

Tierno, B., The psychologist at home, Madrid, Topics of Today, 1997.

—,Everything you need to know to educate your children, Barcelona, Grijalbo, 2003.

Triandis, HC, "Self and Social Behavior in Differing Cultural Contexts," in Psychological Review, no. 96, 1989, pp. 269-289.

University of Sonora,Institutional Development Plan, 2001-2005, 2001.

Vera, J., «Subjective well-being in a sample of university students», in Revista Intercontinental de Psicología, vol. 3, no. 1, 2001, pp. 11-21.

Vera, J.; and Tánori, B., «Psychometric properties of an instrument to measure subjective well-being in the Mexican population», in Notes on Psychology, vol. 20, no. 1, 2002.

Weiner, B., Theories of Motivation: From Mechanism to Cognition, Chicago: Markham, 1972.

Lóbulos del cerebro

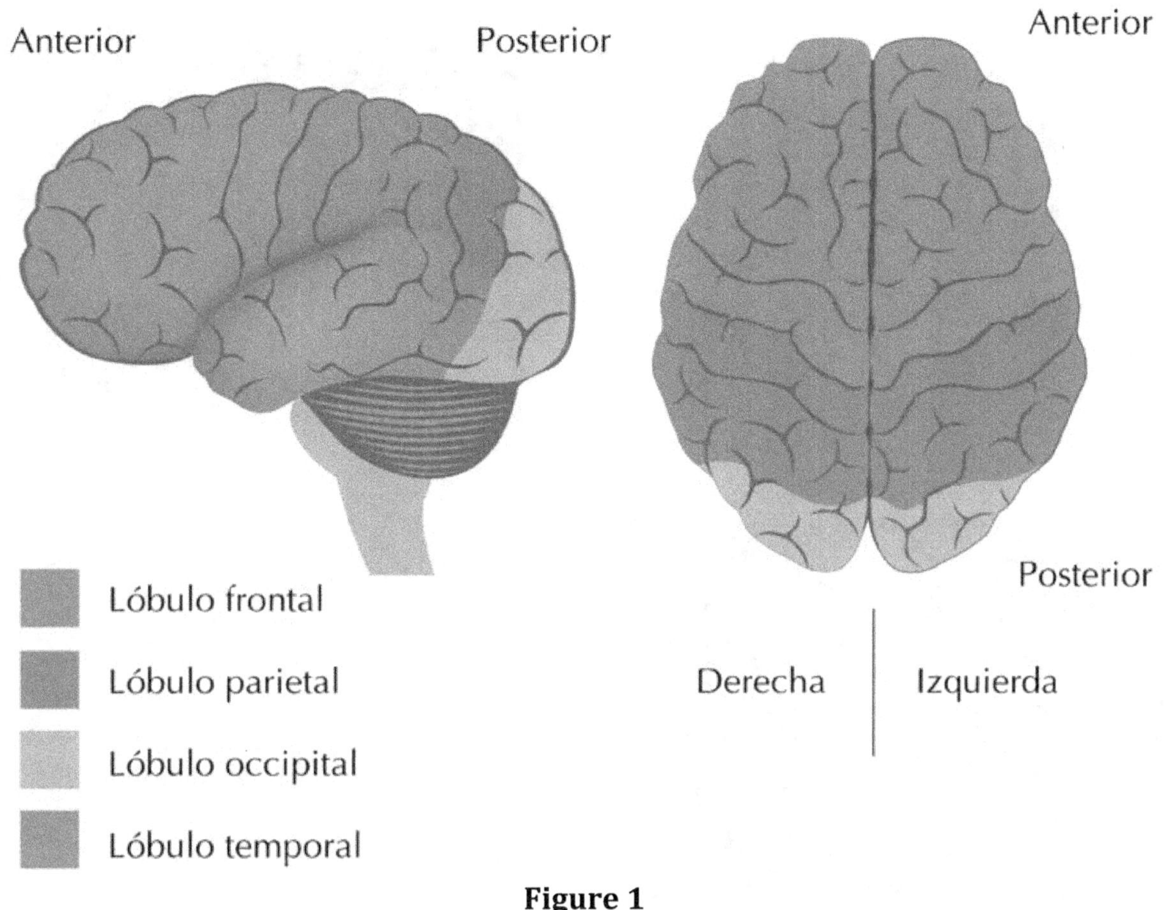

Figure 1

— Keep your eyes on the red bird and slowly count to twenty.
— Next, look at a point in the empty cage and you will see the faint figure of a blue-green bird.
— Do the same with the green bird. A magenta figure will appear.

Figure 2

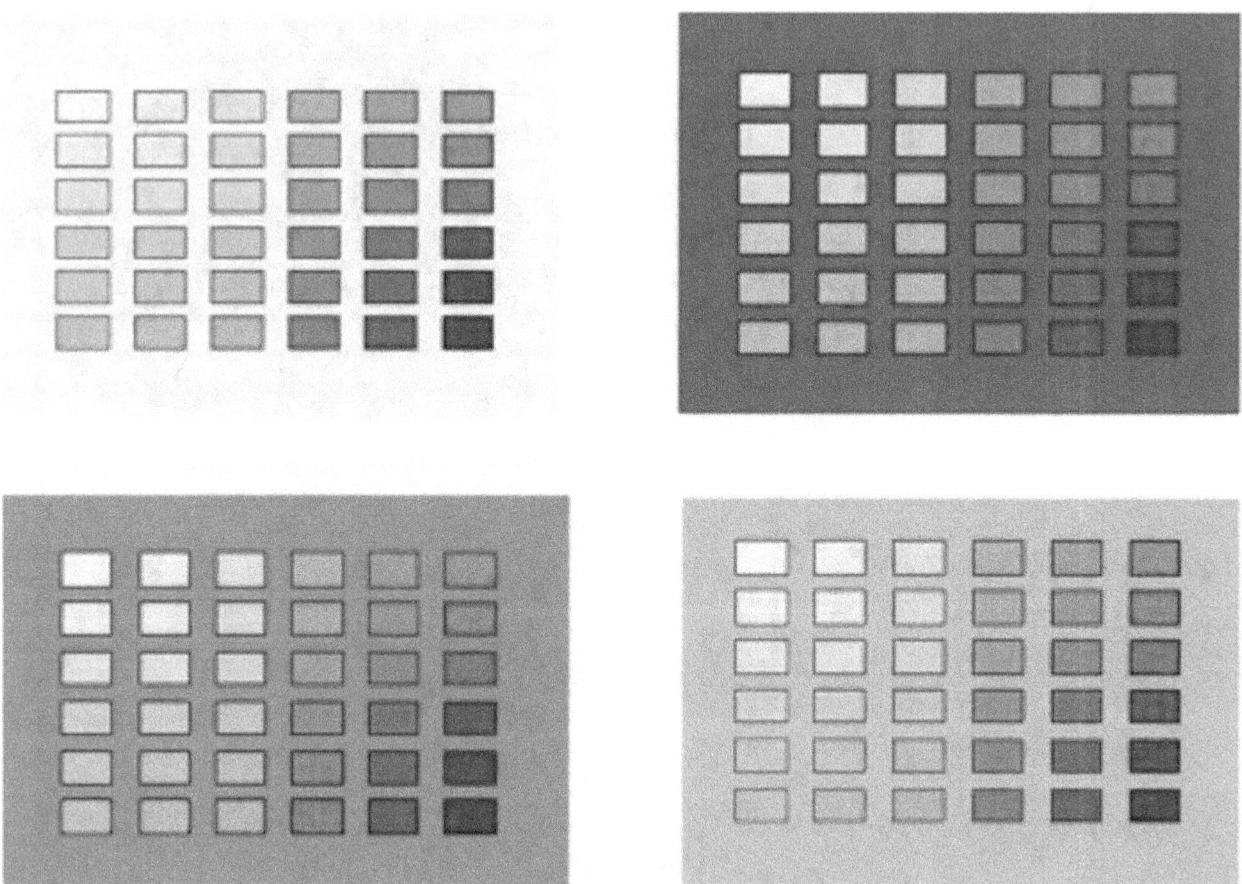

The colors of the grids are the same, but they are perceived differently depending on the background.

Figure 3

Look below and say the colors, not the words.

AMARILLO   AZUL   NARANJA   NEGRO   ROJO

VERDE   ROSA   AMARILLO   ROJO   AZUL

VERDE   NEGRO   AZUL   ROJO   ROSA

There is a conflict in the brain: the right hemisphere wants to say the color, but the left hemisphere insists on reading the word it is seeing.